DRAGON BAIT

DRAGON BAIT

A novel by Robert Flanagan

Book II of The ASA Trilogy

Connemara Press

Yellow Spring, West Virginia

<www.connemarapress.org>

authorHOUSE®

AuthorHouse™
1663 Liberty Drive
Bloomington, IN 47403
www.authorhouse.com
Phone: 1-800-839-8640

First published by AuthorHouse 2/4/2011

ISBN: 978-1-4567-3015-4 (e)
ISBN: 978-1-4567-3016-1 (dj)
ISBN: 978-1-4567-3017-8 (sc)

Library of Congress Control Number: 2011900408

Printed in the United States of America

This book is printed on acid-free paper.

Book cover and dust jacket by Liam M. Flanagan

Acknowledgments

Every author—whether fledgling or hoary master of his art—must acknowledge the great writers who have gone before. In *Involuntary Tour*, book I of this trilogy, I named some whom I credited with inspiration; I would add a few more, expanding the realm of my debt: Feodor Dostoievskii, Frank O'Conner, J.R.R. Tolkein, Tim O'Brien, Leo Tolstoii, Ray Bradbury, and Washington Irving. My etermal gratitude.

Again, thanks to the No Name Writers of Winchester, Virginia: your critiques abide! And to those whom I've never forgotten but failed to mention: English teachers, from the seminal period of high school, wherein the interest and possibility was first aroused, to the many instructors, teachers, and Profs scattered across a number of colleges and universities who confirmed it..

But, as before and always, my premier obeisance is to the force of serving military in this country who have kept us all free to do what we will, however we can manage. Without the protective shield of their sacrifices, all the words—in our books, newspapers, and on parchment in our archives—would be meaningless and worse—already lost to memory. This prevailing mindset is the motivation behind these three books.

Some segments of this book have appeared previously in various publications:

Throughout this, and the other two books of the trilogy, many segments derived from real happenings have appeared for 12 years as subjects of my newspaper columns weekly in the *Hampshire Review*, Romney, West Virginia. As columns about real people and events, they bear the characterization of essays, though not so formal as that may sound.

> Elements of Chapter 8 in *Dragon Bait* appeared
> in poetic form in Volume 6, Numbers 1-2 of
> *Vietnam Generation: A Journal of Recent History and
> Contemporary Culture* in 1994.

Elements of several chapters appeared in prose form in various issues of *phoebe*, the literary journal publication of George Mason University.

Segments of several chapters appeared as short stories in my book, *Peripheral Visions* ,a collection of short fiction; Mountain State Press, Charleston, 2003.

Dedication

Again with book II, as with the full trilogy, this work is dedicated to a once-extant and critical military intelligence organization, the U.S. Army Security Agency. For a more expansive comment in this vein, see "Dedication" in book I of the trilogy, *Involuntary Tour*, Robert Flanagan, AuthorHouse and Connemara Press, 2009.

Author's Note:

The "Author's Notes" in book I, *Involuntary Tour*, pertain once again. Also, to emphasize: to avoid confusion in sequencing of scenes, please **note carefully the place/time** sub-headings in each chapter, as well as some internal shifts within chapters. These are all delineated to provide clear tracking.

Contents

Prologue

Dragon Bait

Fort Ord, California: July 1965

David Winter stared up at the house, number 1026, as a goal of lofty ambitions. He set his mind, pushed off, and hobbled from the car into the open hallway, struggling with the aluminum supports. The twenty-yard walk left him exhausted.

Nickie, ahead of him by moments, had made a quick inspection sweep of the family quarters. She met him at the door, ensuring that nothing at the threshold could trip him up. He was still new to crutches, and she read pain on his face; she knew his depleted state. Seven-year-old Jeremy held onto one crutch, posing the greater risk, but David felt the need for him there.

"You O.K?" she asked, slightly breathless.

"Yeah, fine. Just . . . just gotta work with these things a bit."

She flicked him a smile but her eyes were cloudy, and wrinkles distended the corners of her mouth. He smiled back, knowing her thoughts: silently thanking the gods again for the simple fact of his presence.

But he also knew—sharing her concern, stirring up something dark with feathery, whisking wings that hovered, unseen, just above them—that she harbored unspoken fears for the future. For a time when he might have to go back there. Back to the war.

Back to Viet Nam.

He was just months returned, only on the leading edge of recovery, though encouraged to hope for eventual complete use of the leg. But—there it was! Regular Army NCO, Winter had no illusions. The jungle telegraph already named military personnel being rotated back to the combat zone for a second involuntary tour. Some, of course, had pulled a second, even a third tour at their own request; these universally were personnel without attachments. Not soldiers with close ties to those who loved them, those who suffered the pangs of separation in addition to mortal fears. How could he convince Nickie that it would not happen to him? He'd served out his full tour—well, almost; he lacked a few days reaching DEROS—and wounded, to boot.

No, he convinced himself, he had no worries in that department. He was assigned now to the Army's nearby Presidio of Monterey for a 37-week Russian language course and would no doubt go on to future assignments in Europe. Maybe Japan. Or even something in the states, though he was not anxious to explore the option of Alaska—Shemya was grim! He hoped to settle into some crucial and satisfying role at one of the European sites, and homestead.

The term from Marine days caught him by surprise. *Homesteading* had a negative connotation. Homesteader was a pejorative term for one who, by manipulation, managed to remain at one assigned military location for an extended, inordinate period of time. Contrary to military expectation, even policy, homesteading was not beyond the realm of possibility.

He realized, though, that hope was the weakest sort of peg on which to hang a future..

"How far is it—tell me again—from here to the school? The Presidio," Nickie said, masking anxieties in commonplace.

"About seven miles. Probably take me ten, fifteen minutes to drive it, depending on traffic. Straight shot down Pacific Coast Highway. Piece-a cake." He smiled over the pain, remembering this time to cover evidence of discomfort. Anytime he was with Nickie or Jeremy.

Granting him latitude in his deception, she nodded out the window. "Nice to have a corner lot. Big side yard where Jeremy can play . . . and three bedrooms. How'd we manage that?" She knew Army housing authorities to be parsimonious with space when allocating quarters. If you were married you were authorized and assigned quarters, depending upon availability. For a couple, a two-bedroom, even without children; there were no singles. One child, also a two-bedroom. Two children, still a two-bedroom, unless they were opposite gender, in which case, upgrade to three. Four bedrooms was in the realm of dreams. With only Jeremy, she valued the extra bedroom. Make a study for David, a family room. Useful.

A gift! The Army didn't run to frills.

"It's going to be fine, Nickie." He turned his head and was still. "Listen," he shushed. The front door stood open behind him. "Can you hear the surf?"

She seemed distracted, then cocked her head. "Heavens. I hadn't noticed. Wonder how long it will take to get used to that. What are we, a block from the highway? The ocean?"

"I count it two short blocks. California blocks," he said.

She smiled lazily and came cautiously into his arms. "Well," she offered, abandoning banality. "We have the extra room. Would this be a good time to consider . . . expanding the family?"

The message was slow getting through. "Whoa!" he blurted.

He realized as the words popped out that likely it was not the desired response. He held her tighter. "Pretty sudden, isn't it? This—" he said, awkwardly covering surprise.

But he knew it wouldn't be sudden for her; this would have dominated her thinking for a while, without counting bedrooms. Suddenly confronted, and without exploring her decision, he couldn't comprehend what all that would mean. Here in school, the distractions of an infant while trying to study . . . But then, he'd be almost through the course before her term.

If it happened. What would it mean wherever they went from here? His focus shifted.

He'd been out of hospital four days. They'd only made love, hmmm, eight or nine times. It had never occurred . . . Surely she'd gone back on the pill!

"Sudden is as sudden does," she murmured, checking about for small prying eyes. She tightened her embrace with one arm while her other hand dropped between them.

Assimilating the flush of warmth, the throbbing surge of arousal, he relished the years that stretched ahead: this woman, this child, and—another?

chapter one

Dedicated to the Proposition

Bad Aibling, Germany; June 1968

The Winters returned from the south as from a bad run in Reno rather than a second honeymoon in Italy. Dave, begrudging conversation, barely spoke when I saw him, and I seldom saw him. Temporarily I took over Delta Trick working swings and our paths didn't often cross. My regular, usually unannounced visits to their quarters seemed held in abeyance.

Nickie tried to avoid me the one time I saw her in the commissary. She was absently shooing fruit flies away from overripe bananas when I walked by. She bobbed her head and murmured, "Sergeant Brenner," and hurried away, leaving me searching for the Listerine.

I felt the strain in Casa Winter, though I never saw the two of them together in those next couple of months. Even I, confirmed bachelor of the first water, recognized legitimate marriage crisis. Dave had managed to keep his orders a secret from Nickie back in April, before Rome. I suspect he had hoped, however vainly, that the distractions, the ambiance of soft, decayed civilizations, might mask the harsh fact of his orders for a second tour in Viet Nam. However it evolved, the fact of the orders and their implication was now well known—not well received.

A sense of impending disaster seemed to pervade Winter, ever more intrusively, working on him—a catechism of catastrophe. I thought it likely to do with his marriage, and not the orders, *per se*.

Anyone who halfway put their mind to it could empathize with Nickie. Her man, her love, the father of her children, had come within a hair of checking out during his first Viet Nam tour. Out of his place, ordered to something he had no business doing, he'd bought into a high-stakes game not of his making. The resultant wound, severely shattering his right thigh and leg, leaving him a patient of extensive surgery, treatment, and physical therapy for months, was illogical. But I knew—and he agreed when I proposed the concept to him—that whatever he'd suffered, he had come out ahead. For he'd narrowly missed the wound that killed more matadors than any other: the dreaded *cornado*. Bullfighters' nightmare: severing of the femoral artery. Passage through his thigh of the green-pea-sized morsel of shrapnel had occurred just two millimeters from that critical vessel. Such a wound, on that barren LZ, would have been a death sentence.

And when all the shooting and shouting was over, even after he'd had more than three years to recover from the mortaring—as had his wife, vicariously—I guess I can understand how she could carry the fear of a repeat about with her, wear it like a garment. So the *status* was not all that *quo* involving my man, Winter.

As the Bavarian springtime wore on, his despair was obvious to those of us around him who might have helped. He responded to conversation in a manner implying he couldn't be bothered. As if he were running a race that he couldn't win, puzzling an enigma that couldn't be solved. And I suppose he was.

Regularly polling his clerk, Magic Marvin, and Mister Stoneking, another of his friends, I maintained a sense of what Dave was going through. But neither anger nor sadness nor even stoic acceptance of the orders could make his summer more bearable.

His temper frayed easily now. In the eyes of some, he ceased to be the golden boy of Ops, the one officer who kept all the balls in the air, kept his job, his life, and his commitments on a single plane of equanimity. For a time I feared my very own, personally assigned warrant officer no longer afforded me space in his shrinking world. But we'd been friends too long in too many disparate places for this to be a permanent condition.

During all this melodrama, Dave and Nickie grew apart. Obviously so, to the extent that this very private man soon found himself fending off solicitude or disparagement from those whom he did not consider in a place, nor qualified, nor invited, to make such judgements.

Nickie had begun talking. A lot! As much as I liked Dave's wife, and thought she was God's gift to a friend—if you simply had to be married—she was losing it.

And if Winter was the lead dancer in the great European theater shuffle-off-to-Sai Gon second-tour soirée, he was in good company. Two senior NCOs in Alpha Company, both Viet Nam vets, were alerted for second tours. Archie Krebs, Assistant Trick Chief for Charlie Trick Morse section, veteran Phu Bai and Air Section op, got orders. And others, not Viet Nam vets, found themselves on the road to Indo-China. A new analyst, just in from school stateside, known to no one, lost his head and volunteered. He was gone before the ink dried on his request.

Captain Ernest Lowry, who lived with wife Jeanette in the Winters' stairwell, was tagged. Jeanette Lowry appealed to everyone in the officers' housing area, wives and husbands alike, protesting that Ernie couldn't go to Viet Nam, him being a sole surviving son and all. Unfortunately for Jeanette no one in the housing area had anything to do with the drafting of Ernie's orders. Or the option of effecting their recall. The unwholesome brazenness of the woman's appeal was floating around the O-Club before she'd finished her first morning Bloody Mary. Sergeant Murtaugh, club manager and den mother, opined she was pushing dung up a steep slope, and word was soon all over. Throughout the club ranks, it produced a bad taste.

Jeanette had a valid point, though. Captain Lowry, had he chosen, could have availed himself of that particular Exempt Excuse. It was a matter of filing the correct forms, the entire process a matter of a couple hours' administrative shuffling. And though fellow officers and subordinates might question his motives—legitimate concern about ultimate survival aside—every soldier on involuntary orders for 'Nam would secretly envy him.

Jeanette was simply appealing to the wrong lobby, as Mrs. Lieutenant Colonel Judalon Satterwhite archly pointed out at Mrs. Colonel Aline Ahls's Wednesday tea and workshop for Biafran Relief. Captain Lowry related as much to me later in conspiratorial confidence; Ernie was another officer I'd served with when he was enlisted. But there was only one appeal that might have been effective in this case, and Jeanette was so close she overlooked it: Ernie.

Captain Ernie himself had declined the perfectly legal, triple-S cop-out. Captain Ernie did not wish to play his Sole Surviving Son card. With career intentions vis-á-vis the Army, he recognized the value of a combat assignment in his 201 file. A couple of medals, chance for combat command—all big pluses when records were screened for majorities.

Another element factoring large in Captain Ernie's decision not to oppose the assignment was that he felt he could use the twelve months away from Jeanette and Hank Snow about now. He was beginning to think with a nasal twang.

The summer of '68 played out as a season of frustrations and frayed tempers. I'd made Sergeant First Class in May while Winter was in Italy, and it was a measure of the chaos in his life that it was late June before he got around to congratulating me. For a while I thought he might have subscribed to Mister Barnshell's remark: "Brenner, when you make S.F.C., it will mark the absolute nadir of Army integrity. Final disintegration." But, soldier on!

Personnel shortages made for long, heavy work schedules as the revolving door of Viet Nam cycled men and officers—experienced NCOs and junior officers, mostly—in and out of usually stable tours in the United States, Europe, and worldwide to fill the insatiable needs of that jungle drain. Personnel who eventually trickled in to fill vacated operational spaces in Europe came largely from assignments in the war zone.

Some came joyously. Alive! Relieved to be out of it, even if only for a while. The professionals.

Others came having done their jobs, impatient to be free of the Army and all it represented, putting in their time merely to complete their allotted sentences.

Some came recovering from wounds, physical or psychic, with a wide range of scars from OPERATION DALLAS or MANHATTAN or JUNCTION CITY, or the horror of Dak To. Those arriving in late spring and summer had lived through the unexpected savagery of Tet—the Tet Offensive,1968—already labeled by the media as a major American defeat.

Every cotillion of nay-sayers around the globe had the US and South Viet Nam forces relegated to history's ash can. Done for. Deleted. *Don't bother to police up the battlefield; we'll mail the remains to you. Now stand aside so we can get on with the glorious revolution and don't worry about the rights and hopes and dreams of the millions of poor fools who put everything on the line to make it otherwise.*

Sergeant Bloomer summed up pretty well with his post-Tet assessment: "Journalist mothers suck *benjo* water. You shoulda seen the other guy."

Staff Sergeant Miles Ellison, while assigned to the 371st Radio Research Company with the First Cav in OPERATION PERSHING II, late January in the highlands of Two Corps, caught a small, inconvenient piece of shrapnel in the fleshy part of his leg while engaged in a call of nature in what he thought was a relatively secure area, a concept contradictory to the Viet Nam fracas. Choppered out the following morning, he spent a sluggish two weeks in the recovery ward at Cam Ranh-South. Upon release, he was reassigned to the 404th Radio Research Detachment operating with the 173rd Airborne Brigade in I Corps, just in time to limber up his leg in OPERATION

MUSCATINE. Ellison was wounded again on that outing in April, again by mortar fragments, again in the leg—both legs this time. The cry of "Dinks in the wire!" had brought with it heavy enemy RPG fire, rockets, and mortars, and there was outgoing mortar fire as well, heavier and higher-angle as the action moved closer. There was some question later whether the round that wounded Ellison the second time had come from a VC tube or from one of the friendlies. It didn't matter, but Ellison felt better about it thinking enemy.

"At least there was engagement. I wasn't just minding my own business, taking a dump. We were scorchin' Zips when I bought it," he told me. I wondered how much "scorching" a DF sergeant would have done. But when he left the hospital in the Phillipines in late May, Ellison was transferred directly to Bad Aibling. After the second Purple Heart, though he'd completed only ten months of a twelve-month tour, the computer decided he'd paid his dues.

Others came, some without visible scars but mind and soul and heart seared, will and strength-of-purpose blown away. Constantly mindful of mortality, equally careless of it, they had become hazards in the warp zone; out of the zone, they were only slightly lesser hazards. These walking wounded seemed to work harder in the initial weeks of their new assignment, ". . . like it really meant something," I heard Magic Marvin comment to Winter.

Then, as realization grew that they were now in different circumstances, benign and seemingly lacking emphasis compared to what they had left in 'Nam, efforts slackened. Try as they might, officers and NCOs could never convey the criticality of Cold War conflict compared to the hot variety as practiced in Southeast Asia.

"Men, it's the same game," the troops were told in monthly training. "Our opponents are the same team."

I noted a decided shift here. What the hell happened to *the enemy*? What's this *opponents* shit? *Game*? I found myself using this spent analogy. Only the names and places have been changed to indict the innocent, the leaders argued futilely. Young combat veterans, beyond the naivete of their military origins, scoffed at the professionals' lack of sophistication.

We lifers' inducements were transparent. But our leaders' adoption of the concept of corporate structure, instead of military hierarchy and command, put us on a road to oblivion. Engagements, conveyed in terms of the only conflicts known to the corporate clowns, was leading to chaos. Battlegrounds became playing fields, where the enemy became "the other team"; we didn't have leaders but role models, not commanders but managers. I tried to imagine a fastidiously dressed colonel *managing* a brigade assault on bunkered fortifications.

In expiation of unnamed, often imaginary sins, the ones who'd passed through the trial, and to all outward appearances survived, drank harder and more often, drove faster with greater abandon, fought quicker employing less Marquess of Queensbury in the clubs and barracks and downtown bars, in the cobblestoned streets—in summation, they cared less. They made seemingly bizarre alliances, often for the sake of contrariness: south Alabama redneck bigots palled with Philadelphia ghetto blacks; FTA hardcases drank themselves silly with grizzled, three-war sergeants; atheists debated philosophy with Jesus Freaks. "Man," as the saying went, "in never-never land, nothing else matters. It's how you hang when the shit flies."

Most, so afflicted, would never understand why they acted as they did, but when asked to account for their behavior, often parroted Magic Marvin: "Who gives a shit?"

* * *

CW2 Buford, another Operations Section Chief, was alerted in early June. He was back from 'Nam less than three years. Rotation was coming faster and faster: four years, down to three-and-a-half, to three—and less. Lacking a national strategy, it couldn't be otherwise.

Dick Buford and I had been SP5s together in the Philippines. He was a bachelor, sort of a hard charger. In celebration of his pending release from the ". . . benign bullshit and boredom of the European assignment," as he so succinctly put it, he elected to indulge one last fling.

Buford took Elise Rudemacher to the Officers Club where he plied her with banana daquiries until she was fish-eyed, then fondled her ass around the tiny dance floor until she developed hot pants and dragged him out the door. She wasn't a teacher for nothing.

Miss Rudemacher's legendary '53 Fiat was parked in the colonel's O-Club reserved space as usual, since that worthy seldom attended the revels. Miss R convinced Buford she was sober enough to drive them to her BOQ room at the other end of the post, a distance of only three blocks. But somehow, between the debilitating effects of the daiquiris and stimulation from the ass massaging, the young schoolteacher pointed her machine in the wrong direction, swinging the Fiat out around the firehouse, past the library, racing along the security fence around Operations on the remains of the old Luftwaffe taxiway.

It was never satisfactorily explained why she did not notice that the chainlink fence took a ninety-degree jog to the left, angling out some thirty feet before straightening again. Indeed, since the fence had been that way forever, it was a puzzle. It wasn't as if she was new in town. Miss Rudemacher had taught school at BA and driven men to her room for more than six years.

Neither was it ever disclosed what act Dick Buford was performing on Miss R when they hit the fence head-on at the angle. The Fiat came to rest nosed under the chain link, trapped by the tension of the fence stretched so tightly across the hood you could have strummed a Chet Atkins riff on it. One guard watching this phenomenal train of events from the corner guard post saw the Fiat race by but later swore he saw only the driver of the car.

Whatever Buford's actions or intent, the crash broke his nose against the brake pedal. When the MPs pulled him from the car, bleeding, Buford was stanching the crimson flow with a pair of lavender bikini panties. He never attempted an explanation. Mister Buford was an officer *and* a gentleman.

"And truly," as he later said to a gaggle of curious friends, "ain't no big thing."

A second guard had been in the angle of the fence corner, making his rounds. He saw headlights coming straight at him, heard the tiny engine screaming, and above all the clamor claimed to have heard a long, protracted squeal of feminine ecstasy. Buford, standing around, morosely bleeding at the inquisition in the aftermath, hearing the guard's version of events, asked the man how he would qualify "ecstasy."

When Captain Mims, the OD, got to the scene minutes after the accident, he saw Private Patulski still hunkered down in the dying headlights. "Private," he ordered. "Relax your grip on that weapon. Easy, now. Release the hammer. Point the weapon skyward, please." His commands ran lengthy moments ahead of the guard's responses. Patulski gripped the .45 automatic with both hands in proper police technique, holding the attacking auto at bay within sweep of the pistol.

Patulski wasn't wanting to hear explanations. "She never even touched the brakes," he whined. "She had her foot to the floor, squealing her lungs out. She gol-durn near run me down . . . crazy bitch!"

"Shaking like a dog shittin' peach pits," Chief Warrant Officer Buford intoned through the packing in his nose the following day at work, characterizing Patulski's response. But the MP, it was noted, had held his ground. A contented rumble of speculation swept through Ops.

Miss Rudemacher, whether from rum, shock, concussion, or sexual satisfaction slumped over the wheel unconscious immediately after the Fiat struck the wire. Her large, bare left breast pressing into the center of the steering wheel was of a softness that did not even actuate the horn. Sergeant Bloomer commented on that fact in awe as he eased her from the car, checking closely for lacerations.

Indicative of the nature of that summer, Mister Buford was not called on the carpet for his passive part in the incident, though the Post Commander felt even stronger about loose women and fornication before the eyes of God than he did about the drinking of alcohol, taking of drugs, and other biblical no-nos.

Miss R, for reasons she wouldn't discuss, swore off banana daiquiris. But the Fiat was repaired soon after Miss R, and both were back in service within days, doing what they were maintained for.

I took it all as a manifestation of mass hysteria.

* * *

A week after the Buford-Rudemacher-Fiat triangle episode, the Bad Aibling Chief of Police made an official visit to Colonel Ahls's office. The colonel sent an MP to fetch Magic Marvin, despite the fact that the chief spoke excellent English, and the colonel's *Deutsche* wasn't half bad. Magic Marvin rode in the MP Jeep to the headquarters building, later commenting it was the first time he'd ever been in a cop vehicle willingly and/or sober. He vowed it was the last.

Hauptpolizei Baumann had handled hundreds of such diplomatic missions back over the previous eleven years since his investiture in that exalted position, performing a neat balancing act between the security and welfare of the people of his town, and maintaining good relations with the military post, from which the German community derived significant economic benefits.

Baumann was a heavy, florid-complexioned farmer with a bristling shock of steel-grey hair. Though considered a large man, he would not have stood out in any gathering of Bavarian menfolk.

Except for his hands. When he made a fist, it was larger than the proverbial breadbox. A smile forever frozen on his face, he shook hands with everyone who would meet his courtesy—and few would not allow it, German and American alike. The hard dullness in the eyes behind the beaming face suggested the insistent handshake was to impress you with his strength, his position.

It was an ill-kept secret that the chief had been a sergeant who'd served in an SS mop-up unit in World War Two, an organization whose mission was to leave no witnesses behind in Russia to testify. The chief's pragmatic appraisal of his current role, vis-à-vis the Cold War and America's antipathy toward the Soviets, explained his openness about his history. Practical persons realized that during the war he would not have survived capture by the Russians for more than the time it took to convene a firing party of relatively sober Ivans, and he'd fought, maneuvered, and bribed his way back across the Elbe when the German war effort collapsed. Some particular aspects of his history were not widely known, though most were in our files. The fact of his SS association he spoke of himself, albeit discreetly.

But he was a good chief, good policeman, good politician, and he got on well with *Amerikanischers,* all agreed. And besides, that was all a long time ago. In the shifting allegiances following that war, and in the current stand-off with the East, few Germans held his past against him. Even fewer Americans showed concern about what, for them, was ancient history.

Herr Baumann, however, had come to *Bad Aibling Kaserne* this warm June morning hesitantly. For the first time in memory, he was not sure of his grounds. In the first place, he had no hard evidence. Usually he could name names, places, license plate numbers, list the items broken, quote medical bills, enumerate sheep and fence posts dead-missing-broken: cold statistics of GI fallibility.

Absent such facts, he was cautious. But it appeared to be the weird kind of event he could count on the crazy Americans for, so he'd come despite reservations.

While Baumann, his assistant a *Deutsche* police captain, Colonel Ahls, and the Post Adjutant awaited Marsh's arrival, making stilted conversation in a mix of German and English, the chief felt again a slight awkwardness. In the hot, bright sunlight of an early summer day the incident seemed preposterous. He wondered if in fact *Schutzman* Steichel wasn't nipping the schnapps when he reported what he'd seen last evening. But they were here now, and it did smack of an American production.

* * *

Magic Marvin returned to work in Ops just before noon. He scampered into Winter's office where Dave and I were going over mission tasking changes. The clerk glared at me as if I were something overlooked on sweepdown the previous night, but spoke up when Winter urged him. Marvin cautioned Winter—and me, by unspoken association—to say nothing of what we were to hear. Winter waited. Marsh launched into explanation, and we shortly understood.

After the departure of Chief Baumann from the headquarters following the diplomatic dance session, the colonel had released Marsh from his duties as translator with finger-wagging admonition. "Specialist Marsh," the colonel oozed, "I understand your loyalty to Mister Winter. It is legendary on the post. I admire it . . . and I permit it. I know Mister Winter values your friendship and dedication. However, uhh . . . son, what we're dealing with here is something very serious, something which fortunately does not concern Mister Winter . . . so far as we know. This must not, simply *must not,* be bandied about. We have a fragile situation on our hands."

Marsh reported the colonel had gone silent for a moment, then had gotten down to it.

Bandied about . . .? I marveled.

"'Some believe this an act of divine retribution toward us for our part in this godless war. Rightfully so, if that's the case. But I have to consider all possibilities. It's fair to say we may be dealing with a sick, lost soul.'"

"Not *my* place to comment," Marsh said expansively, likely reading in Dave's and my eyes the kind of hopeful *Why didn't you do or say something?* we might have asked. "The colonel had *something* squarely in sight," he added.

I heard echoed in Marsh's re-creation the same zealous extremism, the undecipherable religious marginalia for which the colonel was famous. Admittedly, in the final telling the colonel wasn't so far off the mark. Though that was to take a while . . . we weren't there yet.

Marsh insisted he hadn't the slightest clue how the colonel had crafted a zealous cause out of what the police chief had relayed to them. But then, no one ever knew where Colonel Ahls stood in relation to the Army, the war, and anything associated with it, between his obsessive quest of a nondescript religion and his sworn military duty.

Magic Marvin said he'd just done the necessary translating, otherwise kept his mouth shut and listened. When the colonel had worked his way around to dismissing him, he waved off the young soldier's salute and walked him to the door, arm around his shoulder. There had been a fatherly touch in the gesture, Marsh reckoned.

"Pig shit, Mister Winter. Just plain, unadulterated pig shit!" Magic Marvin quivered with indignation. "I was about to piss myself with what I'd heard. It needed telling, and I thought I was going to have to do a chorus of 'Bringing in the Sheaves' just to get out of that office."

"Shut the door, Marve," Winter said belatedly. I sat back to listen. "Okay, what?"

"Electric Man."

"Jesus!"

"Electric Man! Yessir! Oh, yessir! Hell yes, sir, and it's wonderful. Did you hear—"

"Marve, this better not be one of your—"

"Sergeant Brenner. Please," Marsh said, putting me in my place. "This clown, this Electric Man, has got the whole friggin' post on their toes for the first time in the years I been here. The Old Man's going apeshit—that alone's worth the price of admission—and the M.P.s are making their rounds like they mean it, for a change."

We knew the clerk was right about that. There was a feeling of highly charged anticipation as if an audience, loving the wild, unexpected, out-of-season first act, couldn't wait for intermission to end, the second act to begin.

The Midnight Marauder, now known officially as Electric Man from his screams in the night when gate guard Waller tried to shoot him off the bike, had done no harm that I knew of. It wasn't his fault that Corporal Waller was trigger-happy and blew out Dietrich's fire engine windshield. Merry-go-rounding the guard post at the front gate in the fire truck caused nothing but ribald comment, despite the shooting that accompanied it. It put the cops on their toes. Mrs. Colonel Ahls was still festered up about Dietrich destroying the flowerbed on the triangle, but that was mere surface tension. Even Captain Meechan's inflammatory encounter had come to nothing.

No, Electric Man had done no real damage. Except to the image the military held of itself. But he *had* added some life to the dreary day-in, day-out mundanity of this backwater outpost. It was a welcome change from watching the going of the doomed, the coming of the near-dead.

"That goddamned Nazi, Baumann," Magic Marvin said vehemently, "said one of his *Schutzmannen*—one of his policemen, Steichel by name—was on patrol last night, standing in a doorway downtown just off the *Platz*, about oh-two-thirty hours, when he sees this canary-yellow dude whip down the *Strasse*, cut straight across the square right out in plain sight. Guy was on a green bike— Steichel was very precise with the colors—and almost went into the fountain. Had on yellow tights and a yellow helmet and cape. Goin' like a bat outta hell. Cop yelled at him to stop. In *Deutsche*, of course. Cyclist never gave him a glance. Just kept pedaling, right on down the road, and the last Steichel saw of him, he was headed toward Kolbermoor. Cop went to phone in and they had *Polizei* all over the district within minutes. But nobody else saw him."

"Why'd Baumann come here with that tale?" Winter asked. Then turning to me, just before I got the answer out, "Wait, Brenner . . ."

Winter's was a fatuous question, and I mouthed the words as Marsh said them, mimicking Baumann; I'd heard them before: "'cause it seemed like something American soldiers would do." Winter, by the look on his face, had heard the snide appraisal too.

Marsh, torn between hilarity and indignity, went on to relate . . . how the colonel couldn't just keep his mouth shut, but had volunteered to Baumann that he, the colonel, understood—that the post had already suffered several instances of the unidentified figure's appearance, and the fact that we had no clue as to identity or purpose . . . and so on, and so on.

"Jeez-us, Marsh. This Electric dude's gonna get his stuff blown away if he don't cool it."

"No shit, Sam Spade," I observed, rather trenchantly, I thought. Winter dismissed me with a head shake, and dug down into the reports on his desk, putting an end to the conversation.

"Aahhhh . . . Mister Winter," Marsh began, the unfinished statement implicit.

"Aahhh," I said, staring in Dave's wide eyes as Marsh left the room. "Mister Winter, indeed. What the fuck? Over."

* * *

Two weeks went by, the mood of expectation punctuated by fistfights at the NCO-Enlisted club. Mutual hostilities between FTA short-timers and career lifers sought a natural outlet in the hot late summer nights. Magic Marvin was a participant, if not the perpetrator, in at least one of those end-of-week cathartic rites.

A Friday night in July. Bavaria was unusually sultry: South Carolina with Alps. Magic Marvin sat at a table in the NCO/EM club, playing Ship-Captain-Crew with the headquarters mail clerk and two medics, and a pair of dice they all knew to be loaded. The only game in town! Marsh had drunk a couple of Maxlrainers and wanted nothing more than to pass a quiet but profitable evening, relieving his three pigeons of their loose change.

At the next table several Viet Nam transferees, all junior-grade enlisted men, were making a casual spectacle of their limited beer-drinking prowess. The young troops had discovered deep reservoirs of hidden talent in the hops-spiced night, and the cans formed a pyramid five high in the middle of the table.

One of them, recently arrived Viet Nam vet Specialist Four Mouton, who had yet to hear a shot fired in anger despite his duty in the war zone, was noticeably louder than the rest. His voice carried across the club, obtrusive above the crinkle of beer cans and the clink of glasses, overriding the hum of conversation and laughter and curses. Magic Marvin was not the only one who recognized the tendency in Mouton, common among rear-echelon combatants, to establish a reputation for himself as, what might have been called in earlier wars, a *front-line veteran*. No doubt he sought that image, but without actual participation in combat, and bereft of imagination, Mouton was not aware of the absence of any *lines* in Vietnam, but went ahead and made a fool of himself before everyone—the ones with Viet Nam service, and those without.

Mouton sought notice, but went about his seeking as one who'd survived the fires of hell, one who had an obligation—a mission even—to preach the given word to one and all, though he would have been unable to define it thus.

Magic Marvin, at the adjacent table, listened for a while. Though intent on the dice, he couldn't avoid the ambient anger.

"Yeah, man," Mouton announced loudly, black shades masking his eyes. "There ain't no sense to none-a it. The goddamned gum'ment done sent us over there, do their shit work. You look at the cas'lties: they're *all* brothers and privates and Puerto Rican P.F.C.s. Ain't no chucks in the bunch." Mouton, black, unfortunately drunk, and angry with his lot, trapped in a predominantly white outfit in white Germany where he had not wanted to be, gave free rein to his spleen venting. To convincingly make his argument in his new-found, self-appointed role of spokesman for the disenfranchised, he grew increasingly loud and derogatory. It was a pose; it might even have been harmless in the confines of the club. But Mouton's tone and words implied taking it beyond the club. And it was all unnecessary.

"Now I done my time in hell—" Mouton lectured, omitting the fact that his *time* was a full twelve months on manual Morse intercept position in the relatively secure confines of the field station at Phu Bai "—'stead of lettin' me go back home to Mo-town, they done send my vur-gin ass over here to honkie heaven. That mu-fuckah, Wint-tuh Man, put me to work on a dumb-ass mission, snaggin' worthless dits. Now who the hell's interested in this Hunkie shit, man? I told him—told him twice—'Man,' I said, 'if I got to be in this mu-fuckin' country, gimme a gun and let me do something. Make me a M.P.'"

Heads were turned now, would-be revelers unable to revel with Mouton's diabtribe carrying across the bar like that of the shit salesman they all judged him to be. It made little difference that Winter's happened to be the only officer's name Mouton knew in his new assignment; it served his purpose.

"Yeah, Mouton," one of the off-duty military policemen at a nearby table called, "that would be a great idea. Give you a gun. Let you show us how you kicked some ass in Tet, right?" The fact that the speaker was also black fed Mouton's rage.

"Ah, fuck you, cop. You sound like that al-bino mutha with the bars. You think I can't handle bein' a M.P.? Shit, man, ain't nothin' to leanin' on the front gate and drivin' around with that blue bubble blinkin'. That mu-fuckah Win-tuh could even do that sh—"

"You talk like a clown with a paper asshole, Mouton." Magic Marvin had clearly sat still as long as he could. "Shitbird, your mouth is overloading your potential. You haven't been here long enough to know what the hell it is you're talking about. Hell, you haven't even been in the Army long enough. Haul your shit, motor mouth."

After the squaring off and the rapid exchange of blows, Mouton climbed up out of the wreckage of chairs and table and cans and stormed out of the club. Frustrated. Deadly.

Marvin returned to his beer, shrugged off the club manager's protestations, and became reflective. After a few distracted thus unprofitable minutes, he got up and left the club. Before the evening was over, Marvin and Mouton returned to the club together, drank a few more beers, and Mouton learned how it was. Action in the club flowed on around them as if nothing unusual had occurred.

Which it had not.

But like other problems with no easy solution, Mouton remained black, in the Army, and in a white Germany. Enlisted for four years to avoid the infantry, and after basic, tech school at Fort Devens, and a year in Viet Nam, he still had more than two years to go when he came to Bad Aibling. A long, slow-burning fuse.

And over there, far to the east, the war raged on, a siren whose background call had nothing to do with wind and song and men tied to masts, but could entice one back by the simple expedient of a terse directive.

The summer wore slowly, September looming large on Winter's horizon.

* * *

"Yeah . . . datelined Prague, thirty June. This journalist says the Warsaw Pact exercises ended today—that's yesterday. He's convinced, and he won't have any trouble convincing me, Pact forces are only in Czechoslovakia under Soviet leadership to influence and squelch the six-month-old growing liberal movement," Specialist Four Toombs read. "Hey—"

His Trick Chief, snatching the paper from his hands, said,. "Mark, get back on your net. You don't even work the Czech problem."

"Your ass! With Soviet Guards Motorized Rifle Divisions flooding Prague right next door, the Czech problem's *all* our problem." He began tweaking the background noise out of his monitor channel. The babble in the Morse bay went on without interruption.

chapter two

Electric Man, Redux

Bad Aibling, Germany; Summer, 1968

Second Lieutenant Dana Holly, newly commissioned from enlisted grade at Berlin Field Station, reported in to Bad Aibling in early July. Winter's name topped the officer sponsor roster, so he was assigned to aid the new lieutenant in getting settled. After walking the new officer through the process, getting him on the list for housing, obtaining details for a driver's license and vehicle registration, and most significantly, making sure he joined the Officers Club—even more important, paid his dues—Winter left the new guy in Temp quarters with his wife, a languid-looking Vasser type, obviously still caught in the throes of revolution. With an overweening sense of impending disaster, he wondered how this lieutenant, cast directly from junior enlisted man to officer, would wend his way through the maze of codified militarism.

Indulging a bit of historical reflection, Winter smiled wryly. If Lieutenant Holly was, as it appeared, in need of close and continual nurturing, the kind a First Sergeant would normally provide a young officer, then he was in a world of hurt. Holly was assigned as Executive Officer of Bravo Company, whose First Sergeant was an old retread, Sergeant First Class/Acting First Sergeant Waldo P. Pepperdine. In a career as checkered as that of the infamous PFC Younkin, Pepperdine's service dated from World War Two, followed by service in Korea and Vietnam. In and out of the Army since 1942, here, twenty-six years later, he needed yet two more years service for retirement with twenty. Passed over once for promotion, he was in a holding pattern. If not selected the second time, he would be forced out of the Army short of retirement.

Winter's perspective on the First Sergeant was enabled by personal memories from 1964 Viet Nam, about September best he could recall. Then Staff Sergeant Winter had been Non-Commisioned-Officer-In-Charge, 3rd Radio Research Unit Air Section. He bunked in NCO quarters, a hooch adjacent to the Orderly Room on Davis Station, Tan Son Nhut Airbase near Sai Gon.

There, late one evening while lying on his bunk, reading, Winter heard loud voices and crashing noises coming from the nearby

Orderly Room. SFC Peebo shouted from the NCO hut next door for quiet. He was ignored. Few were bold enough to ignore Peebo, for he had a testy sort of temperament. As much to see what such non-response might elicit, as to find out what the hubbub was about, Winter, in his skivvies, wandered out front of his hooch.

Through the screen that constituted orderly room walls, he saw Staff Sergeant Pepperdine seated behind the duty desk, frozen in place, staring at a soldier standing before him. The unidentified GI was cut off from view from the belt up by the louvered walls of the hooch. Winter could not see the individual's face, but saw tiger-stripe fatigues and an M-14 held menacingly before him. He heard voices clearly.

"—old piece of shit, don't you give me any crap. I got a gun. I'll blow your fuckin' lights out." The unknown with the bad attitude lifted the M-14 and sighted it at the head of the Duty NCO. Pepperdine cringed, but his gaze held square on his assailant's face.

"Miller, what's this crazy shit? Man, you're already cleared, spos'ta catch a plane in about seven hours. You're finished with your tour, goin' home. Don't pull this shit now, not even jokin'. It ain't funny." The older soldier appeared properly scared, but not ducking his duty.

"Fuck you, Pepperdick. You're new meat. You don't know what this place is all about yet, do you?" Winter recognized Miller then, an op who had worked briefly for him at WHITE BIRCH, but for the past two months was on the liaison team working with the South Vietnamese at SABER TOOTH site.

Sergeant Pepperdine straightened, his voice growing firmer, louder: "You silly asshole. I been new guy in more countries than you got points of I.Q. I got more months in *combat* than you got outta diapers. New guy! I'm not too new to know you're shittin' in your own soup bowl. Man, in all my time, I never seen a dumber move. DEROS tomorrow, and you pick tonight to screw up."

"Don'cha know, I don't wanna go home, Pepperdick. I love it here so much. I can't stand the thought of being without my little yeller ditty-bop friends. Maybe I'll just stay and take out papers. Yeah, maybe I will." The gun was wavering, moving in tight circles, centered on Pepperdine's breastbone.

"So, tell somebody who gives a shit. The Army don't care what you do with the rest of your screwed-up life. Sign on with the friggin' Cong if you want; you're going back for discharge anyhow; just don't do this. Man, they ain't never going to let you go if you make bad like this." For a substandard NCO, under pressure, it was uniquely prudent advice.

Winter looked around at the cluster of troops gathered on the walk. Inside, in addition to the NCO and Miller, he saw another soldier, a new guy he didn't know, dressed out for guard duty, but with no rifle. He quickly put it together: Miller had somehow gotten the weapon away from the guard, and now was confronting Pepperdine with it. Winter looked at the other bystanders; they looked back with blank expressions, or away toward the glow of parachute flares over Gia Dinh. No one made a move. Inevitably, muttered jokes were all to do with Miller's implausible timing.

Winter had to do something. "Miller," he said, speaking through the screen. "It's Sergeant Winter. Can I come in?"

"Fuck no, Sarge. You're no part of this. Stay out. I got a gun."

"I know you have a weapon. What's Sergeant Pepperdine done to upset you?" He wasn't sure about the line to take.

"*I'm* not upset . . . and it ain't him. It's the Army. *He's* the Army. He's the Duty N.C.O. I've got an official complaint and I'm taking it to the man officially in charge of this unit during non-duty hours." Miller's high-pitched, pedantic voice projected instability, but as he spoke he moved away from the door, away from Winter's voice behind him.

"Don't threaten him, Miller. That'll just make things worse. No one's been harmed. If you want to get a hearing, come back in the morning and see the First Shirt. Request a hearing with the C.O. That's the way to log a complaint."

"Oh, bullshit, bullshit, bullshit, Winter. Get off my case. In the morning I go home. I won't have time to see the C.O."

Winter recognized complete disconnect in the lilt of the soldier's voice. An unknown voice from the gathered crowd nailed it: "The lad's clock's not keeping good time!"

Pepperdine, growing increasingly nervous under the muzzle of the weapon, was sweating profusely. But he couldn't pass up response.. "You ain't going nowhere, Miller. You're fucked up as a soup sandwich. Standin' there, bad-ass, big old gun in your hands just like you knew how to use it. And all you can do is try to scare old soldiers and cherries. If you had any balls you'd-a volunteered for a second tour, or gone green beanie or like." Pepperdine spoke in a rush, as if the string of sound was somehow staving off the threat.

"I never heard no tales about you rushing to point a gun at someone who might be armed. Like charlie. You can kill me, asshole, I know that. And I don't wanta die, fur sure. Dyin's numbah ten-thou. But lettin' you shit on me like this, well . . . fuck it!" Pepperdine slammed his fists down on the desk and rose to his feet.

Winter couldn't believe it; the old fool was going to trip Miller's wire. The crowd on the sidewalk went quiet, scuffling back into the shadows, out of the line of fire. Winter looked around, searching for a weapon.

Nothing! All locked in the arms room. Perfect in a combat zone.

Miller jacked the operating rod back, and the *clink-tinkle* of brass bouncing on the concrete floor told everyone the weapon had already had a round chambered. The ejected round bounced and seemed to ring forever on the concrete floor, time standing very still. Miller leaned forward over the desk and pressed the M-14's muzzle just under Pepperdine's chin. Every onlooker imagined he could hear Miller's finger tightening on the trigger. Sergeant Pepperdine's color was a blanched white, sweat standing out on his face like fresh rain. He closed his eyes but didn't move. A low growl spread across the area. It took a moment for Winter to realize it was Miller, a sound from deep within severe maladjustment.

Miller screamed and pulled the trigger, jerking the rifle up toward the ceiling at the last instant. The round punched a small, neat hole in the roof of the orderly room as the crowd—except Winter and Sergeant Alvarez—disappeared. Alvarez went through the door without bothering to open it, taking the screen and cross-braces with him, grabbed Miller and slammed him forward onto the desk. Winter, close on his heels, grabbed the rifle.

And that was all of it.

Miller made no resistance. He moaned and laughed and swore as Alvarez held him on the desk. Pepperdine stood as he was, eyes still closed. Gradually, as if the flesh melted beneath him, he slid lower and lower, angled toward the chair and missed, and was sitting on the floor behind the desk, looking across it into Miller's face crushed against the desk three feet away. There was a babble of voices as the crowd returned, surging like a tide around the orderly room.

Sergeant Pepperdine, staring into the agitated eyes of Miller, said softly, "You poor miserable sonuvabitch. *Now* you got trouble.

Seven hours! Just seven hours from a freedom bird. Now you got trouble. Jesus Christ. *Seven hours.* Asshole!"

Following that night in 1964, Staff Sergeant Pepperdine was regaled for his steel *cojones*, fêted for his *chutzpah* in the face of Miller's madness. The old sergeant, Winter suspected, had done as he had because he'd reached the end of choices. He was too old, too dysfunctional to physically disarm the man. Out of his depth. He was a man accustomed to technical matters and no command responsibilities; and found himself suddenly, literally, under the gun. For all that, and with all the rationale that attempted explanation of the sergeant's unlikely behavior, Winter admired his performance.

But it was a flash in the pan, a single act in a series of one. Observing the sergeant's subsequent performance of duty, seeking any change that could be attributed to his demonstration of grit, was a pointless exercise. Pepperdine was promoted to Sergeant First Class the following April simply because he had more time in grade than any other Staff Sergeant in ASA, worldwide. And because of that questionable preeminence, and despite the attractions of promotion, he seemed reluctant to give up being number one in some queue.

His role at Bad Aibling, following his tour in Viet Nam, was almost accidental, resulting from the untimely departure of the First Sergeant of Bravo Company amid a scandal involving a teenage German girl. Pepperdine, in no sense an effective NCO, was made Acting First Sergeant due to a shortage of non-commissioned officers. If he had ever shown any degree of competence and fortitude, it had disappeared following the 3rd RRU orderly room dust-up.

And Pepperdine was new Lieutenant Holly's First Sergeant.

Good luck to you, boy Lieutenant, Winter observed with dry commiseration.

* * *

"Toombs, didn't I give you specific instructions about bringing outside reading material into the Ops bay? Just last week? Gimme the goddamned paper and get back to work."

"Sure, Sarge. Just keeping up with what our target entities are doing . . . in the real world." He handed the crumpled *Stars and Stripes* to the sergeant.

"You wouldn't know real world if it bit you in the ass, Toombs."

This by-play might have generated some interest among the operators, but it was old hat. The dialogue was a tired, two-man show.

"Yeah, well, bet you didn't know . . . though the Russkies announced a slowdown in extracting their troops after the Pact exercises were over, now, according to the paper, the Pact commander has announced a resumption of the withdrawal. But the Germans, the Hungarians, and the Poles are still hysterical and the Czechs don't have much hope for reducing tensions."

"Do I give a shit? This bay is all G-SOF mission . . . nothing to do with the Czechs. Continuing tensions are job security." The Trick Chief, finding difficulty in maintaining interest in the Group-Soviet Forces, Germany, mission, turned away, glanced at the confiscated *Stars and Stripes* newspaper in his hand, and said, "Toombs, you dumb shit. This fuckin' paper's three days old."

* * *

The summer crept forward. On the base, pressures from short-handed tricks and over-tasked personnel were carried home, adding to domestic conflicts. For Lieutenant Stanley, it was the new-found and doubly startling knowledge that both his wife and his Turkish immigrant girlfriend were pregnant, both approximately the same length of time. For Winter, the stand-off with wife, Nickie, was exacerbated daily with anything military. In general, life on the post in paradise was not the beneficent rapture one would choose. Madness erupted with regularity.

* * *

On a morning in late July, Winter was called to the Operations office. Standing at a brace before Major West's desk was Specialist Four William Cummings, a young soldier from the printer section. Previously a run-of-the-mill printer op—one of the boys, friendly and open—his persona had undergone a major overhaul when he had returned to the states on leave in the spring and had come back to BA with a wife. No one had known he had a fiancée, even a girlfriend.

"Sir?" Winter said, reporting. Clueless.

"Mister Winter," the major opened. "We have here, as you see, Specialist Cummings, William H. This young lad came to me, all on his own, without the blessing of his Trick Chief 's or your permission, so I am told." It was the drill instructor snideness, the sense the speaker was about to disembowel the speakee, that put Winter on alert. Otherwise he had no hint.

"Well, did he?" the major asked politely. "Clear through the Collection Office, Sergeant Butler, Sergeant Brenner, or you?"

"No, sir, not through me. I don't think Brenner or Butler either. What's the problem?"

Major West sat a long moment without speaking. At attention, Spec-4 Cummings, though not up for Soldier of the Month, looked more military than Winter had ever seen him.

"Specialist Cummings wishes to leave us, Mister Winter. Leave our employ. Our association He has hurt my feelings." Sounding in deep despair, West reached forward and picked up a security badge on a chain lying on the desk before him. "He has just told me he doesn't wish to be here with us anymore. Doesn't like us, is my guess. Came in, tossed his shit on my desk, and says he *quits*." There was barely concealed humor in West's sardonic voice.

"Cummings, what the hell?" Winter asked. Other-worldliness always pulled his chain. The soldier held his brace, did not look around at his OIC.

"Sir, I respectfully submit my resignation."

And won't the union boys love this!

Winter waited for further explanation. None was forthcoming.

"You what? Say again," Winter demanded.

"Sir, I respectfully submit my resignation," the specialist repeated.

"That's section-eight talk, Cummings. This is the Army. You don't resign; you can't quit," Winter said, looking at the major as if he might hold the key to this baroque fantasy. West shrugged dramatically. The soldier seemed to be staring at the flag behind West's desk.

Silence.

"Cummings, what *is* this shit? You've been in the Army long enough to know that can't happen. You sick or something?"

"Sir, I respect—"

"Hey, asshole," West growled. "We heard the party line. I think what Mister Winter would like to know—certainly what I am just dying to hear if you can spare me the syllables—is an explanation as to what makes your wants any different from every other G.I. in the world who wakes up every morning wanting to boogie out. Basically, a no-no." Winter felt it the instant West went into meltdown. "You know it. Yet, you walk in here," his voice rose, "throw this fucking badge on my desk, and tell me *you quit*. Do you *really wanna go to fucking jail for the rest of your fucking life?* Or is this some exercise in shits and giggles, just to fuck up my day?" Major West, clearly relinquishing his relaxed pose, leaned forward over his desk, threateningly.

"Sir, I—"

"If you say that one more time, you goddamned little prick, I personally will drag you out of this office and duck walk your ass to the fucking stockade," West roared. "Now goddammit, make sense to me. What prompted this bullshit?"

Winter moved around beside the major's desk, watching the soldier's eyes behind thick glasses flicker from side to side, squeezing shut, blinking. He reminded Winter briefly of Captain Meechan's habit with the eyes. The kid was scared!

"Cummings, stand at ease," Winter said.

No response.

"Cummings, I said stand at ease. It was not an invitation; that's an order." The soldier tore his hands from alignment on his trouser seams and smacked them together behind his back, spreading his feet, effecting a parade rest position. Winter let it go: close enough. The two officers saw a physical tremor sweep over the young man like a shivering spasm from a cool summer breeze. Cummings shifted his gaze to the floor.

"Now tell me what this is all about." Winter's voice was even, encouraging, but short of solicitous. He held his hand out and gestured to West where the soldier couldn't see, a kind of fluttering, easing motion. West exhaled, leaned back.

"Sir, I . . . I don't know how to go about this. I just have to . . . I have to do something else. I mean, I have to quit being a soldier." Cummings dried up.

"What do you mean by that?"

"Sir, I've become aware that I am acting as an integral part of the militaristic hierarchy of the United States's imperial forces, and I'm . . . I have to take a moral stand. I must stop lending myself to these efforts, this machine that controls us all counter to the will of the people."

"Say what?" West exploded. Winter glared at him; the major glared back and continued speaking: "Cummings, that's some goddamned propaganda bilge you got memorized. I smell the choking red fumes of dialectical materialism. So stop the shit. What's your angle?"

"Wait a minute, sir," Winter urged West. He sat on the corner of the desk. "Cummings, when you came to B.A., about the time I came down here from Rothwesten last year, you were a good soldier. Lately, for months now, I've seen you go downhill. It was so subtle I let it pass. I charged it off to the general distemper of this war thing. Looking back, I see more clearly. Lately, you're not so subtle anymore." His eyes came to rest on the peace activist's glasses.

"Yeah, I've noticed the same thing. Those squirrely little glasses, for instance," said West, divining Winter's thoughts. "Where'd you get those silly goddamned little round bifocals?"

"Sir, my vision is twenty-seventy. I must wear glasses."

"You know what I mean, asshole. The fucking bee-bop glasses, the hippie shit. It's a statement. My Army don't like statements." The major's tone promised sincere attention.

"Cummings, what the major's saying is that the Army expects a certain amount of dedication, in form if not in spirit. In fifteen years, in two services, I have never seen anyone, career or otherwise, who loved—or even professed to like—*everything* in the military . . . but they accept the notion that there are accommodations to be made. A balance that must be struck. It's the only way the system can work." Winter had engaged the soldier's eyes finally, saw in them a level of confusion he understood. He thought he also knew, from casual conversation among Marsh and some NCOs, what Cummings' real problem was.

"Mister Winter, I just can't be part of that anymore." The soldier begged for a fragment of understanding.

"Is it your wife, Cummings?" the major demanded, again preempting Winter's thoughts.

"Sir?"

"Your wife, asshole. She the one behind this? You never showed this side before—deserting your post. Dumping on your buddies. What happens if we could let you go? Have you thought where that would leave your friends, the other guys who might not like the Army? You'd force them to pick up your slack." He was quiet a moment. "It's not the work itself, is it? I mean, printer copy is pretty slick work. Not everyone can get it."

"Well, yes sir," Cummings picked up on West's first question. "My wife has her opinions. I happen to agree with her. I don't think that makes her responsible," he said defensively.

"Bullshit, Cummings. She's a goddamned commie lunatic you picked up at some anti-war rally in the states, though why she'd latch onto your wimpy ass is another guess. But she's sure as hell using you for her own purposes." West would cut the kid no slack, Winter saw.

There was a suspicion of tearing in the young soldier's eyes. "Sir, I resent that—"

"Resent fuck-all. Don't be a stupid goddamned dupe, for chrissake. You're pussy-whipped, Cummings. She's probably a hell of a lay. Even in that radical rag-bag shit she wears, anyone can see she's built for speed. Was she your first, Cummings? Is that why you grovel on command?"

"Sir," Winter insisted, "I don't think this is where we should be focusing—"

"Mister Winter, that's all right," the soldier managed. "She told me to expect this. I knew what I'd be facing," Cummings said, glaring at the Operations Officer.

"Don't mistake me, Cummings" West responded. "If your wife's to blame for this . . . sedition, then she deserves no consideration. It's just that with the question at hand, we need to be discussing real world. You're jerking yourself around if you think you can just walk in here espousing discontent and walk out a civilian."

Winter felt exasperated with the major's lack of resilience. There was no place on his ledge for a toehold. None but the standard Army response: court martial, stockade, Bad Conduct Discharge at a minimum, and a burden to carry the rest of the kid's life. But Cummings was giving him little option.

"What is she, Cummings?" West continued. "A real commie? A true-blue Red? A card-carrying fellow traveler? Or just another disaffected campus hippie who's found salvation in pissin' on the establishment?"

Winter understood the major's position. Every man in ASA held high-level security clearances and was privy to reams of classified and sensitive information. And many young soldiers weren't disciplined enough in security to keep everything to themselves. A wife with tainted sympathies could be calamitous. West would envision Cummings' wife as a round-eyed Mata Hari.

The questions continued: West alternately raved and coaxed. Winter tried to make sense, understanding and counseling the soldier, but grew impatient with the line of drivel parroted by Cummings. Straight out of the radical handbook, the language embarrassingly simplistic, any logic circular.

But Cummings was persistent. The event came to a close with the Operations Sergeant sending for the MPs, who escorted the soldier from the Operations Building to the office of the S-2/Security, where his access to classified material and controlled areas was suspended. Cummings was then escorted to his company, where his company commander restricted him to the barracks, allowing him only time to be escorted to his private quarters in the nearby town of Rosenheim to pick up personal articles and clothing.

The MPs, on a mission to save the free world, would not allow Cummings to converse with his wife, a matter of no great concern to her, but which she used to advantage when she later led the rally in downtown Rosenheim.

No one ever learned how she had sought out and found, courted with undescribed favors, quickly married, and accompanied Specialist Cummings back to Germany. For her, likely, the young soldier was an unexpected windfall. She did not relate how her brother and sister anti-war advocates reached their various levels of dedication, nor who devised the scheme of such insidious intrusion into the system. When Cummings was eventually transferred to the stockade at Mannheim for administrative detention, Mrs. Priscilla Cummings followed, moving her activities to that city, to larger support groups within the populace. Everybody moved up one in the anarchy hierarchy.

* * *

"Well, you can't say I didn't warn you," Specialist Toombs whined, staring across the mill at his Trick Chief with a look of vindication. "Now the Russkies issued that 'Warsaw Letter,' Dubcek's in deep *kim-chee* and a Pact takeover is imminent."

The Trick Chief, nursing a hangover from celebrating his wife's defection with her sergeant lover who was transferring to Taiwan, didn't give a rat's ass what the Russians might be doing. And what the hell was a doob-check?

* * *

A week later, Warrant Officer-One David D. Winter stood before the Commanding Officer, the Executive Officer, the Operations Officer, and the Personnel Officer, and was promoted to Chief Warrant Officer-Two. His wife, Nicole, made excuses not to attend the ceremony, thus avoiding complicity in Winter's further slide into arrant militarism.

That afternoon, dithering in the Morse bay in Operations, the new Chief Warrant Officer was alerted by Magic Marvin who said, "Chief, Major West wants you in his office. He said right away. Colonel's there." Winter started toward the hallway, and Marsh added, "Mister Barnshell and Mister Buford, too."

Major West waved him in the door and directly to a chair, and while they all waited silently, suitably impressed, the colonel ignored them while scanning the Read File. Winter loaded his pipe. He darted questioning glances at West and the other two warrants. It was obvious from the blank stares of the latter two that they were in the dark. Major West shook his head and looked away, examining a blank wall.

The commander laid the file on the desk, sniffed and frowned at Winter's pipe smoke. To West: "This all of them?" he loftily enquired, a disdainful inventory.

"Yes sir." West hesitated. "The only Ops officers not sitting on some board or committee or otherwise out of house for now."

The colonel settled himself and spoke in his pulpit voice. "Gentlemen, what I have to tell you does not go beyond this room, understood? You're not to relate any of this . . . to your NCOs—" he stared at Winter "—your clerks, your wives" and looked pointedly away from Winter. "No one! Understood?"

A mumble of assent.

"We have, this morning, ended the mystery of the unknown . . . ahh, prankster, assailant, what have you."

There was no comment. Nervous, sidelong glances.

"I believe the common reference on post is to Electric Man, a title self-imposed, I gather. In any event, we now know who this individual is and the circumstances surrounding . . ."

The three warrants shifted suspicious eyes from one to the other. Winter had the feeling one of the other two was about to be unmasked; he saw reciprocal anxiety in their eyes.

The colonel continued his delivery, and it was obvious he relished the secret he was barely containing. "Early this morning, with the suspicion that some men were hiding . . . *liquor*—" he spat out the word like a worm he'd suddenly discovered in his mouth "—in their lockers, Captain Meechan and his First Sergeant held a shakedown inspection. One of the men, just in from working a mids shift and known to be in the barracks, did not come forward to open his locker." The colonel paused for the drama to heighten.

"Since this individual has a reputation for erratic behavior, Captain Meechan thought he was trying to avoid shakedown for obvious reasons. The barracks sergeant found the man hiding in one of the latrine stalls."

A startling image of some liquor-swilling GI, perched like a defecating owl on the hard rubber ring of a cold toilet, did little to ease Winter's impatience with the colonel's melodrama. Goddammit! Get on with it! he urged silently.

"The man made a pretense of being unable to find his locker key. The First Sergeant sent the supply clerk for bolt cutters, prepared to cut the lock off, but the man produced the key and opened his locker. And inside, a surprise . . ."

Who the hell cared what? It obviously was not booze; the colonel had almost said that. *Who* was what mattered. Who was the Masked Marvel, promoter of *joie de vivre*, the elusive target of Waller's poor marksmanship, the brief but illuminating hope for solution to Meechan's continued existence? Who was the individual who for weeks now had provided an element of adventure in an otherwise drab servitude for hundreds of GIs?

Who was Electric Man?

But the colonel, pacing to a metronome of his own devising, plodded doggedly forward with relish. ". . . inside the locker, seven costumes," he said to the silent officers. "Seven sets of G.I. winter underwear dyed different colors." Winter, painfully aware of the colonel's bias in the scene he described, at no time felt an inclination to laugh at the charade. "Seven helmet liners painted to match the longjohns. Seven U.S. Army bedsheets, cut to fashion crude capes, dyed like the underwear. And a pair of high, black, patent leather boots. Patent leather . . ." the colonel muttered, staring into space. Winter thought of Meechan's fascination with the cape. All kinds.

Colonel Ahls glared at each man in turn: the three warrants who were the spokes in the Operations wheel, West the hub. Winter wanted to scream. If Electric Man worked in Ops—at this point it seemed he did—he was likely in one of their sections, but he would only work for one. How could all three be involved? Why were they all here? *Was machts du?*

"Specialist Five Van Ingen!"

Winter later told Brenner the name had dropped into the room like a thirty-pound elephant turd, and to Winter, had the same unwanted impact. "Van Ingen, Mister Winter," the colonel turned his ire on the new Chief. "The unprofessional *miscreant* you've gone to bat for . . . how many times? . . . Too many times."

In the shock of the announcement, Winter could not assimilate the revelation, but only wonder where the hell the Old Man dredged up *miscreant*, for God's sake! The archaic characterization, however, seemed somehow to fit Van Ingen, despite that Winter understood nothing of what was being said.

"Van Ingen! One of your *linguists*," the word nasty on the colonel's tongue. He continued, his voice rising, his hand pointing heavenward now, calling upon the supreme witness to his long suffering at the hands of such rabble. In righteous indignation, he said, "One of your Viet Nam trouble makers."

At the sneer in his commander's tone with the words "Viet Nam," Winter felt the urge to vault out of his chair and attack the old fool, but was shamed at the knowledge that he would not move. The colonel did not think much of the quality of soldiers coming out of 'Nam. The colonel thought the modern soldier a vast step downward from "old soldiers" of wars past. But then, the colonel lacked the experience to make any such judgements. He had somehow been passed over time and again in his *bid* for a combat command, bids known only through his telling. Oh, it was a troubling issue for him, he admitted: he'd tried hard, urging the Army to send him to Viet Nam, just in the interest of fairness among the rotation cycle of his fellow lieutenant colonels. All that effort, despite his personal feelings about the war. As God willed it, he'd managed also to miss the Korean fracas, and was too young for World War II.

There were those unkind enough to point out, though never to the colonel, that the colonel really didn't know jack shit about combat, about the unique problems of combat commands and combat troops, combat morale and casualties and pressures, about the shifting values and perspective of such troops and what it took to command in the face of this uniqueness. The colonel's contention was that command was command. Didn't make one whit of difference, he'd been heard to propound sententiously, if the command was in Chu Lai or Darmstadt or Fort Riley, Kansas. Remembering those expressions, Winter briefly thought kindly of the Pentagon selection process that had managed to deprive the colonel of the fray, had kept him away from the men he would have doomed.

The colonel was right to the extent that *in anyone's army, it was a wash*: He would have made a miserable combat commander.

"What do you make of *that*, Mister Winter?" The colonel didn't think much of warrant officers either, Winter knew, not being truly officers of the first water, but some bastard breed, some amalgam, neither officer nor enlisted man. He thought the colonel suspected they were a plague visited on him personally by a degenerative Army.

"Suffering Jews and Gentiles!" Buford exploded, turning to Winter.

Guy Van Ingen, Winter thought. Jesus! Speechless, he couldn't answer the colonel. It was as well; the colonel neither wanted nor expected an answer to his sermonizing

"—and no doubt he will try to make some accommodation with a . . . psychiatrist, some other falsified defense," Winter heard him say. He turned toward the colonel and rose to his feet. The blood pounded in his head; his fists were clenched.

"Dave, you can go ahead on back to your section. We're through," West said quickly. "Don't want to miss trick change." He inserted himself between Winter and the colonel.

Trick change was hours away.

"Tom. Major, I—"

"Go! Now! We're finished here." The major's hand tightly gripped him at the elbow. "I need that D.F. report and I don't trust your T.C.s to get it right."

What DF report? He had nothing to do with DF. Pure creativity.

Winter took a deep breath, shifted his glare from the colonel, stared West full in the face.

"Go on," the major urged him evenly.

The Colonel started to speak: "I think Mister Wint—"

"He has to go. Sir." West's tone was irrefutable. West turned away from Winter, keeping his body between the two men. Buford and Barnshell glanced casually at one another, at the floor, the ceiling, inspected the walls, checked the floor again. Both knew Winter and Van Ingen went back a way.

West shoved Winter gently toward the door.

* * *

In his office, Winter told Marsh, "Marve, I'm leaving for a while. Don't know where I'll be. I'll call if I'm going to be gone long." What the hell were they going to do if he walked out of Ops? For a few hours, or a few days? Send him to Viet Nam?

"Tell him to hang in there, Chief."

"Who?" A specious question, he knew.

"Van Ingen, of course, sir."

"You knew, then?"

"Sir! Really now."

"Naturally."

"I mean, really, sir." There was nothing smug or coy about the clerk's demeanor, his store of illicit knowledge. He was not called Magic Marvin for nothing.

Winter stormed out of his office and the operations building-hangar, not knowing where to go. Home was not an option. His mind was suffused with disparate visions. He sought stability and knew he would not find it. Jesus, Guy Van Ingen!

His mind flashed on past service, and he wondered how such a situation would have been handled in the Marines. The Army seemed always to do things differently. For sure, this Army Security life was nowhere near a grunt outfit, but he ought to be used to it by now. Going on nine years since he'd made that change.

Change!

Change of service. Change of direction, of life. Strange, obtuse paths he'd trodden.

Visions of startling clarity of early ASA assignments assailed him in that moment, visceral and ribald fantasies providing a welcome hiatus from the sudden ambiguity of Guy Van Ingen. He walked blindly, and later, would have been unable to say where he had gone physically in his suspended state, but his 201 file would have mapped out where his thoughts had traveled, in search of—for lack of a better explanation, he thought—in search of better times..

chapter three

FTA

En route; August 1960

The flight from Charleston Air Force Base to Asmara took four days on the Constellation.

Between South Carolina and Bermuda there was a box lunch: carton of warm milk, pulpy apple, two subdued and autopsied relics of cold, greasy chicken, a slice of cardboard bread, a piece of cheese only lately wrenched from a rat's embrace, and three crumbling cookies rejected by a soup kitchen. The Spec-5 across the aisle from PFC Winter drank his lunch. Sucking on a straw from a half-pint of Old Granddad hidden in a shaving kit in his lap, the Army specialist sought escape. He was en route to a MAAG advisory assignment at Taif in the Arabian desert and wouldn't see a woman's face or taste alcohol for the next twenty-four months.

There were military dependents on the flight. The SP5 was shortly informed by the Air Force sergeant flight steward to consider himself in custody for having threatened to throw a dependent urchin from the plane. The specialist had only verbalized what everyone on board felt. The child was an abomination and had brazenly interrupted the Spec-5's liquid lunch.

In Bermuda, the inshore waters were azure mirrors. The Class VI was closed so no one could sneak a bottle for the ongoing leg, and there was no time to take one of the tiny cabs or horse-drawn carriages into Hamilton for whatever enticements the city offered. Two hours on the ground; liftoff.

Eight hours to the Azores. Nothing to get excited about, it was obvious why Portugal's interests had faded. Lajes, patchwork green and white; small sad farms, and the transient air base strung up a hillside from the valley airstrip. Box lunches piled in the trash and an open-sided van to the top of the hill for mid-afternoon chow in isolated, Air Force messhall splendor. Back on the vibrating transport before anyone could get acclimated to a stable environment. Not that the Azores was stable, but it showed promise of continuing to float.

Tripoli humid, warm. Linen issue and idiot lessons by an Air Force two-striper at 0230 hours. Reveille by a *muzzeim* in an unseen minaret, the metallic echo of the PA system adding disharmony to the otherwise disagreeable awakening somewhere near 5 A.M. Arab servers in the chow line sneaking bacon sandwiches between sessions on the prayer rug. After takeoff and altitude, the littoral of habitation in Libya was visible as a green swathe running inland for a mile or so from the Med, stopping where the sandy wastes of interior Africa began.

Cairo was a mistake. Had to be! No logical reason to touch down there. The pyramid and sphinx concession was controlled by Colonel Nasser, and he wasn't sharing. American GIs were not even allowed on the sacred sand wastes of the ancient kingdom. The Connie-load of troops was herded into a non-air-conditioned, barn-like hangar and left for three hours without food or water, and a bathroom break was performed above a hole in the ground. And no paper. Jeez-us, talk about anxious to avail oneself of the questionable embrace of the abominable Constellation.

Brit Air Force GCA brought the Connie down on Bahrein Island: super saturation humidity, 90-degree temperature at 0200—what the hell was this Air Force penchant for landings only in the dead hours?—bad breakfast and a boring, five-hour stand-up wait for the early, quick hop to Dhahran on the Saudi coast after the fog lifted. Another landing, daytime this time, and maybe he understood why the zoomies chose nighttime landings. Unreal heat, sun, sand, dust; Saudi civilians in the BX, camel drivers buying toasters and black and white TVs, and not an electric outlet anywhere in the Empty Quarter.

Afternoon movie at the joint American-Saudi military theater; Saudi airmen holding hands, playing grabass in the dark, with liquid eyes promising nirvana of a peculiarly male-bonding style. A quick but bizarre venture in a cab to the nearest town of Dhahran, pit stop for the multitude of ARAMCO oil company workers and families, where he caught a glimpse of Arab justice.

* * *

Dhahran-Al Khobar, Saudi Arabia; August 1960

Six soldiers piled into the '57 Chevy. The driver yelled, threatened, and pleaded, complaining they were too many. They remained unmoved. The inside of the taxi—doors, seats, dashboard, floor and headliner, upholstered in cheap, gaudy carpet—smelled of goats.

Winter, seated next to the driver, leaned away, grateful the aroma of goats was allowed to linger.

US Air Police and Saudi MPs competed to see who could pass the most vehicles onto and off the joint airbase, unimpeded, in the shortest time. Security was just a word. The cab full of GIs exited the base in a swirl of copycat Chevies.

The road from the base at Dhahran along the coast to the town of Al Khobar was thin, uneven macadam, suspended in broken floes on the surface of scorching sand. The afternoon sun provoked a stifling assault: the eye-smarting reek of hot tar and blistered dust through the open left window; from the right arose the smell of salt-water brine and rotted fish.

The driver, illogically imploring them to somehow reduce their numbers, sensing in Winter the leader, turned repeatedly toward the soldiers in the back seat,. He was not to know it, only sense the status, that with one Private exception they were all PFCs. Winter had prior service; years of it, the others were aware. The driver felt it.

The soldiers as a body ignored the Arab, staring out at the few diseased camels chewing determinedly on unseen fodder along the verge. A family of Bedouins walking haphazardly along the center of the road provided inexplicable comic relief.

The soldiers fondled the carpeting in the taxi, pronouncing it cheap and gaudy. They stared longingly over the dry flats toward the aquamarine shimmer of the Persian Gulf beyond.

Each time the driver turned about in entreaty, the packed sedan was at risk. No one acknowledged responsibility for the path they followed. The Chevy raced up the coast road, alternately driving on the right with cars passing on their left; then on the left with vehicles speeding by on the right; sometimes up the middle of the road with dual threats bracketing them.

The flat emptiness of the coastal desert reared suddenly into a jumble of dirty white—square shapes and spires that formed the town of Al Khobar: new and old, filth and dazzling purity, Agip gas stations and thrusting minarets. Unlikely stucco and concrete apartments, their newness fading, were anchored on dirt streets. Sheep roved at will in the streets, in and out of doorways.

Through the streaked windshield Winter caught a glimpse of movement above, a shrouded figure with the grace of a woman, the shy elusiveness of the young. She stood on a third floor balcony, hanging wet clothing on a line stretched between an iron grillwork door and a metal pipe holding the tattered remnants of an awning. As he stared, the young woman glanced at him, jerked the veil tighter across her face, and disappeared into the house.

The taxi continued through the maze, bounced around one final corner, and scraped to a halt in the square of the town. The driver, for the first time showing enthusiasm for his enterprise, stepped from the car and gestured grandly about the square. The soldiers, in bored resignation, stepped into the late sun of the square. It was mostly bare, except for an old man sitting in the dirt, leaning back in the late shade against the wall of a building with a steepled, green-glazed roof. Beyond, a shapeless bundle huddled near a dark stain in the sand.

To the right of the taxi, some forty feet out from a low stucco wall with crenellated crest, a two-pole-and-crossbar affair was erected, suggesting a football goalpost. With curiosity at the familiar, the soldiers strode toward the rack. Beneath the crossbar a cloud of flies partially obscured several objects, suspended like market goods: a large, brown right hand missing two fingers; a much smaller and paler hand that appeared intact; and a human head. Swarming flies made it impossible to tell if the eyes were open in the head, or indeed if it were that of a man or a woman. But it had not been brought to the bar of justice with a clean, humane stroke. The flesh was hacked and ripped about the neck, ugly strands hanging below, drying to jerky in the desert air. Their curiosity satisfied, if assailed, they fled back to the goat-smelling taxi.

Later that afternoon a merchant in a dark back street tried to sell them a carpet which he promised was truly Persian. When they had bargained, and had considered but finally declined the offer, he gave them each a packet of rough but serviceable writing paper. That was for *baksheesh*, he said, and refused payment.

Overnight in the transient barracks, another bad breakfast, it was the only time they had in Saudi Arabia. Shortly, lift-off in "The Desert Rat," a C-54 deployed out of the past, across the great Empty Quarter. Brief, nervous stops with no de-planing—Why the hell had they landed?—in Riyadh, Taif—even the arrested SP5 was not on board to be deposited in this wasteland—Jedda—where a Pepsi with Arabic script, the ubiquitous blue and red logo, cost almost a dollar—then west, over the Red Sea, which, surprisingly, was not Red, to Eritrea, mistakenly called Ethiopia then. .

After a boring hour, Winter felt the aircraft gaining altitude. Anticipating bad weather, he waited and.when the aircraft did not fall apart, asked an airman shuffling cargo around, "What's the problem? Why're we climbing?"

The airman, after moments, finally deigning to answer, said, "We're going in to land."

It was only then Winter remembered the information bulletin he'd picked up in the Fort Devens MI school library about Kagnew Station at Asmara, the city in Eritrea (temporarily Ethiopia) where the base was located. The Eritrean capital spread out on a plateau at 8,000 feet. He later learned they had flown at 5,500 feet across the Red Sea.

* * *

Asmara, Eritrea (Ethiopia): 1960-1961

The long rainy season was past, the little wet three months away. Banks of clouds, mere false threats, hovered along the escarpment rim. Where the plateau crumbled away toward the flats about Zula— becoming in one final, half-serious effort the shores of the Red Sea—the threat seemed imminent. But it had not rained for days. The ditch was dry where the soldier lay.

"You wanna get up, Mac" Winter called.

"Naw, he don't. Can't you tell when a man's in his element?" Harry Spruance spoke with a firmness grounded in experience.

"Get up, Mac!"

"Leave 'im alone. Least he ain't pukin' in the squadbay."

"We can't leave him out here. First Sergeant'll have his ass. And the goats'll eat his clothes."

The myth of the voracious goats—ubiquitous, omnipresent when least desired—was learned early-on during a tour in Asmara, and never forgotten. No one dared ignore the sad tale of Sergeant DeMaione.

"You got a terminal case of empathy, Dave. Or just plain dumbass. Goat wouldn't touch Ratty Mac's clothes, doncha know. Anyhow, didn't you never see 'im like this before? Hell, he looks natural in goat shit."

The object of this early morning discourse moved in halting mimicry of a live being, one hand clawing feebly at the dry, red soil in the streetside drainage ditch. Tiny puffs of dust arose from his efforts. like vapor from a miniature volcano rising from a fissure in the earth's bowels. His fingers twitched in spasm, clutching at something present only in his muddled mind. The twitch reminded Winter of a pianist's finger exercises.

"Get up, you silly shit. Day Trick's making formation. Bus'll be here soon." There was a desperate, almost disbelieving quality to Winter's urging.

"Jesus, Dave, ain't you got no sense of propriety? Man's found a fuckin' home. Leave him be," Spruance insisted. He probed a boot into the scrabble at the roadside, nudging loose pebbles and dirt in a small avalanche that cascaded into the ditch.

Winter heard a whoop and looked up. Teklai stood on the third floor balcony of Operations Company barracks with two other houseboys. The three of them were laughing and pointing, chattering in what served them as language.

"Hell, Harry. He's disgracing us in front of the goddamned Ethis. Let's get him out of there."

Harry Spruance's disdain was clear. "Teklai's been in the ditches," he said. Winter was too new at Kagnew Station to credit the *non sequitur*.

Ratty Mac flailed at the sides of the ditch, going down for the third time. Waves of red dust closed over his sinking body until he became suddenly still.

"Who's that?" rose from the peremptory grave.

"Get up, Mac. It's Dave Winter. Give me your hand."

"You can't drink for shit, Mac," Spruance scoffed.

"Harr-r-ry? That you?" Ratty Mac turned his head grotesquely far in an arc toward the sound, burrowing his nose into dust and rock chips. "Where am I?"

"In front of the company. Get up outta the ditch, Mac."

"Yeah. *Near* the company. Missed by tha-a-a-t much," Spruance chided, holding his thumb and forefinger a quarter-inch apart before Mac's unseeing eyes. Harry held no brief for losers, and he would cut Ratty Mac no more slack now than he would in a poker game in Club 31.

MacGantree had struggled onto his back, and his hands pawed pitifully, futilely at the high, fast-moving clouds that would be over Somalia in an hour.

"Harry . . . Dave! Are my eyes open?" he croaked.

"No, you simple asshole. You're drunk."

"Thank God," the prostrate soldier said, shuddering deeply. "I thought I was blind."

There was a screech of brakes behind them in the street, the sound a worn, tired alarm. Spruance and Winter turned to watch the Military Police advancing on the ditch.

* * *

The headlights flashed skyward, then down onto the dry, rutted ground as the Jeep's right front wheel sank in scree. Lights were almost useless in the ambiguity between dusk and dark.

"Harry, you silly asshole . . . watch the ditch!" Ratty Mac screamed. He was standing, one foot on the Jeep's front floorboard, one knee on the seat, rifle braced across the top frame of the cracked windshield. The .30-06 jolted with each bounce of the vehicle, pinching his arm. "How d'ya expect me to hit the sonnav—look out! Goddamn, he's headed for the *wadi*." The hunter swore on fluently, bracing for the Jeep's turn.

Spruance never looked at him and didn't answer. His glassy eyes were fixed somewhere out in the void beyond the reach of the headlights.

From the back seat, hanging on with fierce determination, Darmanian shouted, "I think it's unlikely, MacGantree, that you could hit the beast should we chase him into a closed room."

"That's what! That's all I need. I don't notice you turnin' loose-a that rail and haulin' your ass up here with a weapon," Ratty Mac sneered back over his shoulder. The effect was lost when the Jeep swerved and Mac let out a yipping scream, maintaining his grip on the windshield by the barest margin.

"You animal, you'll recall I wanted no part of a slaughter at this hour to begin with . . . not after your bout with the bottle this p.m.," Darmanian shouted.

"Ahh-h-h, get bent, you sniveling puke." MacGantree spat over the side of the Jeep as it continued rattling blindly across the flats. "Hey, lifer! Pass me the jug . . . careful-like." Intent on the chase, he did not look back.

There was no answer. The Jeep bounded on like some accursed vessel of the damned, coursing its way across the burning flats of hell.

"Lifer! . . . Dave! . . . *Hey, Winter!* Jeez-us! Is he passed out or somethin', Darmanian?"

"I certainly hope so," the reluctant passenger shouted back. "I am thoroughly disenchanted with his performance in an enebriated state. Fortunately, he does not seem to have the remainder of the liquor, either."

"Fortunate, my ass! We—*There, Harry!* Mac screamed. "You goddamned ignorant Texas asshole. *Watch him.* Watch the fuckin' porker, you good-for-nothing—Now. *Now, now,* you shit. Keep the headlights on him."

The African evening had lived up to the best literary expectations, advancing from a true gen Hemingway sunset, through a murky Ruark dusk with a little Isaac Denison thrown in, and was now, in Brenner terms, stark dark.

"Why don't you simply shoot the creature, MacGantree. Get it over with. This continues much too long," Darmanian said lamely.

"Because, you four-eyed, weak sister," Mac screamed back, "that pig's still fifty . . . yards away, and this Jeep's . . . Oww! . . . bouncin' like a bitch . . . and even though I'm the world's greatest . . . Ouch! . . . shot—"

"Hah!"

"—there's no guarantee I'll hit him . . . and if I do hit him . . . there's no guarantee I'll drop him. And I ain't so anxious as you might think . . . Oww! . . . to get out and . . . *Oww! Fuck!* . . . blood-track a gut-shot boar into the bush at night." The wind whipped his voice off into the vast desert night. Turning halfway round to speak to the back seat, "Hell, I'll just chase this porker . . . all the way south through the Danakil to Djibouti if we have to . . . get him tired enough . . . catch. Then I'll take him." He spat again and cursed again as the Jeep leaped and the rifle barrel pinched his arm on the windshield frame.

"Come on, MacGantree. Have Spruance slow down," Darmanian urged in what he knew to be a hopeless cause, his voice weak against the wind and vehicle noises. "At least, get him back on the road. He's going to kill us." He would have said "please" if he'd thought the word was in the manic hunter's lexicon.

"The pig ain't on the road, asshole! Shit! Don't matter . . ." Mac shouted over his shoulder, watching the nearby road for a moment, then swivelling his eyes to the driver, to the road behind, the back seat, and again to the elusive boar. "Don't matter if he slows down. Harry's too drunk to see anything, anyhow. He could kill us at five miles per. Can't see nothin'." He leaned toward the driver's ear: "To the right, Harry, don't lose him now. He's startin' to show signs . . ."

The battered little vehicle careened around rocks and thorn bushes, miraculously skirting some holes, crashing down into others, missing by inches a line of baobab trees that loomed suddenly in the night, and thundered on along the edge of the dry *wadi* seemingly of its own volition. The driver's effect on the vehicle's path was negligible.

"Come on now, Harry," Mac urged. "His ass is draggin' bad. Get us a lee-e-tle closer and I'll put one up his shit-chute. That's . . . that's it! Come on, you blind Texas dumbass, closer, clo-o-o-ser . . . keep us smooth."

As if sensing the sight blade of the .30-06 between its shoulders, the wild boar suddenly put on a desperate burst of speed and angled to the right, pulling away from the loud, stinking thing behind. The animal raced across a cleared strip, veered back into it, and held there where the running was easier.

"Whaa-hoo-o-oo! We got him now. He's cuttin' right down the track. Watch it up ahead, Harry. The track dips sharp . . . after that rise by the trees." Ratty Mac's voice could be heard more clearly, now the Jeep ran on smoother ground. He yelled back at Darmanian whose eyes were clinched shut. "See, now. If you'd-a-stayed in camp, you'd-a-missed all this fun. Now ain't this fun? Huh? C'mon, boy, admit it," he yelled wildly. "Ain't no book . . . *I told you to watch the fuckin' dip*, dip. Jeesh."

The Jeep smashed into a depression, seemed to pull itself together, and raced off down the slope, clattering over rocks, the right wheels again off the track. At the bottom of the slope loomed a dark patch of brush and thorn bushes edging the track. The makeshift road that ultimately ran from Cairo to Capetown, here undulated through a series of wallows, moderate sumps where animals came to perform their ablutions in the dust.

"Darmanian, you want a shot? Huh? I'll set him up . . . you blast 'im," Mac shouted. He was grinning back over his shoulder with maniacal blood lust when the Jeep struck the first game wallow.

"No, you maniac. I do not wish—"

It was a big game wallow.

"Wha-a-a-a-a . . ." the scream faded away.

"—to be a party to that animal's murder. I simply want . . . MacGantree?" Darmanian realized he was speaking only to himself. *"Maaa-a-a-c!"*

The front seat was empty beside the driver. Spruance held his own, piloting the Jeep negligently down the dirt track, oblivious to everything in the vehicle, blind to anything beyond it. Winter had not been a factor since he first crawled into the back seat and passed out at the start of the hunt.

"Stop the Jeep, Spruance. Harry! *Stop the Jeep, Haa-r-r-r-y* . . . stop the darned Jeep."

The vehicle slithered through dust and gravel and ground to a halt, killing the engine. A dust storm swirled around and over the Jeep, powdering everything with gritty talcum. In the sudden silence, behind them in the black void, a scream pierced the air. "*Har-ry* . . . *Dar-r-man-i-an! Hel-l-lp me. Get me outta hee-e-re! Hel-l-l-l-l-l-lp!*"

Darmanian rose to his feet, preparing to jump from the vehicle and run to the sound of Mac's voice, but he suffered a stab of warning: the unfamiliar desert floor, the vast body of myth and bad reputation about the flats. Mambas and scorpions and fire ants, oh my! He held his place.

He coaxed, threatened, and cajoled the drunken driver, who finally got the engine started. Darmanian guided Harry, backing sixty yards to roughly the point where they'd lost Ratty Mac. The screaming grew louder, more vociferous with each yard in reverse. Darmanian halted Spruance where the screams were loudest.

The reluctant hunter sat in the Jeep, staring out to the edge of the lights diffused on rocks and a tangled mass of thorn bushes. The screams became louder when the vehicle came to a stop, the voice at once entreating, threatening.

"Shut your face, MacGantree, or I'll let you hang there for the rest of your unnatural life."

"Darmanian, you bastard. Oww-w-w-w! When I get *Ouch!* out of here—"

"*If* you get out, MacGantree. If! I wish that miserable beast could see you now. Even the porker's not stupid enough to leap into the middle of a thorn bush." Darmanian removed his glasses and began polishing them on his shirttail.

Ratty Mac was a blur, the night starless and moonless for the moment under cloud. "I'll skin you alive, you goddamned *owww!* puke. You squirrelly little prick, I'll cut off your—"

"In your somewhat colorful exploitation of the venacular, MacGantree—bullshit! The animal is home free, and you, my less-than-eloquent companion-at-arms, are in no position to make threats."

Darmanian shook Winter awake while the de-throned hunter continued, unabated, his abuse of the Jeep's occupants. The two passengers—ignoring the driver whose head had dropped forward onto the steering wheel immediately they stopped—managed finally to extract a lacerated Ratty Mac from the thorns.

Darmanian and Winter removed Spruance's inert remains from the driver's seat, dumping them into the rear. Winter climbed in the back, silent throughout the process, wedging Harry's body into the tiny space on the floorboard between front and back seats.

Algernon MacGantree, a subdued and semi-chastened, thoroughly pained Ratty Mac, eased his torn, bruised body into the right front seat, lately so hastily abandoned. Darmanian retrieved the great white hunter's rifle from the thorns, stared at it with dull suspicion, and handed it to Winter in the back seat who slammed the bolt back, clearing it, and slid it under the seat. Winter glanced at the silent heap that was Harry Spruance, then turned to stare at Ratty Mac's back. Stirred by some recessed bit of memory or sudden understanding, he began to laugh.

As Darmanian, chuckling, turned the Jeep and headed back up the track, Ratty Mac said, "Yeah. That's right . . . that's O.K., you fuckin' clowns. Go ahead and laugh. It ain't funny, goddammit. My ass is like a pincushion . . . *oww!*" He gritted his teeth and picked at thorns that projected from him like tiny, cutaneous antennae. "That ain't all, either," he said archly. "Now we ain't got . . . no pig for supper."

Emitting a mixed medley of moans and giggles, the shabby little force retreated back toward the camp from whence the band of Great White Hunters had so exuberantly issued forth in the early evening.

* * *

I was in the midst of a dream about a land filled with white women and golden ale—a fantasy common to me since my arrival in the Land of the Queen of Sheba—when the sound of the Jeep woke me. I heard the straining engine grinding slowly across the flats while still beyond sight. Tesfai, one of our houseboys from the base back up on the mountain, who was acting cook on this outing, scurried to waken the Ethiopian soldier-guard. I had an uneasy feeling. In the movements of the houseboy there was something furtive. I saw fear on his face. Only then did I notice a pair of local nationals—probably Afars, a minority among the nine nationalities that went to make up the Eritrean social structure—moving slowly but determinedly away from the camp. I wondered what magic our guide-cum-cook was practicing with them.

On the other side of the fire from me, Crazy Bruce lay where he'd slowly slid into unconsciousness earlier.

"Tesfai, goddammit!" MacGantree began yelling before the Jeep's motion ceased. "I told you to watch that Ethi guard." He swivelled around toward where I sat up on the tarp. "Shit, Brenner, you guys let that fuckin' guard sleep all day, and then you let him snooze on us right on into the night."

I was still hazy from the late afternoon boozing and sleep, and the heat that sapped us as if leaching out juices from low forms of life. I was in no mood for Mac's Supreme Dictator act.

"Bite my ass, Mac. Who made you king for a day?"

"Well," he whined, "he's hired to mind the camp. You been asleep, ain't you? What the hell good is it if he's asleep, too? Shiftees could-a walked right in on you. Took it all. Guns, gear, everything. Might-a blowed you away." He was pissed; he'd convinced me, but I didn't know then about the thorn bush.

Ratty Mac jumped out of the Jeep and stormed over to the startled houseboy. "Hey, nigger," he yelled.

"Sor!" Tesfai's impression of British sergeants-major he'd served in previous colonial regimes—ramrod stance, unfocused stare—was funny to everyone but Mac.

"'Sor,' my ass, you sorry black bastard. You get that other black sonuvabitch in gear. D'ja let him get into the booze, too?" he asked, glancing at me as if he really expected me to reply. Unanswered, he shifted his gaze to the wooden chop box with the loose top.

"Sor, no, sor! No boose . . . no wiskey . . . no drink! Only rest . . . guard and rest." Tesfai resembled some Boschian imp of darkness: tiny, his seamed, ageless face screwed up into an unreadable mask. He studied the sky when Winter started gurgling. I couldn't tell if Dave was strangling or laughing. The guard had scrambled to his feet, struggling with the strap of the Enfield. All the time he inched farther from the source of contentious noises and disappeared into the dark of the desert beyond, while Mac raged on.

"Brenner—"

"Screw you, Mac. That's two." He took that as my final comment and turned away. My head was still somewhere between my dream and the reality of this inexplicable circus.

Tesfai, working his way toward Winter, away from Mac's tirade, asked with his eyes about a meat kill, and I glanced over at the Jeep where Darmanian was trying to coax Harry from the floor in the back. I could hear only moans.

Winter said, "Nothing, Tesfai. We had one big jackass all spitted and ready for the fire . . . but we had to let him go."

"Sor!" Tesfai, nobody's fool, could read sign. He rolled his eyes away and jerked his head back toward the dark. He scurried throughout the camp, stacking boxes and cans, moving water jugs, re-stacking boxes and supplies. Make-work.

Ratty Mac stood at the edge of the firelight, pissing on Africa. But, like some vicious, ankle-biting terrier, he wouldn't give it up. "What's that smell, Tesfai? Smells like gazelle," he said, glancing over at the spit arranged over the fire. "Looks like gazelle."

I noticed then, for the first time, the smell of roasting meat.

"Can't be gazelle, Mac," Winter said. "Nobody killed game." But his nostrils twitched; he smelled it too.

"Perhaps something wandered into the encampment and simply . . . expired," contributed Darmanian. He was busy using up a day's water ration washing his face and hands. The only one on the hunt who wasn't filthy, Barry invariably washed using precious water rations. It didn't seem to matter that we were six leagues beyond the back side of hell with no chance of replenishment.

Winter leaned over the fire, checking the spitted meat. "Two guinea hens and a Thomson's gazelle. Wonder where they came from?" he asked seriously. I had the uneasy feeling that something was happening. There was no meat in camp when I lay down with the last of the Tuborg. Winter caught Tesfai's eye, but that old imp looked quickly away, interested in something on the horizon.

"Tesfai, you goddamned old crook. Did you take Bruce's shotgun, shoot this game? While they were gone? You and your buddy?" I said, nodding toward the evasive guard. Ratty Mac's concern had been academic, mine more pointed, but there did not seem to be an answer required to his or my questions. Tesfai stood, staring at the ground, then off into the black void following the trail of the guard. It was impossible to imagine his thoughts.

"And you, Brenner. I don't suppose you saw what happened," Mac said, suddenly sounding shocked and chagrined. "You gonna tell me you slept through the whole thing."

"I'm going to tell you fuck-all, Mac. What part of my message have you not understood?" I could see as well as they what had happened, but it wasn't going to ruin my day, whatever the hell was left of it. Truth was, I didn't know a damned thing about the game. I'd started drinking early that afternoon with Winter and Crazy Bruce and Harry, while Ratty Mac was sleeping off the results of the previous night's bout, and Darmanian had sat and read Swinburne in the shade of the fly tent. By the time Mac had come around, the four of us were well on our way. I wasn't about to admit it to Mac, but I couldn't even remember when they'd left camp to hunt. And why they had taken Winter and Spruance, I hadn't a clue. Neither one could've hit Eritrea with a howitzer.

And we were in the Danakil Depression, well within Eritrea.

But Mac's was not the only concern. "Hey, now, Tesfai," Winter put in, ever the social conscience, "you know that's against the law. Haile's law. You could go to prison for ten years, just for even carrying a gun. I don't care—none of us gives a shit—if you shot up half of Eritrea, and Ethiopia proper, especially for supper—" Winter nodded at the roasting meat "—but we don't know this other Ethi," he added, nodding toward the dim shape of the guard, returned to the edge of the firelight. "For all we know, he might turn your ass in. For the reward."

"Hey, lifer, for shit's sake, leave him alone. He's already bribed the guard, ya know? Probably with our booze and chow. We won't have any trouble outta the guard." Mac, eyeing the roasting game, had edged toward acceptance of all violations, and was careful to avoid looking at the chaste guard, who stayed as far from him as possible. "And besides . . . that Tommy sure smells good." He grinned, still rubbing his thorn-pricked skin.

I don't know how Winter received Mac's offhand assurances, but they did little for me. The Imperial Prison was not a round-trip destination.

But when Darmanian chimed in, offering his own take on why we should just drop it—something about Bruce being in camp all the time, and it was probably he who'd shot the gazelle and the hens. He never mentioned me, a nonentity. Winter must have realized he was out-voted, and gave in; I said nothing. The aroma of the fowl and the dripping Tommy chops trumped any concerns. All damned near starved, we dove for the food without further words.

From deep within the circle of masticating would-be hunters came an explosive pronouncement in military lingua franca: *"Fuck the Army!"* I couldn't tell who the FTA advocate was tonight.

We were munching out, the only sounds the chomping, sucking, slurping noises rising in a circle about the fire. As one, on some hidden signal, we turned to see Harry Spruance, without fanfare, rise suddenly from the back seat of the Jeep, raise his pointing finger to the sky in preparation for oratory . . . and fall forward onto his face in the dust. His right arm and index finger pointed generally in the direction of Mecca across the Red Sea, like some infidel statuary fallen from neglect, paying homage to its Muslim origins. He lay where he fell; I was grateful for his consideration. Those whom he'd chauffeured thought it was justice. Tesfai, no doubt, had other reasons to smile; the guard had no part in it. Crazy Bruce slept on.

It took three of us to wrestle Harry's dead weight back into the vehicle.

When everyone had eaten their fill, including Harry who finally scrambled alert at the smell of chow, and Tesfai and the guard were fed, and there was meat left on the spit, Ratty Mac booted Crazy Bruce in the ass until he groaned and stirred. Still, he would not be awakened. But Mac was insistent.

Eventually, in response to an especially lusty kick, the first casualty of the noon drinking spree rolled over and scrambled to his knees, cursing fluently in some lost language: "Wazzit . . . brft . . . we gon massme offetto frikkin goddampt assho' 'ng frzdge . . . can't seeth' fin' me . . . umph!"

"*Raust, mein Herr!* Get your dead ass up and get some chow before I throw it to the jackals." Ratty Mac's invitation penetrated Bruce's alcoholic buffer. He shuffled forward on his knees toward the fire.

"Gimme coffee," he growled.

Darmanian began, "Do you wish a cupful, or would you care—"

"Gimme fucking coffee . . . kill you!" Bruce glared at Darmanian and we all thought the same thing: Barry had misread the big man's usual taciturn behavior.

Bruce got coffee. No one ever suggested his threats might be idle.

We were content to sit and let the chops settle, swill a Heinneken, and watch with fascination the phenomenon of Bruce's dining. I mean, out here at the end of the line in a country at the end of the line, we all acted like animals of some kind at one time or another. And I would not denigrate our domestic pig by making comparisons, but Bruce—Whoa!

After a bit, I noticed Dave sipping his beer and listening to Ratty Mac who chuckled to himself but aloud. I heard him too, though I wasn't about to ask him to explain himself; he was too willing to do that. But Winter could only ignore him so long until it got on his nerves. "What's got your giggle box upended, Mac?"

Mac ripped some more stringy flesh from the skinny Tommy's haunch he'd held on to, and with a full mouth, making more noise than sense, told us his latest take on new guys.

"Most-a you know the newk, Pettit, right? Well, they had him on the—" He chopped off his speech, looked around at the two Ethis just beyond the dining circle, and readjusted his telling to an unclassified version "—the guys down at the end of my row." Several of the hunters, all manual Morse ops and visualizing the layout in the Morse bay, nodded. "Well, he didn't do for shit there. So they moved him up, side-saddle on my pos. Thought The Mac could straighten his young ass out." He gave over talking while he wrestled with the meat, swallowed, and picked up the narrative.

"So I had him . . . let's see . . . three swings, doing my thing, and you know that ain't the smoothest sailin' on the bay. Then when we went back on days, first day he fucked up two whole hours of a sked. Chatter roll looked like Mandarin. Pissed me off, but—" he looked at Winter "—payin' attention to my betters on how to go along, get along, I didn't come down on the lad. I called him aside when we got a break and sent him to maintenance for a band expander."

"For Christ's sake, Mac. The kid's trying."

"Yeah, I know, Barry. Like you tried. Like we all tried, early on. But I'm not payin' him to try. He's gotta push himself, get his code speed up. Get some!"

"Shit, Mac, you're not paying him for anything," Bruce reminded him. "Who made you leader of the pack?" It was at least the second time that query had been uttered, and when Bruce took time out of eating to talk, it was serious doings, and listeners listened.

"I know, Bruce. I know . . . just givin' him a little of what we all had to go through," Mac said in a tone designed to smooth feathers.

"Sulzer says he catches anyone pulling that shit anymore during work, he'll have some ass." Bruce shook his head, reminding the hunters of a bull bison in a snow storm.

"Yeah, that kind of trick used to be common in every field," Dave added. "When I was in I.T.R., and made some kinda goof—can't even remember what, now—a corporal sent me four miles down a North

Carolina swamp road at midnight to draw two hundred yards of skirmish line at regimental supply. And all the way there, in the dark and back, I was thinking, this can't be right. I must have misheard."

"What the hell's I.T.R.? 's that one-a them Marine things you go ashore in?" Harry had to throw in his two bits.

"Infantry Training Regiment. Like A.I.T. in the Army. If you're infantry, then it's your Advanced Individual Training. And all Marines are infantry. Anyhow . . ."

"Well, go on. What happened?" Once he stuck his oar in, Harry couldn't help paddling.

"Nothing happened. I just looked like a jerk. Well . . . a Gunner—a Marine warrant officer—did chew me a new ass for breaking up his poker game to draw an issue middle of the night—something that didn't exist." There were a few chuckles.

Mac started to get back in. "Yeah, but—"

"Before I went to oh-five-eight school," Birch, who'd been silent throughout to the extent that I had forgotten him, interrupted, "I was in maintenance. Back in maintenance school, the instructor sent me to Electronics Supply, clear on the back side of Fort Gordon, to draw a fallopian tube. To replace a bad one in my set." It was obvious Birch still had a case of red-ass over the trick. I was surprised he'd tell it on himself, he being such a quiet one.

Before the laughter died, Mac said, "What the hell's a fa . . . fau . . . whatever you said?"

Now the laughter was general and loud. Winter said, "Something in a female's plumbing."

Snickers.

Ratty Mac looked around the circle, suspicious. "What's funny about someone sending you to Electronics Supply for plumbing parts?"

At Mac's clueless response, two of the hunters fell out on the ground, rolling cautiously away from the fire. Bruce, who had taken a long pull emptying a bottle of Heinneken, spewed the beer across the fire, steam rising as from Old Faithful.

"O.K. O.K.," Mac said, knowing he'd bitten. "You got me. But what I was trying to get in before all this merriment, is that when I hooked up the band expander and plugged Pettit's phone jack in, he got real excited and jumped on that code. The *real* funny thing is, the asshole's copy has improved about two hundred percent. No, no," he said at the explosion of comments. "It really has. I even took his cans and put 'em on and listened. When I caught myself doing it, *I* felt like an asshole. Course, there couldn't be any change. I knew that. Inside that black box is just a straight wire from input to output. But Pettit thinks the signal's better. I *know* his copy's better. He might graduate to pos in a coupla' more days."

The quality of the laughter changed, and the conversation shifted from the inexplicable to the undeniable. It took a while, but with Holland's finest flowing, and full bellies, the pace of the evening slowed toward a halt. Eventually, Bruce, Mac, and Birch took the remaining bits of the Tommy and went a couple of klicks down the track to a watering hole and staked out for leopard. It was just an exercise; everybody knew they'd get no takers; cat wouldn't touch meat that fresh, and cooked, too. I was asleep when they returned.

I heard them clumping around, giggling about something, but they finally settled down and the last conscious vision I had was the Ethiopian soldier-guard, trickling tiny pieces of brush and twigs into the pit to keep the fire going. He was wide awake; I wondered for how long.

chapter four

Down Among the Sheltering Baobab

Dankalia Province, Eritrea (Ethiopia): 1961

Something woke me. I don't know how long I'd slept, but some-*thing* Jerked me awake. Wide awake. I listened . . . nothing! I sat up and looked about the camp. Nothing moved. It was completely dark and there was no sound.

Completely dark!

No glow, no crackle of fire!

There was no fire and I could not see the guard. Did I miss him in the dark? Unlikely.

A sliver of new moon slipped out of the coastal cloud mass and I could just make out vague shapes: the bulk of the Jeep, a couple of bodies in and out of sleeping bags. Rocks. A bush. Suddenly I was struck by an overwhelming stench, the reek of something long dead.

I was in that half-confused nether land, coming from a sound sleep. I knew, suddenly, what had wakened me, but couldn't reconcile it. I felt a tingle of anticipation, a rush of fear, on the edges of impressions combining smell, a few indistinct snuffling sounds, and the suggestions of movement. Before I could be rewarded with clarity, a bright light snapped on.

Movement off to my right—

A scream behind me—a bark.

Scuffling in the dust and the sound of pounding feet. More sounds from every side—Whines and growls, the snap of large metal traps, and the light swung toward me.

In the beam, between me and the light a few yards away, hunkered a lanky, dun-colored animal with shapeless body, dark splotches, and big shoulders sloping back to distorted, short back legs. A huge dog-like head with flared ears tilted forward, away from the light, toward me! The apparition made a jump in my direction, fleeing the light.

The hyena leaped, its mouth huge, coming to devour me. I couldn't move. I heard a barking snarl and watched the threatening dentures pass effortlessly over me.

Chaos erupted in an instant.

Winter sat up, flicked on a five-cell light. Another huge hyena, almost on him, snapped its terrible jaws with a sound like a .22 rifle.

Yet another hyena, caught by the sudden lights while snuffling around by the three-quarter ton truck, attacked the nearest thing to itself. Its huge jaws encompassed the swell of the truck tire and bit through, fangs and teeth and bone meeting when the tire exploded with a sharp detonation. The heavy-tread military tire, designed to withstand endless punishment on challenging terrain, burst noisily under the tremendous pressure of jaws and teeth designed for crushing elephant bones.

There was panic in the scramble. Voices, shouts, barks, screams. By now there were more lights as more hunters came awake and reacted instinctively.

In the flashing beams were at least seven or eight hyenas, prowling through the midst of the camp, now thrown into their own panic. To the human, panicked confusion was added short barks, snarls, whines, and jaws snapping viscerally on thin air, attended by yelps and the scrabbling sound of heavy claws scratching on gravel, rock, and dirt.

This all happened so fast, I was still caught in my sleeping bag, and had not moved when another hyena jumped past me. I saw Winter in his skivvies race for the truck. He grabbed a shotgun, jerked the pump, and fired beyond the cluster of lights at a couple of disappearing, hairy rumps gallumphing off in a cloud of dust and yells. Finally, a couple of rifle shots.

Suddenly, it was all over.

Deadly quiet, except for the sound of Crazy Bruce slapping out flames where a hyena had run through the near-dead fire and kicked live coals onto his sleeping bag.

The first word spoken was a yell: *"Tesfai!"* It was Ratty Mac's really-pissed scream.

"Sor." Tesfai crouched behind the Jeep, peering over in the flickering light from the refreshed fire.

"You goddamned useless . . . you get that muthafuckin' Ethi guard . . . on the trail of those bi-sexes . . . you tell him . . . *push them all the way outta the province . . . you go with 'im and don't come back 'til they're . . . gone or dead . . ."* Mac was incoherent with rage. He was often incoherent with something, but this seemed nearly justified.

I still couldn't get my goddamned legs to work, couldn't get out of the bag.

"Just . . . he better not come back . . . at all. *You hear?*" As he screamed, Mac danced on one foot, trying to sort out his boots from other footgear hung over the Jeep's passenger-side mirror to keep out nocturnal scorpions.

"Sor!"

The guard was nowhere in sight, gone at the onset of alarm.

Tesfai scampered off into the dark after him, carrying only a battery-pack lamp and his *Shifta* stick. He probably realized, at that moment, just how wrong he'd gone in coddling the guard.

"Hey, man, wha'th'fuck? What's with all the noise?" Harry was standing in the bed of the crippled truck, naked, peering cautiously over the tailgate at the confusion in the camp. Coming out of some dark world of his own making, he stood blinking uncertainly.

MacGantree aimed his .30-06 generally in the direction of the fleeing hyenas, the guard, and Tesfai who'd followed them, and cleared the weapon, carelessly clicking the trigger, letting the hammer fall on what was, fortunately, an empty chamber. The implication was clear. He cursed in a steady, meaningless stream of sounds unlike known language.

I sat, tangled in the bag, listening to Mac's blasphemous outpourings, unable to move my legs.

* * *

Coming off break onto a set of days, Bravo Trick had the benefit of good weather. When he walked into Alpha bay, Winter found a cluster of ops gathered about Sergeant Dolman from the Comm Center. It was unusual to find off-going trick workers, especially from the Mids Trick, still on site. There was often difficulty in getting the off-going Mids Trick Chief to even lap over a few minutes to pass on existing conditions, pending alerts, changes, like that . . . So Winter, now an SP5 and the A-Slash—Assistant/Trick Chief—began his day with a confrontation.

"Okay, guys, what's the hang-up? Got problems? No? Then let's clear it out. You guys from Delta better move; Anthony's not going to hold the bus." He dropped his notebook on the A-Slash pos and headed for the coffeepot. The Watch Office was full of milling NCOs and a smattering of curious hangers-on. " Jeez—something going 'round?" Winter wondered.

Back in the bay, shift change complete, he scanned the Read File, made some notes, and made a pass through both Morse bays. In Bravo bay, once again he encountered a small knot of ops, gathered conspiritorially by the antenna rack. "Hey, guys. What the hell? Don't you have skeds? Nobody up today? C'mon, now. Get with it."

"Did you hear, Dave?" Winesap blurted. SP4 Martin Winesap was the Walter Winchell of Ops, and if there was gossip, it either emanated from his quarter, or migrated to it.

"Hear what, 'Sap? Nobody tells me anything." It couldn't be much; nothing in the log.

"Arlington Hall's asking for volunteers for Indo-China." Winesap's ratty mustache quivered with anticipation, though Winter knew it to be a false impression. The Sap would never get involved with anything that took him away from the Blue Nile Bar and Big Mary Wassaf.

"The hell you talking about? The U.S. doesn't have troops in Indo-China." He was right: no big thing. Another rumor, blowing in the wind.

"That's why they're asking for volunteers, Dave. There's gonna be A.S.A. there."

"Where'd this come from?" Pin it down right now. Put a stop to it.

"Dolman saw it in incoming traffic, just before we came on." Dolman was a buck sergeant, an NCO, thus authorized to drive his personal vehicle to the operations site. He usually came on early so that the off-going Comm Center trick workers could get cleared for the first bus. He had been at the core of the huddle in the other bay when Winter walked in.

"He sure as shit didn't waste any time spreading the word, did he?" Winter said. He disliked the notion of an NCO disseminating rumors in the work spaces, even rumors with substance. He returned to Alpha bay, but did not see Dolman. He went down the passageway to the Comm Center and pushed the buzzer. A steel-gated window slid open.

"Dave. Wha'cha need?" Perkins asked.

"Dolman in there, Perky? If he is, ask him if he'll give me a minute." The window slid shut, cutting off the chatter of teletype machines, the whine of signals falling from space.

The window came open again. "Dave. Somethin' I can do you fer?" Dolman had his hands full of yellow tear sheets that spilled off the chattering machines.

"Yeah, Tommy. What's this I hear about Arlington Hall looking for volunteers for Indo-China?" It was probably nothing, but Winter was thrown when Dolman looked quickly behind him, shook his head, said, "Hang on a minute." He slammed the sliding port shut.

The heavy vault door opened almost immediately and Dolman stepped out, looking behind him. He pulled the vault door closed, caught Winter by the arm, and led him down the hall and around the corner toward the supply room. The hall was deserted. The air solidly comprised white noise and rushing sounds, AM and FM signals clashing, separating, overlapping; a steady chatter of manual Morse emanated from behind one of the Bravo bay steel doors, neither of which was ever opened.

"Keep it down, for Christ's sake," the sergeant urged. "Mister Hollomon was standing right behind me when you asked that. At the window."

"So what? Must be pretty much common knowledge by now. But since we just came on, I wanted to get the story so I can set the guys straight. Instead of having a bunch of rumors and shit floating about, disrupting the bay."

"No. It's not out yet. I just read the message from the Hall when we came on."

"So, it'll be out soon, right?" But as he said it, Winter knew where this was going. And it wasn't a good thing . . .

"No, no. The message is classified SECRET, and if anyone finds out I was spilling the beans before it goes to the head shed and they can announce it formally, I'll have my ass in a sling." The sergeant's eyes were like BB shot. He had let his mouth run away, not good policy for a Comm Center worker. The Mafia practice of *Omerta* was a public gossip column compared to the stricture of talking out of shop when you worked in a communications center.

"Well, I suggest you consider keeping such things to yourself. Do your job; we'll find out when we're supposed to. Hell, I wish I didn't know, now," Winter said.

"Hey, goody two-shoes, just keep your mouth shut. O.K.?" Dolman had suddenly found his stripes; it seemed to surprise him.

"Exactly what I'm telling you, *Sergeant* Dolman." Winter turned and stalked back to the Morse bays, wondering.

For the rest of the day, despite all his efforts to contain the spread, the rumor was the hottest topic throughout the building. In the Watch Office during the lunch hour, Chief Warrant Officer Hollomon commented on the speed with which the unauthorized information had gotten around. He didn't act as if he knew where it originated from, but he must have known, Winter thought; it was his damned Comm Center. Had to originate there.

From one of the NCOs who had been back at S-1 on the main post during the morning, Winter learned the content of the message.

"Didn't say a lot . . . about units or organization, or when, or anything concrete," Sergeant Porfiro reported. "Just asked all commands to very cautiously ask for oh-five-eight and nine-eight-two volunteers for a six-month T.D.Y. to South Viet Nam. Part of old French Indo-China. Didn't specify where. Might be in the embassy or something. I guess that would be Sai Gon."

"Didn't say when?" Winter, uneasy with the illicit knowledge, still wanted to know. He calculated quickly. He had served almost a year here on an eighteen-month tour. If he volunteered for the T.D.Y., he'd probably get curtailed out of here, maybe in another couple months or so. That way, he'd get to be with Nickie and the baby, now four months old, for at least a thirty-day leave before going on to the assignment. The six months TDY wouldn't be anything. Besides, they were stirring up trouble in that part of the world, years now after the French war. Might be interesting to be in on the start of something. He tried but could not envision the map of Viet Nam. Hell, he had only the vaguest notion of what constituted Indo-China. Somewhere down near Burma and Siam—Thailand.

"Nothing. Two oh-five-eights from Charlie Trick came in and asked about volunteering, right while I was standing there. Personnel Sergeant had a shit fit. The message was SECRET. Word's not even officially out yet. Somebody's weenie's gonna be in the wringer over this before it's over. Comm Center somebodies." Porfiro looked knowingly at Winter, raising his eyebrows.

Nobody seemed to have a clue where Viet Nam really was, though they could find Sai Gon on the wall map in Ops; there was no denotation for a country called Viet Nam. A bloc of territory, generally named Indo-China, spread over a sizeable portion of the landmass floating to the west of the South China Sea. The Asian map bore a publication date of 1951.

* * *

But Porfiro was right. Within twenty-four hours, following a line-up of 058s and 982s at the Personnel Office, all volunteering for six months in Southeast Asia, the colonel issued a bulletin, posted only within classified spaces in the Operations building. The single posted sheet announced that the need for personnel for TDY deployment to an Asian site had been cancelled. Personnel were to make no references to whatever they thought they knew about such a subject, neither within classified areas, nor—certainly not, it was implied—outside sacred bounds.

Dolman, after a few days of unexplained absence, appeared in the billets wearing corporal stripes, and nevermore crossed the threshold of the Ops building. Without a clearance—the host ship which his loose lips had sunk—he found employment in the motor pool, and it was only at the end of his own 18-month tour in Asmara when Dolman had a chance to further investigate the attractions of sunny Sai Gon.

* * *

Bravo Trick worked its first night of a set of Mids. At 0317 hours, SFC Sulzer, the Trick Chief of Morse who was again Acting Watch NCO, scurried into Alpha bay. Standing at the back end of the bay, he ran his rabbit eyes over the reduced crew at the consoles. It was a Friday morning, coming up on the holy day for most of their target entities. They were expectantly slow that night, and Sulzer had manned the positions that required it, sent four men back on the last trick change bus to work a set of Days, gave three the night off, but thought his Assistant Trick Chief should have the remainder busily snatching dits.

There were no dits to speak of. From San'a to Mogadiscio, Cairo to Kigale, the air waves were empty. One of the semi-conscious ops, a new guy, blindly following SOP and twirling the dials, had almost fallen asleep, tip-toeing through a melancholy network of nautical stations—mostly tankers and freighters in the Med and the Red Sea—and was mesmerized by the clean, professional sound of the maritime Morse transmissions. Clearly not his targets.

Not spotting his A-Slash Winter, Sulzer shouted out in his "tea and cotillion voice"—as Darmanian termed it; he would know, coming as he did from that rarified strata—"Hey, new guy, what's ya name?"

At the nonconformative response from the PFC who was typing hurriedly, the rotund sergeant shouted, "Well, no shit you can't hear me. Get the cans off your ears."

When the startled operator had removed his headset, Sulzer said, "Now that you can hear me—you can hear me now, can't you?—good! So, get off that shipping channel shit! We don't do shipping. Let the goddamned squids handle that."

The Op, too new to know better, demurred: "But, sarge, there's nothing up but ships. Why—"

"Because, dip-stick, you hang out in those maritime bands across the Med and Red Seas, you're gonna run across some goddamned raghead asshole that's fucked up his boat and wants somebody to come drag his heathen ass outta the briney. And if you do snag a goddamned S.O.S., I'll be writin' up goddamned paperwork for a goddamned month. And we'll be tyin' up the Comm Center with goddamned alerts to everybody from NATO to goddamned Disneyland."

The chastened operator's head sunk between his shoulders; he clapped the earphones loosely on his head, and faded into the twilight realm with the other bored operators. Two-and-a-half more hours, he thought, before early skeds began filling the bay with noise and priorities.

Winter walked in from Bravo bay and Sulzer was reminded why he had come: to spread charm and cheer among the troops. "Listen up, all-a youse."

Oh, hell, Winter thought. This is going to be a ball-buster. Whenever Sulzer effected that South Bronx collective address mannerism, everybody was in the shit.

"Somebody, wake up Phillipson," Sulzer urged the bay in general.

No one reponded. No one moved.

"Pettigrew, wake Phillipson, will ya."

"Not me, Sarge. Crazy Bruce don't like to be woken. Waked. Awakened." The op looked away as if that would disappear Sulzer.

Winter walked over to Bruce's pos, tapped him gently on the back, murmured something no one else could hear, and Bruce raised his head. His eyes were clear and unclouded, his very pronounced American Indian face utterly devoid of expression.

"Yeah, well," Sulzer tried again, "Listen up, all-a ya. Just got a rocket in." He hesitated. "And not the one got all you glory hounds excited about going to kill gooks." He looked over the ops who were obviously trying to ignore this interruption to their rest. "Youse guys what are short . . . Old Man, how many days you say you got left? Short timer . . ."

SP4 Currie didn't bother looking at Sulzer. "Nineteen and a wake-up, Sarge."

"Now see, that's a lie, Currie. You got . . . two hundred and . . . two days. Two oh two," he reiterated, anticipating the specialist's response.

"No way, sarge. My DEROS's the twenty-fourth. October twenty-four."

"Your eighteen months up then, is that it?"

"Right you are, Sarge. Gonna spend my last four months in the Army at balmy Camp Polk. That's Loo-easy-anner." He smiled across at Phelps.

"Well, you see, Currie, that's where you're just flat-out wrong." Sulzer's smile was last photographed on a guard in Sing-Sing. "But it may not be a fault with your math. You just might not know about the rocket. The rocket says . . ." he hesitated, exhibiting all the charitable good will of a debit insurance salesman putting the close on a two-dollar accidental death policy. "The rocket, from ole J.F.K., hisself, says all you boys—" he swept the bay with his hand "—every swinging Richard now serving in an overseas post is hereby, gratuitously, extended in place . . . for six months. One hundred—"

"Bullshit!"

"Get outta here, Sulzer," came from down the row.

"That's crap, Sergeant Sulzer."

"The fuck you say—"

"—and eighty-three days. Which means for you, Currie, and you . . . and you . . . and you and you and you . . ." Sulzer stabbed his happy finger at a roomful of ops who were suddenly awake. Suddenly aroused.

"Sergeant Sulzer, Sergeant Sulzer—"

"Sergeant Sulzer," Winter's voice cut through the babble like a scalpel through a chancre sore. "I'm not short. I have more then five months to go. Does that mean—"

"Yeah, Specialist Winter. It means you got eleven months left. You're a long way from even double-digits." He seemed happy with the news. "You prol'ly got time to make Spec Six."

Through a rising tide of angry denunciation and uncontrolled blasphemy directed jointly at the Hyannisport Hot Shot, the Pentagon, the Army, and the gloating sergeant, questions flew fast and furiously, emulating outright denial.

"Knock it off!" Winter sang out, and when the uproar dropped to an angry muddle, asked, "What brought this on, do you know, Sergeant?"

"Thought you'd never ask. Yeah, matter of fact, I do know. Seems Eye-van the Terrible in East Berlin rolled his tanks up to the Friedrichstrasse crossing . . . what you boys call Checkpoint Charlie—" Sulzer never missed an opportunity to roll out the inflated history of his tour there, and subsequent knowledge of Field Station Berlin "—making bear-like noises. That pissed off our people; we cranked up some tanks and moved in facing them. Right now, both of us, Russkies and Amerikanskis, got heavy armor eyeball-to-eyeball, about one hundred fifty-to-two hundred meters apart. And a beer fart's about all it's gonna take to start World War, Act Three." Sulzer looked smug, though Winter was sure he was not as blasé as he wanted to appear.

"Does it mean you're extended too, Sarge? How about that?"

"Me too, Phelps. But . . . " and a chorus of voices, anticipating, spoke with him, "—I found a home here. I lo-o-o-ve the Army." Sulzer continued on his own, "Since I don't wanta hafta fight this one all alone," he said in a thinly disguised hint at his involvement eight years earlier in the Korean fracas, "I figured youse guys—" he was back at it, Winter noted, "—would wanta hang around and he'p me out. I sent word, askin' Jumpin' Jack to extend all-a youse so's you don't hafta embarrass yourselves, get your wives and mommies and girlfriends all P.O.-ed by volunteering."

His little bunny eyes behind the pink frames of his Army-issue, Coke-bottle bifocals were bouncing like bird shot in a tin cup.

"See how good ol' Sergeant Sulzer is to you ungrateful private soldiers."

In the midst of the hubbub that drowned out printer chatter drifting up the hallway, Crazy Bruce began rising from his chair like an emerging dome of barely contained volcanic lava.

Sulzer remembered he had other destinations he needed to visit and dispense his happy news. He backed toward the hall door, saying in a voice devoid of the Bronx, "I've not been here. You didn't hear this from me," he muttered quickly and turned and fled.

Jeez-us! Winter thought; everyone's developing loose lips.

Military discipline is most effective when military personnel have no alternative, Winter knew. Military discipline, without being acknowledged, kept Sergeant Sulzer alive. As expressed by PFC Darmanian, "Sulzer would have been dead or disabled months ago if not for Micki, his unlikely-but-remarkably-statuesque wife . . . the fact that his absence would deprive one and all Kagnew Station soldiers of the vicarious delight provided by her world-class body, universe-class mammaries." As long as Micki Sulzer remained a factor, and paid regular visits to the pool in one of her dozen-or-so bikinis, SFC Sulzer's mean persona was allowed to flourish in relative safety in East Africa.

chapter five

Four Floors of Whores

Massawa, Eritrea (Ethiopia); 1961

The freighter had once been white. Now, rust stained the hull in broad swathes down from each port hole, each seam in the steel plating, each aperture in the riveted bulk of the vessel. SANDOVAL stood out in flaking, three-foot-high letters on the stern; beneath, in less prominent style, PANAMA. She was nestled into the chipped concrete of the deep water pier in Massawa, tressed up close with hawsers that threatened to part with each slop of tidal movement.

On the pier pallets, piled high with ecru-colored bags, were themselves stacked in defiance of physical laws. Each bag bore a red-white-and-blue shield superimposed with two hands joined in eternal felicity. Printed beneath were the words "A gift from the peoples of the United States of America."

Beyond this pier, extending out into the Red Sea, other dock areas hosted other ships—a white-hulled freighter from Poland, shiny with care and newness; a black-hulled liner with two blue bands, home port Piraeus—and a motley collection of fishing boats, speedboats, pleasure boats, Arab lateen-sail *dhows*, and a destroyer escort of the US Navy.

Dockside, a busy crowd of officials swarmed about a low platform where a microphone stood alone. The mike was dysfunctional; like the occasion it was not what it represented itself to be. There were curious stares from the natives gathered along the edge of the stone-cobbled street that bordered the dock, standing with blank stares out of coffee-colored faces. They stood as storks, one leg folded, crooked up and anchored on the other; black mobiles draped in white.

Along the waterfront, sometimes-fishermen hawked bizarre bounty of the sea from boats and carts on the quay and, between entreaties to the crowd to buy, they watched carefully the unfolding of this drama, unmindful of the blistering sun and punishing humidity of the port city.

A Land Rover packed with armed Ethiopian troops squealed around the square scattering idlers at the streetside tables before the one café and along the curbless, broken asphalt street. Following hard on the military escort came a long black Mercedes with dark windows. Behind the limousine, a military open-bed truck of ancient Italian vintage with a body of troops. The Ethiopian pennant flew from the military vehicles, the arrogance of their occupation perhaps abrasive to the watching Eritreans, but those blankly staring hosts were silent. On the bumper of the Mercedes, another kind of pennant flew: a red field with a gold-imposed hammer and sickle.

The Soviet ambassador to Ethiopia stepped from the Mercedes. Flown north from Addis Ababa to Asmara the day before, and driven earlier today down the winding Massawa Road to the port, dropping eight thousand feet in a matter of some one hundred fifteen kilometers, his was an effective entrance. He was quickly joined by the emperor's ministers from the darkened vehicle and the group, surrounded by the Army troops, moved quickly to the platform and the dead microphone.

One pallet of the grain stood at hand to the dais. The Ethiopian minister stood beside the pallet and spoke without mechanical aid, using the languages of the land: first Tigrinya, then Tigré, a short burst of coastal Arabic, finally concluding in English while he gestured toward the sacks of food grain and enclosed the Soviet minister in his slightly fractured remarks: ". . . and we have our friend and ally, the mighty and glorious Soviet Union, forever in our hearts for their generosity and love, for their comradeship and socialist duties fulfilled, in providing this food for our suffering people. Our gratitude, and our desire to welcome our friends to greater participation in our search for fiscal independence, And in return, we offer them a greater role in the development of our mining resources and our ports of Massawa and Asseb. Now, let us hear from the signal person himself, the Ambassador of the Union of Soviet Socialist Republics. Your honor. . ."

The short, stocky man in the dark suit, sweating freely at the noonday ceremony, began to speak in the Amharic tongue, slowly, smoothly. Onlookers stared, glanced shyly at one another, and wondered why this august personage spoke to them in the language of the accursed Ethiopians to the south.

Across the water from the American destroyer escort came the sounds of several stereo systems, playing as many different kinds of music, the discordant cacophony overridden by Elvis's nasal entreaties. The music was the only element of American interests actively represented at the hijacked presentation, but the watchers on the dockside, and the readers of the native language newspapers— even the English language paper in Asmara—did not miss them, and the consensus was sincere gratitude to the people of the Soviet Union in their common plight of western exploitation.

Ratty Mac and Winter, potential American reps but determinedly quiescent, seated at the edge of the dockside street at the only café beneath the meager shade of a tattered umbrella bearing a Cinzano logo, remained quiet.

As the Soviet Ambassador was quickly driven away, Winter, so softly only MacGantree could hear him, said, "Kinda tugs at your heartstrings, doesn't it?"

* * *

Asmara, Eritrea (Ethiopia); October 1961

Harry Spruance was not noticeably a bad match for the Army. A Texas boy, he seemed well fitted for service, duty, and country as many before him. Only quirky circumstances in an untimely progression conspired to set Harry on a collision course with what was never meant to be his destiny. The fallout was to echo down the shaky ranks of ASA for years to come.

Harry worked in Analysis Branch, Bravo Trick. A devil-may-care lad, he was more stereotypical than not. Essentially prime cannon fodder, he never promised to rise in the world of spooks and techies beyond what his unfocused efforts afforded him as reward for minimal effort.

Harry was barely adequate. As a common sort of soldier, he had no clear vision of his future, thus no cares associated with it. He made little money, spent it all each month, and often—not unusual at his rank—spent more than he made. He ran short. He went into debt, a debt which had to be paid off come payday, thus initiating a fresh cycle of indebtedness.

The specialist fourth class had few recurring expenses: haircuts, shoe polish, cigarettes at a dollar a carton, the occasional can of Barbasol, laundry fees, kick-in for the houseboy fund, and his club bill. He did not buy stationary and postage stamps; he never wrote anyone. Though his club bill usually represented a significant percentage of gross income, it was not out of order for his rank, his mindset, and his placement on this post at the ass end of the world.

Beyond these petty accountings, the bulk of Harry's pay went to one or more of several whores who worked the shabby bars near

Kagnew Station. As had happened previously on occasion, due to lack of planning and caught up in a budget crisis, young Harry's financial wherewithal went into the toilet three days before payday in October. So when he made his weekly foray to the crib of Little Annie, it was knowingly without funds.

Her bar name, as one of the "Annie girls," was a misnomer; and she was not even the smallest of the lot, consisting of Blue Nile Annie, Big Annie, Fat Annie, Dirty Annie, and Cathy, graduated from the Annie Archives to stand apart for her exalted talents in the fellatio follies.

When that autumn evening and Harry's commercial love affair expired, he explained to Annie that he had no money. This was not a crisis; he often before had faced the same dilemma, and Little Annie knew he was good for it. As there were many other GIs who practiced the same sort of promissory commercial sex, a custom of sorts had become institutionalized.

In Eritrea (Ethiopia) during the late years of Haile Selassie's reign, American GIs were welcome guests. To ensure a soldier or sailor, netted by local police for some alleged egregious activity, could identify himself to the authorities for who and what he was, all military personnel carried picture identification cards printed in English and Tigrinya, a local language. Effectively a sort of *Get Out of Jail Free* card, these were prosaically known as "Ethi ID." Ignoring the latent purpose, usually the only time necessary to show the Ethi ID card was payday. Each soldier in the pay line was inspected for haircut, facial hair, dog tags, military ID card, and Ethi ID.

As a temporary hedge against insolvency, GIs might deposit the Ethi ID with a bar, a bar girl, or any enterprise. The holder of the card was assured of getting his or her money, for the GI had to have, and be able to produce, the card for authorities at a given time. The tricky part was that such a temporary deposit was usually made with the intention of redeeming it on payday, after funds were in the hand of the card owner; however, the card owner must have the card in hand to show to the pay officer in order to get paid. A tricky sort of balancing act.

But improvisation, thy name is soldier!

Some GI who had not pawned his card would get into line early, draw his pay, and loan a buddy enough to retrieve his own card so that he could then get paid, loan to someone else, down the line. On payday, the holders of the debt markers would be waiting outside Kagnew Station front gate in a gharry-cart taxi, displaying a veritable sheaf of Ethi IDs, ready to effect their redemption for the debt amounts. A mutually beneficial accommodation.

* * *

Winter approached MP Sergeant Henby and received permission to visit Harry. He went through the single door into the holding area, an imposing-sounding title for a single room with accommodations less stark than they might have been. Harry sat in a brightly colored deck chair stolen from the Massawa C.I.A.A.O. Hotel. GIs pronounced it as an acronym, "chow."

"Now you've done it, asshole," Winter growled, taking in Harry and the stolen chair.

"Hmph! Hello to you, too, Specialist Winter. Come to gloat?"

"Not likely," Winter said, looking around. "I could spend a few days resting and relaxing here myself, if I could afford the tab."

"Hmph!"

"So . . . you gonna tell me the story, or what?"

"How'd you get in here? Prisoners can't have visitors, except for the C.O., the Chaplain or a medic. Or their supervisor. Where do you fit?"

"Harry, Harry. My sad, benighted country boy, you're not devious enough, my lad. You're not going to make it in this military life. That's a fact." Winter took the only seat available, the unmade steel-framed bunk. "I told Sergeant Henby I needed to see you. He knows I'm A-Slash on Bravo Trick . I guess he must have assumed you're in my Morse section."

"Even an Assistant Trick Chief might have trouble gettin' in. But, that's not here, or over there, either. You just gathering info to gossip on?" Harry seemed in a decent frame of mind. "You might-a come sooner. I'm about to get out."

"Yeah, I heard. You're going to serve your time in Mannheim. Well, at least, when the three months're up maybe they'll leave you there. In Germany. Transfer you to Herzo or B.A."

"No, no. I'm getting out. Charges dropped, sentence rescinded, all that good shit."

"Lying bastard!"

"Am not. My clearance's up and running, right as rain."

"Har-ry—"

"Do you even know the whole story, Dave?" At Winter's display of confusion, the inmate wasted no time. "Obviously not. You know, maybe, most everything that happened prior to the courts-martial."

Harry then proceeded to enlighten Winter on all that had occurred, including what he already knew of earlier events.

"A few days before payday I'd left my Ethi ID with Little Annie. When I got off Mids payday morning, I caught a gharry and went straight to her place. Annie didn't answer the door. Some local street boy opened up . . . shifty eyes and bad teeth, ba-a-a-d breath. On the other hand, he didn't speak much English either." He nodded, confirming a suspicion.

"I just walked in, assumed he was a relative or something. Annie never had a pimp. So when I headed toward her bedroom, this asshole grabs my arm. Now, Dave . . . I don't care to be manhandled even by white people, let alone some Basgh-living, lowlife darkie. But I didn't give him trouble; I was really trying to understand what he was sayin'. Finally made out he wanted to know who I was. I told him 'Harry.' 'sall he needed to know, whatever his interest. He pulls out a little red note pad, says I owe Annie seventy dollars. American! *Seventy!* 'My lad,' I said—"

"How the hell'd you ever run up such a tab? With Annie, for Go—"

"Listen to me, man. I didn't owe Annie no seventy, American *or* Ethi. I said to him, 'My lad, you're obviously fucking with the wrong Harry. I owe Annie fifteen Ethi.' As I'm explaining the facts of the matter, I'm staring at his hand on my arm. Trying, you know, to give him a hint. But he don't take hints."

Winter listened, mesmerized as Harry's tale built to an obvious climax; he was, after all, locked up here for a reason.

"He let loose on me, spraying a barrage of gobbledegook, sounded like Amharic, Arabic, Tigriniyan, Italian, and bullshit, all mixed up together.. Not a word of English in the whole broadcast. He moved to block me from Annie's room—his strongest weapon was that witherin' breath—and that's when I figured we had nothing more to talk about. Stupid shit. He ought to've known . . . Texas boys don't stand still for a shakedown, especially by someone of the dark persuasion."

Winter didn't speak, just nodded with understanding. He did understand. "Darkie" was a term his immigrant grandfather had used to denote a person of color, though in his Irish brogue it was without antipathy, meaning no degradation. Likely not the case here.

"When I finished with him, I went in her room. Annie was sitting on her bed. Her face was marked up, one eye swollen. Had my card in her hand. Got the card, came back to post, got paid, took a cart back downtown, paid off Annie and added a coupla bucks Ethi for any damage in her place. I figure the guy forced Annie to take him on as partner. Had his own agenda. Sayin' I been cheatin' Annie all along. Hell, Annie's lucky to be getting my business. She's not pretty, got no knockers . . . but she is clean. Smells nice."

"Yeah, you're a horny but discriminating swordsman. Right?"

"Whatever. But that goddamn pimp got his own back. He did that, damn him." Harry looked reflective. "A week or so later when he could walk, he came to the front gate and picked me out of the lineup book. Helluva thing, that book,"

Harry shared the view of every serving soldier, sailor, dependent, and all other persons of a democratic bent, that the US government's policy of posting in a book in the MP shack at the main gate photos of every man stationed at Kagnew Station, was going a bit far in the realm of appeasement. Anybody could—and occasionally did—walk in off the street, idly flip through the book, and point out the *guilty party*, whether true or not, whether anything had ever occurred or not; and if the identified being had no alibi for the time/date in question, he might stand for a charge.

"That's when they come and got me outta Ops."

"Okay. I knew some of that. Most of it. I was at the trial yesterday, too, when you were convicted of—both assault and battery, and robbery, was it?" Winter said.

"Yeah. Claimed I not only beat him up when he was just doing the job Annie paid him to do," he stared with raised eyebrows, "but I took four hundred Ethi off his unconscious body. Shit! That sucker never saw four hundred Ethi in his life. I didn't take nothin' off his smelly body. Wouldna' touched him."

"I believe that, but how is it that you're now exonerated of all these criminal pursuits? The courts-martial convicted you. Guilty or not. Why're they letting you out?"

"Well, I was settin' here last eve . . . in shock, my mom would say. I never thought this thing would ever reach courts-martial, let alone conviction. It was an obvious hangin' court to appease locals. I didn't ask for a civilian attorney for my trial, thinkin' it'd be a waste of money. No way would they find me guilty . . . such an obvious scam. But later last night, after the conviction and sentence, I realized I'd been walking around with my head up my ass. I argued with the M.P.s that I had one phone call coming—they do that in the movies—" he smiled facetiously at Winter. "Henby caved in. I called Gran'pa Spruance."

Winter, aware Harry had a grandfather, knew him only from Harry's past references to "Gran'pa."

"Was that your best shot?" Winter asked, skeptical.

"Gettin' out, ain't I?"

"Well, sure . . . I guess. I don't *know* that."

"Take it for gospel. You might not-a known, Gran-pa's from up on the Pedernales. You probably heard talk of that, home ground for our Vice Prez. Gran'pa always refers to him as 'that damn pissant Johnson boy.' Still, Gran'pa claims kinship with some of the Baineses."

Winter stared, awaiting some link to a logical explanation.

"Sorry, got sidetracked. Anyhow, this morning, a few hours after my call home, the Provost Marshal came in and told me I'm on my way back to the company. Back to Ops. Only reason I'm still here now is I gotta wait for the doctor to confirm I'm not all beat black and blue by the M.P.s. I told 'em, 'Hell, I drink with all those boys. They wouldn't lay a glove on me.'"

"So, all's forgiven and forgotten?"

"Said nothin' about that," Harry pointed out, squinting up at Winter. "I ain't forgivin' nothin', and I won't be forgettin'. This fuckin' Army has dumped on me something fierce, and there's gonna be a reckoning. Sooner or later. Sooner . . . maybe later."

* * *

Following restoration of common sense, the incident became the catalyst in the making of "Hatin' Harry," a spurious title applied to Specialist Spruance for the abiding hatred that grew out of his embarrassing and, he thought unnecessary, ill treatment by the Army. In the remaining year that Harry served in Eritrea (Ethiopia), try though he might, he was unable to satisfy his quest for revenge. But he held it loosely in abeyance.

So thoroughly consumed was he by anger, hatred, and need for revenge, that when he had served out his overseas tour—and in order to eliminate the remaining seven months' obligation on his term of enlistment left to serve in the states, and contrary to all odds against his eligibility to do so, *and* completely beyond the comprehension of anyone—Harry reenlisted.

For six more years.

In the Army Security Agency.

He could have reenlisted, taking as few as two, but local wisdom considered his ire was such that merely getting back at the Army once would not do the job. Hatin' Harry needed room to work.

Harry interrupted his reenlistment swearing-in ceremony by Lieutenant Colonel William "Bourbon Billy" Keyes, Commanding, and informed him and all present that they ". . . better cinch up your skivvies. It's comin'. It's comin'." And if none present within the headquarters understood or gave credence to his dire prescience, everybody in Operations did, recognizing this prophetic utterance for a vendetta of biblical resolve.

* * *

Massawa, Eritrea (Ethiopia); October-November 1961

Dockside in the shadow of the minaret, Martine hesitated, staring across the street and up at the squat, round tower beyond, a crumbling remnant of times past when Arabian *dhows* blew seasonally before the wind from Jidda on the Saudi coast to Eritrea and back with the moods of the desert-born *mistral*. He breathed deeply, inhaling the rich effluvium of oil, gypsum, and fish, the moldy reek of heavy, wet hawsers lashed like thickbodied snakes about stone bollards, the iodine tang of the sea-savaged wooden wharves. He knew the histories of nearby warehouses by the essence of spices—cayenne, East Indian curry, black and white peppers, nutmeg, saffron, ziggani—residual from bales and bags stored there over centuries when Massawa was one point on the trading trapezoid with Pemba, Madagascar, and Zanzibar. But lacking historical context, Martine merely thought the whole place stank.

The Red Sea night air enveloped him like a damp, rank carpet—hot, humid, close. The distinctive reek of camels hung strongly on still air. A coastal beacon swept monotonously across lowhanging clouds, and he knew the skies would open soon. He could smell rain, already on its way from Lake Tana in the Ethiopian highlands, could feel its electric preview in the hushed, expectant darkness. He cringed, anticipating. He hadn't long to wait.

A beer bottle shattered on the street in front of him and he heard laughter and Hatin' Harry's insane giggle above the dissonance of a Sudanese band on the roof patio of the tower, struggling through the unfamiliar rhythms of the Everly Brothers' "Cathy's Clown," and he knew he dare not wait. Two more brown glass grenades hit the street; fragments sprayed his legs. His body was vibrating with tension as he sought to gauge when best to sprint for the doorway without exposing himself to a bottle barrage.

Abandoning caution while awkwardly shielding his head from the deadly missiles, he dashed in an labored crouch across the jettyside street. The cobblestones were littered with goat and sheep dung and myriad shards of Melotti bottles thrown from the tower four floors above.

Martine burst through warped planks of the ground floor door, screaming, his pentup anxiety released in the crash of the door—screaming until doors were smacking open on every side and all the whores on the lowest level were screaming back at him from all the evils of their lives, real and imagined, as they burst out of their cubicles and ran around the circular passageway incessantly in a scene of mad, operatic hysteria, as if there were no exit.

Martine did not worry about the effect on the whores down here. Only Ethi sailors, Yemenese fishermen, and other coastal dregs—including the occasional economyminded GI from MESA—shopped the ground floor. The girls here were lowrent, offering little in their amoral arts and sinful sciences beyond several exotic forms of venereal disease, tuberculosis, occasional beriberi, intriguing but deforming elephantiasis . . . who knew what-all? Nothing better was expected of them. They were, after all, ground floor.

Had he sought the high class of the trade, he need only go north to the second floor, or on up. On the third level—classy—they even washed between servicings. Four was the premiere objective—quasi-jazz band and warm beer. Truly, Top o' the Mark. But reflection was absent regarding this four floors of whores.

The clamor of insane chaos reverberated around the circular hallway, amplifying, further distorting the acoustics of three octaves of screams echoing off dank walls, until it seemed by din alone to gutter the candles ensconced in niches in the stone at each cubbyhole entranceway. Girls on the floor above, responding to the madness in kind, began slamming out through flimsy doors, screaming.

The violent response, the instantaneous frenzy he'd triggered, so alarmed Martine that he flung himself about and burst back outside into the hazardous alleyway in retreat, his passion foregone. A terrified Somali black marketeer, his dirty, sheet-like garment streaming behind him in the murky night, having experienced the worst kind of *coitus interruptus,* was just ahead of the soldier going out the doorway. The Somali entrepreneur was incoherent, but he was fast, and the two Don Juans ran in self-contained fright and confusion, each unaware of the other's existence though they ran in tandem only yards apart—one pair of Hushpuppies, one pair of bare, callused feet—slapping the sandy mud and broken stones down the dark street toward the harbor.

* * *

Asmara, Eritrea (Ethiopia): November 1961

"Where's Sergeant Henby?"

The military policeman at the front desk answered, "He's in Keren, sir. With Rantz—"

"Shit. I forgot. Shee-e-it! Shit. Shit. Shit." The Provost Marshall's indelicate litany echoed up the hall with a certain rhythm.

"Yes, sir." Corporal Spohn returned to his dog-eared paperback.

"Where's Corporal Banks?"

"He's on break, sir. Massawa."

"That's where I need to send him. What the hell's he doing there without checking with me. That doesn't do me any good . . ."

Spohn tuned the captain out.

There were a few moments when the corporal thought the spasm was over, but soon, "Get me Corporal Piedmont." The less-than-commanding voice had acquired a pout that superseded even the reluctance of his order.

"Sir, he's on patrol in the Basgh. With Estes."

"Well, goddammit, who else is available? I got an emergency; I need a driver."

"Just me and Copley, sir. He's right here. You want him? Or me?" he asked with misgivings.

No response.

"Sir—"

"Radio Corporal Piedmont to come in to the station. When he gets here, put Copley on patrol in his stead. Send Piedmont to me."

Spohn could envision the Provost Marshal, nodding his head at the logic of his own manipulations; the captain was a force to be reckoned with.

* * *

Corporal Piedmont shifted into second, scattering a small herd of goats setting up housekeeping in the middle of the town's square. "Goddam him," he cursed aloud, glancing at his watch, "that young idiot captain is going to cost me my ass yet." The sun was already down below the mountains in the distance. He continued bitching to the mosquito-filled dockside air.

Why drive all the way from Asmara down the mountain to Massawa, just to bring a fucking courier pouch to squids on a tin can? Don't these assholes have radios? He glanced in the blotched rearview mirror, watched the American navy destroyer recede through a tangle of goats and children standing on one leg and a shambles of crumbling sheds and shacks along the dock on the Red Sea harbor. By the time he cleared the edge of town, visibility was in that nether land between dusk and dark. And no stop at the C.I.A.A.O. Hotel for a beer. No time!

The drive inland, across the coastal desert, took him more than an hour. By the time the mountains enveloped him, and he began the switchback climb, it was close to 2100. The Jeep was running sound. He'd filled the gas tank before he left Kagnew Station to come down, and it was only seventy-or-so miles here. He thought of those odd dynamics: seventy miles, but it took four hours. The goddamned Massawa Road dropped seventy-five hundred feet in the first forty-five or so miles from Asmara. The road was not the problem; the road was good; it was the ten thousand goddamned switchbacks that held you back. The dreaded Nefasit switchbacks.

Now the day was gone. Gotta make time! he urged himself.

How many times had he repeated it, stressing it in the safety classes for GIs he taught monthly at training: "Don't go off the hill within two hours of dark! Even though Ghinda is less than two hours, what if you have a flat or vehicle trouble? You *will* become a victim. During daylight hours, you're all right; no *Shifta*, seeing you're American, will stop you; the bandits know you'll be armed. But in the dark they can't tell you're American. They know we don't drive the mountain in the dark. They stop everything that moves at night. Do not . . . I repeat, *Do not!* get yourself stopped by the *Shifta*. You'll lose every penny you have, your clothes, cameras, radios, fishing gear, rations. And especially guns. They're always looking for weapons. Don't help 'em out. Plus, you could lose the big one—your ass. If there's less than two hours daylight left, stay put. With two hours you can at least make the Halfway House. If you're here on the plateau, stay here. In Massawa,, remain there overnight. Anywhere else . . ." he shrugged.

And after all that "be warned" safety awareness, that dip-shit captain sends me down the mountain, alone, too late to get back in daylight, and won't let me overnight. Bastard. He slammed his fist on the steering wheel. *Bastard!*

But he dare not be distracted by stupidity. He was in the shit now, and he would practice what he preached: Stay alert!

The Jeep growled steadily upward. Piedmont checked his watch again. Past 2300. Ghinda was now behind him. He needn't have tried to stop there anyhow; Halfway House was shut up tight and dark. Against the hazard-filled night, no one would have answered the door. Piedmont clutched the wheel, calculating how many kilometers to Nefasit: he reckoned about twenty-three. Though it wasn't much of a village, at least a police check point was positioned there. Sometimes there were even policemen. Or the Ethiopian infantry troops that counted for police in Eritrea. Even better.

When he slowed for the hairpin turn beneath the overhang that always felt threatening—as if it might collapse into the roadway on a whim—and he saw the figure step into the road, his mindset led him to assume Police. The figure wore a hat like the Ethiopian Second Division troops wore, visible in silhouette like a Stetson, brim flipped-up on one side like an Aussie. But when the Jeep lights swung toward him, passed over the figure, the corporal was startled.

This was no policeman!

The slight man, wearing a police-style hat, was dressed in a *shamma*, a once-white, torn, sheet-like garment that he wore wrapped about his entire body, from neck to ground. His feet were shoved down into laceless sneakers of some cheap design, threadbare and filthy. He wore a broad grin, teeth gapped like the battlements of some medieval castle, and indicated with his right hand for the vehicle to stop. In his left hand was a .303 Enfield, World War II vintage, but in the lights it shone with oil, not rust. Piedmont slowed the vehicle to a crawl.

"Oh, fuck!" he muttered. "*Shifta*." And they never traveled alone. He jerked about, looking for additional bandits. The Jeep slowed almost to a halt. He spotted another *shifta*, emerging from the rocks behind the first; and back to his left rear, even above the diminishing sounds of the slowing Jeep, he heard a scuffle of stones: another. At least three, maybe more.

The first bandit approached the still-creeping Jeep from the front, shielding his eyes against the headlight glare. He shouted at Piedmont in Italian: *"Alto!"* and gave a chopping motion to turn off the lights. With the rifle he gestured toward the roadside at his feet, not quite pointing the weapon at Piedmont. *"Ferma qui!"* The corporal squealed to a stop. He left the lights on.

"Sono americano," Piedmont called out to the gunman.

"Come? Americano? È solo?" The man shifted the rifle to his other hand, shielded his eyes with the freed hand, muttered what sounded like "Hansab" to his traffic stop, and said over his shoulder to the man behind him, *"Ferengi."* He appeared very nervous. Not surprising he speaks in monosyllables, Piedmont thought . Doesn't speak good Italian, and had assumed he was stopping an Eye-Tie. His own training-briefing scenario playing out. *Ferengi.* No shit, a foreigner, he translated.

"Si, solo. Ho fretta. Non mi secchi, per favore." A babble of Tigré—or Tigrinyan; Piedmont couldn't tell one Eritrean language from the other—came from the dark off to his left where he'd heard movement.

An answering cackle from his inquisitor. *"Che cosa?"* A harsh bark of gutteral laughter.

Hell's bells, the MP thought; this is going nowhere good. This fucker doesn't give a tin puppy's shit if I'm American, official, in a hurry, or whatever.

As the man stepped out of the glare of the headlights, he was shifting the rifle once more. He asked again, *"Come? Che cosa!? È tutto?"* He was two yards away now and Piedmont smelled his rank, smoky, unwashed essence.

"È tutto! That's all," the corporal replied, and shot the *Shifta* in the chest. The .45 slug slammed the slight body back off the side of the road, dropping it in scree. Piedmont whipped the automatic toward his left, saw the second figure less clearly than the first as it ran toward the Jeep, and fired twice. The man's right arm was high in the air, waving something. When his body hit the tarmac, a curved sword clanked loose from his grasp, clattering onto the roadway.

Piedmont leapt from the driver's seat and, crouching, ran toward the third man who was frozen at the edge of the headlights. The corporal had thought him unarmed, but he saw the bandit turn and start hobbling away, an improvised crutch made from a crooked stick under one arm, a long gun in his other hand. He'd only made a few shambling steps when the MP caught up to him and shot him in the back of the head. He pitched forward into the rocks he'd emerged from. Piedmont could make out in the nimbus of headlights an old, wired-together shotgun caught under his body. The bandit's legs thrummed in the scrabble of dust and rocks for several moments, and then it was still on the mountain.

* * *

Piedmont drove into the circle of light provided by the spotlights at the Ethi Police checkpoint at the edge of Asmara. The soldier at the door, watching carefully to see who might have ventured out on the mountain this time of night, gawked at the sight. He called out as he stepped out the door and two more Ethi cops came from the small structure. They began jabbering, pointing, questioning, all in a state of hysteria usually reserved for mystical rites.

The military policeman they saw at the wheel was in summer khakis, his helmet clearly proclaiming his function, and the Ethi police never treated him as a threat. They were consumed with the sight of the three bodies, one tied across the hood, two piled in the back seat next to the radio, and the disheveled state of the Jeep: a solid sheen of dark, dried blood on the back side behind the driver and across the hood, down onto the left front wheel. A loud cackle of laughter broke out when one of the Ethi cops pointed to the minor cluster of weapons piled in the back next to the dead bodies.

* * *

The Provost Marshal captain sat in his office by himself, envisioning the decline of his career. He was waiting for a call from the colonel's office, and he damned well had no excuses. As much as he now regretted sending that hot-wired goddamned Piedmont on the courier run, he was short-handed. He'd had no choice. Still, he'd been warned about Piedmont from the previous Provost Marshal. He could hear, out at the desk in the front entrance, two MPs and a Spec-5 named Winter from Operations Company, nagging the rogue corporal to talk about his escapade.

Piedmont had returned to Kagnew Station less than five hours ago, the captain reflected, and already the man had orders cut for one of the armored divisions at Fort Knox, and was scheduled out on tomorrow's MAC flight to Dharhan. Now the captain's short roster would have to provide two duty MPs to guard the corporal overnight. He was being transferred to keep him alive;

the *Shifta* underground network was not sophisticated, but it was ubiquitous . . . and jealously efficient.

And he could have dealt with all that if the goddamned corporal just hadn't insisted on claiming the two-hundred-fifty-dollar (American) reward the Ethi government had posted for every *Shifta* apprehended or killed. He'd had to get USAEUR approval and shake out a Finance clerk in the middle of the early morning hours to have Piedmont a check cut for $750. And he didn't know how he would finagle the Ethi government into paying the money for bounties back into a US facility—not with the collector of bounty already gone from country.

Damn! Why hadn't he taken that Provost slot offered him in TUSLOG?

chapter six

Draw Is Not a Game of Chance

Asmara, Eritrea (Ethiopia): December 1961

Winter's billet space, a room on the third floor of Operations Company building, offered four-man accommodations. Identified as room number 31, located two doors away from BRAVO Trick squad bay, Winter shared it with only two other soldiers; one bunk and locker were empty. Company policy reserved rooms, which offered a modicum of human privacy, for senior personnel, however lowly their place in the overall scheme of the world outside. Within Operations Company, that amounted to any NCO, even a corporal or a Specialist Fifth Class and, depending upon personnel manning at any one time, even sometimes a Specialist Four with accumulated time in the command: an "old guy," likely someone nearing the end of his assignment.

Marty Spicer had made Spec-5, but chose not to move from the squad bay, as he had only a month remaining before DEROS, and rather than leave his 20-month homestead with buddies, he urged the First Shirt to give the room to someone else. Top had not found anyone deserving, so the mattress stayed S-shaped on the empty wire frame, and the wall locker collected dust through the vents.

Winter, Assistant Trick Chief on BRAVO, was at home in room 31 only during off-duty time on his trick schedule. Tricks had been frozen. Whereas earlier the tricks were known as rotating tricks, for the obvious reason of their rotation in a scheduled movement through a complex scheme: a set of six Days, a break; a set of six Swings, a break; a set of six Mids, a break; and back on Days. Some personnel worked a regular day trick—a shift that, though normal in most of the world, was only one out of four in the world of ASA.

Now, personnel were assigned to Days, Swings, or Mids, in a permanent configuration. Occasionally, personnel from one trick would be seconded over to another trick to work a set, usually men from the Mids section, whose work schedule was lightest due to most target entities still retaining a propensity for sleep. Often, personnel off Mids would be sent to pull a set of Days to augment equal manning in the greater demand of daytime activity.

A period of mayhem and confusion ensued upon the transition of tricks. A major change, where earlier under the four-rotating-trick system a Trick or Trick Platoon or section was cohesive: the entire trick worked together and went on break together, and the integrity of the trick was paramount. Now, breaks were scheduled for individuals at varying intervals within each trick. Four tricks were reduced to three: Days, Swings, Mids—ALPHA, BRAVO, and CHARLIE. The old permanent day workers merely melded in with Days trick, and were all considered day workers. The old DELTA Trick was broken up, its personnel scattered across the extant three. As he had always been assigned to BRAVO, Winter was at home with them in their new role as full-time Swings workers.

Winter liked Swings. He liked to sleep late in the mornings, leisurely arising in time for mail call, a late breakfast/early lunch at the club or messhall, and time for personal things midday before catching the Trick Bus to Operations at sixteen hundred hours. He also liked that at the end of a swings shift, around midnight when the bus had brought the trick back to the post, the messhall was still open so the on-going Mids and, when relieved, off-going Swings could eat midnight chow. The chow was better than average in the post messhall, and midnight chow was a culmination of any leftovers from other meals during the foregoing day—regular breakfast, lunch, and dinner—plus anything one would expect at the regular breakfast: omelettes, biscuits & gravy, ham, eggs, bacon, toast, pancakes—the whole phantasmagorical magilla.

* * *

Due to sometimes strained manning levels of personnel, and counter to the intent of the billeting plan, not everyone in room 31 worked the same shift. They were out of step. The room had become a sort of odd-man-out place of banishment for men from any trick's billeting scheme.

One roommate, SP5 BJ Billerikus, was a printer supervisor on CHARLIE Trick; the other, Pat Simonson, a Watch Office clerk-corporal working straight days. Winter, of course, represented the Swings drones. Because of the differentiation in working schedules, men were awake, in and out, and sleeping at odd and differing times. It led to a testy merge of living conditions, naturally resulting in exploitation of the room's primary function.

Billerikus and Winter were both avid poker players, and on occasion they effected a small game, drawing in other equally willing participants when and where found. With a game in progress within the limited confines of the small, fourteen-by-twelve-foot room, the odd man, trying to sleep or write a personal letter to some long-longing girlfriend far away, or in Winter's case to his wife, could find the atmosphere distressing. Such stand-outs would often remove themselves to another venue, crashing on an unoccupied bunk that belonged to another soldier working at the time the would-be sleeper needed a bunk. Letters could be written in the latrine, if needs must, the Dayroom, the Service Club, or in the Post Library, if one really wanted quiet.

Over time, the unregulated living became more ingrained, the poker games more common; then more and more alluring, often involving men from *any* trick, and the game took on a life of its own. The ideal game was six players; they often played with as few as five—even four, for short periods—and could accommodate up to seven. But the evolving ground rules set those as outside limits. Other rules—on the types of games played, "house rules," an accounting system to allow play during fallow periods between paydays, and other unwritten but well understood and doggedly enforced guidelines—slowly became a part of the culture in Club 31, an epithet applied to the on-going games of chance in Winter's room.

Silly-ass card games such as Mexican Standoff, a form of Showdown which allowed for no skill, no tactics—you turned over your dealt-down cards, one by one, and there you were—Baseball, and other frivolous allowances of many and varied wild cards, were outlawed. Three games were allowed, one being specified by the dealer when the deal clocked around the table to him: five-card draw, five-card stud, and seven-card stud. On rare occasions one Joker was allowed in the deck by common consent of all at the table, but could be used only in pairing with aces, or filling a straight or flush. The calling of Low-Ball was allowed: it just reversed the objective of the prime hand, not the nature or odds of the game.

Paid only at the end of each month, and paid embarrassingly little they thought, most players came to depend upon a scheme of benign indebtedness in order to play. Winter, whose pay almost all went home to support Nickie and Jeremy, might have been a non-participant from a financial standpoint, except that he was a wise and cautious player, never betting on the come. Not depending upon hunches, or even worse, hopes, Winter was a consistent winner. As a tenant of the room, he became the recognized house manager of the game and the venue. And he kept the books.

Players came into a game with money or, lacking funds, they borrowed against the house. Their indebtedness was marked down in a scuffed journal for the chips they were advanced. On those occasions when a game was in progress—and that had become *All The Time!*—when Winter was not present, some other responsible individual by common assent took up the bookkeeping task. It was a simple task, just noting down money coming in to the house, and chips, representing money, being dispersed out to the players. Then accounting for the chips turned in at the end of the game. Winter always did the final monthly accounting summations, and it was to him that the debts were repaid, and he who paid out what the house owed. The scheme could only work through mutual trust and accommodation, and a couple of players who, over time and for various reasons or circumstances, tried to work the system to their advantage were forever banished from Club 31.

As the fame of Club 31 spread, soldiers began to expect a game-in-progress at anytime, day or night, rainy season or dry, with room 31 participants or visitors. Room tenants always had a seat in the game if they so decided, but often the game was six men of disparate work tricks, varying personalities, and eclectic tastes made manifest in table talk. Beginning back in the summer months, Club 31 had begun a regularly attended game. When it began in common circumstances, no one could know its persistent promise. It had been running now for some five months, plus.

Room tenants, as well as game drop-outs—busted, drunk, or just tired—would fall onto one of the four bunks in the room not occupied by its owner or some itinerant visitor, whether he worked, was at the club, or even in the game. Non-players could sleep right through the incessant flutter of cards and sharp, explosive curses that erupted at the end of momentous hands played. Houseboys, during daylight hours, came into 31 reluctantly and hastily made up bunks, emptied ashtrays always overflowing, swept up empty soda and beer cans, pizza crusts and leftover food ordered and delivered from the NCO Club across the street, and the inevitable detritus left from an atmosphere of malingering overindulgence. Club 31 became an institution.

* * *

Earlier in November, with a game in progress while Winter was working at Ops, the door opened and a new PFC, lugging a duffle bag and a B-4 bag, edged into the crowded room. He received the usual silent appraisal from everyone present over the first few moments. The PFC stood in the door, glanced around in seeming annoyance, and finally spotted the unused top bunk, except that it was now being used by two non-playing bystanders awaiting a seat in the game. Fatigue jackets, bush hats, two six-packs of Heinneken, and a pair of highly polished combat boots was spread around the two observers on the bunk springs.

The new man gave an imperious nod at the two on-lookers and edged forward. They ignored him and cast their eyes back on the Old Man's hand which they could read, and wondered if he'd improve on the three deuces he held. A great five-card stud hand, but unfortunately, the game was now seven-card stud. The new man, if such he was, to them represented only a curiosity. For one thing, he was a PFC, and though some of the players and on-lookers held the same rank, they at least knew they didn't belong here; they just came for the life's-blood games.

"Hey, guys, can I get to the bunk?" new man said testily.

"Nope. We're watchin' the game," Hammacker said.

"But this is my bunk." The new guy's voice held an unfortunate edge of whine within.

"Get outta here. Ain't no PFCs living in rooms, especially *new guy* PFCs. Especially *this* room. Go away."

"No. No kidding, this's my bunk. First Sergeant sent me up here."

"What trick you on?"

"I don't know. I just got in, got processed. The plane was late. Blew a tire in Jedda and we had to wait for the airdales to fly a spare over from Dharhan and change it out. I didn't finish in-processing until just now." New guy provided more information than they wanted.

Hammacker and Smith looked at each other across the litter of the top bunk.

"Sounds like a fuckin' scam to me," Smith said disdainfully.

SP5 Kennedy, senior techie on CHARLIE's maintenance crew, said, "Are you sure he said this room?"

"Room thirty-one. Absolutely. First Sergeant said it's the only space available in the BRAVO billet area. Squad bay's full; all the other rooms are full, and Top's shooting for integrity in billeting by trick everywhere else. So he put me in here, though he said it might be temporary." His voice held a plaintive quality. No one could tell if he wished it so or not.

Kennedy, accustomed to dealing with inconclusive situations, nodded and said to the two recalcitrant bed-sitters, "Well, in the absence of Dave and the other Thirty-one tenants, I guess you better let him have his bunk."

Hammacker and Smith nodded as if they expected nothing better, and hopped down. They left the scattered detritus on the steel-wired bedframe.

New guy set down his bags, picked up a fatigue jacket which bore no rank but a nametag, and said, "Salzer?" When a player looked up, New Guy offered him the jacket. When Salzer didn't reach for it, the new man let it drop to the floor. He went through the other items, one by one, and eventually everything that belonged to someone in the room was back in their possession or on the floor. The Heinneken didn't suffer from disdain. Unclaimed items new guy piled outside the door in the hallway while the six poker players watched silently, dealing, accepting cards, betting and checking, raising, and asking for cards in the game of draw, through the facility of grunts, terse comments, head nods, chin thrusts, fingers held aloft, and other silent signals.

When New Guy opened the wall locker, he laid his duffel bag aside and zipped open the B-4. Stenciled on the duffel bag in large white letters was the name DAMSON, B.R..

Hours later, when Winter and Simonson came in, New Guy was asleep in the top bunk. The poker game was ongoing as usual, the hubbub of clinking glasses, rasping beer farts, and giggles and guffaws a moderating background to his stertorous snores. Winter threw his field jacket onto Billerikus's bunk, and nodded soundlessly at the sleeping new tenant.

"New guy name-a Damson. Top sent him up here; got no other bunks," Kennedy offered as he got up to give his seat in the game to Winter. Dave sat down without reply.

"Feisty little fucker," Kennedy continued. "Complained about the noise and the crowd when he got in his sheets. Wanted privacy and peace and quiet. Man's in the wrong line of work, and due for a little attitude readjustment."

"Hmph!" Winter sniffed, glaring at a busted hand. "Give me three. Off the top, Smith."

The game went on, as did the world in the Horn of eastern Africa. Damson settled in to an uneasy existence in room 31. Some of superior rank, even some of equal grade, took exception to his presence in a room—especially *that* room—while they lingered in obscurity in the squad bay or in other rooms of lesser attraction.

* * *

Damson made no effort to make friends, either with his roommates, others on his trick, or anyone in the company. Because the four roommates all worked different shifts—oddly, they were one each from ALPHA, BRAVO, and CHARLIE tricks and one straight day worker—there was little occasion for them to spend much time together, except for the siren call of the poker game, still on-going in its twenty-seventh week. No one ever accompanied Damson downtown; he never asked anyone about the status of female accessibility; and he seldom visited the EM Club, where many of the men took meals and drank cheaply. Billerickus explained to him one day, without any request to do so, about the club's many attractions.

The Army—in its efforts to keep the troops on the base and away from the high VD rate downtown, along with minimizing the incident level of violence with or against local nationals—conspired with the clubs to provide easily affordable beer and whiskey, cheap food, and a venue for various sporting, gambling, and entertainment endeavors, as well as occasional floor-show entertainment. US military facilities overseas were exempt from state laws that outlawed gambling. The slot machines were no more onerous than any downtown Reno dive, plus, the profits were ploughed back into the club to further the prospect of low prices.

Beer was ten cents a bottle, and the beer available was premier: Heinneken, Tuborg, Löwenbrau, Beck's, and sometimes Smithwick's ale. At Happy Hour, an unusually common daily event in the clubs, beer was only a nickel. Whiskies were good and plentiful, and the 25-cent bar charge was similarly reduced for Happy Hour. It was only a few non-drinkers who shrugged off the liquid enticements of the clubs, but the food was good and the menu was ever-changing.

On the rare occasion when he went to the club, Damson invariably sat at a table by himself. If he ate, he did so alone; and after, if he drank, he stayed at the same table and ordered from the bar. He never went into the bar proper, played shuffleboard or the German variant of it, never risked a quarter in the slots, never joined the card games that cropped up there, nor the chug-a-lugging contests that were a matter of course.

Then on the tenth of the month Winter, who was on break, walked into Club 31 to find a four-hand, desultory game in progress without enthusiasm. While Winter stood, unresolved as to whether or not to join such a labored affair, the door opened and Damson came in. He nodded to Winter, but said nothing. Winter, not speaking, nodded back. The poker game was being played in silence. Damson never played in the game. The entire space of Club 31 hovered in white noise.

After straightening his locker's contents, and while loading his pipe, Winter was struck by a sudden desire to shuffle some shit. "Damson," he said, "where you from?"

The PFC, startled, looked at him curiously and finally answered, "Mississippi."

"No shit. My home, too."

"Oh, yeah?" Damson responded without enthusiasm.

"Jackson." Winter waited for the normal comeback of the other man's hometown.

Nothing.

"How 'bout you? Where you from. Where'd you go to school?" Winter wasn't exactly on tenterhooks for an answer, but though men in the service often ran across others from their home state whom they'd not known, it almost always offered an ice-breaker to interpersonal relations. Winter was tired of living in the same room with this iconoclast jerk. About them in the room, the conversation went unremarked.

"Greenwood."

"No shit! I started first grade in Greenwood," Winter said, warming now to the subject.

"Really? What year?" A spark of interest.

"Uhh, let's see, it would have been nineteen forty. No, forty-one. Started in forty-one."

"That's truly odd," Damson said. "I began school in nineteen forty-one. We must have known one another; there was only one grade school." He had stopped flipping through the pages of a paperback and stared at Winter. His unusual verbosity continued: "Where did you live? In town?"

"Yeah, can't forget that. Lived on the corner of George Street and Washington Street. A natural memory tag."

Damson's eyes opened wide. He caught himself with mouth gaping, closed his mouth, and stared at Winter's nametag as if it would tell him something beyond the name. "You're Davey Winter! My God, you're Davey Winter! You lived in that duplex on the corner with the screen porch."

"Of course, what—where'd you live?" The enervating but sinking feeling in the pit of his stomach told him before he murmured, "Damson, B.R. Gawwwd-damn. Billy Ray Damson. Jeez-us. Shit! You lived in that big, two-story brick apartment building just two doors up George. My God!" Winter could only stare back at the astounded BR Damson.

When the dam broke and Damson began spilling his lot of pent-up conversation, and Winter could not come to terms with the irony of this encounter, the hubbub became intolerable to the poker players accustomed to small talk and less. One of the players, a Headquarters Company drudge who didn't even know who lived in this room, and who was pissed because he was already down more than eighty bucks despite the two-buck limit on raises, suggested the two long-lost buddies take their fucking drama outside so the rest could get on with some serious gamesmanship.

They did as he asked, too stunned at their awakening to take offense. They took the outside stairs down to ground level and headed for the club. Once identification was established, both experienced a flood of childhood memories.

At the age of six, in the late summer before the onset of war, the two had been the closest of pals, living two doors apart in the sultry delta heat of Mississippi. They'd gone crawdad-dragging together, fished together, and played a modified version of something akin to baseball, though their version could only afford four players on each team. For seven or eight months, they were inseparable, and were usually, in the afternoon when school let out, together before the radio in one's house or the other, listening to Sky King or The Lone Ranger.

When Davey's father, a heavy-equipment man working on a government project to build an air base in Greenwood, moved on with the job to another location in Jackson, they'd moved to a house between Jackson and Clinton and he'd transferred to Clinton Elementary School. The two pals were heart-broken at the distancing. Left behind for more than twenty years now was his bosom buddy. And, of course, like all young southern men too proud to acknowledge the anguish of parting, and being so young, they did not write. Contact was lost in both directions.

And now, inexplicably, on a mountain in the Eritrean highlands in East Africa, halfway around the world, they shared a room, and had done so in ignorance for more than a month now.

It called for a drink. They had one.

They had several.

Ratty Mac and Trotman shepherded them back from the club and into their bunks, while not disturbing the on-going poker game.

For the next few days, they got together whenever they could, though they worked different tricks. They went downtown Asmara and had a meal at the Italian restaurant, their speech laced with southern slang and euphemisms—which each had sought to rid himself of—and the delight at this untoward and reawakened friendship held them in awe.

But after only a few days of the sort of *bonhomie* expected in the circumstances, the misty attraction of common histories lost its warm and fuzzy aura. Once childhood memories were exhausted, they quickly discovered they had nothing of interest in common, other than the one incidental occurrence of having been pals in a distant land. The drinks and hasty visits to the club stopped. By mid-December, Damson was as much an enigma as he'd first seemed, and he appeared equally committed to that end. And Winter, initially bothered by the failure of their reunion to jell, shrugged it off, recognizing that life was such a funny bitch. No accounting for it!

Club 31's marathon poker game continued.

* * *

Asmara, Eritrea (Ethiopia): December 1961

The double-doors at the end of the Bravo Morse bay burst open. A Spec-4 whom Winter barely knew—the Comm Center worker was married, had finagled his wife over from the states, and he lived off-post in civilian quarters—stood framed in the doorway, holding his eyeglasses in his hand and staring myopically across the bay, his mouth open preparatory to speech.

SFC Sulzer, the Trick Chief, appeared behind him, grasped him by the neck chain holding his security badge, and yanked him backward into the hall. The door slammed.

Ops on position, some actively copying code, others sweeping the bands seeking targets, others sitting patiently awaiting upcoming skeds and smoking, all stared about, questioning one another with curious stares. Now what? No one said anything. With Sulzer, it was always prudent to let events play out without over-stimulating the environment with questions.

In a few minutes, the door inched open and Sulzer slipped into the bay. He looked across the full length of the work space at Winter who sat at the A-slash position, head of the room, and his gaze was unreadable. When Winter made no response to the non-event, even when it was obvious that Sulzer sought his presence, the Sergeant First Class walked the length of the bay between operators in various states of dress-undress and various stages of operational integrity. He walked up to Winter's position, sulking at his assistant's lack of prescience. Or lack of interest.

"Dave," Sulzer murmured, leaning over the console.

Winter stopped twirling the dial on the R-390 HF radio.

"Dave, we got trouble." Sulzer's bunny eyes behind his thick pink government-issue glasses were big and twitching. Winter had a flash of concern and then, knowing Sulzer's penchant for games, let it slide.

"Yeah?" he said, staring across to Ratty Mac's raised eyebrows.

"Come out in the hall." Sulzer moved through the side door, breaking an unwritten rule which said that particular door was never opened, for it was nearest the front entrance of the Ops building and the sounds of manual Morse might more easily be distributed to the outside world.

In the hall, Sulzer whirled on him and said, "A message in the Comm Center says there's been a coup in Addis. Ethiopia's in the hands of some group of nutcakes using Haile's son as a figurehead." He stopped in awe and confusion.

"Where's the king?" Winter snapped. Like most, he despaired of referring to Haile Selassie as Emperor, despite that he now ruled both Ethiopia and Eritrea, by UN fiat. He grasped the situation immediately. Coups were only effective if government operations could be affected, and in Ethiopia proper, as well as here in the mandate state of Eritrea, that could only happen if Haile Selassie was somehow out of the picture. A coup in the capital of Addis Ababa, far south in Ethiopia proper, might or might not be convincing.

"Haile's in Brazil. On a state visit. A bunch of Army officers and government civilians, using his son as bait for the population, took control of the government. They've closed the airport in Addis so Haile can't get back in country."

"So what do *we* do? What are our orders?" Winter couldn't imagine that they could just go on as usual, snagging dits while the world about them was upended.

"Don't have any orders. Just the info. And an alert notice. And a request to stand by for instructions." The pink bunny eyes in the pink GI glasses were anything but humorous.

"Gotta go," Sulzer jerked out. He spun about and dashed down the hall toward the Watch Office where he usually hung his hat on swings.

Winter returned to the Morse bay, uncertain what, if anything, he should do. Well, headquarters, waa-a-a-y back in Virginia, at least knew about it. And they'd said stand by for instructions. That implied there might be some . . . an unusual state of affairs.

Ratty Mac stared at him with a huge question mark on his face while he continued banging on the mill, and the chatter roll crept out of the machine filled with inexplicable figures and numbers. Winter shook his head. Brenner came forward from his now-dormant pos. "Something?" he asked.

"Nothing to talk about. Just yet . . ." Winter answered, and Brenner went away. He would know, as would any of the old hands, that something was afoot, but whatever it was had not reached the level for necessary distribution.

Nevertheless, within minutes, activity in the hallways outside the bays picked up. Soldiers, many not where they were supposed to be, flitted up and down, carrying with them a sense of urgency. Voices grew anxious. Loudermilk, who had gone to the latrine, returned to the bay and announced loudly, "Hey, we're under attack!"

Winter jumped up, trotted down the aisle and grabbed him by the T-shirt. "Milk, what the fuck are you doing? You trying to start a panic or something? Whaddaya mean, we're under attack?"

"Shit, Dave, it's true. Haile Selassie's been killed in a coup. Addis is under communist control, and they're coming to drive us Americans out of the country." His eyes were wide in a startled, convinced stare.

"Milk, you asshole. Haile Selassie's in Brazil. He can't even get back in the country; the airport's closed in Addis. Stop spreading goddamned rumors. Man, that's just what we don't need," he emphasized, realizing the cat was out of the bag.

About him, nervous ops began sloughing off their skeds; leaving their positions, they ganged in the aisle, voices jerky and high with nerves.

"O.K., O.K., you clowns, get back on pos. *Sit down!* I said," he ordered when movement was slow. "Now, listen up. There has been word about some level of coup attempt activity in Addis Ababa . . . but the king's in Brazil. He's O.K. We're O.K. Nobody's coming for us. At most, it's an in-house, political thing. We just sit tight and nothing happens."

"Yeah, but—" a chorus of complaints and nay-saying erupted across the bay. It took Winter ten minutes to quiet the troops, mostly upset because living as they did in a vault and cut off from outside communications, they never knew anything until after the fact. Many feared that such a time might be after the fact of their existence. Only a handful of men in the company had ever experienced a war, or combat in any capacity. And their fears were very real.

Late in the shift, an analyst from down the hall broached the doors again and shouted, "They're sending Russian airborne troops to capture Kagnew Station!"

This generated a mixed response. Some expressed satisfaction with that scenario, calling out, "They're welcome to it, bitch." Some said the fucking Russkies couldn't even hit the top of the plateau with their airborne; others worried when the American soldiers would be issued weapons. Most knew there were no weapons at the Operations site; and even if they got back to the post and the company, the armory did not come up to the standards of a good weekend duck-hunting club. The Russian airborne rumor took hold. It was not fully panic time yet, but the troops in Ops were becoming increasingly restive.

* * *

Back on post, the Adjutant, Captain Poteris, went to the Officers Club and did his best to convey to Lieutenant Colonel "Bourbon Billy" Keyes, through his accustomed alcoholic haze, a sense of concern he felt was validated by circumstances. When the notion of this thus-far undefined threat broke through the colonel's whisky indifference, he was transported immediately back to the Nettuno Landing in Italy and the feisty encounters with German armor then, and later up the Italian peninsula. Keyes had been only moderately successful as a young infantry sergeant then, but he had parlayed the Fifth Army's eventual success into s semi-successful career. As

Commanding Officer of the 4th USASA Field Station in Asmara, Eritrea (Ethiopia), he idled now in neutral, in STANDBY mode, awaiting retirement.

The mission of the personnel assigned to Asmara's Kagnew Station, the American post in the capital city of Eritrea, was a critical one, and the operations performed there covered a wide range of Middle Eastern, Mediterranean, and African political and/or military activities. Keyes recognized little of this. Living up to his sobriquet, he kept bourbon sales in the O club at a steady but high level, and the cronies he surrounded himself with knew little more, certainly not enough to enlighten him.

When Poteris was finally able to convince the colonel that something serious was afoot, the one-time infantryman tried to emerge from the onus of age and indifference. Keyes clambered to his feet, yelled for his driver, and motioned a couple of cronies to accompany him. At the motor pool, two startled duty mechanics were rousted into action, and managed to get the armored personnel carrier started and, clanking forward on rusty tracks, chewing up the recently laid asphalt of the motor pool. With one of the mechanics driving, Keyes and one of his sycophants climbed aboard, and the behemoth crashed forward down the street toward the front gate.

There, the guard alerted by the second mechanic, the gates were open and the APC clanked forward from the staid backwater of Kagnew Station into the streets of Asmara town. Down the hill, past the front gate whorehouses and bars, turning left on Princess Menen Boulevard, past the school, the colonel, his loyal aide, and a scared driver made for the Basgh, a sprawling, turmoil of neighborhood that constituted poverty living at its worst. Somehow—no one would ever know how or why—the colonel had presumed that sad quarter to be the focus of threat. En route, to the shock of his aide and terrifying the driver to the point of tearful despair, the colonel stood through the open top hatch, cranked a round into the .50 caliber machine gun, and opened fire against the high wall bounding an area of classier houses. The heavy bullets pocked the wall, and swept up to the edge and roofline of the houses beyond, but fortunately were blocked from creating a tragedy in the homes attacked.

It was a night of confusion and fear. Monstrous over-reaction by the drunken officer and illogical rumor-mongering accounted for a severe case of international terrorism, practically unknown at that time. When the colonel finally either passed out, or sobered up enough to realize the significance of his mindless acts, the shooting stopped. NCOs and officers squelched the Russian airborne rumors, convincing the troops that Russia did not even have aircraft with an operable radius that could ferry paratroopers to Eritrea (Ethiopia)—a distortion of fact; a lie, in reality—the steam went out of the fearsome threat.

Haile Selassie, old campaigner, flew from Brazil back to his countries, landed at Asmara where he was placed under the protection of loyal 2nd Infantry Division Ethiopian Army troops—in Eritrea functioning as a police force during the enforced mandate period—and drove in an armored column south to the Ethipian capital of Addis Ababa. There, with the presence of their God-on-Earth fully revealed to them, the population who'd been confused and lied to and mis-directed into support for the coup, came around politically. Haile took command. The plotters, including his hapless son, were rounded up. Most of them wound up fertilizing the arid coffee slopes; and many more, tangential to the actual coup attempt, would pay the price for having even tentatively wrong associations. The son was relegated back to obscurity.

For days afterward, men and NCOs walked about the Operations spaces and the billets, eyeing each other with shame and misgivings for having subscribed to the falacious goings-on.

chapter seven

Anomaly, Flavored Spanish

Asmara, Eritrea (Ethiopia): March, 1962

"Come on, Dave. Go downtown with me to the Eye-Tie café," Brenner suggested.

"The Italian restaurant?" No one ever called it by its real name, The Sorrento.

"Sure. Where else is there? And after we eat, the Internationale Club has a bevy of Spanish dancers giving a show six nights a week. New in town. Better catch them now before they get bored, cancel the gig, and go back to Saragossa." Brenner was only half kidding.

"O.K, why not? I have damned little money, Luther, maybe enough for spaghetti, and the tab at the International. I won't be drinking much."

"Ahhh, Winter Man . . . your beneficent angel, Brenner, has you covered. At least for a couple of Saint Georges." Had he but known it, reminding Winter he'd be drinking the local brew anywhere beyond the confines of the post, almost lost Brenner his accomplice.

Others had learned of the Spanish troupe, and Winter and Brenner had to wait a full ten minutes at the front gate for a *gharry* to return and take up its taxi post, so busy had they been ferrying GIs into town. At the Internationale—a tongue-in-cheek attempt at a sense of grandiosity for the converted warehouse—a crowd larger than anything Winter had ever seen there was noisy and active when they arrived. Their seats were inauspicious, the view of the tiny performance arena almost blocked by a carved plaster, imitation Spanish architectural column. But before the show began, two GIs, at the edge of the chipped wooden dance floor—one, Signal Corps from Middle East Signal Agency (MESA), and one from the Navy Communications Facility, decided they couldn't tolerate one another for the duration of the performance, and their enmity erupted into a fistfight. Two MPs, assigned to the crowded venue by a supervisor of unusual prescience, dragged the two away to Kagnew Station. Brenner, followed by Winter, dove forward and claimed their table.

The announcer was the same, smarmy Lebanese transvestite that effected good French, a little Italian, a lot of Arabic, damned little

Tigrinyan, and no English, who had been playing to small crowds at the Internationale Club for as long as Winter or Brenner had been aware of its sometime attractions. Once, the place had featured a quartet of Turkish strippers, obviously whores swept off the streets of Istanbul, each of the four ugly to a fault but with redeeming physical features of unnaturally large breasts, large buttocks, and one with the most pronounced pudenda imaginable, where visible through a massive forest of black bush. The Turks lasted four days, before some unrecognized force for good taste and/or Christian pretensions shut down the show and whisked the party girls off on a quick flight to Khartoum. Since the Turks, nothing worth seeing. Until now.

Maybe.

The music was taped. The lighting was iffy and inconsistent. But the dancing was electric, and the dancers, goddesses. Winter and Brenner stared at each other, marveling. Where in the hell . . . *how* in the hell had this backwater ever attracted this caliber of performers? The dancers—six in number—performed with precision, with enthusiasm and grace, and were unstinting in their time on the floor. After a gypsy *flamenco* number, a *jota* from Aragon, or a sultry *malagueña* of Valencia, even the hint of enthusiasm in the applause kept them on the floor for continued performance. Or brought them back, when allowed to slip away.

Winter and Brenner stayed for almost two hours, and the girls were on the floor for all except ten minutes of that time. And they were lovely, to a person. One tall, statuesque dancer bore the attributes of classical dance training. She had a haughty look as she performed, but both GIs recognized that as legitimate Spanish hauteur. At the end of each number, she nodded to the crowd along with the others, but unlike the other dancers, never smiled.

Winter thought a shorter dancer, slightly plump, but with a gorgeous face, impressive bosom, and spectacular legs would have been his choice. Unaccustomed to Brenner's encounters with females—he had never seen him chat up a bar girl, even in the Blue Nile where it was almost impossible not to—Winter was surprised to see Brenner stand and follow the tall, haughty dancer off the floor and down the tiny hallway into the dressing rooms. Winter stayed where he was and waited. Surely, Brenner would be back in a moment, cast out as any undesirable.

Fifteen minutes later, Brenner returned with two women. He introduced the tall beauty to Winter as Dulcie, and only then did

Winter see the cute one he'd admired, standing quietly off to the side. Brenner urged her forward. "Marianna," he said, "meet David." She was not shy, and offered her hand which was firm but soft. Dulcie stood by, measuring Winter's behavior. She might have intuited his intentions, had he any, but even Brenner did not anticipate any back sliding from "straight Dave." He knew that the hold of his wife and child was too well affirmed.

* * *

I didn't really expect Dave to agree when I suggested the four of us leave the Internationale Club and cart back over to the Sorrento. He smiled, was his usual gracious, unspeaking self, declined the invitation, and that left only the three of us to fit in one *gharry*.

Later, when the mediocre dinner had been endured—just the meager *antipasta* for me, as I'd already eaten—and the bottle of Chianti finished, I managed to convey to Dulcie that I would escort her to wherever she was staying. She had three words of English; Marianna had none. But we seemed to understand one another. It might have been my look of entreaty, rolling my eyes back toward the smaller girl while struggling to find out if I could be alone with my choice. Dulcie laughed a lot now, a surprise to me, as she had been the soul of cold professionalism in the Club. She indicated the Hotel Assab, one of the better small hotels downtown in a town where there were few hotels. Nothing was indicated for her associate, but I was sure they were together.

When we went out to the street, and while the girls were climbing into the cart—a tricky proposition as the horse began, for no apparent reason, to toss his head, shy backwards toward the cart, and whinney loudly—I noticed a pair of men come out of the alley next to the Internationale Club. One was tall, emaciated looking and frail, with a wispy white, pointed beard: a sort of long, lank Van Dyke, with long, pointed and drooping mustaches. His hair, likely white also, was hidden under a round hat that was shaped like a bowl and sat loosely on his head. In the sidelight from the Internationale's lighting, the cover had the dull sheen of metal.

With this strange apparition was a much shorter, rotund figure, who had all the appearance of a clown out of uniform. His belly hung over a broad, leather belt that passed through no loops on his trousers but was simply wrapped about his girth with determination. He had a peasant's air about him, and seemed jolly and unconcerned with whatever he witnessed on the street. Both late-night figures were other than locals. They might have been Mexican or American, some European race, and then I realized . . . they were likely associated with the dance troupe. Maybe bodyguards, for here the troupe was off in the wilds—well, maybe not wilds, but certainly remote parts—of Africa where they might face many sorts of threats and dangers, not uncommon with women's plight on the fringe of the Arab world.

When I had handed Marianna into the cart and turned back, the two men had gone. Or, I thought reasonably, maybe they'd been only a distortion in my vision. My mind was not on men, strange or copacetic, right then. I hopped aboard, the driver lashed the bony mare across her withers, and we set off at a pace less than breakneck, albeit likely the best the emaciated beast could manage.

It was after eleven when we pulled up in front of the Assab. As I herded the two girls to the door after dismissing the driver with a couple of bucks Ethi, Dulcie held me at the door. Suddenly, she had more English than I'd come to believe. While Marianna rang the bell and waited by the door for entrance, the tall dancer pulled me aside and said, "To-mor-row. You come. Here." She pointed to the cracked sidewalk where we stood.

Being an unavoidable wiseass, I said, "Here?" and pointed down exuberantly at the sidewalk.

She shook her head. "Hotel. Assab. Two—" she held up two fingers in case my English was weak "—clock. Bring Creme de Ment. Room tutu." With that, she pecked me on the cheek and fled into the barely opened door.

Tutu? Ahhh . . . room twenty-two. *Creme de menthe?*

I looked about. There were no *gharries* on the street anywhere. I began walking toward Kagnew. Creme de Menthe—Tutu? That must be the most bizarre parting line in the history of theater. I didn't know if the Class VI store on Kagnew Station even carried Creme de Menthe. Did anyone really drink that syrupy shit? Champagne would have been more in line with the scenario, or even brandy. How about Courvoisier? I offered silently. Or B-and-B? I knew both were on the shelves in liquor sales. But, Creme de Menthe?

* * *

At two the next day, I made my mandated appearance. The blank-faced clerk at the hotel desk—the dining table-work bench that served as a desk—pointed me to the elevator and said *"Tre!"* when I asked for the room of Miss Dulcie. Realizing he meant the floor, I punched the button labeled "3" and realized, only when I'd ascended past three floors, that here in Eritrea they subscribed to the European floor-numbering scheme. If I'd walked up, I would have stopped a floor below and been, no doubt, frustrated in my search for Darlin' Dulcie. The desk was on the Ground floor. Next flight up, what we in the US would call second floor, was in Europe designated first floor. And so up. Dulcie's room was on the third level, call it what you will.

When I knocked, another of the dancers opened the door, smiled broadly, winked at me, and stepped back into the room. Beyond, I saw Dulcie sitting on the edge of the bed, performing some sewing/stitching magic on a costume. The dancer who opened the door and one other, who sat across the room—all of them engaged in the meticulous maintenance of their working finery.

Dulcie stood and put her sewing on a small table. She spoke to the other two and without a word, they gathered up their domestic work and went out the door. I heard another door open farther down the hall. Dulcie shut the door and gave me another peck on the cheek, a copy of the one the evening before. I pulled the bottle of Creme de Menthe from the paper bag I'd carried it in—I counted myself fortunate the Class VI did carry the viscous aperitif; I might have been left standing in the hallway with nothing to add allure to my presence—and proffered it to her. She smiled, took the bottle, and immediately found two small glasses. I declined, but she nodded encouragingly and I accepted the liqueur which I had no intention of drinking.

Dulcie raised her glass in a small toast, smiled in a Mona Lisa sort of way, and when I raised my glass, she clinked hers against mine. She tossed back the drink, set her glass on the table with her piece work, and by the time I'd lowered my glass, she was naked.

Amazing! I hadn't seen the breakaway action with the robe, but I only had minimal work to find myself in the same condition of *deshabille*. There were no lights to extinguish, no door that required locking, no other awkward, anxious preparations. We were on the bed before I could have spelled it.

I needn't waste space here, describing what was a furious but fantastic two hours of indulgence. A sense of wonder, initiated with her instant disrobing act, stayed with me through the afternoon. Her body was all it promised to be; no surprise, as I had seen most of it in her gypsy dance costume. She was a passionate but sweet lover, and seemed highly sensitive to my feelings and responses.

Later, in unstrained easy though labored talk, struggling through her language reach, when I asked how she had come to invite me to her room, she told me she had "want to have American lover." It seemed unconscionably simple, and I did not pursue beyond what she offered. At the same time I was aware; she might have been sharing this afternoon with Dave, or Old Man, or any other American who'd had the *chutzpah* to ask her out. Nothing special about old Luther; just Johnny-on-the-Spot.

It did give me a slightly anxious moment, thinking on the implications. Was the Creme de Menthe only the prelude to bigger payments? Cash? Gifts? Military secrets?

Admiring those gallant long legs and that generous bosom, I hated the thoughts that coursed unwillingly through my head. I thought I must be wrong. But I was prepared to take that chance.

Without any mention of her future, or *ours*, however, I came back that evening to the Internationale, sat through another performance, had a drink—not Creme de Menthe, but a harsh bar scam drink called "Whisky"—but she would not allow me to accompany her to the hotel. I looked about, trying to identify anyone with whom she might have created a new alliance, but saw nothing suspicious.

I scoured the inside of the club and outside by the alley again, for the two men who'd shown up the previous evening. Earlier that day, when I'd left the hotel mid-afternoon, I'd seen them coming out of the Catholic church. The tall one, upon seeing me, made a surge in my direction, looking as if he would attack me, but the short, round one grasped him about the waistline and pulled him away. A string of strident Spanish invective followed me into my *gharry* and down the streets to Kagnew. I felt vaguely threatened by this inexplicable behavior of strangers.

When I returned to the hotel the next morning with another bottle of the green liqueur, the desk clerk informed me that the troupe was gone. They'd taken an Ethiopian Air Lines flight to Yaounde in Cameroon. That seemed no stranger than the entire set of events, for which I never discovered an explanation.

But that second bottle of Creme de Menthe sat, unopened, in my wall locker until I gave it to Tesfai as a going-away gift when I left months later.

* * *

Keren, Eritrea (Ethiopia): June 1962

Swainson was still driving when they came off the mountain road and entered Keren. He wasn't drunk, but the Tuborg stock count was down from when they'd left the plateau. Back on the mountain in Asmara, Swainson, a maintenance technician, was viewed as a non-entity, a man totally without personality. He had no roommates, no friends—no enemies, even. He barely *was*. Winter had made the case to let him come along on the break, and already he was questioning his altruistic inclination. For a hunting party, he would have tendered no such invite: Swainson had a strange glint in his eye and could not be imagined with a loaded gun.

The SP5 radio mechanic insisted on entering Keren through the silver market, the long way 'round. It's all he'd talked of, all four thousand feet and 91 kilometers down the mountain. He'd never been in Keren but had heard tales. No one in the party argued. There was always action in the market where the local raw silver was fashioned into baubles and sold or traded, and there were camels, donkeys, monkeys, and whores on the block.

As they merged with a flail of livestock and a crowd of "Lascars, Levites, and likely Lithuanians"—Brenner's depiction of an Ethi market—the Jeep was suddenly blocked from further passage. Pedestrians, in an emotionally charged display, surged aimlessly about the dirt square. The vehicle could move forward only with the risk of crushing little coffee-colored people.

"Back it up, Son of Swain. Back. Back. Now! Crowds are not your friend." Brenner's head swivelled, measuring the masses as he spoke.

Swainson backed and filled until he had cleared a small circle, turned and drove back the way they had come. Following Winter's directions, cutting through a narrow alley, they came out on the far edge of the square away from crowds and sped off through the noon sun toward the R-and-R Center.

Passing the Nefratiti Bar, Winter motioned the driver over when he saw Ratty Mac and Dalgren sitting out front in the meager shade of a dusty, diseased palm. A baker's dozen Melotti beer bottles stood on the rickety table before them.

"Hola!" Winter said.

"The fuckin' Greek cavalry's arrived. Look, Dalgren," Ratty Mac laughed manically, "the Greeks. 'Hola,' my ass."

Dalgren frowned.

Winter did not respond; he found nothing lovable about the malcontent private either.

"What's all the hoo-rah?" Winter asked, nodding at the milling crowd across the square.

Mac squinted, focused, and said, "Remember that Ethi major from Massawa that was arrested after the coup attempt last December? In Asmara? Guy they tried and sent to jail for thirteen years for his part in tryin' to overthrow Haile?"

"Yeah. Somebody's brother. Minister of the Interior's or something," Winter recalled.

"That one."

A few moments' silence lengthened into an awkward hiatus. Everhardt, the other passenger, ignored for hours, was still asleep in the back seat and began now to squirm, his body objecting to inaction.

Winter waited for Mac's explanation, gave it more than enough time. "Well, what about him?"

"Ethi military're pretty advanced in human rights. After courts-martial and conviction, any soldier has the right of appeal."

"Yeah, so? . . . "

"So the major appealed his thirteen years. The appeals court agreed he got the wrong sentence."

"Did they let him out? Is that what the hubbub's all about?"

"They hung him." Mac took a long swallow of Melotti and belched.

"Hanged him," Brenner corrected him. Winter stared.

"'s what I said. They hung him. Leastwise, that's what they call it. Put that fucking wooden collar thing on him—"

"Garrot," offered Brenner.

"—turned the screw, and choked him. 'bout a half hour ago. Right across . . . there," he specified, nodding toward the densest crowd.

"Jeez-us! Appellate action," Winter commented.

"Grabbed me by the balls, too," Mac admitted. "I thought they'd've cut his dingles off at the first trial. Surprised he got extra months to bake in Keren's doss house."

* * *

The sun was setting in the gap between Mounts Samana and Amba and the towering peak of Sanchil. The Dongolaas Gorge, where the road to Agordat, and Kassala in the Sudan, ran past Fort

Dologorodoc, was in shadow. A gaggle of American soldiers from Bravo Trick at the 4th USASA Field Station in Asmara sprawled across the tiled porch of the Keren R-and-R Center, the latent ambience not revealing of the building's storied past. But everyone knew the history. During the brief period of Mussolini's exaggerated new Roman Empire—forcibly incorporating Abyssinia, Somaliland, and Eritrea in the 1930s and trumpeted as Italian East Africa, a serf state in the spirit of *Pax Italiana*—the structure had housed an Italian army officers' brothel. Under the American Army's current tenancy, many judged the neighborhood had declined in status.

Passing on drinks handed to him by Tessanai, the barman, Winter noted one fluted champagne glass containing a light brown mixture. Intrigued, he raised it to his lips, and drank. A voice beyond him whined in complaint and Winter passed the glass on to the disgruntled recipient. Someone's idea of a Brandy Alexander: real brandy, but cheap, harsh spirits; the supposed half-and-half was only canned evaporated milk; and powdered instant coffee stood in for creme de cacao. The taste was so far from its intent, Winter declined to point out the absence of nutmeg.

"Yecc-ch-h."

"Well keep your lips outta my friggin' cocktail, Winter." It was Pruitt, who'd been in Keren for more than a week on leave. Winter could only judge the degree of his lonely depravity by the mix he was reduced to drinking.

"You could-a told me, Pru. I promise, I'll never do it again."

A three-quarter-ton truck ground up over the rise and turned in at the ostentatious tile pillars framing the open gate. Colver drove and Winter recognized a couple of Navy people with him. No accounting for taste, Ratty Mac always reminded him.

Colver jumped down, slapping dust from his shirt with his hat, and strode forward to where Winter reclined on a splintered raffia settee. "Dave, heard you'd be here. Got something for you," he said, digging into his shirt pocket. He pulled out a folded sheet of white typewriter paper.

"What is it?" Winter asked. More transfer documentation, he assumed. He was fixated on the fact that when he returned to Asmara after this break, he was to begin clearing post. With a port call date of 27 June, he had exactly one week and a wake-up left in Eritrea. Home to mama!

The headquarters clerk didn't answer but handed the sheet to Winter. Colver reached for a cold Heinneken and flopped on the tile floor, caressing it, scrabbling in a large pocket for an opener. No one invited the deck apes to join them. Winter didn't press Colver for information; he understood he was in possession of an illicit document.

Winter unfolded the sheet, eyes scanning across a full page of text, seeking immediate explanation. The letter, dated 07 Jun 62, from Headquarters, Army Security Agancy, Arlington Hall Station, Virginia, was an INFO copy of a letter addressed to the Dean of Engineering at Milwaukee School Of Engineering, Milwaukee, Wisconsin. Winter's head swam as he read the opening paragraph:

> Dear Dean Unkelmann:
> The Department of the Army, under its Enlisted Training Program in Civilian Educational Institutions, has selected Specialist Five David D. Winter, RA 19 650 141, to pursue a course of study at your institution such as would eventually lead to a baccalaureate degree in Electronics Engineering.
>
> We would appreciate—

The words blurred. He looked to the bottom of the page. Signed by a Major General Kleppinger, Department of the Army. Winter felt pressure in his chest, realized he was holding his breath, a sense of electrifying excitement stifling thought. His head swam.

"What is it, Dave?" Brenner asked. "You look as if you'd seen a naked Ratty Mac."

"I'm not going to the battalion."

"And that would be . . . which battalion?"

"The Three seventeenth. Fort Bragg."

"Say what?"

"I figured you'd like to see that," Colver spoke out. "Might be days before the head shed got around to informing you."

"I got the goddamned college program," Winter exclaimed in wonder, on his feet now. "I'm going to school. In Milwaukee. Hot damn! Wisconsin, not North Carolina. I'm not going to that frigging brown-boot army post and jumping out of airplanes. Three seventeenth A.S.A. Battalion (Airborne), my ass."

Brenner appeared perplexed for only a moment, his mind computing rapidly.

"Through the college program, I thought you asked for International Relations at Stanford. What's in Milwaukee . . . besides Marquette? Is it Marquette?" He shared his friend's excitement.

"No. I said . . . M.S.O.E. Milwaukee School of Engineering. It doesn't matter what school. But I know this place. Takes up a city block, uptown, near U.W.M. Used to drive past there when I was on liberty back in 'fifty-five, when I was in Electronics School at Great Lakes. No-nonsense engineering school. Hot damn!" Winter looked up, his grin too wide for his face. "Jeez-us, Nickie will just shit. She's heard me talk about Mill-Town for years. She'll get to live it. And no piney woods and ticks."

"Engineering. But you asked for . . . ?" Brenner watched Winter reading down the page, his lips moving. He didn't indulge his inclination to chide his friend in harassment.

"Hell, Luther, can't bitch about this. Kennedy wants engineers. We're going to the moon. I'm going to learn to be a rocket scientist. I can do Stanford and world-wide good fellowship later. Don't you realize what a boondoggle this is?"

"I can identify with not jumping out of perfectly good aircraft."

chapter eight

Unaccountable

Milwaukee, Wisconsin; November 1963

The fields that stretched south, bordering the long driveway back off south 27th Street, showed a golden patina of fallow promise. Green would come again, a given in Wisconsin.

Winter tapped the dottle from his briar, crushing it underfoot in the scattering of dusty snow and crushed blue stone and, satisfying himself no spark survived, returned to the warmth of the apartment. Jeremy was sleeping, finally; Nickie now busied herself in the tiny kitchen. She glanced up at his entry, smiled without speaking, and returned to the anxious quick movements inside a pan with a slight clatter, an exercise that promised well for dinner.

David touched her arm on his way to the drop-leaf shelf that served him as a study desk. "Lake wind's picking up. Going to get cold quick, now."

She said over her shoulder, "TV weatherman promised no more snow soon. Winds off the lake are going to make us forget that. But, can't depend on projections." This enigmatic judgement was without humor. Nothing funny about winter in Milwaukee.

David Winter was home this weekday, a Friday, catching up on school work, but cutting two classes. He and Nicole had discussed his voluntary heavy load when the semester began. Taking more credits than required, even recommended, led to a fast accumulation of hours, but it was a bitch in those crunch times that always seemed to catch a student off his stride. Now, with his math and technical subjects going well, he had fallen behind in English. Not that anyone would mind, either in the school management or in the military's control group at Fifth Army. They had sent him here to study Engineering, and more than a small number of the staff academics at Milwaukee School Of Engineering thought of the humanities as fluff, for show-and-tell only, something tacked on to the real courses of Physics of Light, Engineering Principles III, Geometry of the Spheroid, and the like.

But Winter, here in this windfall assignment, was not devoted to the math and sciences of his curriculum. Given a choice, he would have been struggling in some humanities discipline. Such was not in the Army's interests; and that is where the institution and their determined soldier-student parted ways. David Winter pursued his assigned curriculum with real commitment, but he was equally dedicated to the English course. He considered this paper assignment not a task, but an opportunity.

His subject for this, his last paper this quarter, drawn from early interest in Irish poetry, was William Butler Yeats. He'd read Yeats all his life, and if there was any poet whose lines he could quote, the Bard of Connaught was he. And yet, his fairly extensive familiarity with his subject seemed to work against Winter's aims for the paper. He knew about Yeats, as he had told Nickie, "just enough to be really dangerous." As a consequence, he was finding it difficult to winnow down the vast array of subject matter and focus on this one, brief-glimpse paper.

It was not all a private indulgence—focusing on the humanities class at the possible expense of his primary assignment—but also reflected his English professor's interest in Winter's misaligned priorities. Doctor Young, whose age and name gave meaning to the literary device of irony, had earned his doctorate in 1903 at Harvard. Re-employed out of retirement as Professor Emeritus of the minuscule Humanities Department at MSOE, he had found in David Winter a long-sought disciple: an engineering student who thought beyond the electronic circuit.

Doctor Young allowed Winter extraordinary freedoms in his class, knowing he would not abuse the trust. Winter repaid him by pushing himself to the limit in readings, research, and writing. He might have to go out from this educational experience and function in a technical arena, but he would take with him as much knowledge of these other interests as he could manage. And somewhere down the line. . . .

After more than a year here in school, he did not favorably anticipate his future departure from MSOE. He could do without the demands of Engineering and whatever other pressures he placed upon himself, but he would be sad to leave this town behind. Nickie, too, found life in the Midwest to her liking. His wife of some five years, she had only suffered one assignment with him in what he called "drone zones," towns like Jacksonville, North Carolina, San Diego, and others which he'd warned her early-on could lead to divorce or suicide. It was only marginally a joke. Those, and other similar towns—towns immediately adjacent to large military bases—because of a proliferation of watering holes, bars and pawn shops to rid a GI of his money and treasured goods under the pressures of low pay—plus the not-uncommon abundance of loose women, and not-so-loose-but-someone-else's-wife-who-strayed, and such threats—did not make for pleasant assignments.

Milwaukee, blue collar "Mill Town" for its heavy industrial base, was a bastion of solid Midwestern values, family strengths, and warmth. The Winters had been made to feel welcome, even as obverse-culture southerners, such that they might have been returning relatives. They loved the definitive communities, including the lower middle class where they lived in South Milwaukee. They were not lower class here, simply financially less exalted. From both their backgrounds, David and Nicole felt at home here.

* * *

Nickie had not interrupted him for his normal lunch hour; she saw his efforts, tying him to the research, hunger pangs ignored. Sometime after one o'clock, David Winter stretched and rose from the uncomfortable straight-back chair. He headed for the table and the sandwich Nickie had left for him, wrapped in waxed paper. The ice had melted in the tea, and the moisture on the glass was drying. But this late break, and eating by himself, would salvage his train of thought.

Seating himself with a scrape of the chair, he cringed, fearful of waking the baby who was teething and fretful. He heard Nickie, who would be aware of his belated move to the table, turn on the television. It blared out and she quickly lowered the volume.

It was only moments past the time it took for the old, second-hand Emerson Black-and-White to warm up, his tuna fish and Swiss cheese half devoured, when he heard a loud gasp from the living room.

"Oh, God! No!" Nickie moaned.

David jumped up at the sound. Rounding the stand-alone half-wall into the living room, he was in time to see Nickie drop to her knees before the television. Both hands were over her mouth. She was white, her face drained of blood. He saw tears, welling into sudden pools in her wide, staring eyes fixed on the screen.

At the same time, he heard the familiar voice on the broadcast, speaking in uncommonly ponderous tones, "... and it is now reported that President John F. Kennedy, thirty-fifth president of these United States, has died at Parkland Hospital in Dallas at approximately twelve-thirty Central Standard Time of an assassin's bullet."

He looked to her for explanation. What kind of horror movie had she turned on that could—would dare—employ such a plot line? He watched her face for a change of expression.

* * *

Caught in the stream of memory, David Winter glossed over the frantic catastrophe that had been his tour in Viet Nam, catching the war at its inception. Without conscious direction, he seemed to jump from one non-military educational environment to another.

* * *

Presidio of Monterey, California: March 1966

Winter had progressed well past the halfway point in the 37-week Russian language course. His vocabulary was extensive, his cursive writing excellent, but dialogues gave him fits. No matter how many hours he studied at home at night or the weekend, he invariably found himself bouncing the two-part dialogues, scenarios of incredible banality, off another student in the early mornings before class. This last-minute scholarship, performed on the porches of the old wooden school buildings that marched up the hill from the bay of Monterey, was demanding, frustrating, and no less embarrassing.

Russian had for years during the Cold War been the dominant language taught at the Defense Language Institute on the Presidio army post. Now planners and administrators, teachers, logisticians, and post engineers worked overtime building temporary structures, converting warehouses, garages, paint sheds, any and every kind of building capable of housing classrooms, and formulating lesson plans given over to the new linguistics lottery winner—Vietnamese!

Winter, evacuated more than a year before off a hot LZ in 'Nam, through the 32nd Air Force Dispensary at Tan Son Nhut, to the Navy Hospital in Cho Lon, to an Army hospital in Japan, and settled finally in Letterman Army Hospital in San Francisco, had emerged bent but not broken. During the months his reconstructed leg and hip in traction kept him a prisoner on the ward, he was visited by an ASA career counselor who came to advise him about his future, offering him essentially any assignment ASA controlled. Relying largely on Judge Monaghan's enthusiastic take on that culture, Winter asked for Russian language training.

While he was in the hospital, Nickie and son Jeremy had come to San Francisco and found a tiny, cheap apartment so they could be near. His wife, despairing since his wounding, became enthusiastic about his choice for language training, a move she saw in the selection of Russian as removing him from the hazard of further duty in Viet Nam.

When released from Letterman, he was transferred a short ride down the coast, assigned to The Presidio's Headquarters Company doing make-work while recuperating, and months later, when capable of returning to full duty, he was assigned to Russian Class 66-37-5.

No! Thank you, but he had no interest in the many-toned language of the peoples of the two Viet Nams. He looked with curiosity at those new students, marching or strolling past the old Russian classrooms, on their way to learn a language that had only one use, and that in-country Viet Nam.

Winter, exempt from formations, still walked with a severe limp, relying on a cane when the chilly, damp winds off the bay were especially grueling. With every twinge he felt an unreserved antipathy for that inhospitable land where his pain and suffering were manifest. He still had nightmares of the hours spent on that LZ awaiting extraction, and could come to terms with the dreams only with the severest mind-numbing sorrow. If he needed a further reminder, his hip and leg bore the scars and the lingering pain to serve that end, not letting him forget the war. And if he could somehow manage to come to terms, now that he was home, away from it, there was still Nickie's pain. She had suffered every pang of his own. Her eyes had lost that effervescent, smiling glow he'd last seen when he left Jackson for Viet Nam in early sixty-four.

But over the winter months the monarch butterflies returned on their annual pilgrimage to Pacific Grove, the town next door, as close to the Presidio as Monterey itself. Trees were flocked with the magnificent gold and black flutterings, and the lepidopterous harbingers could be found as far away as Cypress Point and Carmel across the peninsula. Sunday morning outings to Fisherman's Wharf, feeding insatiable gulls and deadbeat sea lions was always a treat for Jeremy, and if David Winter could not keep up, the child never let him fall far behind. Winter's pace was measured, a condition of his rehabilitation, but it made for a comfortable speed for Nickie, now seven months pregnant, glorious in that fecund state. He saw her world righting itself as the time of that terrible homecoming faded into gray past, and the promise of new life grew within her. He recalled fondly the day she sprang on him the idea of having a second child, the day they had moved into quarters at Fort Ord.

Now, Jeremy's forbidden downhill glissade in the blooming ice plant meant consignment of his trousers to the trash, for there was no getting out stains from the crushed succulents. But David could not bring himself to punish, even chastise, the child. Every day he thought of that LZ, how close he had come to missing these childish manifestations of independence. Visions of dead Vietnamese children, their homes rendered unto dust and debris by one side or the other, retained the power to horrify and depress him.

But there was a complacent sense of security, too. With his impending graduation into a new career field utilizing the Russian language, future assignments would almost assuredly be in Europe; likely Germany. But whatever his new assignment—there were a lot of slots out there in Russian—it would not be in Viet Nam.

It was with a great sense of relief that Winter learned from Staff Sergeant Butts, the ASA Liaison NCO at the Presidio, that following a five-week TDY en route in Virginia, his next duty assignment was to be Germany. The site was not yet fixed, but would be Germany. Probably Berlin or Herzo-Genaurach, Butts thought.. A promise of three full years

* * *

Rothwesten, Germany: 1966

In early autumn, Headquarters, Army Security Agency, seeking success through reorganization, invoked the "Shazam Shuffle" among those operational units in the Hesse District responsible for intelligence on the East German border and immediate surrounds. The 184th US ASA Operations Company at Rothwesten segued into the 319th USASA Battalion and became instantly dormant; the personnel were transferred to the equally newly defined 17th USASA Field Station and took on the 184th's forsaken role. The common belief that this was a good thing—that of becoming a strategic asset and foregoing the pain-in-the-ass drudgery of tactical operations within the five-kilometer zone—was not immediately borne out by results.

Assets had been used interchangeably among the 184th and its sister tactical elements along the border over many years. Radios, generators, 292 operations vans, antennas, trucks, and AB-105 towers were shipped indiscriminately from one unit to another as needs dictated. Accountability did not accompany the equipments: there were no records.

When 17th Field Station set about its lawful assigns, created as it were out of whole cloth, its newly denoted commanders, logistics shufflers, and bean counters unrealistically asked with what were they to do their job. By extrapolation within the TO&E, equipments that should now be their own, were missing. They likely could have been found in the hands of other newly crafted Field Stations—the 18th at Bad Aibling, the 16th at Herzo-Genaurach and their subordinate border sites, all strategic assets—or the remains of the 319th, extant. But no one looked. Meanwhile, equipments in hand belonged to other, currently unidentified units who were in the same dilemma, vis-à-vis accountability.

Into this confusion and mythic state of presumptive compliance, Headquarters ASA at Arlington Hall, Virginia, promptly added an unsettling element in the form of the dreaded IG inspection. Under the guise of regular, annual harassment, The Hall sent the Inspector General team to ferret out all problems, as well as millions of dollars of mislaid, lost, stolen, and otherwise unaccountable and unaccounted-for equipment.

While troops wandered homeless and confused from dilapidated work spaces to ancient billets on the old German *Luftwaffe* base at Rothwesten, newly appointed officers and NCOs were thrust into bureaucratic harm's way in more ways than they could imagine. It was anticipated that inspection would unveil the depths of disorganization, the lack of command and control in the European tactical elements, and would expose the ennui and disinterest rampant among the border troops. But it was equally expected that logical inspectors would recognize the chaos as temporary, and not use it as a God-sent opportunity to abuse the troops.

But then, that would be logical inspectors . . .

First Sergeant (Acting) Arthur A. Abbot—a Sergeant First Class by rights, banished from Operations for technical ineptitude, who made top soldier in A Company as a punishment of sorts—was visited with a penultimate mandate: get this one right, or your next review leads directly to a second and final pass-over, a condition having nothing to do with religious observances. This was a not-unusual state-of-affairs within the Army's new promotion policies.

Imposing his inflated authority, eager to demonstrate his grasp of military responsibilities, Abbot was hopeful he could flim-flam his way to retention. But, upon reflection, and had Abbot been playing with a full deck, he would have realized that in his bid to stay in the game, ASA troops might have been the worst cards he could have drawn to.

The enlisted men's barracks had not been upgraded since the Kaiser first dedicated Rothwesten as an imperial *Flughafen* fifty-two years before, when tenant aircraft were Spads—biplanes and triplanes of the Imperial German air forces. The most obvious area of lingering malcontent lay with the latrines, where huge white, porcelain toilets had held their own for too many years. It was up to local national—in this case, German—maintenance workers to keep these ancient jakes functioning. And so they did. But to the *Deutsche* plumber, called out from his snuggery during a snowstorm to bring a toilet back on line, appearance was not of critical concern. The toilets functioned, but they bore the evidence of many years' urine stains, present as dull orange, high-water marks on the porcelain bowls. Nothing would remove these stains, neither bleach, scouring powder, nor various abrasive or astringent cleaners. One enterprising PFC had resorted to fingernail polish remover; another to gasoline—the resultant explosion so minor it did not even crack the porcelain—but without positive effect.

As the IG executed his witch hunt upon the fledgling field station with glee, it was inevitable he would take exception to the persistent evidence of generations of the passing of German and American beer in the toilets. It had become quasi-policy, reconfirmed by every IG who passed through the ancient *Wehrmacht* indoor outhouses in USAEUR, that toilet stains inevitably produced demerits. So common was the problem of "yellow peril" in Seventh Corps that it was a presumptive *Gotcha!* for every IG team, even against those units maintaining otherwise exemplary conditions.

Knowing this, First Sergeant Abbot sought divine intervention, irrationally hoping to find a treatment, a miracle that would set him above all previous victims of inspector irascibility.

Abbot assigned Specialist Four Harvey (no middle initial) Broadbent, a day-worker from the antenna maintenance crew, to devise a solution to the IG's persnickety ways. Specialist Broadlbent, though no standout as a soldier, had a reputation for creativity and persistence in menial tasks. "BB" set his mind to the task upon assignment to the toilets.

In the following days Broadbent could be found, dextrously applying ineffective abrasives and scouring agents, followed by liquid soaps, soft cloths, ammonia water, and alcohol with little or no positive results. On the day of the pre-IG walk-through he was up early, and when the ongoing day trick had shaved, showered, shit, shined, and shoved off, he put the latrine OFF LIMITS and went through the motions again. His efforts, if not resulting in banishment of the stains, were an assurance of clinically sanitary bowls.

After hours of waiting—a common affliction with IGs—a bull colonel led into the suspect latrine a gaggle of associate malcontents. These hand-picked ball-busters, all similarly inclined unreasonably to pick at nits, found their attentions never devoted to practical, effective matters contributing to military readiness, but merely to harassment of soldiers of all ranks as a result of the inspectors' own personal insecurity and chicken-shit personalities. The team had only just come from busting Captain McCall's chops over his newfound company's physical plant, a thing McCall dismissed in his mind, attributing the poor showing to The New Order during the Austrian Corporal's reign. No amount of military smartness was sufficient; every facet of preparedness in Alpha Company was for naught.

When First Sergeant Abbot led the IG team into the second floor latrine, a place for ablutions of the Linguist Platoon, all known as devil-may-care reactionaries, he realized he had not put Broadbent through a rehearsal. What the hell! Everything else had gone so badly this morning, he thought, the SP4's efforts must no doubt have resulted in some degree of improved readiness.

Broadbent was standing by in a stiff brace, greens pressed and lint free, his glossy dress shoes locked at an angle of forty-five degrees, heels precisely six inches from the base of the first toilet in the gleaming row of potties. He snapped to attention, his taps cracking loudly in the echoing silence of the stone chamber, and snapped an admirably crisp salute. "Sir, Specialist Broadbent reports latrines of First Platoon ready for inspection."

The colonel, slightly taken aback by the soldier's enthusiasm, never returned the salute, but harrumph-ed, hmm-ed, and mumbled, then stepped past Broadbent and leaned over the first toilet. As an old hand at IG-ing, he was entirely familiar with the problematic, ochre-colored bowls, and though a stupid man, a waste of space as an officer, he understood: the stains were forever. But as the IG, he felt he had to break balls. And he didn't like this Sergeant Abbot either. An SFC! First Sergeant, indeed.

"What the hell is this, Specialist?" the colonel roared, straightening with a malevolent glare blending anger and disgust. "You reported this latrine ready for inspection." He pointed a regal finger toward the bowl. "Do you call this ready for inspection? These toilets have obviously not been cleaned. They've not been touched. They are filthy! Just look at those urine stains," he demanded, fully aware and approving as the USAEUR Sergeant Major wrote up the malingering Alpha Company's First Sergeant.

"Do you not see what I'm talking about, Specialist?" the colonel bellowed at Broadbent's silence.

The unruffled specialist looked intently at the toilet, bent forward, ran his finger around the inside rim of the bowl, licked his very clean finger, and said, "Why, no, Sir. That crapper isn't even salty!"

* * *

First Sergeant Abbott did not continue to seek service retention, but abandoned his servitude along with any hope of making E-8. He reported an elevated glucose level in his blood and water, previously undiscovered, and took medical retirement at 19 years.

His replacement assumed the elusive and fruitless dream of accounting for all missing equipment on the field station's inventories. When the IG and (Acting) First Sergeant Abbott were finished with Alpha Company in their various ways, things fell back into routine.

* * *

Kassel, Germany; November 1966

Specialist-Six Wicklow Saunders, being unmarried and discontent, was assigned to the 17th US ASA Field Station and lived on the *Kaserne* at Rothwesten, a small village several kilometers outside the city of Kassel in the district of Hesse. After an evening of determined boozing late in November of that year, when the freezing rains settled on the brick and cobblestoned streets in a glistening, deadly sheen, Saunders, aiming for the base at Rothwesten, made his way erratically out the main street from the meager sampling of bars in downtown Kassel, along the route paralleling the trolley tracks. Saunders was out alone, long past duty hours. No one was ever able to explain just how he came to drive his old Mercedes at undiminished speed off the street, through a steel-barred gate, and down 28 concrete steps leading to a *Strassenunterführung*, a below-street passageway designed for pedestrians.

Two disinterested *Polizei* pulled him from the wreckage, called for an ambulance, then realized he was American and called the post. The duty medic sent the ambulance to the Kassel police station to retrieve Wicklow Saunders, and put in a call for the duty Doctor, Captain Mosbacher. Marion Mosbacher was not at the dispensary, and not in his quarters, so the medic knew to reach him at the Officers Club, a post-prandial hideout adopted for common usage by the elusive doctor. Captain-Doctor Mosbacher suffered severely from non-professional *and* professional criticism of his medical skills. Drinking helped.

The medics in the ambulance applied a compress, struggling cautiously to create a tourniquet of sorts for Wicklow Saunders's most traumatic injury—the area where his right ear had been sliced off by the glass when he put his head through the windshield. They wrapped the ear in gauze and gave it to Saunders to hold. His degree of inebriation ensured he did not go into shock; indeed, due to a natural tendency toward the maudlin, Saunders deemed it amusing.

Doctor Mosbacher waved the medics into his emergency room. "In here. In here. Bring'm inshide . . . inside. There. Do I know you?" he asked Saunders, leaning into his macerated face.

"Don't know. Who're you, Doc? Hah!"

"Don't be . . . don't be . . . he's a wise-ass, men," the drunk surgeon informed his medics. The two ambulance attendants looked at each other, one grimaced, the other shook his head, and they left without speaking. The duty medic stood by, and when Saunders finally, rather adroitly, fell onto the metal stool, the medic cut the bandage from his head.

"Hell, Doctor. He ain't got no ear."

"No shit?" the victim screamed. "Oh. No. I got the ear," Saunders assured them, fumbling in his pockets. He stared about in mild surprise when he couldn't find the gauze-wrapped bundle, and began to cry. "Well, I had the ear. I had an ear. No shit, guys. I had the ear. Somebody took it."

"Siddown, soldier. Lemme see." The doctor pushed his glasses up on his nose and bent close, probing with his finger in the area of gory excision. "Cut the fucker right off, dint it? I mean, we got us a Van Gogh here, guys. Bleedin' like a cut whore, too, ain't it. Hmmm."

A driver-medic walked back in the emergency room and tossed a dark-stained bundle of gauze on the table, "Yo, man, don't leave yo shit in my amb'lance."

The doctor unwrapped the ear, stared at it, and asked Wicklow Saunders, who by this time, was weaving on the stool like a Rawalpindi union Local Nr. 6088 snake charmer, moaning low and whistling a tune that was almost recognizable to the medic, "Soldier, is thish your ear?"

"I don' know. Mus' be my ear. It's circul . . . circumshtantial, but . . . I'm missing an ear. I have one ear. I *had two* ears. Now, I'm missing an ear. You have there an ear which you don't know the origin of . . . ears are not issued at quartermaster . . . ergo, that's gotta be my ear."

"D'you want it back?"

"Yes. Most as-sured-ly. My head's uneven without it. Dispropro... dispropart . . . crooked. I'll tilt to starboard without it. Or ish that port?" Losing the humor, the one-eared soldier asked seriously, "Will you replace it for me, Doc?" Saunders had not been given any anesthetic, but was inured to pain through his foresight in drinking his way across Kassel. Doctor Mosbacher was feeling no pain, so he had no need for anesthetic; he had fortified himself for his trial in much the same manner as Saunders.

* * *

It was generally considered a miracle that Saunders's ear grew back at all, the lapse of time from severance to re-attachment extensive as it was. The question on post became, "What is the half life of a severed ear?" But grow back it did, probably great thanks to the cold night. It grew back crooked and gave Wicklow Saunders the appearance of constantly holding his head on an angle, but as that conformity was preferred to the doctor's initial placement of the ear back on the head upside down, thus backward—a momentary error the doctor assured the soldier was only a slip of the hand, as he assessed the dexterity necessary to reconstitute Saunders's correct appearance—Saunders went away, if not happy, at least whole.

The German police thought the episode of the ear paid for the violation of the law. Command would never raise the issue of incompetence in an Army doctor when they were so difficult to come by. The Army could not charge Saunders without Mosbacher's chancey role coming out, and as a result, no charges were ever brought. Against anyone.

The Mercedes was a write-off, but stayed where it came to rest, blocking the passageway for weeks while the American military, the British authorities whose military occupation zone Kassel fell within, and the German civilian police, all argued over territorial dominion. Wicklow Saunders, in the meantime, in a world-wide personnel hiccup, was converted from Specialist Six rating to Staff Sergeant, both enlisted grade six, but now with hard stripes so that his flair for military pomposity could more easily be assuaged.

He refused ever to discuss the incident of the ear, since that was in another life. But he was still an imperfect soldier.

chapter nine

Prosit Neue Jahr!

Rothwesten, Germany: December 1966

Lieutenant Colonel Fox burst into the duty room, a space used by Duty NCOs, duty drivers, and the Officer-of-the-Day, adjacent to his own Commander's office,.

The colonel glared at Shipley, sitting on the duty bunk reading a mystery novel. Fox began waving his arms, prelude to speech, as if the momentum needed to carry the words must be generated by his extremities. "Who called you? Goddammit, Shipley, who called?" His face worked its way purple.

"Called me, sir? Why, whatever do you mean?" Specialist Five Shipley deliberately placed a German 5-*Deutsche Mark* banknote as a bookmark in the fold of the book and laid it carefully on the pillow. He looked back at the officer in apparent confusion.

"You know what I mean, goddammit. Every time I come for you to drive me to one of the sites, I catch you awake." The right arm, slack for a moment, began windmilling again.

"Yessir. I *am* the duty driver. It's my role to stay awake . . . in case you need me." The soldier was careful to keep his voice even, the tone away from *disdain*—not broaching the arena of a violation. A disdainful act, word, even a look or one so construed, could bring a charge of "silent contempt," a draconian, one-size-fits-all element of the Uniform Code of Military Justice. A staple in the UCMJ for years, the charge had lately fallen from use as defense attorneys had begun to eviscerate it of its all-encompassing power to punish a multitude of otherwise unprovable sins. The charge had for many years been technically abused, but when leveled, was almost impossible to refute, until Judge Advocate General defenders began taking their jobs seriously. In his condition, Colonel Fox was not above invoking such a charge.

"You know . . . you know what the hell I mean, smart-ass. Whenever I leave my quarters in the night, someone calls around, alerting you people. There must be a whole roster of smart-asses, reading sign on me, alerting sleeping guards and Duty NCOs. If I ever prove . . ."

What he proposed to do in that event, the colonel never said. He stood blinking, caught in the revealing glare of creeping sobriety. The realization emerged that he was beating a dead pony.

The colonel was known to take a "wee dram" before bedtime. Half Chiricahua Apache, and totally responsive to the alcohol intolerance judgement, even a wee dram took the colonel to places he'd prefer his rating and reviewing officers in Frankfurt not know about. Not inevitably, but on enough occasions to remove it from the surprise category, when he went to bed in that condition he shortly awoke with the blazing conviction that every one of his nine-hundred-or-so troops—men *and* officers—were goofing off on him. In the mood of that frustrating possibility, he would set forth with religious zeal to ferret out the renegades.

He would dress—invariably waking his wife and begging her pardon—go to his headquarters, alert the duty driver, and have himself driven to one of the outlying sites without advance warning of a command visit. This could produce extraordinary forays. The drive to Mount Meissner, a VHF/UHF operations border site a few miles outside Kassel-Rothwesten, was little more than an hour from the headquarters. Easy run.

Farther away, Wobeck, another border site, was close to two hours; he'd still arrive in the dark. And if his objective was even farther, to Gartow in the far north near Lubeck, it could be a four-to-five-hour drive. Weather became more of a factor nearing the North Sea.

There were also a couple of DF sites, small three-to-five-man sites providing direction finding on signals of interest reported by the intercept operational sites. These were so small, so minimally manned, and were almost never a source of problems, the colonel seldom gave them the benefit of his presence.

The 17th US Army Security Agency Field Station in Rothwesten with its widely flung subordinates was a compact little kingdom, and LTC Fox relished the mantle of king. As such, he could indulge himself in a few privileges. For these middle-of-the-night excursions, when the colonel climbed into his official sedan, duty driver alert behind the wheel with a thermos of hot coffee from the messhall, the CO promptly fell asleep in the back. The last thing he did before sacking out was to inform the driver of their destination. Then, and only then, did the driver know which site was going to be in the barrel. This night, the colonel had muttered, "Gartow."

And yet, like his unsuccessful attempts to catch duty officials in slack mode within the headquarters, farther afield, wherever he had himself driven, there he was with a fully alert work shift awaiting him. The colonel, for some unknown reason, never adopted the ASA standard of referring to work shifts as "tricks." Days, Swings, and Mid Tricks. It often made him appear an outsider, but it would have been a mistake for anyone to make that assumption.

There was no radio in the army sedan. Though the driver now knew the destination, he had no opportunity to alert anyone. By the time of arrival at his destination, sleep—whether a quick nap or several hours in back seat bliss—had restored the colonel to his better self. That was no small transformation.

A fair man, a favored commander with valorous exploits in his past which he would never divulge but were known by all, Colonel Fox was dedicated to his mission and to the care and well-being of those in his command. Not at all the image he projected when drinking.

Still, there remained the simple question: How did the Duty NCO, the duty driver, or the site NCOs and operational leadership know when he was on the prowl? And where he would pounce? Inevitably frustrated, the colonel's theory was that a conspiracy of enlisted men kept watch on him, thwarting his designs. In a skewed reality, however, it was otherwise.

Major Bartholomew Dowd, Field Stations Operations Officer, third-ranking officer in the command, lived directly across the street from Colonel Fox's government quarters. Bart Dowd—thirteen years later still suffering the after-shock of traumatic, early infantry service, often in sleep drawn back into hellish conflict on a ridge line in Korea—was an insomniac; at best a light sleeper. Major Dowd was also, in his saner moments, something of a wag. As prior-enlisted, he understood the finer points of harassment. Feeling the colonel's midnight rambles constituted such, Dowd, restlessly observant of the colonel's nighttime activities across the street, would pick up his phone and give the duty office a tinkle. At these times of night, conversation often was not even required.

Still, for the very few souls who were aware of this quirky situation, it did not explain how, as with this early morning icy road trip to Gartow, the site in the far north was alerted. The persons who could answer that conundrum were even fewer, limited to site chiefs . . . and Mrs. Colonel Fox.

Erica Fox loved her husband. She knew him, trusted him, and in her benign but lingering girlish love, almost revered him. Never blessed with children of her own, the colonel's wife made her family of the young men who served in her husband's command. She knew they too thought of her husband with great fondness, if not love. She also knew that her half-Indian husband's lack of tolerance for alcohol was well known, and not a measure of his real worth. To save him embarrassment, and likely salvage the service careers of some promising young soldiers, she conspired to prevent her husband from "overstraying his command," as she lovingly expressed it to her closest friend, Hannah, Mrs. Major Dowd.

His kindly act of consideration—informing his wife at the time of each nocturnal arising where and when he would be making visits—never occurred to Colonel Fox as the key to the eponymous and vast conspiracy.

* * *

Gartow, Germany: December 1966-January 1967

Winter committed his body to the brief agony of the shower. Outside the tiny summer cottage which he shared with Captain Goetz, the temperature was minus nine degrees, Celsius. Inside, the temperature had surged up to roughly minus five degrees, C. after he'd climbed from under the *federdecker* and got a fire going in the oil stove. Hot shower water was the niggardly product of a flash heater, a European marvel which saved on electricity. It also avoided the comfort of a hot shower.

A flash heater did not heat water to be stored awaiting use; only after the flow of water was turned on did the electric circuit kick on and warm a thin stream. The bather received a small trickle of very hot water or, if one sought a boisterous spray, the water temperature proved inversely proportional to the elevated pressure. An unsatisfactory arrangement, it was what it was.

The summer cottage here on the Elbe River was usually occupied in season by vacationing Danes, Swedes, and even Germans. Its only attraction now in the dead of winter, agreed Captain Goetz and Sergeant First Class Winter, was the scant six-minute stroll to the Gartow Operations Site, twenty seconds by Jeep, making the Commander and NCOIC immediately available to work.

Hopping stiffly from the shower in the frigid room, his body wracked by freezing spasms, Winter saw the bathroom door had eased closed. He pushed it open to let in what heat there was. A thick, rank fog quickly flooded the small room, sending him coughing and choking toward the stove. The stove top, around the eye plate, and at the seams of the stovepipe, leaked a noxious, black cloud.

Jeez, not again, Winter thought.

The first time the stove was fired after they'd moved in, the diesel mechanic at the site had sent his gofer down with a five-gallon can of fuel to fill the stove and get the two site chiefs settled in. The gofer, Private Coykendall, a reject from operational duties due to his inability to obtain a security clearance, was unaware of differing fuel categories. Oil's oil, he assumed. He went into the wired enclosure, grabbed a jerry can of fuel, drove to the cottage, and filled the stove's tank. When Captain Goetz first lit the stove, it was quickly confirmed that diesel fuel, though a POL product, was not designed for use in stoves. The cottage filled with smoke and soot, blackening all surfaces, including uniforms and civilian clothing of both men.

Winter's first thought now was that Coykendall had done it again, perhaps in angry response for his restriction to the site and his *gasthaus* quarters in Gartow village for other thoughtlessness. Then he remembered, the errant private had been transferred to the brown boot army at Hohenfels for ever-greater transgressions. An ineffective and unlikeable soldier, it wasn't commonly noted that he was gone. The site now had a new diesel mech assistant.

Kee-rist, could two of them have been equally ignorant? Winter mused.

He knew the odds: they could!

Winter shut down the stove, dressed quickly in the falling temperature, left the door and windows propped open, and walked in the dark up the road to the site. He dreaded walking this road in the dark. Surface ice, channeled and broken by heavy military trucks, made walking difficult, and it was like greased glass where unbroken. It was why Captain Goetz, though he liked the exercise of the walk, chose to always take the Jeep in winter.

In the truncated period of light in these extreme northern climes, Winter rather enjoyed the walk. He could admire the variety of structures the north Germans used as home-barn-utility buildings. Here, where the winter Siberian winds had no natural barriers, constant squall conditions could be damning. Farmers built their barns and houses under one roof, allowing care for their stock through the winter without exposing themselves to the arctic conditions. The homey ambience in winter, with smoke spiraling up from chimneys, was attractive.

In the dark, early hour now, he could see nothing of a bucolic nature, and was left with disturbing memories of bitterly frigid night movements in Korea.

He arrived at the site in plenty of time. Mrs. Fox had called a little after 0130. Even if Shipley drove all-out, which he was not apt to do in this weather, the colonel's sedan could not reach the site at Gartow before five-thirty or six. It was now just minutes past five.

Winter entered the Ops van, saw two positions manned, nodded and went out. In the Control van, Captain Goetz was scribbling in the logbook.

"Newk put diesel in our stove again," Winter growled.

"Aww, shit! Who was it?"

"Dunno. The new kid, what's his name? Damn it! Steiffell should have clued him in after Coykendall."

"We'll take care of it later. Colonel's about due," Goetz said.

"Yeah, O.K. Anything up?"

Goetz, in their commonly shared house, had earlier arisen at the phone call from the site, which had received a call from Mrs. Fox. Afraid he might oversleep if he lay back down, he'd read by a weak light in his bed, wrapped in the heavy German bed cover, until an hour ago, then dressed and drove to the site before Winter could make himself get up. There were two duty Jeeps for site use. One was kept at the site to convey personnel back and forth to the village of Gartow, where most had rooms in local *gasthauses*; the other was commandeered by Captain Goetz for his personal convenience.

Goetz said, "Up? As in working comms?" He shook his head, No!

* * *

Colonel Fox breezed in minutes after 0600, bright-eyed and bushy-browed, content to note full manning and an alert site commander and NCO. He had lost the ability, even the urge when sober, to catch his troops in violation of rules.

Following his pre-dawn arrival and unfulfilled suspicions, Colonel Fox nodded at his sedan. "Let's get some breakfast." It was just past six thirty in the morning by this time, but the farming- and working-class Germans would be crowding the *Gasthof Brauner*. The colonel was an enthusiastic guest there whenever in the north. One unkind driver suggested the colonel forced the mean trip to Gartow merely to submit to one of Fritz's monstrous breakfasts.

Seated around a rectangular, dark, bare wooden table with a pair of dour, Lower Saxony milk truck drivers, Lieutenant Colonel Fox, Captain Goetz, SFC Winter, and the driver, SP5 Shipley, bowed to dictates of local custom, washing down the hefty *Bauern Frühstück* with the first beer of the day. Their farmer's breakfast was rapidly disappearing. An impressive melange of eggs, chopped ham, potatoes, onion, and two kinds of cheese, scrambled and mounded on each plate with a basket of fresh, sliced pumpernickel, a small tub of butter the color of egg yolks, and a plate of sliced tomatoes, the source of which no one could account for at this time of year, Fritz's *Frühstück* was worth the drive to Gartow.

Colonel Fox, in the field, adopted a liberal, egalitarian attitude and would break bread with any of his troops. He insisted on it. During the free exchange of conversation, after the two German truck drivers departed without a word, Shipley said in a sudden blurt, "Dave, weren't you in Asmara?"

"'Sixty-to-'sixty-two. Why?"

Colonel Fox looked on with mild interest. He noted his driver's unmilitary address to the NCO and, knowing them to be friends, ignored it. The other officer noted nothing out of place; five-to-seven years before, Captain Goetz had been a student at San Jose State and that distant 4th ASA Field Station in East Africa meant nothing to him.

"You must have known Sergeant Balence. Frank Balence—"

"Sure, I know Frank. He's in 'Nam now," Winter said. Frank was one of the good guys.

"I just heard he was killed. Last week, sometime." Shipley looked down at his food.

"Aww, no-o. Jeez-us. What . . . he wasn't out in a support platoon. He was an analyst, in the Field Station at Phu Bai. How'd it happen?"

"Way I heard it, he was pulling a stint on the perimeter, supervising an M-60 crew and a couple riflemen. So Benquist tells it. A sapper, trying to wriggle through, got caught in the wire, armed his pouch, and flung it. It fell on Frank's hole. Got him and another guy, not one of ours. Not A.S.A."

When he tuned back into the flow of conversation, Winter heard Goetz lamenting the hazard of the winter fog in the Gartow area.

He shook off the sad news and tried to make sense of Goetz's point, not an easy task. They were in arctic conditions, a product of which, in terrain with ample water, is fog. End of equation. WTF-O? he wondered irritably.

Besides, the colonel didn't give a rat's ass about fog. When he traveled, someone else drove. He slept.

Winter became focused again when he heard the colonel agreeing the site could go to fifty percent manning over the New Year. The team had deployed to Gartow over the winter to recover and reconstruct Soviet, German, and Polish communications links, which traditionally changed schedules and identification at the New Year and shortly after. Gartow was a significant tribulation in deep winter to support personnel, as to movement of supplies and equipment, and it was considered by the rank-and-file as a no-brainer. No one really believed Ivan would try to push armor across the Elbe, in the winter or any other time. Conventional wisdom offered the attractive alternate route of the Fulda Gap, much farther south, and with broad, rolling plains eminently conducive to tank traffic year-round.

"Allow the men a couple days break, if you like," the colonel offered Goetz. It was a part of the more attractive side of the commander. He'd been in Operations long enough to know the New Year's period would be slow.

Colonel Fox delivered his parthian shot on the street as he approached his waiting sedan. "Sergeant Winter, I see you've all your I-s crossed and T-s dotted for the warrant board." Winter did not presume the colonel intended a pun; he kept his silence. "Paperwork crossed my desk yesterday. Just so you know, you got a hell of a fine set of recommendations from everyone involved, your boss Mister Etheridge on up. I didn't break the chain; I signed off with hearty approval. Good luck! See you down there in March." He saluted before Winter could get his hand up. Likely returning Goetz's homage, he thought; don't mean nothin'.

* * *

As rats fleeing a plague-ridden Chinese junk, site personnel split to the winds. The departure on pass the last day of 1966 resulted in personnel striking out in all directions, leaving minimal manning in operations. Captain Goetz, leaving the integrity of the site and mission in the hands of his NCOIC, SFC Winter, while knowing Winter might also have plans, departed early for the British Zone headquarters at Celle. He had friends among the Brits; they had invited him for the revels. It *was* their zone.

Two ops and a security guard took off for Luchöw in a Volkswagen that sounded doubts for a round trip. Winter, in the doldrums about Frank Balance, reluctantly agreed to accompany Steiffell to Hamburg. The generator mechanic staff sergeant intended celebration in the Reeperbahn, an area in the old seaport with a world-renowned Red Light district.

Winter, though they'd been deployed only five days, beginning the day after Christmas, called to his quarters in Kassel with a New Year's message to Nickie. He responded to her laughing query, assuring her his visit to Hamburg was one of curiosity only. Then Steiffel was anxious to get on the road, and Winter let himself be led on a potentially wild and licentious night. Only potentially, and that based on Steiffell's lascivious mutterings.

Instead—after a harrowing drive west and north to the Sodom of Braunlage, then onward where he then lost track of Steiffell early in the evening in the North Sea Gomorrah of Hamburg—Winter was relieved to be alone. He didn't worry; he marked where the sergeant parked, and had Steiffel's spare car key. It was a given they'd meet up sometime after festivities.

Winter strolled the Reeperbahn, the district named for its principal street, one of bars, cafes, whorehouses, restaurants of every persuasion, nightclubs—often indistinct from one another. No question, the meat-shop displays of naked female bodies and barely-clothed female bodies and luscious female bodies behind plate glass windows fronting the street were enticing. A dish for every taste: every size, color, and specialty. Should one have inclinations in that direction, the glassed-in ladies left no doubts about the wares offered for sale.

Some were alone in their splendor; others paired. In some cases, a trio or quartet, knitting or playing cards. Most incessantly did their nails, their unclothed goods displayed in natural settings for perusal. Soft lighting; salacious cleavages, front and back. Catering to a minority whose tastes incorporated a custom popular among north-country clients, some of the women had underarm hair as thick as the pubic displays, and many proudly displayed unshaven legs.

Standing in the vicious damp cold, observing the talent seated in obvious warmth and comfort, gave added emphasis to other aspects of their allure. Winter could understand their attraction. The women were invitingly, some distractingly beautiful. He looked, smiled, waved back at their wriggling fingers, and moved on.

A short visit to a busy, obviously popular club offering another kind of sex shopping, left him equally disenchanted.. The action had a cold, commercial air. Each small, round table held only a black, rotary-dial phone and a placard bearing large, two-digit numbers projected prominently above. The scheme was immediately obvious.

Customers, male or female, entered after paying a small fee, took a table, ordered a minimum drink, and checked out the talent. If they spotted someone, other sex or the same, in whom they were interested, they dialed on the phone the two-digit number above that party's table and spoke with whoever answered. Depending upon the success of the call, the caller might provide their own table number. The callee would look about, locate the caller's number, check them out, and things progressed from there. Or not. Winter, spellbound by the simplicity of this social ploy, finished the watered-down scotch and sidled out the door onto the street teeming with Polish, Latvian, and Russian mariners.

He was asleep in the car parked near the canal when Steiffell staggered back. Standing in silhouette, weaving against a weakly illumined gray winter skyline, the generator mech's condition was obvious. Winter judged the shade of red of the generator mechanic's eyes and held out his hand.

Steiffell dropped the car keys in Winter's palm, then emulated Lieutenant Colonel Fox. He was asleep in the backseat before Winter had negotiated his way from the docks.

* * *

When the general bail-out had occurred at the Gartow site that last day in December, the NCO left in charge was Staff Sergeant Spruance. Winter, who had known Harry for years, since Asmara, did not always think of him as "Hatin' Harry" anymore, now that the soldier had more than six years service. Spruance had, against all odds over that interval, metamorphosed into a dedicated, selfless practitioner of soldiering skills. So much so that Winter had no qualms about leaving him in charge of Gartow operations. Harry was straight.

Harry was STRAC!

Late in the day a printer operator, monitoring the single teletype channel that connected the border site to the Field Station at Rothwesten, called Harry into the commo van and handed him an *Info Only* message relayed from Arlington Hall Station. "Know him?" he asked.

Spruance took the tear sheet, skipped the boilerplate down to the text which informed of the death, in combat in Vietnam, of one Balence, Frank F., Staff Sergeant, USASA. Harry read the rest of the meager information through misty eyes. He had not been present at the breakfast when Shipley informed Winter of the death, and had not known.

Ol' Frank.

He and Frank had hoisted a few together in Asmara, Massawa, Keren, and the Halfway House in Ghinda. Come to think on it, he was sleeping off a wet session in Frank's bunk, ground floor in the Massawa R&R Center on the Red Sea, when he was bitten on the hand by one of their non-paying guests, a wharf rat judged the size of a warthog.

No, now he thought about it, that's not right.

He hadn't been bitten in Massawa. That was Ratty Mac. In Balence's bunk.

Harry was bitten later, in Asmara, down in the *Basgh* quarter by Black Beauty's three-legged cat while sleeping one off on her rug. The cat's rug, it turned out. Yeah, that was Mac in Massawa. No one ever figured out if that rodent assault was the genesis of "Ratty" Mac's nickname, or if the apt descriptor was due to his disheveled and unwholesome appearance. And every time Mac had to take one of those shots in the belly—twelve or thirteen in all; Harry remembered because his cat bite led to the same result—Mac had cursed and consigned Balence to a ". . . bleeding, burning, hell's own asshole of despair and blistered hemorrhoids," blaming him for the rat, who Mac swore, regularly shared Balence's bunk.

Harry'd had no one to blame.

Ol' Frank!

A short while later, Harry checked the Ops van. Just a couple of guys on pos, but he knew the night would be slow, and if he needed them, there were a few more ops in Gartow village, priming for the new year with a brew. Not everyone had gone away. He knew five or six others had gone to the nearby small village of Schnackenburg on the Elbe River when word had spread of a New Year's dance there in a stock barn-bar—Americans welcome. As the quiet evening on the site dwindled down in tandem with the year, Harry thought to check on his troops on pass. Having been left in charge meant—he was in charge.

Driving the duty Jeep, Harry slipped and skidded his way down the road slope for the few kilometers until he saw the lights of Schnackenburg village. It was snowing lightly by the time he arrived.

Harry, previous visitor to the tiny burg, drove cautiously down the main street—the only street—and was careful when he turned to look for parking. Schnackenberg was merely the nipple on the tit of West Germany which protruded into East Germany, separated from that latter, sad fiefdom by the Elbe, a deeply cut, fast flowing stream that was put there by God and the Eighteenth Engineers to act as a border between West and East Germanies. Indiscretion could lead to an icy plunge into the un-guard-railed river. He found a spot in someone's front yard, locked the chain on the Jeep's steering wheel, and walked fifty meters to the dance.

Along the way, paralleling the river, Harry realized he needn't have worried. Almost midnight, the temperature had reached its nadir; a measure he estimated at fifteen below, C. That translated to a soundly nippy night, and he gauged the thickness of the ice on the Elbe at probably twelve-to-fifteen inches, considering how many days now the temps had been negative.

Inside, the *Festhalle* was wall-to-wall. He spotted a couple of soldiers from the site immediately, but he stood inside the door and continued surveillance. The talent, as he referred to the few local *Frauleins*, seemed plentiful tonight—all those who had not fled the limited opportunities here in their river village for a better-paying job in Bremerhaven, Hamburg, or Bremen. Some who held those distant jobs were likely here as well, home for the New Year.

Echoing Harry's thoughts, there arose a series of loud shouts, *"Prosit neue Jahr!"* and clashes of steins and mugs, glasses, cups, hunting horns brimming over. *Happy New Year!* my ass, Harry thought, glancing at his watch for confirmation. Here am I without even a goddamned brew. He turned toward the makeshift bar to remedy that distressing situation.

Harry made his rounds. He nodded and spoke to the few Germans he recognized. He nodded and spoke to another few he had never seen but who looked friendly. Results were not encouraging. Harry had not expected them to be. Unlike Winter, who was only up here for the annual comms change, Harry was an old hand on the border. He hardly knew how to act outside the 5-K zone. And he knew the stand-offish ways of these northern Germans.

Eventually, his *bonhomie* exhausted, and having located all the troops he had expected to find here, he took his stein of *Bock* and settled at the table with Spec Four Trout and the new kid. Must have been Trout who enticed the two Leavenworth bait over. The new kid looked scared, glancing about steadily at the tumult in the closed space, as if under attack. But it was just the locals, celebrating the river outside that defined them as *West Deutschers*, not *Est.*

A few liters later, long after the two *Kinder* had sauntered on seeking their own kind, the new kid passed out with his head beneath the edge of the table. And Trout wasn't looking good. Hanging on, but weakening, Harry judged.

Another village lass, one of the barmaids, came and sat with them. Initially, Harry bought her a *Schnapps* and hoped she wouldn't get too friendly or stay long; he was with his charges, and she was anything but good looking. But later, the *Deckels* stacking up indicating the increasing number of drinks taken at the table, the bar maid began to grow in allure. It was amazing, Harry thought, how these *Fräuleinen* benefitted from large quantities of beer. Their appearance—his drinking.

Harry had been trying hard to maintain an even keel. He told the two soldiers about his friend Frank Balence early in the visit. Later, he re-told the remaining Trout again about his *dearest, lifelong* friend, Balence. He had tried to tell Marike when she sat down, but Harry's German, good enough to get him food, lodging, drink, and laid, was insufficient to historical reminiscenses. Marike drank like a fish, and Harry gave up about Balence, mesmerized by her zeal with the stein. But in the back of his mind, his lost friend festered.

Sometime in the new year, hours past the witching hour—Harry somehow had missed the point of the whole evening—he found himself in a treacherous situation. His moves on the barmaid of steadily improving appearance had gone for naught. She could have told Harry, had he been curious or sober enough to listen, that she could give him pointers on appearance, behavior, and manners less-than-captivating. Such advice would have been wasted on Harry; he'd never counted himself a looker. Or very smooth, either. Screw'm!

With Marike gone, Trout fisheyed—Harry was sober enough to enjoy the pun—and the new, still-unidentified soldier now fully under the table, the Acting NCOIC felt the coming together of disparate emotions, none comforting. Ol' Frank was dead. Everyone else was off in Hamburg or Celle or Luchöw having a good time, and he was stuck here in Nowheresville with the duty. The desperate object of his current affections had spurned him to return to the bar to carry heavy, dripping steins.

Ol' Frank was dead . . . and thinking of Frank brought back Asmara. And Asmara always brought back . . . Damn it! Harry still, five long years after Asmara, had not managed to even things up with the Army for his politically motivated maltreatment.

Harry was a confirmed lifer now, a career soldier with qualms and merit. But the seeking after revenge was a matter beyond that equation. The revenge was a vow. An obligation. Nothing personal. And reaffirming his vow in the new year, somewhere in the back of Harry's mind, a tiny ember of inspiration glowed into life.

At first he did not grasp the notion of his emerging thinking. Something he'd seen or heard, something—recent. As recent as tonight. Whatever mote was piquing his interest was ju-u-ust there. Just beyond his conscious awareness.

And then, in a sudden, blossoming eruption of enthusiasm, he was on his feet, heading for the door.

The River. The Elbe!

Frozen over.

In his mind were yet no details, but the state of the river subliminally offered clear opportunity.

Just beyond the river, just across the ice, was Ivan. Many, many Ivans. Ivan of the Guards Motorized Rifle Division. Ivan of the Guards Tank Regiments. Ivan of the Illustrious, Glorious Air Divisions . . . lots of Ivans. Some of them not two hundred yards away. And the river was iced over.

* * *

When Winter parked Steiffell's Opel before the wire at the site in the first hint of daylight, and left the sleeping sergeant in the back seat, the first thing he checked was Operations van. Nothing happening. The Russians were sleeping off New Year celebrations, too. But he did find an adequate number of Ops present. He didn't attempt to measure their sobriety, but asked where the NCO left in charge, Harry Spruance, could be found.

He got no answer.

The duty Jeep was gone, so Harry might have gone into Gartow for some reason. Winter let it go. Steiffell's Opel was commandeered for a duty vehicle, shifting men back and forth from their quarters to the site and later, back the other way. By the end of the New Year's day shift, though, when Harry had not shown up and had not called, Winter became concerned. The men who'd spread out for the holiday were straggling back. No one had seen Harry. The captain arrived, and when he asked Winter directly about ". . . all present or accounted for," the sergeant was forced to deal with Harry's absence.

"When were you going to tell me, Sergeant Winter?" the officer asked after listening stoically.

"Hell, I thought he was just on an errand or something, Captain. I just talked to Milrose who saw him at the dance in Schnackenburg. Site and Ops were adequately covered . . . but Harry was down there, having a few brewskies. They said he came in there checking on the men. But he stayed And then disappeared. Sober, they thought. No one knows where he went."

The captain looked at his NCOIC, contemplating actions he must take. Inside the 5-kilometer zone as they were, this close to the border, any disappearance was of command concern. He picked up the phone and dialed Field Station headquarters.

Just as the OIC hung up after reporting the missing NCO, someone knocked on the frame of the van. "In," the captain shouted. Spec-4 Bizzell came in and hesitantly approached Winter and Goetz.

"Uh, Sergeant Winter. Sir. Thought I'd better tell you something . . . about last night."

"Yeah, Bizzell? What is it? Anything to do with Sergeant Spruance?"

"No. Uhh-h, don't know, sir. Guess it could be." He scuffed the toe of his boot on the gritty, metal flooring. "I was sitting pos last night—there was just a couple of us. After midnight, sometime later—don't know exactly when—the few of us hanging around got a scare. Sirens started wailing, over there," he nodded east. "Several. And then whistles. We could hear clearly. It was so cold, the air was like one big conduit for sound. We ran outside, thinking maybe the Russkies had decided to come after all. Maybe drunked up for the New Year. The sky across the river, over the Guards Tank Army marshaling grounds, was criss-crossed with searchlights. Then we heard automatic weapons fire. Just a few short bursts. Tracer rounds across the sky. Green.

"Tanks were cranking up. Cold as it was they got several started, and from the top of the AB tower—I climbed up there to see what I could see—I saw them moving about, their lights flashing. Small vehicles, too. Ivans were running, and I could even hear shouting. Barely. Then flares started to pop. Floating down over the landscape, they gave everything a weird, spooky feel." The burst of his enthusiasm spent, Bizzell went silent.

Winter had visions of the scene: the far bank of the river glaring a flickering nimbus, like a football stadium viewed from a nearby hill; vehicle lights flashing. Flares. He felt a cold shiver he could not escape. Harry gone. The gunfire! Harry's part in this—

"Finally quieted down. Trucks and tanks and cars stopped racing around. Flares went out. Lights went off. . . . don't know what the hell," Like the flares, Bizzell faded out.

The captain, leaching out every item of info he could get from the nervous operator, made notes on the back of a logbook. At his nod, Winter set into effect an all-hands muster. He called into the village, around to the farms where soldiers rented rooms, and generally got the word out. Within forty-five minutes, all hands were mustered on the frozen ground outside the vans; all hands except those actually sitting pos, and Winter had their names. All hands were accounted for—except Staff Sergeant Harry B. Spruance. Sergeant Spruance was missing.

Sergeant Spruance was AWOL.

But Winter's anxious prescience was spot on.

* * *

Four days later the Russians released Harry to American authorities at the Helmstedt check point. The soldiers at the Gartow site never saw him again. He was seen sparingly for a short time on base in Rothwesten. War stories trickled down—gossip being the same in the military as in civilian life, only more so—and thus, with his "Lost Patrol" shtick, everyone knew Harry finally had exacted vengeance on the Army.

The facts known were added to informed speculation, mixed with a touch of asperity or delight, depending upon the light in which an individual held Harry, and all stirred to produce an answer soldiers could live with. The consensus was that Harry, in the doldrums from the news of his friend's death, had indulged himself with a drink. Drinks. *Several* drinks. Balence's death, the alcohol, plus the shake-off by the bar maid—if, indeed, that held any meaning at all—had left Harry in a testy frame of mind. Overlay that with festering memories of Asmara betrayal. All who knew Harry knew of the Asmara debasement.

How best to cause the Army to atone for past inequities? It was a challenge they all knew Harry bore about himself, like an olive-drab Typhoid Mary. For Frank Balence. For the troops stuck on the hilltop at Gartow, slated as a doomed and to-be-abandoned tripwire for the Soviets' invasion of the West. For Harry Spruance, courts-martialed on bogus charges in Asmara, Eritrea (Ethiopia). How best to enact vengeance ?

Embarrass . . . humiliate American Army officials. But how?

Why, attack the Soviet Army of course.

The one-Jeep racing advance across the frozen Elbe had so startled and confused the intoxicated Soviet tankers that they responded, not to Harry Spruance's mini-assault, but to all the propaganda and bedtime stories about the evil ogres from the West of their childhood. They reacted, chased him, lighted him up, shot at him . . . and finally, caught him.

On the fourth day after, likely as tired of Harry as US soldiers were known to become under his aggravating intransigence, Ivan gave him back. They had been celebrating a new year that night, expecting nothing but a shortage of vodka and continued doldrums of duty in a foreign land. What they got was a pent-up Hatin' Harry in a particularly unattractive mood.

The regiment which Harry attacked had been transferred to Group of Soviet Forces-Germany from their home base in the steppes of central Russia. The land here was nothing like Mother Russia, and the unpredictable frivolities of the mad American soldiers was unnerving. The Soviets, mostly Mongols from Central Asia, and miners and steel workers from the Urals, appreciated Harry's unique seasonal outburst far more than did their Europeanized Russian officers. They had no problems with conflict hangover.

Heightened tensions subsided. The Alert Status was reduced two grades. The matter was dropped.

By direct edict from USASAEUR, the matter *was dropped.*

* * *

In the spring, along with the flowers, a unique sight blossomed on the Soviet side of the Elbe: an American Army Jeep, painted in broad red, white, and blue stripes daily raced up and down the river road along the bluff across from the town of Schnackenburg and, on a clear day, could be seen from the top of the AB-105 tower at the site with powerful glasses. The lost Jeep bore a long white banner, fluttering from the radio antenna, that read, "Happy New Year Sgt Harry." The English spelling was flawless, though, as Brenner pointed out, they'd dropped a comma.

Observing personnel swore they could hear, loud and long from across the river, unlikely, unaccustomed sounds of mirth. The taunts would continue until the site closed and the ASA TDY personnel rotated back to Rothwesten at the beginning of spring.

And the Russians kept the Jeep.

* * *

Major Dowd glared at the ringing telephone on his clerk's desk. He said, "Please, God . . . let that not be the C.O. again."

The clerk picked up the phone and spit out the required salutation. Dowd watched the man's eyebrows climb, and then turn toward his boss, who shook his head.

"Yes, sir. I'm answering in the Operations Office. No, sir. Major Dowd is not here, sir." The clerk did not sound distressed. This was old hat for him; he was well accustomed to the major's waggish ways.

"Sir. Yes, sir." He held his hand over the mouthpiece and said to the major across the room, "Sir. It's the colonel. He knows you're here. He asked—I had to acknowledge. So do you want to talk to him . . . or will you scoot—"

Dowd jerked his phone from its cradle. "Yessir, Colonel, sir . . . I am working on the goddamned quarterly activity report now." He waited briefly. "No, sir. *Right* now. As of this red-hot moment. And I could get this bitch done if I didn't keep getting interrupted with these goddamned phone calls."

There was strained silence.

"Yes, sir." Dowd replaced the receiver carefully, shifted the pen to his other hand, and resumed writing.

The clerk glared challengingly at the ceiling, awaiting the lightning.

chapter ten

The Rock

Rothwesten, Germany; February 1967

Back from the far northern border site, Winter, with wife and child, lived in Harleshausen housing complex located, oddly enough, in the Harleshausen district within the city of Kassel, capital of Hesse District. The complex was decent living. Comprising four sets of concrete and brick apartments, spread in a standard pattern with six stairwell-accessed apartments opening off three stairwells per building, configured on three floors, the buildings served well for married NCO and EM quarters. An additional two sets of temporary quarters, consisting of a large number of individual rooms originally designed to house servants for the American occupation forces' families in the late 'forties and 'fifties, were located on the fourth floor of each building. The American grade school for dependent children in the Kassel-Rothwesten area was adjacent to the four housing structures. In addition, there were seven separate houses occupied by officers and one DA civilian that stood across the *Strasse* from the high-rises. For the most part, this far from the flag pole, these quarters were occupied by warrant or junior commissioned officers.

By the time Winter had made Sergeant First Class in the late fall before, he had come to know several of these officers and was invited to join the car pool which ferried them back and forth to the site at Rothwesten some seven miles away across patchworked farms and dairyland. Most enlisted and NCO personnel who lived in the stairwells worked trick work, and such schedules kept them to their own transportation schemes. But Winter, soldiering in the Management Branch with only three other asssignees—CW2 Garth Etheridge, OIC; SFC Burt Carmichael, NCOIC; and SP4 Willie Ketona, a clerk-typist—worked straight days and thus was a viable candidate to share the rides, and the driving, with a small group of officers.

One of the drivers, CW2 Ambler, was the Field Station Comm Center OIC. A friendly sort only a year-and-a-half removed from life as an NCO, he saw in Winter the possibility of a similar benefit for the Army and ASA. On an unusual, muggy morning in February, under the influence of a warm southerly wind from Africa, and driving with the window open, listening to the bitching from two other warrant riders in the car, he said, "Sergeant Winter—Dave—have you considered going for a warrant slot?"

"What? Is there a slot open?" He knew little of the politics or practicalities of warrantship.

"Well," Ambler chuckled, "doesn't exactly work that way. "You've never checked up on the warrant program?"

"No, sir. Never have. I guess if I'd stayed in college in 1964, when the Army sent me to engineering school, I could have come out with a commission, but failing that, I . . . nope. Never did. Why d'you ask?"

"Well—I'm talking a bit out of school here but nothing classified, *per se*—an admin message came through the shop yesterday announcing open application for warrant officers, Oh-five-one. It specified generally when the boards will be, and depending upon applications, they'll shortly define where. The word will probably be out today from the head shed, because this thing has a short fuse. I think they're making three Oh-five-ones . . . worldwide, of course. You're primarily an Oh-five-aich, right?" Ambler asked.

"That's right. With the language trailer."

"Uh huh, and they didn't mention any Nine-Eight-Eight warrant slots. But they did indicate there would be three openings for Oh-Five-One, the Oh-Five-Eight warrant. Likely make one in Europe, one in the Far East, and one stateside."

"For career purposes, I probably should look into it," Winter acknowledged. But he realized he probably would not do so. He didn't allow himself to get excited about what was likely pie in the sky. He'd been enlisted too long to believe in fairy tales.

"Why don't you talk to Garth Etheridge about it," Killington said. The civilian was the only non-military resident in the housing area and worked in Operations with the rest of them. He was not a usual rider in their fluctuating roster of car-poolers; his Peugeot had died on him again and desperate to get to work on time, he'd flagged them down by the *Lebensmittel.* Now a carbuncle on the ass of the military body—a civilian employee—Killington was a retired Master Sergeant, but in his new role, stabled in the officers' corral.

Winter considered Killington's a worthy suggestion. He got along fine with his boss, though Etheridge was an ELINT warrant, a skills area Winter had no experience of. They'd had no ELINT in Asmara or Viet Nam that he knew of. He wondered about radio finger-printing.

The key, though, was that Etheridge was a warrant officer himself, and likely possessed current awareness of the process.

* * *

Such proved the case, and after an intial discussion soon after that early-morning suggestion, Winter broached the subject to his OIC. Etheridge seemed pleased he'd been asked, and was able and ready to tell his new SFC what he thought might be useful to him, should he choose to pursue that course. He told him, first off, that he, Etheridge, would be pleased to recommend Winter as a viable warrant officer candidate. That was encouraging, considering he'd worked for him only about eight months.

* * *

Rothwesten, Germany: March 1967

In the Field Station Operations office, Winter encountered Brenner. "What are you doing down here? You covered in Gartow?" he asked his fellow sergeant. Winter ostensibly on TDY, honcho-ing the Gartow site over the winter change, was back on post only for the warrant board.

"Captain sent me down," Brenner said. "Ran off the dike."

"Ahhh, shit, Luther. Don't you know better'n go into town and drink? You tear up your car?"

"Wasn't drinking. Just foggy. Hell, it happened yesterday, right after you left. Captain didn't write me up right away, but you know his policy: anyone runs a vehicle off a dike gets sent back to The Rock. He finally gave in to it late yesterday afternoon, 'against his better judgement,' he said. I had to pack it in, *et voilà!*, here I am. And no, I did not tear up my wheels, thank you kindly for your concern." He smiled at Winter with a smug expression.

"What?"

"The recall doesn't matter. I'm transferred to B.A., effective in a couple of weeks."

"Jeez-us, if you have to go, Bad Aibling's not bad banishment."

"Within every catastrophe . . . So, how'd the board go?"

"Bizarre rituals. Don't know why I let Ambler talk me into going for warrant anyhow. They asked me shit had nothing to do with the M.O.S., nothing to do with leadership. Or Army for that matter. Weird stuff."

"Confirms my thesis. You want to be an officer, you must know weird shit. Don't have to know anything else." Brenner was resolute. Brenner was also Brenner, and as such would cut his friend no slack.

"So, how'd you swing Bad Aibling. The Garden Spot of Europe is usually a sop for some politically connected yo-yo."

"Who says I'm not?" Brenner replied in faux umbrage. "So, what's with the board?"

"Well, don't mean nothin'. Only three of us from Rothwesten met the board. Me, from Management Branch, Cabiness from Maintenance, Marshall from the Morse shop. Not taking anything away—he's a good N.C.O. and a good operator—but being black, Marshall will no doubt get the nod. Make Oh-Five-One. Been a long time since Cabiness worked manual Morse, set pos; he's reaching. And I saw the Telex. A.S.A.'s only making three Oh-five-ones, world-wide. They sure as hell won't make more than one from Rothwesten, if that. The Pentagram's pushing blacks. No discredit to Marshall, but it sure'n hell gives him a leg up." But Winter was OK with the way of things in the Army. It was the only wedge of society in America that offered minorities a chance at equality. "I'm headed back to Gartow in a few minutes."

"Don't give you much time with family, do they? When'd you meet the board?"

"This morning."

"Did you even see *die Frau und Kinderen?*"

"Last night. Had a night at home to get a uniform ready 'n' all for this morning. Renegotiated marital arrangements with Nickie. Hugged the boys. Gotta get on back, though; with you down here, there's only Block in Gartow to keep the Captain out of trouble, with Harry gone."

Brenner looked at Winter with evasive eyes, then looked away. "Stay on the main road."

"What?"

"Don't go down by the river, through Hann Munden."

"I've got no intention . . . Why the hell would I go through Hann Munden? I'm going up the autobahn—"

"Yeah, just . . . just don't go there . . ."

Winter sensed uneasiness, unusual for Brenner. He leaned on a file cabinet by the corner of the Ops Sergeant's desk. The Master Sergeant stared at them in turn with a morose look tempered with disdain. Winter said, "O.K. What's with the wave off? No Hann Munden?"

Brenner hesitated before answering. "I drove down through Wobeck yesterday to drop off some maintenance stuff for Smitty, and decided to take the back roads on here. Between Göettingen and Hann Munden I had some . . . a strange experience." His eyes were moving.

Winter, alarmed by this new Brenner, said, "Well . . . ?"

"Driving along the river, the fog was even hairier than Gartow. I should have stopped. Couldn't see diddley. There's nowhere you can go on that road that will get you lost, but the few times I thought I knew where I should have been, I didn't recognize anything. A couple of times I came into a lighted area, like there was a street lamp. But there aren't any lights on that road, except in the villages. But I swear, on the open road I passed several lamps—old-fashioned gas lamps—flaring in the fog." He went silent. He wouldn't meet Winter's eyes.

"And. . . ."

"Twice I passed horse-drawn carriages. With sidelamps, windows all curtained up against the fog. Did you ever see a carriage on that road?" Without waiting for a reply, he said, "Like being in Lancaster County, P.A. Gave me the golliwoggles. Began to think I was hallucinating, but that can't be. I got here all right. Eventually." Brenner, speaking fast, as if straining, holding his breath, rushed on. "Passing through Hann Munden, I could see weak lights from behind curtained windows. The few times I saw any semblance of humans, they had . . . they appeared to have yellow eyes. Glowing."

"Glowing, yellow eyes?"

"Only about nineteen hundred by the time I got opposite the post, down in the valley. It was dark as the inside of a cow. But none of the farmhouses had lights."

"Gimme that bit about the eyes again."

Brenner was quiet. "Not a light. Anywhere."

"And you weren't hallucinating! How many'd you have at the Red Cat? How many at Wobeck?" Winter smiled ruefully, shaking his head.

"Hey, asshole. I just got sent down to The Rock for what is normally a booze-related incident. I'm driving on dark, foggy, icy roads. D'ya think I'm going to be hitting the sauce?"

"Well, you better stop reading fairy tales for late-night fare. You're smack dab in the middle of Brüder Grimm country, as you so often remind me. Don't let 'em get into your head."

"Assuredly, Kemo Sabe. Thanks for the vote of confidence. And may your board results be in the toilet. Remain a slug like the rest of us," Brenner said, moving away.

* * *

On 19 July 1967, in Rothwesten's Field Station Headquarters, Sergeant First Class David D. Winter was commissioned Warrant Officer-One. CW4 Wally Stegner, Field Station Personnel Officer, immediately bestowed on him the brown neck scarf as soon as Colonel Fox stepped back. Nicole, after pinning the bar on his collar, kissed him rather wantonly.

Stegner seriously reminded all present that only Warrant Officers and Generals wore the brown neck scarf. The old Warrant leaned close to Winter and whispered, "Caca-colored."

* * *

Munich-Bad Aibling, Bavaria, Germany; September 1967

The last week in September was given over to *Oktoberfest*. The drive from Bad Aibling to Munich was fifty-one kilometers up the back road, same thirty miles by autobahn. No difference to split. Officers, suffering the full range of pettifoggery at the hands of a capricious commander, were not allowed to drive to the festival; the fear—well founded—of a fleet of alcoholic drivers on the late-night return on the autobahn was too much for the Colonel. A driver from the motorpool, invited to work non-duty hours for pay, the trifling sum taken from Officers Club funds, agreed to convey the officers and accompanying females to the affair, refrain from partaking of the primary event—drinking—and convey the merry-makers safely home. Well done!

With warrant officer came a reassignment for Winter from Rothwesten to Bad Aibling. He followed his friend Brenner by only a few weeks. He'd been a member of his new command for three weeks, and this was to be his and Nickie's first big social "do."

Following an afternoon and evening extravaganza when leaving the *Oktoberfest* grounds, the all too-aware and totally sober sergeant driver pulled the busload of Americans into the path of an erratic

Mercedes as it passed unheeding of a red stop signal. They all became victims of the fest.

In moments, police were all over the scene. No one was injured on the bus. The Mercedes driver, sizing up the large, green Army bus and seeing *Deutsche Marks* in a glow against the shadows, claimed severe back injuries. But no evidence could be found, and the summoned white ambulance with the large red cross was sent back to its nesting lair. Still, the proper police, not readily available, had not arrived.

Only a certain category of designated police officers could investigate traffic accidents, and only a special subcategory of that group could investigate incidents involving foreigners. So the bus sat. After the initial flurry of concern over injuries, of which there were none, then worry about baby sitters back at Bad Aibling, about which nothing could be done, the mood lightened. There was no rushing the matter. The drunks were already asleep. Those who had imbibed lesser amounts, but were yet beyond rational social intercourse, alternately dozed, sang, and argued. Husbands, wives, officers, girlfriends milled and mixed, conversations finding fertile ground in common despair. No one was allowed to leave the bus.

Eventually, the proper authorities arrived on the scene and began their considerations. Major West, half in the bag but still vociferously deploring the plight of the trapped party-goers, stepped off the bus despite protestations from the attending *Polizei*. One of the newly arrived investigators, wearing the mandatory leather greatcoat and rimless glasses, argued with the loud-mouthed officer—who spoke good German, but not *polite* German—until, having been maneuvered past some personally established demarcation in relations, he ordered West back onto the bus and the bus to follow a lead motorcycle officer to the police station in the district.

West and the driver were escorted into the station house. Time passed and they did not return. All the while the busload of Americans sat and waited, their olfactory senses assailed by the smell of roasting chicken and *pomme frittes* from a *Brathendel* next to the cop shop. The eatery did a land-office business with the sobering busload of Americans under the close supervision of a German patrolman.

It was finally Frau West, with no German at her command, who went into the station and retrieved the situation, convincing the cops of the futility of it all. The cops no doubt by this time were tired of the rambling, angry tirades of the Major and the whining of the driver, and sought a way to defuse the situation, which was not a situation at all because the American driver was not at fault. It was a matter of face. A matter of bureacracy and multiple forms. *Deutsche* records.

Cissie West brought forth the major and the driver, and the bus departed in an injured funk. Three hours late getting home was still better than a fatality report for the abstemious colonel, who of course never went to *Oktoberfest*.

By mid-November, the matter was forgotten.

* * *

The day after Thanksgiving, WO1 Winter, now Manual Morse Section OIC at the 18th USASA Field Station, Bad Aibling, left with a select crew of operations personnel—soldiers with skills in several technical specialties—to be the Operations Officer, the number two man on a handpicked team conducting a hearability study at Augsburg, some fifty miles away. Similar crews, many of them picked by Winter and CW2 Garth Etheridge at Rothwesten, commander of the test team, would arrive from Rothwesten, Herzo-Genaurach, and Frankfurt, in addition to the Bad Aibling troops. It was a gathering of professionals. Their task was to determine the suitability of Augsburg to function as a field station in future field operations.

It was a demanding assignment, and Winter returned home only three days before Christmas, for the holidays. Final operational test analysis and the writing of the Test Report with conclusions and recommendations would follow before the new year. For now, he was home.

On Christmas eve, David and Nickie bundled the boys into Bavarian kinder capes and hats and walked in the afternoon from the post to the village, little more than a couple of miles, in deep, fresh, clean snow. Squeaky when they walked. The air so crisp and clean it hurt the sinuses. Tears froze on cheeks before they could drop.

German children dragged sleds and ice skates through the powder, their round, red faces glowing, their babble warm and recognizable, if not always understood by the *Amerikanischers*. Downtown, the shops were festooned with greenery, striped canes, and gnome-like characters from folk tales. In the bakery windows were displayed seasonal offerings in competition: enormous gingerbread houses, chateaux, castles, each bakery seeking to outdo its fellows.

As the light of the day faded, and the street lamps came on, a Dickensian quality overlay the scene. Smells of baked sugar cookies and *Kuchen* and rich German coffee saturated the pedestrian-filled streets. There was no vehicular traffic, and when the Winters left the *Gasthaus* where they'd had mulled wine and hot chocolate and pastries, and made nice with their host and neighbors, they headed home in a crystal night with a billion stars to guide them.

Houses built to the edge of the walkway along the street, which turned into the road to the base, presented their own, separate homage to the season. Evergreens inside were festooned with lighted white candles. From the town came the sound of bells, striking every quarter hour, and over a loudspeaker, carols in German filled the air.

Their way across the dark countryside for the last quarter mile to the base lighted only by a brilliant half-moon and the stars, the Winters walked slowly, favoring the two tired children who begged to be carried. When talked out of it, Jeremy held up the full distance; Adam was dead weight in David's arms. They could see the lights of the gate ahead, Christmas tree lights of the post beyond.

"I'm going ahead with the special assignment request," he said, vocalizing his decision.

"Oh, Dave. If that means we'll have to leave B.A. . . . " Nickie began.

"I know. It's a choice. I love it here, love to stay. But from what I hear from Frankfurt, I stand a pretty good chance of getting it. West will give me a positive endorsement. I think the Old Man will, if only because it would get rid of another agnostic. I need to make my move while I have a fair chance of success; they have openings so seldom. But once someone gets into the unit, they never leave."

"But you don't know where we'd go?"

"Not many bad ones in that business. Oslow, Copenhagen, Athens, Bangkok . . . there are more than twenty different sites. No, I don't know. But one big thing . . . it'll mean I won't be on the Pentagon's list for Viet Nam, anymore."

A Motor Pool duty driver had run a tractor through the post, scraping the roads clear of snow. There was a feel of letdown when they stepped out of the deep comfort of the countryside drifts onto the bare cobblestones of the post road. But Nicole was smiling.

* * *

Bad Aibling, Germany: December 1967

When Colonel Ahls announced that officers and wives would ride the bus to the New Year's celebration in the lodge at Chiemsee, fifteen miles away, a collective moan arose in the Officer's Club. The outburst threatened to obscure Scott McKenzie's rendition of "If You're Going to San Francisco," a song with bittersweet stigma attached, given its implications to the body of officers who either already had, or soon would, pass through that fabled city by the bay en route to Oz East.

Another bus, for God's sake! The common complaint was that, forced into similar compliance for Oktoberfest three months earlier, the night had proved a disaster. Major West still awoke every morning, and went drunkenly to sleep every night, bitching over that episode.

Still, riding the bus, not having to drive, freed one to drink oneself silly if one chose, without concerns for maneuvering a vehicle back to post over icy, elusive roads filled with Deutsch celebrants. So Winter was neither hot nor cold about the colonel's dictate. The only concern he had was that should a crisis arise with the children while they were away, and he got a call from the baby sitter, and he and Nickie should be forced to return to BA, he'd be without transportation. But others had that same consideration; and the adjutant assured him he could commandeer an MP vehicle in that case, or call for a lift from the post. Soothing words aside, it was the colonel's order. A done deal.

As a celebration, New Year's on the lake was brilliant. The food was excellent, a given: typical *Bayerischer Deutsche* fare; the booze, beer and wine flowed with true holiday abandon—no one ever expected the Russians to attack over the holidays. All those atheist troops would be celebrating the season, too—and the women were beautiful.

Especially radiant was Lieutenant Colonel Satterwhite's wife, Judalon, exposing as she did some ninety-two point six percent of her magnificent bosom in one of the most daring gowns seen in a Christian land since the Crusades. Brigadier General Avraim O'Brian, the Army's European Chief of Chaplains and a guest at BA's Chiemsee revels, put aside God and the pulpit long enough to develop eye strain seeking out Judalon's other seven point four percent, an ultimately fruitless pursuit that some said was responsible for the permanent tic Chaplain O'Brian later developed.

Winter had been a Warrant Officer for five months, a member of this command for just over three; socially—officerly—he was still a new guy. He knew all the officers, and had met most of their wives, but couldn't say he knew them. Nickie knew the CO's and XO's wives, Mrs. Major West, and the other wives who lived in the same stairwell with the Winters, but few other women on the small post. As a coming out for both, the night shone with promise.

Returning home on the bus at 0230, Winter threw up two bottles of Liebfraumilch and an excellent prime rib dinner into a series of paper party hats Nickie had collected to take home to the boys. It was to Winter's credit that he managed this *faux pas* with so little disturbance that only Hermione-the-Harlot, the wife of Captain Abercrombie in the seat in front of the Winters, was aware; Captain Abercrombie was unconscious. But each time Winter opened a window to dispose of a brimming hat, the complaints from other passengers were loud and sustained. The night was bitching cold.

New Year's traditional Commander's reception, in-quarters, was scheduled for 1300 hours—ten and a half hours away. Uniform was Class A "blues," the same dress uniform Winter had done his partying in the night before. The only one he owned, it bore evidence of the new warrant officer's intolerance of German wine shaken, not stirred, by persistent feats of terpsichorean bedazzlement with his wife. 1968 did not bode well for the young officer.

* * *

While the 18th USASA Field Station officers worked off their hangovers in the days following New Year's, a fair segment of the population in a vastly different culture barely beneath the Southern Cross made plans for their celebration, belated by Western standards.

They called it Tet.

chapter eleven

That Summer in Prague

Bad Aibling, Germany: Summer 1968

All water under the bridge. An uneasy flood of disjointed remembrances, from all those many years ago down to earlier this year, left Winter in an edgy, depressed mood.

"No. That's bullshit!" he muttered. His mood derived from that springtime drive through the Tirol when he'd belatedly informed Nickie of his orders for return to Viet Nam. To say she'd gone ballistic didn't pay the craft of gunnery any compliment, vis-a-vis pejorative metaphors. And September bore inevitably closer.

But some pre-existing conditions also impacted his days. Winter drove to the BA dispensary and learned that Van Ingen had been removed to the Mental Hygiene Clinic in Munich. Informing Major West, Winter then called Nicole, told her he was off to Munich to visit one of his men in hospital, hung up quickly to avoid her non-response, and departed.

He took the back road to Munich, the same thirty miles as on the autobahn but less stressful. He had never cared to drive at one hundred-plus miles per hour. The scenic drive through manicured forests and sculpted farms was bereft its usual entertaining focus; his mind roamed through all the bins of chaos about him, even before the onset of his runaway conflicts.

When they had first moved onto post at Fort Ord, his first assignment after Viet Nam and his wounding, even as he was beginning to heal from his wounds, he'd been able, if not to put Nickie's fears to rest, at least to assuage them to a workable degree. In 1965, he and everyone else was sure the war would be over soon, and the question of being ordered to 'Nam again did not arise. Especially with the new MOS language trailer designating him as a Russian linguist.

But that was three years ago, and those heady days of new promise had ground down to a barren pall of disillusionment.

His focus, like a ping-pong ball in a metal box, bouncing from image to image, tracing his movement through the early Army years: Fort Devens, Asmara, college in Milwaukee, then . . . Viet Nam. Early days.

And after all that—he managed to shade out those dark recovery days of March through July, 1965, in Monterey. Bad memories. But then came Europe: Rothwesten and Gartow; and then Bad Aibling, where he had transferred when commissioned warrant officer. They did love it here.

But that was all in the toilet now, possibly his marriage, too. Several months since receiving those fateful orders, Nickie had settled into a glacial mode of accommodation. She no longer glared at him as if he'd poisoned her dog, but still avoided unnecessary conversation. Nothing for it but go with the flow; he'd done everything he could.

As the military hospital came into view near Munich, he thought of the revelations yesterday by the colonel, identifying his longtime friend and fellow Morse-ARDF Op, SP5 Guy Van Ingen, as the elusive Electric Man, who brought a whole new meaning to the term "veteran."

But now, today when he arrived at the clinic, he was not allowed to see Van Ingen. No one from Bad Aibling except the post commander, XO, post surgeon, and chaplain could visit. Winter located the senior staff doctor in the psychiatric clinic and badgered him into discussion.

"I've known him a long time, Colonel. We were together in "Nam."

"Then you're familiar with his trauma."

"I don't know about . . . I was unaware he'd suffered any trauma," Winter said hesitantly. "He wasn't wounded."

"He has all his limbs, vision, hearing, that's true," the doctor admitted. He paused to light a cigar, walking away down a hallway, forcing Winter to follow. The colonel drew deeply on the cigar, then peered intently at the forming ash. "What do you know about a 'carload of burnt corpses'?" He looked just past Winter's face when he asked the question.

"Nothing. He never . . . a carload? Not a plane load?"

"Don't know. Could be a plane, I suppose. A 'load.' Was there something involving a plane?" The colonel's questions seemed casual, academic. Winter felt no such dispassion.

* * *

He and Van Ingen had been Specialist Fives together in Viet Nam, working at WHITE BIRCH Ops in 1964. When Winter was promoted to Staff Sergeant and transferred to run the Airborne section, Van Ingen volunteered for Air, qualified, extended his tour by six months, and followed soon after. They worked well together; there was mutual respect; and they spent off-duty time together. Neither was a heavy drinker, and they found common interest in various cuisines in downtown eateries, and in scouring the markets for gifts to mail home. Van Ingen was unmarried but had young siblings.

Shortly after he began flying for Winter, Van Ingen rode one in. It was only the second plane ASA had lost in the war. The small unarmed plane took ground fire in the main fuel tank. Mr. Orezco, with skill and cunning, took out half a farmer's new rice crop and his only water buffalo, but the pilot and Van Ingen climbed free of the plane into the muck of the paddy and were picked out by a rescue chopper within half an hour. After that, Van Ingen seemed less enthusiastic about flying, though he made no move for relief from flight status.

Van Ingen's problem with the bottle began on the day he sat in the co-pilot's seat in a Beaver RU-6, waiting in the runup area for takeoff on a morning mission, and while idling away the wait whistling tunelessly into the intercom to tweak Lieutenant Branch's hangover, he watched the C-47 ahead of them roll onto the active, run up its motors gathering speed, and disintegrate into a fiery heap of refuse in an instant, a deathtrap for twenty-two Vietnamese paratroopers and the four-man American crew. Van Ingen and his pilot, the young lieutenant, non-participant voyeurs, were trapped there in the U-6. They sat helplessly as the cargo aircraft burned and exploded fifty yards in front of them. Branch leaned out the door and was sick on the tarmac; Van Ingen didn't show such consideration for the ground crew.

The disaster was at first assumed to be caused by a mortar round or RPG; an accident board later concluded it was an unsealed fuel cap. The strip was closed until the charred mess could be bulldozed off to the side. Branch and Van Ingen's flight launched late on the adjacent, parallel strip and their schedule brought them back at noon. By one-thirty, Van Ingen had made a dent in the Club bar stock and couldn't stand up. He had not stopped drinking since, though after language school and subsequent assignment to Bad Aibling, he'd become crafty with his drink in deference to his job and his OIC friend for whom he was again working.

Winter was now the Collection Officer, having as his responsibility the Morse, printer, and linguist sections, a total of some three hundred-plus operators. The slot called for a captain, but the officer holding that slot had gone to be CO of Headquarters Company, when that Captain CO flew to CONUS on emergency leave to succor a dying mother, and had been reassigned to Fort Meade to put him in close proximity to his parents' home. Winter was the only other officer in the Collection Branch, and was moved up into the slot.

* * *

Winter stared through the colonel, his mind flashing back through the kaleidoscope of Viet Nam, remembering Van's work.

"Van Ingen's performance, since he arrived at B. A., has been . . . not stellar," Winter acknowledged. "He came here straight out of language school where he studied German. That was following his Viet Nam tour. He was always a good operator; he became a good linguist," and he hesitated, adding finally to answer the colonel's expectant pause, ". . . but there were days when he didn't make it to work on time, days when his Trick Chief had to cover for him at trick change. Even I had to cover for him on a couple of occasions.. Days when Van was physically present with the trick, but out of it . . . to some alcoholic degree." He paused, looked inside himself, and when the doctor did not speak, said, "I wonder if by covering for him, I've contributed to his problems. Or was it the inevitable baggage he brought from the war?"

"Those are aspects we might consider in his treatment," the colonel said, committing to nothing, Winter knew.

He knew, at the same time, that Van Ingen suffered from command irresponsibility consistent with Colonel Ahls's shallow appraisal of the problem. But what *was* the problem? Neither the Army nor the command had ever given Van Ingen psychological consideration. He'd sustained no wound in Viet Nam, and like many others not physically marked by the war, and in such pristine condition, could not be a war casualty. Marked by the system didn't count. Winter began badgering the doctor on this point.

But when he made mention of *shell shock,* lip service paid to its successor *combat fatigue* and now new euphemisms, the colonel closed him down. Brenner often warned Winter of his habit of making rash assumptions based on things as ephemeral as truth and conscience. This lack of competent evaluation was not a matter of Army policy, but of personalities among the treating medical staff in the general military quorum. Mental issues got short shrift and were generally avoided in polite conversation.

"And you—none of you who knew him, worked with him, his boss and his commander, his chaplain, friends—no one ever suggested he seek help?" the doctor asked. A strange tack, Winter thought. Maybe this colonel was not part of the problem.

Winter felt a sudden stab of guilt. It made him feel—*helpless.* Already missed the boat and can't do nothing! A double negative felt about right. He said, "Colonel, that makes me feel . . . like I guess you meant it to feel."

"No, no, Chief. Wasn't meant to be laid on you. It's . . . ahhhh . . . the system. The war. I want to blame someone, something, you're right. But not you. Not any-*one.*" He crushed the fresh cigar in a brass ashtray on a coffee table, threw the splintered stump into the waste can, and turned back to Winter with a blank look.

"Will I be able to see him? Later?" Winter asked.

"Give me a call tomorrow. I'll let you know how he is. Depending on his condition. . . ." Giving Winter his phone number, the colonel left it there.

* * *

Good Soldier Woijczek was in superlative fettle. Private First Class Mladczik Vlad Woijczek, native-born *Amerikanischer* from Three Ponds, Georgia, had Magic Marvin cornered when Winter returned to the Ops area.

Woijczek, admittedly an enigma, was a uniquely frightening one. Borderline mental, he was regarded with wonder and apprehension by fellow enlisted men, NCOs, and officers alike, though he was not so bizarre as to remain beyond the reach of the draft. And so Woijczek, brilliant in his own strange way, genius on some scales, had enlisted, willingly subordinating himself to a system staffed with persons of near-imbecilic proportions.

The Personnel Officer at Woijczek's in-processing center, tasked with one of those orders which was not really an order to "get rid of the psycho," understood that the soldier was a near thing to a true *idiot savant*; but the various psychological profiles, faced with Woijczek's evasive irrationality, melded into an imprecise matrix of confusion. Without confirming medical evidence to support a section-eight discharge, the Army reckoned as how they would keep the odd fellow. They gave him to ASA without requiring his extension to four years of servitude..

Woijczek had become a walking encyclopedia of Army regulations, field manuals, maintenance guides, and various lists, catalogs, and directives, and memorized as well the entire Uniform Code of Military Justice. He did not contribute anything useful to the bare fact of his memorized knowledge. He couldn't, for instance, repair any equipment; he could not take a field manual and conduct a relevant operation with it. He just knew the contents of every document concerned with all such exotica. It was his knowledge of the UCMJ, however peripheral, that scared off those who would rid the Spartans of this affliction.

When Winter walked through Magic Marvin's outer office, Woijczek was reeling off data regarding, as best the bemused officer could tell, something from Army Field Manual FM 20-15, *Pole and Frame Supported Tents*.

Winter heard, ". . . letter D period Pitching period The tent can be pitched by four men in approximately figures three zero letters minutes period paren figure one close paren letters Preliminary Instructions paren figure one comma figures three three close paren period paren letter A close paren Spread tent on ground period Check to see if liner is in place semi-colon if it is not in place comma spread it out beneath—" Winter, passing a transfixed Magic Marvin with glazed eyes, hurried on into his office, fearful that any innocuous statement could be proximate cause to involvement.

Magic Marvin later told Winter he'd merely commented to Woijzcek that with the weather so fine it looked to be a good upcoming weekend to go camping at Eibsee, above Garmisch. Camping induced the vision of a tent, a synaptical connection, diatribe. . . .

* * *

Winter never saw the Munich colonel again. His phone calls were never returned; his queries went unanswered. After one frustrating episode of phone tag with the faceless proles at the hospital, Winter, with icy restraint, eased the receiver back onto the cradle and sat, fuming quietly. His clerk, alert to his OIC's mindset, rapped on the frame, though the door stood open. The distracted warrant officer glanced up, motioned Magic Marvin in, and watched with curiosity as the soldier glanced back into the outer office and pulled the door shut.

"Sir?"

"What? I didn't call, Marvin."

"Yes, sir. It's . . . I think you're overlooking something," he nodded toward the phone.

As if following one of those connect-the-dots puzzles in the Sunday paper, Winter looked to the phone for a clue. None there. His eyes, veiled in anticipation of one of Marvin's sleight-of-mind facilitations that gave rise to his *nom de militaire*, slid back to the clerk's face.

Magic Marvin understood implied permission, and proceeded to earn his keep. "Sir, I know you haven't forgotten it—" he said with arch emphasis "—but you must debrief Specialist Van Ingen."

"Hell, Marvin, that's not my job. You know the S-2—"

"Excuse me, sir, but S.-2's not responsible for BASTION GREY. Not *solely*. You are, as O.I.C. And only you have operational access— besides, of course, Major West and the C.O."

Winter puzzled over the statement for a moment, looking for what he thought should be obvious to him. Nothing! "What?" he said inanely. "Elec—Van Ingen doesn't work the B.G. site." When he said it, he sensed the threat of false information in his statement.

"Sir, Van Ingen's the number one *alternate* linguist for BASTION GREY. He works Ops, but he *is* standby for work at the B.G. site. He's cleared for it. And you're the officer who must debrief him on operational . . . matters." The intelligence project, conducted at a separate operational site two miles away, was so highly classified, Winter understood Marsh's pause.

The clerk's point was immediately taken. "By God, Marvin, take two Privates from petty cash for yourself. Another Coop de Gracie!" Winter snapped his fingers. "Call up front, see if Major West is entertaining. I'd like an invite. Call for my carriage."

Marsh raised furry eyebrows and regarded Winter blankly for a moment, in light of his playfulness. "You have an open door, Mister Winter. I just spoke with the Ops Sergeant."

Of course you did, Winter thought. The incredible thing was that his magical clerk could relay that information with no hint of smugness. Winter left for the Operations Office in such a state of enthusiasm he left behind both his old Cardiff Senior briar pipe and his equally rank coffee cup, two items of usual *must have* when visiting the holy see.

* * *

The specialist seven medic was the first super grade soft-striper he had ever seen. The spec-seven led him to a junction in the hallway and stopped, facing two doors, each bearing the name-plate of a colonel-doctor. Winter wondered if one of those offices housed the colonel who had lied to him in the hallway on his last visit, the one who didn't understand telephone communications protocol. He could only ask the specialist for a "shrink colonel." The colonel had given him a phone number, which had been answered once by a UI voice, but leaving a message got him nothing. At the time of their meeting, the colonel had been wearing scrubs without a name tag and never mentioned his name. Winter knew he likely would never know. Both doors were closed and looked apt to stay that way. The medic looked at each in turn, but made no move of clear intent.

Winter walked away from the medic, leaving him standing, undecided, before the Lady-or-the-Tiger choice. He found a nurse major, got directions, and found the ward he sought. A quick conversation with a doctor who stood at the nurse's station reading a chart started the process. In less than ten minutes, the doctor was back and took Winter to perform his debrief. When he opened the door to a quiet, cool room, the doctor made no move to accompany him inside. West had done his job; the skids were greased.

The blinds, partly closed against the bright sun, gave a bizarre, corrugated look to the soldier in pale green pajamas slumped in an easy chair, reading. He slowly placed his finger between the open pages, folded the cover over, and only then looked up. His face betrayed no surprise.

"Van . . .?"

"Hi, Dave. I knew you'd be here." Statement of fact.

"So you say. Well, let me tell you, buddy, it was a close thing."

"Never a doubt. D'ja need Magic Marvin's help?"

"Matter of fact." Winter laughed quietly. The eternal enlisted network. He wasn't surprised, though; he hadn't been an officer so long he had forgotten how well it served.

"I can guess why you're here." Van Ingen didn't smile; his eyes crinkled as though he might. He waved his boss to the only other chair, an upright iron and wood monstrosity with a link to Prussian domesticity that guaranteed unique discomfort.

"Yeah, I needed to check out the fruitcake section. Before the season." Winter smiled ruefully when he spoke, knowing he took a chance in so openly confronting Van Ingen's state. But he was convinced he knew his man. They'd run the long course together. The endurance of that bond demanded Van Ingen get every benefit of any doubts. And Winter had no doubts.

"I'm really glad you're here, Dave. I can't talk to these people," he said, waving his free hand to encompass the extent of Army medical benefits. "The shrinks . . . all that witchcraft and chemical cocktails. I'm still on the edge of zonked from last night's dose. I just want to—"

"What've they told you? About a prognosis, or is it too soon? Are they telling you anything?" He knew the answer to that before Van Ingen shook his head.

"Have the doctors here, or any of our officers—field station officers—talked to you about any charges? You know, for the things you did . . . and I have to admit, *soljer-san*, I don't *know* what all you've done. But I can't imagine we're talking serious crime here."

"Jeez, I hope not." Van Ingen's eyes, only slightly myopic from the cornucopia of mind-altering drugs, or extension of the malady that drove E-Man, pleaded. "I can't be sure what they have in mind. I don't think I did anything wrong. Maybe I could be leaned on some for my uniforms, mis-use of government property or some such shit. But I haven't hurt anyone . . . that I know of. Certainly, I never meant to harm anyone. Just the opposite."

"I've not heard of any injuries. But let's get the teensy-weensy shit out of the way first." He wasn't sure if he was trying to keep light a necessary military encounter, or just making stupid statements to bridge an officer-enlisted gap. But, no, he knew it wasn't the latter.

Thus began an-hour-long, painful dialogue in which Winter tried to find the right questions to ask, and Van Ingen scrabbled through his drug-muddled mind to provide answers. Winter asked about the seven different colors of costume—Were they for the days of the week?

"Simple answer," Van Ingen said slowly, obviously having to concentrate on the words he would use, "is that they represented— wearing a particular color—a response to one of seven common crimes. Crimes committed within range of my influence."

"Your influence," Winter managed without inflection.

There was no expansion on the phrase. What did that mean?

"Well, I had a TransOceanic radio and I acquired the local German emergency frequencies and codes—" Van Ingen did not explain the surreptitious maneuverings that provided him that information, but it was not a difficult task for someone of his profession "—and I monitored police broadcasts, responding, dressed in the color appropriate to the crime: murder called for the green suit, a costume I never employed; blue was for traffic accidents—" Winter thought of the night Electric Man had run afoul of Meechan. "—orange for robbery or assault, and so on. Black, for the most heinous crime. That

would be child abuse of any kind. Never had to use that one, either."
He said it with overtones of relief..

He lightly described how he'd acquired "extra" helmet liners and
painted them; the longjohns from Clothing Sales; the sheets he'd
purloined from linen exchange, a loosely controlled exchange of
dirty for clean on a weekly basis which invariably lost dozens of sets
of linen each month: the supply staff sergeant nearing retirement
boosting his retirement prospects.

Winter, feeling a deepening sense of despair toward his friend's
innocent descent into unmilitary behavior, abruptly pulled up when
Van told him they'd found the gun.

"Gun. What gun? Jeez, Van, you didn't carry a weapon?"

"No, I never. I told you, I never used the black or green outfits.
Those were the only two authorizing me to carry a weapon."

"Where'd you get it?"

"Remember the old thirty-eight Iver-Johnson on a Peacemaker
frame that I carried in 'Nam? You remember, that kid lieutenant
gave me such a hassle about 'non-standard weapon' and told me I
couldn't carry it on missions."

"I remember the kid lieutenant. The one who—"

"The same," he said obliquely.. " Same gun."

"In case you hadn't noticed it, Van, Germany's no longer a
combat zone. Not for a couple of decades now. You aren't authorized
a personal weapon in the billets. Where was it?"

"Don't ask. It'll just get someone else in trouble." Van Ingen
seemed contrite.

"Do you mean you had accomplices?"

Van Ingen did not respond; then suddenly stood and said,
"Mister Winter. I'm sorry. I can't talk to you anymore." A strange
light illuminated his eyes. "I only tried to do some good." His eyes
crimped shut and tears squeezed out onto his cheeks. "You must
discuss this with my doctor . . . or my attorney."

They were the last words the specialist spoke to Winter, who,
after continued appeals, recognized intransigence. After stumbling
his way through the debrief, which was his excuse for access to
the patient, he left, finding his way from the clinic in a daze. But
cataloging the various incidents and adding on the weapon, though
seeking to be supportive, Winter couldn't avoid the list of charges
compounding in his mind.

Winter left the clinic, still short on understanding. He had the
uneasy feeling that this might be the last time he would ever see Guy

Van Ingen, and he was saddened by the fact. And it was true that he had debriefed his silent operator for BASTION GREY before leaving, but if he ever had to stand before a court or board and testify to the competence of the debriefee to understand his debriefing, Winter knew he'd have to waffle that one.

* * *

Three days later, another trip to the Munich hospital proved fruitless. A clinging captain-nurse with grey teeth informed him that Van Ingen had been med-evaced stateside, but she didn't know where. He returned to Bad Aibling and went to the Dispensary, where a friend, a captain-doctor nominated Post Surgeon, would normally be the one to follow the case of Van Ingen.

"Benny, have you heard anything?" Winter asked.

"He's gone to Valley Forge. It's going to require a long period of treatment. All I can tell you."

"I have to know: what will happen to him? Why didn't we see, why didn't we notice something sooner? How did it get this far?" Winter stood in the surgeon's office; he couldn't sit, couldn't stand still, but paced about the office so that Captain-Doctor Trilling was forced to continuously work his chair about in a circle to face him.

Looking back later, Winter understood that Ben Trilling, friendship aside, had fed him pablum. Lots of "you knows," when he didn't; "it's understandables," and it wasn't. Lots of misdirection and medical closed mouth. Which meant the medicos hadn't a clue.

Envisioning the pile of aluminum and rubber and charred flesh beside the runway at Tan Son Nhut, he thought it had been a long time catching up. Winter knew that the crash-fire was a wound, as surely as a jagged piece of Urals steel through Van Ingen's skull. He knew little about survivor syndrome, but instinctively knew the answer lay there.

In the background, a modulated tone of reason flowed through the captain's non-explanation like a sine wave of rational-to-mad extremities. But there was no feeling that on the other end of the glib diagnosis was a man of flesh and blood with mad delusions.

Winter thought of the practical aspects of Van Ingen's dilemma. Other than the one sighting by *Schutzmann* Steichel in downtown Bad Aibling, he had never definitely been known to have been off post in his role. Discounting the front gate *pas de deux* with guard PFC Waller. But somehow in his watchdog role, between the initial alarm, getting into costume, and reaching the scene of action, a waning of resolve, a loss of purpose obviously occurred. His attention span appeared irrationally sporadic, his overall response episodic.

The doctor chuckled, surprising Winter with something relevant. "With what we know now about his avowed mission—" and Winter didn't know 'what we know' "—it would have been inconsistent for Van Ingen to attack anyone. Even Meechan," Trilling sighed, a concrete statement for once, his listener thought. "Too bad. It's almost surely a fact that when Van Ingen, en route to one of his emergencies—an automobile accident, I guess it was, since he was wearing blue—when he came out the window and crashed through the bushes that night in front of Headquarters Company, he was as surprised as Meechan was at the confrontation. It was late at night; he wasn't expecting anyone, hadn't thought about it. He was fixated on the accident."

"Meechan said he had a knife. Or a bayonet."

"A flashlight."

"No shit! How d'ya know?"

"He always carried a flashlight. It was a part of his . . . *uniform*. Dave, what do you know about his attack on Meechan?"

"I was O.D. when it happened. Ernie said the guy—Van Ingen, Electric Man—charged out of the bushes, raised his hand—" He stopped, his eyes focused on a point above Trilling's head.

"You see it, don't you?" the doctor asked. He waited for Winter to speak. Confronted with silence, he asked, "What's the first thing a good soldier does when he meets an officer outdoors?"

"Salutes. He salutes, by God!" Winter jumped up, his face a mix of emotions working. "He didn't wave a knife at that dipshit. He had a flashlight in his hand—and he saluted. Hah!"

"That's how I read it. The upraised arm, swinging, was an attempt to free his hand of the cape. The mask or weird glasses Ernie Meechan reported turned out to be a pair of skiing goggles."

"A salute, by damn! A soldier, through all that." Winter was smiling as he doggedly but futilely continued questioning the doctor about Van Ingen's future.

* * *

Winter was unable to learn anything further about Van Ingen. But he understood that Van Ingen was no different from any of them who cared.

"It'll be a wonder if any of us can get through this bitch and retain our sanity," Winter commented to Magic Marvin one morning in early August. During this period, despite command attempts to low-key the entire affair, from first sighting to the wall locker shakedown, the post buzzed with several versions of the story. None of them, Winter thought, as strange as the truth.

It might have become a *cause celébre* of the highest order on the tiny post, but two days after Van Ingen departed Munich on the Air Force Nightingale flight, priorities were realigned by external events.

* * *

"Toombs, for a goddamned know-nothing slacker, you got my attention. I gotta give you credit. You got it right—more or less," the Trick Chief said grudgingly.

"What do you mean?" Toombs, as was often the case, was not engaged in his primary task of pursuing Soviet communications links. He welcomed conversation.

"The Sovs finally did it. Yesterday, nineteen-forty-five hours. Brought in transport aircraft, de-planed officers and lead men. Then their fifth column at the airport drew guns and took over: runways, tower, borscht concession. The whole enchilada. Rounded up all civilians and held them in the departure lounge while AN-24s landed Soviet shock troops: Kalmyks, Mongols, other barbarians. They marched on Prague from the airport." It seemed, somehow, to satisfy the sergeant. When he overheard the remarks, Winter thought it merely a reaffirmation of the sergeant's commitment to duty.

American and NATO allied forces ratcheted up from Defense Readiness Condition Three to DEFCON 1. The troops in Operations who had bitched about the dead-ass European mission suddenly found themselves up to their knickers in all the excitement they could handle.

Communications were slim and diminishing; normal Czech broadcast facilities were either shut down or dramatically altered. But a more insidious flood of communications in harsh military jargon speaking German, Polish, Bulgarian, Hungarian, and Russian in extraneous dialects, filled the air. Heavy armored movement, special train movements of unusual routing, airborne troop envelopment activities, massive air operations—all gave the lie to the Soviets' and their Czech Communist Party stooges' lies about friendly, WARSAW PACT cooperative maneuvers.

In the midst of the Czech suppression hysteria, CW2 David D. Winter reached the end of his Bad Aibling tour and prepared to move his family to the United States. There he would settle them in housing, arrange certain civilian matters, and move on to the war zone without them. Because of the Czech flap and his own part in helping man an understaffed Operations Group, he did not have the luxury of the customary five days to clean and clear quarters, ship his personal vehicle, clear post, and catch his flight home. A sergeant just in from Second Field Force, Bien Hoa, traveling to Bremerhaven to pick up his own incoming automobile, drove Winter's VW wagon to the port and shipped it for him on prearranged paperwork. Winter was on duty at Operations until noon of the day before they left for Munich to catch the US-bound flight.

On the day of departure from BA, driving out the front gate in an army van en route to the Munich airport, the driver halted and Winter watched SP5 Magic Marvin Marsh walk out of the guardshack. He'd been waiting for over an hour, though Winter was not to know that. Marsh saluted Winter gravely. They had already said their goodbyes, shaken hands. The departing officer and his sons shouted goodbyes again. Nicole languidly waved a limp hand.

Magic Marvin grinned and flicked his eyes skyward.

Winter looked, saw nothing. He leaned out the window and searched as the van passed through the gate. Atop one of the heavy iron balls crowning the front gate pillars was jauntily perched a bright orange helmet liner, sporting a large E painted in da-glo red. The helmet faced off toward the mountains and looked a permanent fixture.

The spirit of Electric Man was alive at BA. Deriving from that impish dedication, the Wine Troll confidentially vowed to Magic Marvin that he would follow Winter's lead to Nam. As soon as he sobered up.

chapter twelve

The Prodigal

Bien Hoa, Viet Nam: September 1968

Chief Warrant Officer David Winter walked down the ramp of the charter 707, anxious with curiosity. He understood that all he knew from before, all he'd read and heard since, had left him unprepared for return to Vietnam. To its already ugly provenance the war had been appended a familiar cachet in the three-plus years of his sabbatical—transport upgrade.

Instantly breaking a sweat in the tropic pressure cooker, Winter faced an unbroken landscape of vehicles: trucks, forklifts, vans, line carts, sedans, Jeeps, and crash vehicles racing about and across the airstrip, stirring dust on access roads, congesting in the parking areas. A dusty blue-green patina, comprising Air Force blue and Army olive drab, overlay the busy military airfield at Bien Hoa. The stench of vehicle exhaust and the heady lingering kerosene effluvia from jet engines blended with the scorching heat and oppressive humidity and, in a spasm of Asian vindictiveness, sucked the breath from new arrivals.

The reception process was as before, only more so. Bad-tempered privates and airmen tossed duffel bags and luggage from the aircraft hold onto the blistering white concrete apron with abandon. Winter recognized novice military travelers by the anguished screams as their personal goods smashed onto the pavement. Like other old hands at the game, Winter had packed nothing that could be destroyed, broken, or bent, short of incoming shellfire.

With an overriding sense of déjà vu, thrust suddenly back into the maw of the most-hated things in creation, Winter's mind tended toward overload: *Christ! I forgot. I never went to Peoria! I never raised Angus beef. My chute never opened!* With a surge of resolve, he forced an override on digression.

Processing in-country was an unavoidable given: drug lectures, official warnings inevitably providing a roadmap to a shopping list of dealers; personal safety, essentially spelling out the territorial limits beyond which one was strongly advised not to progress; and hygiene, a treatise on VD, malaria—chloroquine, proguanil Tuesday noon meals—and forty-seven varieties of dysentery. Fam-firing of weapons would come later, after all bodies reached assigned units.

Ba-mui-ba beer, a vile Vietnamese brew labeled with the unlikely name "33" was the subject of a separate alert. Every incoming GI—FNG or recidivist—listened with disdainful skepticism, and promptly ignored the suggested ban. The presenter finished his pitch, delivered in a flourish of insincerity. He left the podium, returned to the relative cool of permanent party quarters, and popped the cap on a *Ba-mui-ba*.

Officers and NCOs showed up in ones and twos, like hyenas to a wildebeest kill, calling out names over the assembled troops sweltering beneath the metal-roofed open shed. The hyenas sought individuals or groups assigned to specific units: 5th Special Forces, 1st Aviation Brigade, 101st Airborne Division, 4th Infantry Division, 173rd Airborne Brigade, 5th Mech, 82nd Airborne, 9th Infantry Division, the 25th "Tropical Lightning," Americal, Big Red One; engineers, medics, communicators, and others. Navy, Air Force, and Marine personnel, siphoned off in smaller herds, were then subdivided into gaggles in their own esoteric schemes. There was a home for everybody, but not bodies for every home. Captains and sergeants went away empty-handed, their charges gone astray somewhere in the pipeline. Another flight due 1445.

A Vietnamese Army sergeant with child-like facial features stood alone, off to one side, listening. He appeared to be waiting for someone; he only lacked a call board. Winter noticed him when he first took his seat for briefing, then paid him no attention until he saw the ARVN NCO leading two young American lieutenants away toward a side gate. Winter felt an immediate uneasiness: the two lieutenants didn't have the look of advisers, who alone might be assigned directly to Vietnamese units; even then, they would have been met by USARV headquarters people first.

Winter stepped up to the high plywood counter where an Army master sergeant reigned over In-Processing. His gut told the returning warrant officer something was off-key. The way the ARVN soldier stood was disquieting—watching, not mingling or speaking with in-processing personnel, not asking anyone about personnel he might have been assigned to meet, not even interacting with other ARVN. His reticence, hanging back, was suspicious. If he was there on legitimate business, how had he singled out the two lieutenants? He couldn't have known the two, who had "new" written all over them. In alerting the processing people, Winter didn't worry he might come off looking silly, that he might be experiencing Return Jitters. There was a nagging conviction that the ARVN sergeant had been waiting, not for two specific lieutenants, as much as for two *types*. New, inexperienced. Untutored. Unwarned. *Unweaned!*

The master sergeant ignored him for agonizingly long moments, as Winter observed how chaos and one-upsmanship ruled, the impress of bodies. Many incoming personnel wound up in outfits where liaison people were simply the most aggressive. Obtaining replacements was a piratical enterprise, and competitive as a press gang.

Feeling increasingly anxious, Winter's eyes followed the backs of the three men—two newk lieutenants and one presumptive ARVN—disappearing toward the nearby parked truck. He banged on the plywood counter. The master sergeant glowered at him, unabashed by impatience in a mere warrant officer; he was accustomed to haggling with full colonels. His imminent retort was interrupted by a noise beyond the shelter.

A Jeep loaded with QCs roared up to the parked three-quarter-ton truck and squealed to a halt in a swirl of dust, just as the second of the lieutenants climbed aboard. A half-dozen Vietnamese Army Military Police—*Quan Cong*—piled out of the vehicle, weapons at the ready, and rushed the little knot of three men and truck. Without the niceties of civilized discourse, without even a goodbye, the ARVN sergeant abandoned his two lieutenant charges and bolted for a row of nearby latrines.

"*Dong lai! Dong lai!*" A string of commands in Vietnamese were ignored by the runner: he didn't stop or otherwise respond. Hunched over and zig-zagging, he was at the door of the nearest latrine when the QCs opened fire. The first burst of .223-caliber rounds stitched across the fleeing man's back and he pitched forward through the screen of the door. There was sudden silence . . . then pandemonium.

The incoming troops near Winter ran for cover—any cover. An officer shouted, "*Hit the dirt.*" A sergeant sitting on a nearby bench rolled off onto the ground, reached into his AWOL bag, and jerked out a chrome-plated Walther .380. He crouched warily behind the concrete base of the bench and waited for whatever came next. It was not his first tour in Vietnam. Nor his own, Winter acknowledged, addressing his own position parallel and adjacent to the ground.

The two officers cut out of the herd by the pseudo-ARVN remained fixed in the vehicle, fear and confusion on their faces. One waited for permission to breathe; the other, more adaptable, climbed down, walked toward the latrine to watch the QCs moving up on the fallen body. One of the QCs poked the still figure gingerly with his rifle, then viciously, stabbing the downed man's ribcage with the barrel and sight blade. There was no response. Holding the barrel directly against the body, the Military Policeman, who looked like a child himself, put his foot underneath and flipped the body over in the dust.

Climbing from cover or open exposure, troops thrashed about, attempting to sort out what had just taken place. A babble of excited voices rose above the sounds of the airfield behind them. Out of the inconclusive muddle one voice stood out, clear and harsh, an unsolicited critique. "They just killed that man," protested a slovenly-made-up draftee masquerading as a soldier.

"It's what we do, private," said a captain, too old to be a captain, lifting himself stiffly from the concrete. He turned away, rubbing his elbow, shaking his head. Muttering, "Asshole!"

The QC officer holstered his .45 and knelt by the body. The front of the dead man's khaki shirt was soaked with blood. There were rips and rents where rounds had passed through him, the ground beneath him blotched with gore. No doubt he was dead. AR-15 rounds made tiny holes going in; coming out, tumbling, they left bloody hamburger.

Winter still lay on the ground. A soldier standing beside him gripped the wooden counter, his knuckles white, his face green. He began retching, gently, inevitable sickness imminent. The master sergeant screamed at the young soldier, "You silly shit! Get your ass outta my area . . . *Get out!* . . . *Move*, get away from here, you goddamned—"

The young soldier turned away and sprinted for the grass.

The senior NCO then turned and glared, growling at Winter rising from the ground. "Yeah, Chief? Now what is it I can do for you?" he said. The master sergeant had not moved from his place of duty at the podium.

Winter stood, brushed at scuffed khaki knees, gave a disdainful snort at the NCO's façade of cool, and looked at the huddle around the bloody corpse. He said evenly, "It's taken care of, Top. Thanks." He nodded at the corpse, "'preciate it."

Welcome to Vee-et-nahm!

Winter walked back to the bench where he sat down heavily. His mind hop-scotched to the Army transit area at Travis Air Force

Base in California where Vietnam-bound personnel were processed aboard flights to Tan Son Nhut, Bien Hoa, Cam Ranh Bay, or Da Nang. A sick joke displayed on the wall, a poster crafted in white and garish green and black: VACATION IN VIET NAM! A smiling infantryman, ripping off a full magazine with explosive graphics, leapt across two sprawled bodies of obvious Asian lineage dressed in stock black pajamas. The gunner appeared enraptured, having a fun time. But the subtle humor—the perverted message of the poster—left Winter unmoved. Somebody, not wrapped too tight, had found an outlet. Okay then. Okay now.

A young PFC crawled from under the bench, looked sheepishly at Winter, and sat down by him, glancing nervously out toward the shooting gallery. "Why'd they shoot him?" he asked.

Winter answered slowly: "Well, soldier, you just saw your first V. C."

"Viet Cong? The enemy? You mean—"

"Old V. C. trick: put on an ARVN uniform. Waltz in here looking like you know what you're doing, find a couple of cherries, and tell them you've been sent to meet them, take them to their units. In the confusion, being new, they probably wouldn't—*didn't*—question him. I noticed him hanging about. The truck stolen, same with the uniform. He probably spoke just enough English to name a unit, probably a major parent organization. He told them he was sent to pick up two lieutenants, and they went with him. He might have struck out first time, second, even third . . . but waiting, patient, he'd eventually likely hit pay dirt." He nodded affirmatively toward the two lieutenants.

The PFC looked stricken. With just a little bad luck, or a shortage of newk officers, some newk *enlisted man* might have been selected . . . and I might have been it, Winter imagined his thinking.

"That easy?" the soldier asked. Obviously, the ploy would have worked with him.

"Just that easy," Winter said with conviction. They both could visualize what the outcome of that would have been. "You watch," Winter said. "Pay attention to the guys in the shed area. Watch how they bunch up. Notice how many of them appear lost. Hell, it'd be the easiest thing in the world for a trained VC to lead a couple of these sheep astray."

The young soldier's mouth hung open, his eyes wide.

Winter said, "Now, for a while, it won't be as easy. Everyone on the alert. They'll start pre-briefing on the aircraft before landing, and there will be posted notices about the area. But after a while, when nothing happens, things'll get lax again. That Top Sergeant up there will have his mind on moving bodies again, and leave it to fate or someone else to protect them."

Almost immediately, the master sergeant called over the PA and directed all personnel to return to the area of the shed where he relayed briefly the facts of the attempted snatch. The two target lieutenants stood beyond the shed, talking to an American MP major. From body language Winter knew the Newks were being subjected to a reaming. Gullibility is a punishable offense.

The PFC got up off the bench and moved back with a group of enlisted men, all wearing the 4th Army patch: fresh out of training. Winter saw him talking to the group, describing with violent hand motions what had just happened.

A US Air Force ambulance backed up to the latrine area. The QCs picked up the body of the dead guerilla and flung it into the back of the meat wagon. They got in their Jeep and drove off, laughing.

* * *

Winter struck up a conversation with an Army captain wearing Military Intelligence brass and aviator wings. The two of them, along with two MI branch NCOs, were soon called out of the group by a private in greasy fatigues who drove them to Long Binh, where the two NCOs were put on a bus for Sai Gon. The two officers were assigned a bunk and spent the night in a squad tent.

Over a beer in the Long Binh Transient Officer's Mess, the captain, who wore no nametag, stared at Winter's ribbons. "If I'm not being too nosy, may I ask where in-country you won your Silver Star?"

Winter, always reluctant to talk about it, tried by-passing the question: "Not in-country; not *this* country."

"Yeah, I see the blue-and-whites. Korea?"

"Eleventh Marines. First Mar-Div."

"But you've served in-country here before, also, haven't you?" reading Winter's bio in the colored cloth ribbons above his left pocket.

"'Sixty-four, sixty-five. Third R.R.U."

"The Prodigal returneth. Hail, Aaron; slay the fatted water buffalo," the captain said, smiling to ease the . . . what? Joke? Didn't qualify as a pun. Wasn't much of a joke, Winter thought, smiling bleakly.

* * *

The following morning, the two officers rode a three-quarter-ton truck into Cho Lon, the Chinese sector on the southern edge of Sai Gon, and were dropped off in a courtyard adjacent to two tall, modern, decaying buildings. The courtyard was posted as parking for the 18th MP Brigade. Jeeps, tracked and wheeled armored personnel carriers—APCs—filled the yard. The 11th something—Winter couldn't read the entire sign; the corner appeared to have been shot off—was quartered in one of the buildings. The driver directed the two officers to the other structure; it had no distinctive markings.

Inside the foyer, signs proclaimed the 509th Replacement Company Transient Bachelor Officer Quarters, an element of the 509th United States Army Radio Research Group (509 USARRG). Winter and the captain were assigned an empty room on the third floor where they found bunks and wall lockers. Dropping their baggage, they returned to the lobby with their records and copies of orders and were issued sidearms: .45-caliber, M1911A1 pistols with ammunition pouch and two magazines.

A Spec-5 came from behind a makeshift hotel desk and told them, "Stand by at 1230 hours for a ride to Tan Son Nhut, sirs. To Headquarters Company at Davis Station. From there you'll be transported to the Five-oh-ninth headquarters located next to Tan Son Nhut on the J.C.C. Joint Command Compound's where the Zip, Aussie and American headquarters are located."

"Where do we mess?" Winter asked.

The Spec-5 looked at his watch. "B.O.Q. mess is a restaurant a block and a half from here—take a left from the parking lot, to the end of the block, another left and follow the flies. They open in about fifteen minutes. Or, you can wait and eat at the Five-oh-ninth Headquarters Mess at Davis Station. I'll give you directions—"

"Thanks, I know it." Winter turned to the captain and said. "We may want to check out this restaurant. Odds are against the Five-oh-nine. Used to be good, but P. J. Philpott will be gone, and he was the only mess sergeant in the world granted *carte blanche* by G.I.s. We'll get plenty of exposure to Five-oh-ninth chow, anyhow."

The captain smiled skeptically.

They headed out the door. "Hold that ride for us to Tan Son Nhut, Specialist."

"It's a bus. He don't wait," the clerk predicted.

"He don't wait, *Sir*," the captain admonished. "Hold the bus." They headed out to lunch.

Winter stopped on the front landing of the BOQ and used the better light to examine the weapon he'd been issued. The slide was loose, and the one magazine with a spring that provided spring action had rust on the case. When he shucked the seven rounds of ammo from the magazine, he could hear the grate of grit, sand, and dirt. He quickly ran a handkerchief over the magazine, banged it, loading aperture down, on a concrete wall; then wiped off each round, and reloaded the weapon. He prayed they would not be attacked.

MPs rotating through meal break milled about the courtyard. They were all young, heavily armed with sidearms and M-16s, some with 12-gauge riot guns, and one carrying an M-60 machine gun. Each Jeep mounted an M-60 on a steel pipe stanchion above the drive shaft housing. The APCs, not just playing at war, were rolling armories.

The MPs wore on their left shoulder the yellow-and-green patch of the 18th Brigade, a Military Police unit that had cut its combat teeth in the Tet Offensive eight months earlier. Many of the MPs wore other patches on their right shoulders, indicating combat service with other organizations. First Air Cav and 82nd Airborne patches were common, but Winter saw a couple from the 9th Infantry Division, one each from the 4th and The Big Red One, and a blue diamond with stars—the Southern Cross—framing a "1" that bespoke service in the First Marine Division.

Boarding the bus after lunch the officers threaded the aisle as a few enlisted men scattered to grab seats near the front. Winter sat next to a window halfway back the length of the bus. There were only about a dozen men on the bus when it pulled out for its run to the airbase north of Sai Gon. Through the frenzied squalor of Cho Lon the bus driver, a PFC wearing threadbare tiger-stripe fatigues, honked and threatened and intimidated his way in a gradual northward push.

At a traffic circle by the fish market on the river, the bus became trapped in a hellish snarl of traffic, deadly smells, and cacophany of noise. Noonday heat exacerbated the incredible stench from the market. Just when the driver thought *he* might throw up, a Jeep loaded with ARVN Marines cut through the crowd behind the bus, scattering bodies, vehicles, and consumer goods in their path, leaving a wake of screeching peasants and merchants and animals, pulled around the bus, and motioned for the driver to follow.

The PFC wrenched the wheel over and tagged onto the Jeep. "Watch out, now," Winter shouted over the din to the captain across the aisle. "ARVN Marines don't give a rat's ass if they run over a few coolies; they're meaner than our own and the people fear them like the plague."

"From Winter, plague, and pestilence, good Lord deliver us," the captain intoned pointedly, glancing slyly at the warrant's name tag. Winter made no response. This captain's just full of humor, he thought, remembering the fatted boo line.

In a few moments they were clear of the jam, heading north on Plantation Road, passing open fields, rolling toward the base. The Marines waved and fired a burst of automatic fire into the sky when they turned off across the fields on a narrow track.

Clearing the press of crowds—the threat implicit in them—was a psychological release. But even removed from the oppression of the fishing docks piled with fish guts and heads, yesterday's fish, rotted bait, and assorted offal in the adjoining alleys, there was little relief from the industrial-strength stench of the city, broiling in one hundred-plus-degrees sun. Densely cluttered with every kind of vehicular traffic, the streets stank of ineffective combustion, diesel engines, and charcoal burners. Only slightly less offensive were otherwise benign odors of waste, dirt, charcoal fires, urine, feces, rotted vegetables, and the incomparable sweet reek of the tropical clime. Despite competition, the fish market retained title as the worst offender.

Everywhere, in the streets of Cho Lon, into the edge of Sai Gon, along the road that ran west of the city, every traffic artery— boulevard, street and alleyway—was clustered with olive drab, green, and blue trucks, jeeps, and staff cars interspersed with the omnipresent blue-and-cream-colored Renault taxis, motorized cyclos and the hand-drawn cyclos. Winter, nose pressed against the grenade screening across the open bus window, saw on the streets fewer cyclos—foot-powered, three-wheeled bicycles used for cheap transportation—than in 1965 when last here. Mesmerized by the bustle, he noted an evident phenomenon, a general upgrading of status. It seemed everyone who had walked in '65 now had at least a Honda motorbike; those who then had ridden a Solex or Vespa now drove a Datsun; those who had a Renault before or a Peugeot were now driving Fords, Pontiacs, and Mercedes. Damn! Ain't progress wonderful! Winter mused. Everybody move up one.

The Navy bus halted at the intersection outside the gate at Tan Son Nhut. As the traffic eddied about the bus, where passengers were trapped and helpless in the flood of vehicles, animals, and people, a green lieutenant near the front of the bus drew his .45 and began nervously fingering the trigger. Everyone around him became nervous in turn, and two NCOs sitting nearby got up and moved toward the back. An occasional local child, walking or cycling by the bus, would pound hollowly on the sides to watch and laugh aloud when the new troops cringed or dove to the floor. Nervous, armed green troops gave real meaning to the term "implicit threat."

"Get outta here, you fuckin' little Vee Cee urchins. *Di di!*" The driver picked an M-16 off the floor next to the gear shift and waved it threateningly at the squealing children in rags.

Jeez-us, thought Winter. The ghost of Tet's not laid yet. Eight months, and we're still jumping through our ass at loud noises. But it was not a condition to be abated by logic, decree, or legislation.

"Hey, Winter! That you, shitbird?" came a shout from outside the bus. Winter looked down into a Jeep infested with GIs in jungle fatigues; legs and arms protruded outboard like oars on a Byzantine galley. A sergeant first class in the right front seat cradled an M-16 over his knees while his eyes swept the tide of bodies pressing close around them.

"That's *Mister* Shitbird," Winter yelled, his eyes taking in the faces turned now toward the bus. It took him a moment to isolate the moon face behind thick, pink-framed GI glasses in the shade of the helmet brim, but there was no doubt about it. "Ashfinian! You wretched asshole. What's this shit?" he pointed to the warrant officer bars on the beaming officer's collar.

"Glass houses, Winter. You, too." Mean-Mutha Ashfinian had left Vietnam two days before Winter was wounded, three and a half years before. Both were staff sergeants then, and shared a hooch.

"Yeah, I know," Winter shouted. The cries of peddlers, constantly racing engines stalled at the junction, cries from kids hawking Pepsi Colas and *Ba-mui-ba* outside the screen of the bus, drowned out Ashfinian's next words and Winter added, "They give these damned things to just about anybody, it seems. Who're you with, M.M.?"

The Jeep had begun to edge forward, separating from the bus, even as Ashfinian urged the Jeep sergeant driver to slow down. The driver, tired of trying to do what he was supposed to do and being berated for it by a sweating clown, finally told Ashfinian to talk or walk, but to leave him alone and let him get on with the business of delivering them from this death trap. The driver was not anxious for a grenade in his lap, and despite threats and entreaties from Mean Mutha, continued to edge the Jeep forward through the wall of coolie flesh. Still, the driver was enlisted; and Ashfinian, though not an authoritarian, raised eyebrows.

He shrugged at Winter and shouted back at the bus: "I'm at Five-oh-nine H.Q. Give me a call." Ashfinian waved over the crowd, and as the Jeep surged away Winter heard, in a loud, W.C. Fields whine, "And like you, Dave, I doubt the wisdom and efficiency of any army that would make me an officer. A-*dee*-o-o-o."

Approaching gate number 2, the bus passed a small French cemetery at the road junction. A sergeant seated behind Winter leaned forward and pointed out where the VC had holed up in the nearby burial ground during Tet, using stone markers for cover while laying down fire on the gatehouse. "Charlie was so firmly entrenched that it took a couple of five-hundred pound bombs from an annoyed Skyraider to settle the issue." The stones had not been righted or replaced.

American Air Policemen and QCs clustered at the gate. One AP boarded the stopped bus. He looked squarely at each passenger as he worked slowly down the aisle. As the Air Force cop approached, he was looking beyond Winter at something farther back in the bus. Winter saw the airman's eyes narrow, watched his hand slip to his hip to rest nervously on the holstered pistol, as he continued edging toward the rear of the bus. Winter turned to look.

On the next-to-last row of seats a short, skinny Oriental in unadorned jungle fatigues sat looking out the side screen. He wore no name tag, no unit insignia, no indications of rank, no "US Army" tape on the fatigues. He stared out the window, ignoring the AP and the silence that fell over the bus. As the cop moved down the aisle, two Air Force officers seated at the rear, got up and edged past him toward the front of the bus.

"You," the guard called out, stopping short in the aisle.

No response.

"You there, Zip. What you do this bus? No belong. . . . Stand up! *Di-di!*" He gave a fluttering motion with his hands, urging the small Oriental from his seat.

The Oriental's face turned toward the AP, his hard, flat stare showing no expression, eyes burning with intensity.

"Dung thang!"

The Oriental sat quietly. The Air Policeman unsnapped his holster and put his hand on the butt of the .38.

"I said, stand up, fella. Everybody—"

"Airman, your Vietnamese pronunciation is truly fucking terrible," the small Oriental man said. "But I mean, numbah ten-thou. Christ!" The nondescript passenger turned his gaze away, promptly ignoring the guard, whose jaw dropped.

"Yo," the cop managed, "who're you? Let's see some I. D.," he said more firmly.

"'Yo, shit, man. That's 'Yo, *Sir.*' My name is Ito. Chief Warrant Officer-Two Ulysses Simpson Ito. United States, *et cetera.*" He handed the confused airman a green identification card. "Hey," he waved his hand in a dismissive signal. "No hassle, man; all my gear was ripped off at Bien Hoa yesterday, incoming. I borrowed these threads at transient billets in Long Binh."

"You reporting in-country?"

"You mean, Airman, 'Are you just reporting in country, *Sir!*'" Ito snapped. That second reminder to this AP was the third time within an hour that Winter had witnessed an officer chastising an enlisted being for improper military respect—the proprieties. Country's going to the dogs, he thought.

"Uh, yessir. I mean . . . that's okay . . . sir." He handed the green card back to the officer, reluctantly offered a shabby salute, and retreated from the bus.

Outside, an ARVN corporal continued circling the bus, using his long-handled mirror to view the underside of the vehicle. There was an awkward silence. No one looked at Ito.

"Still checking for booby traps and smuggled bombs?" Winter, his eyes following the ARVN corporal, said to the sergeant behind him. He had presumed earlier that the NCO was not just a new kid on the block, and Winter sought information where he could find it.

"Shee-it, sir. They pulled two *Cong* out from under an ARVN deuce-'n-a-half just last week. Cats were carrying enough plastique to do 7th Air Force Headquarters. Yeah, they still check. You here before?"

"Sixty-four, -five. Here at Ton San Nhut, with the old Third R.R.U. It's all changed, though. Except the check point."

"I don't know the Third," the sergeant said. "I been here five months. Thirty-ninth Signal."

The captain across the aisle spoke up: "The Third became the Five-Oh-Ninth Group in build-up a few years back. The Chief's old Air Section has now become a full aviation battalion, the Two-twenty-fourth."

Winter smiled at the captain. "We're gonna build a decent table of organization in this war yet. And how come you suddenly know so much about the Five-oh-ninth? For a new guy."

"Didn't say I was new. Been in country a while, but I'm usually on T.D.Y."

The bus was cleared and drove on through the steel and concrete baffle. Winter pointed to the gate guard in camouflaged fatigues and said, "Look at that shit. Guards on the gate in no-see-me suits, and they never leave the perimeter. Back in sixty-five, the goddamned Air Force A.P.s were the first ones to get jungle fatigues and jungle boots. All the grunts and guys in the field were still sweating it out in standard issue fatigues—long sleeves, starch, and all. And the leather boots rotted faster than they could be shipped in."

The captain knew that tune, and responded. "Air Force contract says they can't be assigned anywhere over fifty yards from a flush toilet."

The soldiers laughed at the old saw. The airmen on the bus, officers and men, grinned uneasily.

"Gospel!" the captain insisted, and from him it did not sound like a joke.

Winter laughed easily. The captain asked, "How long you been here . . . this time?"

"Let's just say I've got three sixty-four and a wakeup."

"Ouch! The Prodigal does return, but is presently in hurt mode."

"Well, have to start somewhere. I have little ambition." Winter made a vague gesture back toward the billet in Cho Lon. "I'll be moving out to Tan Son Nhut as soon as I report in."

"Good luck," the captain said with scepticism.

Winter looked the question. Then said, "So you been here awhile?"

"Eight months. I was with the One-fifty-sixth in Can Tho. Got shipped up here to Group to fill in for a major that got med-evac-ed. Been in that Cho Lon B.O.Q. for three weeks now. No space out in the B.O.Q.s around Tan Son Nhut. I'm John Swift," he announced, ending an odd two-day interlude of anonymity. He held out his hand.

"Dave Winter. Nice to know you. Ever serve with A.S.A. before?" he asked, glancing at the aviator wings on the captain's blouse.

"Yeah, in sixty-six, sixty-seven. With the One-thirty-eighth in Danang. You regular A.S.A?"

Winter hesitated. He said grudgingly, seeing the wary look on the captain's face, "Uh-huh, Operations. Coming from Germany. Bad Aibling. You got some problem with A.S.A?" Winter asked.

"Not especially. I just prefer the real Army."

"Takes all kinds. But A.S.A. keeps grabbing you up, sending you to exotic places, right?"

"Yeah. Army's a bitch."

* * *

Davis Station had not changed much. The old gate into the compound by the mail room and enlisted-NCO club was closed with barbed wire, traffic baffles, and a sand-bagged machine gun position. A new entrance opened from the road directly into the motor pool where all vehicles parked; no vehicles were allowed into the billets and Orderly Room area. Winter recognized the logic of that—no one wanted a mobile bomb parked next to his hooch.

The road that boxed a rectangle around the tropical huts within Davis Station was still unsurfaced, though a layer of used motor oil had been applied to suppress dust. An additional hooch had been constructed in what used to be a cleared concreted area next to the club, so there was no more volley ball. The tennis court was still there, but inaccessible due to a littering of metal shipping containers, Conexes, and cargo pallets, some stacked atop other bare ones, others holding unidentified materials—all without pattern or discernible order but wherever forklifts had dropped them. The tennis court nets were gone; the chain link fence around the courts was sagging, the green-painted concrete pitted from incoming. Winter could only remember the tennis court enclosure as the area where local nationals—Vietnamese housegirls, cooks, mechanics, and others—had been held without outside contact during military scrip exchange periods. He looked across the road to the ARVN Ranger training camp, expanded with new buildings, a new obstacle course, and exercise field. Progress everywhere.

Winter reported in, turned over his records, and assumed the standard Army pose of waiting. After twenty minutes, during which he saw the clerk with his records on the phone, looking across at him in that particularly blank manner that indicated Winter was the subject of a close-held conversation. Winter was beckoned back to the desk, handed his records, and invited to get a Jeep and driver from the motor pool and report to the 509th Group Headquarters on the Joint Command Compound.

He rode leisurely back across Tan Son Nhut, past the new 7th Air Force Headquarters, past the truck park and antenna field of the 39th Signal Battalion, then back out gate number 2 where they joined the traffic snarl in front of the nearby compound. A line of vehicles inched its way through the gate, each one halted at the entrance to allow the team of QCs and MPs to check ID cards and bomb-check beneath the vehicle and under the hood.

Passed through, Winter was driven along dimly familiar streets, much the same as in 'sixty-five: bare dirt compounds; scraggly, vaguely Asian trees; improbable flowers in unlikely settings. They passed the stump of a tree where a Huey, one unfortunate evening in 1964, had fallen from the sky and was speared through the open ports by the tree trunk. The engineers had used chain saws to recover the unusable remains. SABERTOOTH, the Vietnamese Operations center, looked even dingier, otherwise the same. And then, the 3rd RRU . . . or where the 3rd had been.

The driver, a silent PFC who smelled strongly of witch hazel and whorehouse perfume, pulled the Jeep into a "No Parking" zone and sat behind the wheel, looking nowhere. A maze of buildings crowded in where the single old, chipped and stained structure housing WHITE BIRCH had stood, a place that had served as the Operations site of the 3rd. Only the narrow end of the old building was viewable, peeking from the newer, higher, wider, cleaner structure that formed the present headquarters. When Winter exited the Jeep, the driver, without a word, backed out quickly, and roared off in the direction they had come.

Passing through the nearest entranceway, Winter found himself in the S-2 shop. A Security clerk looked up, told him firmly he was not to use that door except in emergency. Following a pathway through a hedgerow of desks, Winter joined a group of officers and senior noncommissioned officers being processed for in-country assignment; and the bored but efficient manner of the processing told him something about the Sai Gon attitude toward the war.

A young captain glanced perfunctorily at Winter's 201 File and reached for a folder. "Hmm, let's see. Got a slot for an Oh-five-one in Bien Hoa. Another in Phu Bai. Any preference?" he asked, as if Winter would be granted any say.

"Captain, my orders indicate assignment to the Two-twenty-fourth. Eventually, to one of the aviation companies." Winter's voluntary statement was his only chance at destiny control.

"Hmmm? Oh, yeah. Got that in your orders, sure as shit. Lemme see . . . uhhh, just says Five-oh-ninth—"

"There. Paragraph six," Winter pointed.

"Uhhh, okay. You know somebody there or something? Why d'ya want to go to that specific outfit?" The captain didn't appear very disturbed by Winter's specificity. "You been here before, I take it."

"Sort of. Matter of fact, I do know someone, several, in the Two-twenty-fourth. I'm experienced in aviation, passed my flight physical, and was selected on the basis of my fit for a particular slot. Maybe that has something to do with it," he said, his tone barely short of snotty.

"Yeah, well, it might. If Colonel Sizelove wants it to. Makes a shit to me, Chief.

Here . . ." he was thumbing through a separate folder. "Oh! Yeah! Matter of fact, we got your name here on a hold list for the Two-twenty-fourth. Better?" he grinned up at Winter.

"Better."

"Maybe. There's an S-2 flag on the assignment. What's that all about?"

"Does S-2 talk to me?" What *was* that all about? "Hell, I don't know, Captain."

"Better go see the security people. Hmmm, you haven't processed through there yet, anyhow. Ask 'em." Winter was dismissed, as if seated at a table not of the personnel captain's serving, knowing he would surely return anyhow. It was the only cafe in town.

The clerk made him wait while the S-2 finished debrief of a pilot caught cohabiting with a suspected Viet Cong agent-slash-bargirl, losing his clearance. The pilot, a young first lieutenant came out the door with ashen features, his eyes fixed on the long, empty corridor ahead of him. The clerk openly commented to the S-2 captain, "That won't change anything, sir. He'll be back shacked up with her within the hour."

"Yeah," the captain agreed. "But now he can only whisper sweet nothings into her commie ear about sweet nothing. He's going to the Thirty-Fourth, flying ash and trash. Let her get vital information from that. The QC are watching her anyhow, and if the goddamned lieutenant hadn't been so stupid about the whole thing, we could've worked something out." He glanced at Winter significantly.

"Mister Winter," he said, flipping through the record jacket the clerk passed to him. "Come in, my man." He indicated his office with a nod of his head. "Interesting situation with you. You've heard, I gather."

"I've heard nothing."

Inside, Winter sat across from the captain who flipped slowly through the file. "Chief, I'm sending you to the Two-twenty-fourth Aviation Battalion, further assigned to the office of the S-3, Plans and Operations. They have notions about how they're going to use you."

"Will I be flying?"

"No flying. Got a flag on your file. You were on a project in Europe, let's see . . . uhhh, BASTION GREY. Sound familiar?" The captain looked up at Winter across the file, squinting.

"Yeah. A thing I worked before the Czech invasion. But that's been months."

"Still a security clamp on the project. And anyone with access to it. You can't be allowed to fly over enemy territory, where—in the ridiculously improbable circumstance of hostile fire or platform malfunction—you might be thrown into unwanted contact with our adversaries." He made the pedantic recall of directives sound plausible. "And since all of Viet Nam, south *and* north, is enemy territory, at least hostile territory, that means *no* flying." It seemed clear to the captain; he didn't care for flying. "Problem with that?"

"I thought I'd go back on flight status: I've got experience . . ." and Winter launched into a litany of rationales. "And I can use the flight pay."

"Couldn't we all. Beside the point. No can do. The Two-twenty-fourth can't be too bad, though. Billeted at the Newport. Chow at the Thirty-Fourth Open Mess, or any one of the others in the area. Close to Tan Son Nhut, which cuts down on your travel, ergo, cuts down on your assassination index. Anyhow, that's it. Out of my hands." He tossed the file aside, closing the matter, then abruptly changed the subject. "You know Billy Bartok in Frankfurt?"

Winter, distracted by cascading perturbations, shook his head. He'd heard of the officer but had never met him. "What's my next processing point?"

"Personnel Officer, but he's up-country today and tomorrow. Come back, see him anytime. Go ahead, check with the S-4 and get on the billet list. They'll push you on." He stood, shook hands, and said, "Sorry as it is, it's home. Welcome back."

chapter thirteen

Crossroads

Vietnam: September 1968

A rumpled CW2 named Thurgood informed Winter, "Hell, Chief. Who you kiddin'? There ain't no quarters available at the Newport B.O.Q. Or B.O.Q. One." His smile was cruel. "Stay in Cho Lon, catch the bus out to Five-oh-nine."

Winter groaned, thinking of the harrowing, time-consuming ride to be faced daily.

"Nope, no idea when somethin'll open up. Billetin's a bitch. And besides, they's lots-a names 'head of yours on the list." The billeting officer couldn't understand why nobody wanted to live in Cho Lon. "Hell, I love Cho Lon. Pussy's cheaper, the bars ain't crowded, get hit less by the V.C. I wish they'd let me stay down there and—"

Winter tuned him out and left the billeting office with a feeling of despair. Better and better. First, no flying. Now this . . .

After processing, Winter caught a ride back to Tan Son Nhut and walked from Davis Station down the flight line to 224th headquarters, former headquarters of the 3d RRU when it was the entire Army Security Agency in-country. Now, ASA's covert presence was the 509th Radio Research Group. Det-J in Phu Bai was now the 8th RR Field Station; the Air Section of the 3rd had morphed into the 224th Aviation Battalion, and the five scattered flight elements had become Aviation Companies. A two-hundred-man headcount in 1964 had grown to some six thousand in 1968. There was opportunity for everyone. But he couldn't fly.

He reported to the Admin Officer of the 224th, was welcomed, introduced around the headquarters, and taken in to meet his boss, the S-3, Lieutenant Colonel Marshall Northcutt. The stylish name plate on the door alerted Winter to expect the very essence of Prussianized military elegance. Colonel Northcutt turned out to be a pipe smoking, grey-haired, fatherly gentleman who seemed sincerely pleased to have Winter, and welcomed him into his family with deference.

"You're the first officer we've had assigned within the Two-two-four headquarters who's career A.S.A.. You can teach us a lot, I'm sure. We need it." He bumbled on in a folksy manner. "We're basically a bunch of airplane drivers, and most of us have never been around the Agency before. Half the time, we just take directions from the back seat—the operators—and pilots don't know why they're doing what they're being told to do. I'm sure," and his eyes twinkled as he puffed quickly on the briar, "I'm *fairly* sure, Mister Winter, you can imagine the potential in that situation for, shall we say, less-than-optimum performance." The colonel widened his eyes dramatically, as if he'd surprised himself with introspection.

Winter surprised *him*self by readily agreeing. He remembered Third Air and the problems they'd had when he took over the mission. He hadn't thought of it, but had he done so, he would have felt assured all those things would have been worked out. After all, *we learn from our mistakes!*

There was a knock on the door. The colonel called, "In!"

A CW3 in flight suit ambled into the room. He saluted the S-3 with a typical aviator gesture, which The Mad Cajun used to say was as if a bird had flown up your tailpipe, was blown out fluttering to the ground, singed and defeated. The newcomer said, "You wanted me, Colonel?"

"Boyd Smiley. David Winter."

Winter felt cheated with so little time alone with the colonel. He had not had a chance to bring up the question of flight status. The S-3 could not change his status, not so long as the S-2 forbade it, but he'd wanted to register his druthers in any case—a thing the Army could not have cared less about. It did not seem the time to do that. And the colonel surprised him again.

"Dave—Is it Dave, or David?"

"Either, sir."

"O.K., Mister Either, I had a brain storm when we learned of your assignment here. Boyd and I've talked about it, and thought it could work, depending upon the A.S.A. officer we got. Your background and record give me confidence. Here's the drill: the Two-twenty-fourth has five operations companies, in addition to us, the headquarters. They're scattered all over the four corps. They're far enough apart, hung out on the end of the communications chain, their flight environments different enough, that we are really running five different kinds of operations. We have no standards, either in flying or in the intel work." Winter listened as the colonel unearthed long-standing problems.

"Boyd's an I.P.—instructor pilot, as you know—and you're thoroughly versed, I presume, in spook things," he allowed a tight flash of grin, *"plus,* the big factor, your being A.R.D.F. experienced. I'm putting you and Boyd together as my Operations and Flight Standardization Team. Except for maybe the First R.R., where they have a different mission, you two will T.D.Y. to the other four companies, fly with the crews, and pick out the best from each— the best operational procedures, best flight rules, the optimum in security, communications, even emergency procedures. Escape and evasion. Anything that will better our performance. We'll put it all together and make it battalion doctrine." He sat back in his chair, his head swathed in dense clouds of pipe smoke. "What do you think?"

Winter thought it was—chancy. Every unit adopted the best procedures for their target regions. How could you standardize something as disparate as the flat marshes and rice paddies of Four Corps and the towering peaks in Eye Corps? He glanced at Smiley. The pilot said nothing, but his eyes were dancing. A short man, he looked fit but lean. His flight suit hung about him like green skin on a man who had lost half his body weight.

"Sounds reasonable, sir . . . I, uhh . . . maybe you don't know about me not being able to fly, though." Winter did not know what it would mean, shooting down the colonel's plan.

"Forget that," the colonel said, waving a dismissive hand.. "We've informed H.Q., Five-oh-nine, that you'll fly only in administrative and instructional capacity, minimal risk of hostile overflights. Course that's B.S., but it's the kind of B.S. they like: gets them off the hook, puts the bear on us . . . to thus mix my metaphors. We must just keep you out of unfriendly hands, must we not? If you're shot out of the sky, Smiley," he said, turning to the pilot, "you'll have to take time out of your Mayday routine to perform an excision on Mister Winter." His face, a study in colonel look, indicated only slight amusement.

Discussion of general tactics, the philosophy they would work to, and plans to immediately implement the scheme took the rest of the day. A sergeant was summoned, someone the colonel said was ". . . an old hand at the A.R.D.F. game" who would be allocated to The Team, as required. When Staff Sergeant Jack Albrecht reported to the colonel's office, the S-3 appeared to take personal pleasure in reuniting old friends. He'd learned Albrecht and Winter were acquainted upon first receiving notice of Winter's pending arrival and background, and subsequently hatched the standardization scheme. Winter recognized the crossroads phenomenon relegated to this one-year tour. At some time in Vietnam, you'd meet everyone you ever knew in ASA.

Jack Albrecht had been an operator at WHITE BIRCH in '64, and after the required six months on the job, extended his tour and requested transfer to the Air Section on the same day Winter had been promoted to Staff Sergeant as NCOIC of the section. When Winter was wounded and medevac-ed out six months later, Albrecht was well on his way to becoming one of the best airborne ops in country. Now, more than three years later, he was still in country. A Spec-4 when Winter first knew him, Albrecht now wore Staff Sergeant stripes. The confluence of the careers of the three men comprising the team augured well for success.

Dismissed and leaving the S-3 shop, Winter said, "Jack, let's get a *Ba-mui-ba* and catch up." He glanced briefly at the colonel, acknowledging the presence of Regular Army; but the colonel didn't seem to feel his army threatened by the NCO and warrant officer's socializing.

Colonel Northcutt said cryptically, "Watch out for Dragon Lady."

Winter looked quizzically at each one in turn.

"C'mon Dave—Mister Winter. I'll fill you in." Albrecht motioned him out the door.

In the Jeep, taking the unusual route out the civilian entranceway to the airport, cutting back over toward Kong Ly, and thus back to the Tan Son Nhut gate, Albrecht, driving, related the saga of the latest *cause célèbre* in the Capital Military District—Dragon Lady. "Not a figment, for sure, she's right out of 'Terry and the Pirates'."

Winter let his ignorance hang there, without comment.

"Been going on for more'n a month now. Zip chick in a black *aow-dai*, putting the come-hither on G.I.s, then blowing them away. Right on the street. She works the downtown Tu Do-Tran Hung Dao area. And once that we know of in Cho Lon. Uses a forty-five, probably taken off her first victim. The only survivor of her attacks, a pill pusher from the Air Force Dispensary, said she's a looker. Got more tits than a Zip's authorized, more gun than she ought to be able to handle. But she's killed three, confirmed; wounded one; and there's a couple more possibles. But then," he added hesitantly, "those might be results of black market or drug deals gone sour. They were back street. Most of Dragon Lady's work is down-town. Right in front of God and everybody."

Albrecht maneuvered the vehicle through a knot of Vietnamese and Americans at Gate Number 2, zig-zagging his way through the roadblock baffles of concrete and wire. He ignored the Air Policeman's desperate hand signals, and shot forward down the road past the satellite communications site, 39th Signal Battalion.

"How do they know so much about her and can't stop her?" Winter said. "How often does she hit?"

"Well, four-to-six times over the past month or so. Maybe some before that, but no connection for sure. Maybe once a week or so," He said solemnly. "You're better off gettin' laid with girls out of the bars and known houses. Stay away from the freelancers on the street. Naturally," he added graciously, "you won't be interested in that sort of hanky panky anyhow. But for the single guys and Don't-Give-a-Shits, it's a risk. Far riskier than incipient V.D."

"You're still single," Winter observed, looking at Albrecht's empty ring finger. "How's it your butt's still intact? I remember you working your way through every bar and whorehouse in Sai Gon."

"*And* Cho Lon. Days gone by, my friend. Days long gone by. I live a quiet existence: . just me and my mission birds . . . and Thuy Co, and the children." He kept his eyes on the road.

Several moments of suspended silence went by. *Children?* "Thuy Co? That same bargirl you hung out with when I left here in sixty-five?"

"I don't refer to her as a bargirl, Dave. She's a wife in everything but the eyes of MAC-Vee. Got two kids, too. That a bad thing, you think?" His voice said it mattered.

"Shit, don't ask me. Not my call. I can't keep my own life straight. I'm sure'n hell not taking on anyone else's." He sought some plateau they both would be comfortable with. "She's a beautiful girl, as I remember."

"Not so beautiful as she once was. Another reason she don't work the bars anymore." Albrecht kept his eyes fixed on the mad, ever-changing pattern of traffic about them.

"What do you mean?"

Deep, reluctant sigh. "Had a . . . an *incident* a couple years ago. A cousin of hers from down in the provinces, part-time VC, found out she was shackin' with a G.I. Guess he thought he'd restore the family honor or something. He came to the bar one night, had a couple of his buddies with him. Heroes of the fuckin' revolution. Assholes ran everyone out but Thuy, they thought—" Albrecht swerved the

Jeep violently to the left to avoid a sailor in dungarees, sprawled into the edge of the road, barely visible in the weak headlights. Winter watched his hard face in the glow from lights of a passing vehicle.

"I was out back at the troughs," Albrecht continued in measured tones.. "When I came back in the bar, I heard shouting. I didn't know what it was all about, but these fuckers had Cong written all over 'em. They were not chic, you dig? Country boys. And mean. One of them looked about fourteen, but the pistol he had in his belt was big enough. I hunkered down, come in at the end of the bar, and grabbed Mama-San's shotgun from under there. Took out the biggest one—turned out to be the cousin—and hit the kid I could see had a pistol. The third one grabbed him and dragged him out the door. On the way, the second one I shot flipped a Chicom grenade back into the bar. I hit the deck. Thuy was already down under a table, but the blast tore loose some floor boarding. She caught a jagged piece of plywood across her face." They were entering the Davis Station motor pool as he drew to a close.

Silence.

"Well, is she all right?"

"All right? . . . A relative term, my friend. She's still Thuy. Sweet as ever. Good mother, great lover, dutiful daughter to her mother." There was silence as he pulled into a parking space, killed the motor, and added quietly. "But she's not a real beauty anymore."

* * *

The morning runs from the Replacement Company in Cho Lon to headquarters on Tan Son Nhut were redundant, whether on the bus with its minimal protection, or in an open Jeep or semi-closed cab of a six-by or three-quarter-ton truck, vehicles without even grenade screening. Nothing new to see or learn; always the ubiquitous threat hanging. Forever the crowds of suspicious figures carrying nondescript bundles which might contain salad greens or C-4 explosive. No less threatening than other factors was the incredible stench at the fish market.

For a while, several officers of the 224th and the 509th headquarters shared a Jeep. This polyglot group chose a different route every day, through the city and out to Tan Son Nhut along Tran Hung Dao, or Plantation Road, or even round-about through Gia Dinh. It was a conscious risk, the longer route, but the air, never a rose garden in Sai Gon-Cho Lon, was immeasurably sweeter. Traffic was less. And it made for change.

After two weeks clustered in a closed room without air conditioning—the only classified space available to them in 224th headquarters—Winter and Smiley had devised a basic questionnaire and operations technical guide for use in their project assessment. "O.K.," Winter said, closing the folder with their hard-delivery baby inside, "Let's take this mother on the road, see how it plays in Kankakee."

In mid-October, they took a non-mission U-8 aircraft and Smiley flew them to Can Tho in the Delta. Can Tho, home of the 156th US Army Radio Research Company (Aviation) was one of four companies assigned to the 224th Aviation Battalion, all performing the same airborne direction-finding mission in the four Corps Tactical Zones.

En route, Winter rode right seat with Smiley. Clear of Tan Son Nhut control, he switched to intercom and said, "Been here; done this."

"Roger that." Then, in an aural double take, Smiley said, "What? Done what?"

"Riding right seat. Mostly in-bound from missions, back in the Third. You remember, whether you were with the R.R. or not. In the early days we were short of pilots; there *was* no co-pilot, no back-up. Mission birds carried one pilot; one operator. After a few weeks flying, I originated a notion of, helped establish the policy for, non-pilot operators to sit right seat on the way to and from target areas. We got whatever instruction there was time for on flight procedures, communications, emergency actions—whatever might increase our chances of survival in an already unbalanced equation."

"Ever do you any good? Any of your people?"

"Don't know. Didn't help me in my great gettin' up morning. 'course I wasn't flying when I made a hash of my TDY to the black mountain, near the end of my first tour, March 'sixty-five. But by then, I was confident that if the pilot I was flying with on a mission was hit by ground fire, or took sick or, as happened to one of our pilots in Da Nang, suffered a heart attack, I could at least point the airplane back in the direction of the home field. Or some alternate paddy or pasture. Squawk a Mayday, alert Air-Sea Rescue, and get the thing down."

"Well, for sure, you could almost *always* be assured of getting it down. It's what airplanes have a tendency to do when they lack proper piloting or sufficient power," Smiley said.

"But I even thought I might do it and walk away from it. As Stoetzel, one of our pilots used to emphasize, during the many mission hours we spent together, 'Any landing you can walk away from is a good one. It might look like a controlled crash, might *be* a controlled crash, but if you can write it up, it was a good one.'"

Boyd Smiley was a good if careful pilot. That came from being an IP, Winter knew. Or vice-versa. Smiley made nice smooth turns, lined up on final with plenty of distance for corrections—did all the things the book said do. That made him an aberration in the world of Army flying.

Most Army pilots Winter knew were heavy handed, "highway flyers," pilots who had come to flying from careers as mechanics and chemical services sergeants, dental technicians, infantry riflemen. Most never mastered the intricacies of navigation or instrument flying, and if there was no highway, railroad track, or stream of water bigger than a *benjo* ditch to follow, they might not be able to get the aircraft back from whence it came. Or to other places it sought to go.

But they were gutsy airplane drivers who would take the ship where it had to go to do its job, whether transporting generals and visiting firemen in and out of secured flight facilities, hauling ammo to a besieged garrison of ARVN in the mountains of Two Corps, recovering bodies and wounded from hot LZs, or any one of a thousand other varied tasks they were asked to perform—fixed wing and rotary. They drove the aircraft past specs on mission, and they kept it on the flight line during needy periods way past required maintenance downtime. Winter knew they didn't necessarily abuse the craft, but they sure as hell used them to exhaustion.

Winter already knew some of Boyd Smiley's history. The CW3 was on his third flying tour in 'Nam. He'd trained with the now defunct 11th Air Assault in Georgia and rotated in-country with the Air Cav in late 1965. One tour flying gunships, then back by request to fly Dustoff, and afterward to Fort Rucker where he learned to speak navigation and was IP trained. On his current tour, he had arrived in Vietnam two weeks before Winter, the fifth tour for the pair of them.

Delta: the epitome of flat. *The Delta* in Viet Nam was no exception. Approaching Can Tho, capital of IV CTZ in the delta, it seemed to Winter they could see the river and the city forever before they got in range to radio the tower. As he'd remembered, it looked beautiful from the air. Up here, everything smelled fresh: no flies, no scorpions, no dung underfoot, no smell of urine in the air strong enough to blister paint.

Winter had been in Can Tho only once before, in the days before Radio Research had a company there but would sometimes set a bird down for refuel during a long, round-about mission from Tan Son Nhut. He remembered nothing about it except the river. Now he relinquished the yoke to Smiley who made all the right moves and put them on the ground with minimum risk and discomfort. As they taxied into a space alongside two Caribou cargo planes backed up to a canal on the edge of the parking ramp, Smiley swung the little plane around on its tricycle landing gear, yanked the flaps once up and down, and chopped the power.

"There we have it," the pilot said decisively. "Averted death and destruction again." He looked over at Winter and said with a straight face, "I fly good. I land for shit. Usually, I tear us to pieces by this time." At this he swung the door upward, grabbed his log and flight bag and, climbing out onto the wing, deplaned.

Smiley knew his way around Can Tho; Winter thought it well he did. They were not met at the plane, and were forced to walk from the ramp to the 156th along the runway, carrying their bags. In the Orderly Room, they learned that they were not expected until the following day. The commander, Major Johns, was flying a mission; the XO was on R&R in Australia; and the First Sergeant was on bed rest in his quarters, accommodating the recuperative effects of bicillin as treatment for an elusive but recurrent Asian malady. The only officer available was a Chief Warrant Officer-Four Millar, the Maintenance Officer. The clerk told them he could be found in his office in the nearest hangar.

They found him there. Asleep. They left him as he was, and considered themselves welcomed to Four Corps.

The next morning, following a surreal evening of steady illumination flares and starshells blazing in the night sky, but never hearing a shot fired or a round impacting, Mister Smiley flew co-pilot with the CO on one mission bird. Mister Winter flew right seat in place of a co-pilot with Lieutenant Petersen and an operator named Sachs on another aircraft

Winter's pilot, Petersen, was new in country, still coming up to speed with the mission. The op, SP5 Sachs with more than a year on the job, seemed good at his work, but he operated by no known set of standards, not unexpected since there *were* no standards. It was what the team, hopefully, was there to fix.

Winter kept off the intercom as much as possible during the mission, listening, asking questions only when necessary, and only then between target fixes. When the pilot-operator team was engaged in performing their mission—a procedure which came up only five times during the four-hour flight and lasted ten-to-fifteen minutes each—Winter kept his mouth shut, watching, listening.

Sachs had talked to him before lift-off and told him things he already knew. The Delta was a challenge to navigate, with water everywhere, changing with the seasons. Most maps, even if they had been updated from the original French survey maps, showed the waterways as they existed in some sterile, static past, never relevant to the mercurial state they demonstrated in any given season. The streams, as perverse as people, overflowed their banks, re-routed themselves, and in general went wherever erratic climactic and geophysical conditions directed them.

"The pilot, after shooting an azimuth on a target communications transmitter, rolls the bird onto the port wingtip," Sachs continued his prolix lesson, not knowing the warrant officer had pioneered many of these procedures. Winter didn't embarrass him. "Pilot eyeballs the ground, attempts to locate the plane on the ground's relative surface at the point from which the bearing is taken."

Winter knew it was a dartboard method at best, often impossible to tell where ground base was under the aircraft. Every piece of the earth looked like every other piece. One stream looked pretty much like another, and their numbers were infinite. One shabby village resembled every other ratty village. As Brenner had paraphrased Leo Nikolaevich four years before, "Blown bridges are all alike; every intact bridge is intact in its own way." Winter never mentioned his familiarity with the original of that quote before Brenner applied it..

Winter watched the pilot spotting grease pencil marks in a cute design on the map's plastic overlay, but could see no reality in his efforts. The fact that they formed a pattern at all could be attributed to the pilot's designs in flying a circle about the targeted area, providing cross-bearings.

On the way back in from the mission area, while the lieutenant struggled to keep them aloft, Winter asked the operator about the ground refs.

"Any good? I hope to shit in your mess kit, Mister Winter. Of course our ground plots are good. Why, the lieutenant's a real old hand at navigating, and we've got all this fine new state-of-the-art equipment and all. I don't see how you can ask that question." The engine roared uncertainly for a moment, pitching the craft wildly to starboard while yawing to port, but the pilot righted it as Sachs rolled his eyes.

"Sir, we haven't the goddamnedest notion where we are ninety percent of the time. It's not the pilot's fault; he just isn't good enough. The maps aren't good enough. The country eats it. What can I tell you?" He began stuffing his maps in the mission bag.

"Don't you have inertial nav gear on this bird?"

"For what it's worth. But the Army got a handjob," he said firmly. "We run up engines for takeoff, zero the dials before we turn onto the active, and during the flight, as we turn and roll and bank and pitch and yaw, the machine's supposed to go through all those perturbations with us, moving the dials east for every bit of eastward movement, south for southward, *et cetera*."

Winter impatiently nodded his head; he understood the logic of inertial navigation.

"The theory is that wherever we are when we take a shot, we record the dial readings—"

"But you didn't do that. You grease-penciled visual landmarks on the map, just as we did four years ago."

"No shit, Sam Spade . . . sir. Sorry. We do what works, Chief. As poor as that is. Theory with I..N. is that those dial readings can later be readily translated into geographical coordinates. If we return to the same place we took off from, the dials should, in theory, zero out; when we land, should be nothing but zeroes. Fuck me! We take off from Can Tho, fly this mother for half an hour, go back and land in Can Tho, and the readings tell me I'm in fucking Des Moines. The longer we fly, the better chance we have of getting to something resembling real geographic location. But that's only because a billion errors tend to average out."

They were in sight of the field now and the lieutenant was busy on the radio. Winter remained twisted around in the seat, listening through the intercom.

"Whatever it requires to fix this mother ain't happening," Sachs continued.. "We *think* the problem's because of the flat turns we make taking shots. The system's not stressed for that kind of G-forces. But the bottom line is, we still have to use eyeball and grease pencil. And that's for shit in the Delta."

* * *

There was no one in the 156th that Winter knew from other tours. The three days he and Smiley spent in Can Tho were long days of work, rack out after a few beers with whomever was around the BOQ hooch, get up, eat a greasy breakfast, and go fly. Can Tho, located in the center of the delta of the Mekong's many tributaries, had easily the most debilitating climate of the four company areas they would visit. Humidity beyond concept. The Standardization Team was not unhappy when they went wheels-up and flew away from the 156th's Area of Operations.

* * *

In Sai Gon, Dragon Lady made the AFRN news again, killing an Army sergeant inside the front door of the Catholic cathedral on John F. Kennedy Plaza. How she could have lured her victim in, presenting herself as a prostitute on the very steps of a cathedral, made even atheists angry. Elusive again—still—she was yet to be identified or apprehended.

chapter fourteen

Dragon Lady

Vietnam: October 1968

Two weeks later, with three of the four aviation companies surveyed and only minimal ground fire encountered thus far, Smiley set the bird down late on a Friday evening at Da Nang, the largest airfield in South Viet Nam's north. They taxied past rows of Marine helicopters: fat, sluggish CH-46s, older UH-1s, lean, shark-like Cobras. Long angular echelons of fierce Phantom F4 fighter-bombers that belonged to both Marines and Air Force sat adjacent. Other revetments harbored C-123s, C-130s, Caribou/C-7s, A1Es, F5s, F-101 Voodoos, F-105 Thunderchiefs—anything that would fly and carry hurt or haul *Dreck*. Two C-9 Nightingales for medical evacuation languished unattended in a large open taxiway; Hueys and Sea Knights for rescue and Dustoff operations, "Loaches"— LOHs—for Command & Control and recon; OV-10 Broncos, O-2s, and ancient, tiny single-engine "Grasshopper" L-19 artillery spotter aircraft . . . all were scattered as if spilled from a careless child's toy box.

Across the field, Winter saw civilian aircraft, charter planes hauling troops into country, hauling reduced phalanxes of leftovers away from the conflict. And away off on the distant edge of the field, in a segmented and bermed-ramp area, two small U-8s of the 138th Aviation Co. (RR) squatted delicately, like tiny, ankle-biting canines that aspired to the regard given their attack dog cousins. Winter knew the rest of the company's aircraft were deployed to, and worked out of, Phu Bai. These two were likely down for maintenance, or used as training or admin aircraft.

Following all the exigencies of landing on someone else's patch, arranging re-fuel, securing a tie-down site, dropping their gear in the BOQ, and finding their way to the general mess, the two warrants went for a late meal at the 138th messhall. Barely in the door, Winter spotted a familiar face. "John. John Glencannon," he called over the buzz.

"No shit! Winter Man." The Master Sergeant heading for a table, turned, made his way across the messhall and tossed his tray on a table where four men sat playing cards. "Heard about you making warrant," the NCO said. "Congratulations," he added, shaking hands with vigorous pumping motions. If the two men, longtime comrades-in-arms, were surprised at such a circumstantial encounter across the endless miles and months and events of military service, they did not speak of it. Among those serving over time, Viet Nam, with its one-year tour of duty, had become the great crossroads of the world. A soldier was more apt to encounter past acquaintances there than in all other unlikely places combined.

Glencannon was a short, broad Irish-American with glacial blue eyes and a florid complexion comprising myriad broken blood vessels acquired from Irish forebears' national pastime. The chevrons on his sleeves—three up, three down—covered the length of the fatigue jacket sleeve from his shoulder to the bend of his short arm, disappearing under the jungle fatigue jacket's rolled cuff. The army had converted its rank symbols to a non-glare metal insignia worn on the collar points of fatigues, making obsolete the in-your-face dominion of yellow cloth chevrons, but Glencannon was slow in letting go of institutions.

"Hey, Top," one of the card players whined, "can't you see we're using this table."

"*Hey?* Hey, yourself, asshole. Go outside and check the sign. It says 'Messhall,' nothing about a fucking casino. You wanta eat, I'll move my shit. Otherwise, bag it." He turned back to Winter, dismissing the truculent complaint. Then he looked back and added, "And just a note to the wary . . . not advisable to yell 'hey' at senior NCOs, turd."

"Irish John Glencannon, want you to meet Boyd Smiley. Boyd, my erstwhile aviator avatar, John and I have been to see the elephant." Winter made the droll introductions and the two shook hands. Smiley winced. The rolled up sleeves on the top sergeant's jacket were stretched tightly over massive biceps. And when he smiled, it wasn't quite a smile. It was a facial picture that implied, Okay, I'm pretending to be civil because the Army expects me to be civil. But I don't know you and consequently, I don't particularly like you. After I get to know you, if that unlikely scenario should eventuate, I *know* I will not like you. So bear with this little façade and we'll get through it and go our ways.

But Irish John was okay. Winter said he didn't *always* like John, only about ninety-nine percent of the time—enough to compensate for the times when he was a real, live motherfucker. And he could be. They'd pulled too many shifts and too many passes together not to have come to an accommodation, each according to his particular lights.

"What're you doing here, Big John?" Winter wanted to know.

"I'm not. Not here . . . not assigned here." He nodded toward some ephemeral kingdom to the west, maybe north. "I'm at the Field Station. Phu Bai. Just here a couple days T.D.Y."

"No, I meant *here*. Viet Nam. Thought you were through with 'Nam. I heard you got your second 'Heart' in sixty-five, after I was gone."

"Yeah, you dog-ass sorry mother. When you got short-sheeted on that L.Z. in Three Corps with your skivvies down, you know what happened, don't you? *I* got shipped down to fill in for Morrison, who was sent to replace you as N.C.O.I.C. of Air. Morrison was due for R. and R., got pissed for getting pre-empted after making arrangements, and suddenly *he* can't pass the flight physical. Despite two years of flying. But Colonel Meador said he had to take the slot anyhow, be the NCOIC and not fly, and the section just went short one op.

"Being down in Sai Gon was okay, at first," he grinned, shifting his squat bulk around backwards in the chair, resting his arms across the back. "Good chow, some good booze, some good . . . hmm, social benefits. But bad shit, too . . ."

* * *

Sai Gon, Viet Nam: 1966

SFC Glencannon wrenched himself out of the tiny blue-and-cream-colored taxi, paid the driver, and stepped onto the ramp leading down to the deck of the *My Canh* floating restaurant. The vessel, a river-going barge in a prior incarnation, was docked at a private pier on the Sai Gon River at the end of Tu Do Street. Its fortunes improved by the change of function, the *My Canh* had developed an enviable reputation for food and service. Visiting firemen were hustled down to the floating restaurant, and senior US government officials and military officers made it *de rigeur* for social dining. In the eyes of rankers, it was unfortunate that the *My Canh* subscribed to certain egalitarian perks of capitalism: allowing military enlisted persons, local nationals, even ladies of the evening to partake of the exotic fare.

The elevated rank of many of the restaurant's customers also attracted attention in another sector, results of which were that it had been the target in three bombing incidents. Such activities had a tendency to put off service for a while, but blasé was enough of a lifestyle, and personnel turnovers sufficient, to keep the tables filled. It was a rare evening when one could walk in and be seated without a reservation or influence—*viec hoi lo*. But no one made a reservation, fearing that such offered a perfect opportunity for pre-planned terrorism.

As Glencannon descended the gangplank, a youth pedaled up behind him on a blue-and-white, vintage French bicycle and stopped to talk to the QC on guard at the head of the gangplank. The lad shook hands with the Vietnamese military policeman, and they exchanged pleasantries. The youth leaned past the QC and spoke to an elderly woman seated on the ground, a pile of tiny banana-shaped fruits, another pile of mangoes, and one of green nondescript water plants before her. The ground to the side was dark with the spittle of betel juice, and she rigorously pursued that addiction while she cawed and craned at the youth, waving her arms and cackling at his boyish humor.

The youth settled the bike carefully against a lamp post and walked over to crouch before the old woman, who was his aunt, bargaining with her for some of the plantain. While the QC busied himself doing his job, warily scanning the street for would-be bad guys, the youth took one of the green banana-like fruit, peeled it and began to eat. He looked sharply behind his aunt and shouted to another vendor, moved to join him, and eventually moved on down the concrete embankment along the river.

Glencannon was a frequent diner at the quayside eatery and never had to wait for a table. This evening was no different. The waiter seated him on the outside of the craft, away from the shoreline, so that he would have, when it came, a clear view across the river to the sunset beyond. It was still early yet, the heat, super-saturated with foul humidity, hanging like a forest of wet wool smothering eyes, nose, face and body, inundating the senses. Electric fans on stands, strategically spotted about the open deck, kept up a movement of air that was the closest thing to refreshing one was likely to find outdoors in Viet Nam.

One of Glencannon's eternal complaints about duty in the Orient was the absence of Irish whiskey, *uisce beatha*. Despite his complaints, the owner of the *My Canh* would not stock Jameson's or Bushmills, so it was generally Johnny Walker black when he ate here.

Mid-way through Glencannon's second drink, waiting for the clams, he sat facing the far, sunset side of the river, when suddenly behind him the shore side of the restaurant, without prelude, lifted awkwardly in a roaring explosion, and pitched onto the river bank, crashing in grotesque mimicry of a huge, broken mechanical toy. The blast sent sheets and slivers of glass, splintered wood, shards of fragmented metal, and flame and shock waves across the width of the decking. Interspersed with the shrapnel of the boat were customers, customer parts, the remains of three waiters, and the bartender. There was a long moment when there was only the frenzy of the explosion, and its immediate, technical results. Human reaction took milliseconds longer to set in.

Agonized screams filled the air, the sound as damning as the blast. Glencannon, his eardrums ravaged by the explosion, was spared the vocal outburst as he slid slowly to the deck of the restaurant, a sudden dizziness welling over his senses at the instant of the pain in his head. It was only later he would know of his broken arm, three fractured ribs, and extensive lacerations and contusions, in addition to the skull fracture. The ribs and arm abuse resulted from being struck by a segment of the bar torn loose and catapulted across the deck; the fractured skull occurred when his head got in the way of another skull flying asunder in the blast. The decapitated body of the barman was partially shredded, the clothing torn completely away, and with the absence of its most identifying features, was thus the last victim identified following the attack.

A US Navy Lieutenant Commander, seated also on the river side of the restaurant, was only slightly grazed by a loose metal strip from the cash register, and when he knew his dinner partner, a secretary from the US consulate, was all right, he moved into the midst of the carnage, organizing efforts to get people clear of the boat, onto the bank where the ambulances, when they came, could more rapidly attend them. He had also to deal with the panic that followed the blast, when every survivor who could run, walk or crawl wanted off the boat. He cleared a body from the gangplank entranceway and directed a file of dazed customers up the narrow passage toward the shore. Only a few had cleared the boat ramp when the blue and white bicycle exploded, creating a new killing zone, sending hundreds of steel pellets lately removed from an inoperative US Army Claymore mine, in enfilade down the axis of the restaurant gangway.

From a spot on the second floor of his third cousin's laundry shop nearby, the youth who had placed the bicycle so casually, so unerringly and perfectly oriented, watched with disinterest the thrashing of his aged aunt who was caught in the primary blast and disemboweled by a severed fan blade.

Unfortunately for the newly recruited party member making his bones with the fourth bombing of the *My Canh*, an attack with the added fillip of a backup killing strike utilizing the bicycle, the *Quan Cong* he had held brief discussion with on the quayside was not even touched by the blast. The QC, who disliked the particular intensity of the two blasts, coming one on the heels of the other as they did, was able to remember everything that preceded the blast. And he remembered specifically the bright, cheerful lad who spent his time in pointless discussion when he might more willingly have been engaged in play or in the alternate recreational pursuit of begging.

That the boy would be eradicated with little fanfare by a QC squad was never known to Glencannon, but he never questioned the outcome of the experience. He considered he had taken his chances going to the *My Canh*. The Viet Cong had already announced, by their previous efforts, that the restaurant was considered a prime target. They never paid their VC tax.

* * *

"So," Glencannon said, raising his glass of iced tea without ice, "here's to life in the Green Machine. May it ever be so fucking humble." His eyes came nearest to a smile since they had sat down in the crowded messhall.

Winter knew Glencannon's story was not that unusual. The senior sergeant had come back to 'Nam, and even he still did not know why. He hated it his first tour, mostly the climate and the totally indecipherable language of the natives. He volunteered to return for a second tour, was severely wounded under unexpected and non-combat action circumstances, which could really upset one's personal view. Yet, here he was. Third tour. One of thousands.

Winter wondered how many career personnel, like Glencannon, had volunteered for a second or further 'Nam tour,. If there were as many as he suspected, why was the Army working overtime recycling those who had already served a tour and were not volunteering to return? The policy smacked of some kind of personal vendetta at DA level. But he couldn't for the life of himself remember anyone there who even knew him, let alone had it in for him; and he could not really believe such a plot on such a grand scale. He did not, however, discount the improbable simply on the grounds of improbability.

"Who's that officer, John?" Winter asked abruptly, nodding toward a table in the far corner.

Glencannon, twisting his body along with his head to accommodate the thick column of muscle connecting, said, "Which one? The lieutenant sitting with the . . . don't see any rank on the other man. Must be a private. Or a spook. That one?"

"Yeah. Old for a first lieutenant. Do you know him?"

"No," turning back ponderously, Glencannon was succinct.

"Ever see him before? Him or the . . . private?"

"No. Why? What's with the lieutenant, Chief? You officer-conscious, now you're wearing bars?" Glencannon turned to look at Smiley for reaction. He got none.

"Yeah, it's an obligation you take on." Winter grimaced, trying to recall . . . "It's just . . . I think I've met him." He felt self-conscious with his banal response.

"Hmmph!"

There were a few moments of silence, and Winter, glancing at Smiley, felt, suddenly, an oblique need to fill in some blanks. But he spoke only to the NCO.

"You wouldn't know, John, but . . . uuhh, Nickie and I . . . we're not together right now." The moment the words were away, Winter wanted them back. Wrong context.

"Well, no shit, Sherlock. None of us seem to be with our squeeze, 'right now,' as you so delightfully put it." Hardcore. Winter knew John understood him, but would run out his string on a *faux pas* any way he could.

"Yeah, yeah. You know what I mean, you bloody enlisted swine. I mean, for some time before we left B.A., re-settling, the whole cucamonga, we were . . . *not together*. Without the soap opera shit, suffice it that I no longer fit her image of a husband and father. A *responsible* husband and father." He wasn't looking at anyone right then, peering inward.

I'm not touching that one, Winter could imagine Glencannon thinking. It was the generic pattern for too many marital horror stories he'd heard over his career. Nicole had reached the end of her enlistment. Did not re-up for the joys of military homelife. Another one down the tubes, with or without allotment conveniences. *Say-o*-fuckin'-*nara!*

He said nothing.

Smiley sat silent, uncomfortable, reluctant to engage; unable to walk away.

"Started in B.A., when I got my orders . . ." Winter reflected, then added, "don't think I'll go into that. Just . . . when we left Germany, things were on a downhill slide. We decided to take a house on the Gulf Coast. Not knowing what might happen over here, I insisted on *buying* a house. I . . . thought it was likely there was divorce in our future, insisted on buying." He thought of all the well-reasoned logic he had put into that decision, finally realizing Nickie did not care where he left them, did not care if they bought or rented.

"Uhh, 'scuse me, Chief, but what's all this domestic shit got to do with the old lieutenant in the corner?" Glencannon's expression of banal disinterest left him open for any answer.

"Hell, gimme a chance, will you, John. There's a connection."

Glencannon glanced at Smiley, whose eyes were focused on Liechtenstein. .

After a few dithering moments when he could not decide just how much to bore his two friends, Winter said lamely, "Before I left for the west coast, she got rid of my books."

After a silent eternity, into an awkward void Glencannon said, "You're going to have to expand on that a bit."

Winter did not answer immediately, remembering the unpacking. Nickie always did the kitchen, bathroom and bedroom because it was her call, placing everything where she would want them for convenience. Like always, he unpacked his records, and started on the books. He knew he shipped too many books about, but they were a major part of his life. His responsibility.

Winter glanced over at the coffee urn; immediately a Vietnamese swamper trotted over with an aluminum pitcher of coffee, filled their cups, and trotted away. All three sat in silence.

Winter remembered the day a week after they had moved into the new house in Long Beach, a short couple of miles up the coast road from Gulfport. He left the house to go to the Harrison County Highway Patrol office to register and get plates for the new car they had bought upon arrival in the states. While out on that errand he had gone on for other chores that needed doing before he left. He'd told Nicole the day before what he planned, she'd made no response, and he took the boys with him. He had sprung for a hot dog lunch, and they were away from the house some five hours. Winter wasn't sure how much of this memory string he spoke aloud.

"When I came into the house through the den—" He stopped, realizing he was speaking out of his thoughts. His audience waited.

He had known, right off, that something was not right. It only took a moment to realize—there was not a book on the shelves. He had just spent the best part of two days sorting and shelving them, so it was a shock. He called Nickie. She answered but did not come into the room. He found her in the kitchen and asked about the missing books. His mind, confused by the physical absence, flitted through possible explanations: shelves had to be painted, fixed; books needed cleaning—a dozen far-fetched ideas ran through his head. But not *the* answer.

"She just . . . she got rid of my books. You remember, John, how many books I had."

Afterward, he could not recapture her words precisely. Nicole, when confronted, said she had given the books to Catholic Charities. She had called the office of a thrift shop, talked to a woman, who was apparently uneasy about the circumstances, and passed Nicole over to a priest who was in charge of the outlet . And right away, Winter remembered with fresh anger, the sky pilot, whom Winter thought of as Brother Emasculation, found a truck and a helper, a barber from next door to the shop, and they came immediately out to the house, piled everything into boxes, and hauled them away. "All in that four-plus hours I was gone."

The two listeners, still without comment, waited. Winter felt the silence like an accusation. No! He did not know what he thought it meant. It meant nothing. Only, Nickie had lately accused him of drawing his military inspirations from books on war and history and such. He could not tell them all of it; it would not be fair. Not to mention dealing with it again in his mind.

Without meaning to, he blurted out, "I mean, every damned one of my World War II collection. Fiction, non-fiction. Poetry. Shirer to Joseph Heller, James Dickey to Randall Jarrell. And others. Willi Heinrich. . . ." With the naming of the German author of the Gunner Asch series, he seemed to have run down, the tension in his springs released. The cogs not meshing. The silence was not strained, but it was silent. For a while.

"Like I said, Dave," Glencannon said tersely, "what the hell's that got to do with the old lieutenant? Sorry 'bout your readin' material, but you screw around with wives, matrimony and all that shit, you gotta expect short shrift."

Shrift for the hard-pressed storyteller was short indeed.

And Winter knew it was the best response he was ever likely to get.

"Yeah. Yeah, you're right. But the connection . . . when I boarded the plane at Travis—I'd left Long Beach next day after the book thing, drank too much on the flight from New Orleans to San Fran. Hung over on the bus ride up to Travis—and when I boarded the flight, things were not altogether clear. I do remember it was one of those chartered military flights, a Continental seven-oh-seven. I was damn near in the pilot's back pocket. In row one, what's normally First Class section. Aisle seat. The one to my right, the window seat, was unoccupied. Even after the plane was otherwise fully loaded, far as I could tell that seat was still empty. We'd started taxiing when the pilot locked the brakes, they ran a mobile stair up beside us, and a lieutenant and one other guy came aboard. That lieutenant," he nodded toward the elderly officer at the nearby table, "or someone who looked for the world like him, took the window seat by me. Immediately, we began taxiing again."

Winter's voice had taken on a different tone. A changed pace. He sounded a changed person, someone farther away.

"The second passenger . . . him I never saw clearly. He went toward the rear compartment. Guess there must've been a seat for him. They wouldn't've allowed him to board, otherwise, would they? FAA rules. No 'standing room only' on ccommercial or charter flights." His cryptic sarcasm went unanswered.

"To carry on with your 'connection . . .'" Winter said pointedly, nodding to the NCO.

In the background, what had been a continual drone of voices at the table where money was changing hands had grown into something more, a slim notch below disturbance. Argument over the way a Spec-5 had tried to check and raise, apparently, in a game which disallowed such *laissez fare* play.

"*Knock it off, Assholes,*" Glencannon bellowed. "I'm listening to a sob story, and I cannot abide competition." The Vietnamese kitchen swamper scampered for the storeroom.

In the ringing quiet which followed, Winter picked up the story. "From Travis to Hawaii, not a word from this lieutenant. He wasn't sleeping. And it wasn't as if he gave me the cold shoulder. He just sat, staring straight ahead. Sometimes out the porthole. He read some.

Big book. Old, leather-bound. Author's name stuck in my mind. A. de Gaul. Like the general. De Gaulle? Anyhow, he got nothing from me, either. I didn't need hand-holding and, as I think I mentioned, I wasn't feeling too good.

"Everybody off at Hickam. Some passengers left the flight there, but when we took off, every seat was filled again. When I'd taken my seat, the lieutenant was already back aboard and talking to this short, round private. Must have been the one who boarded with him. They may have been on orders together. Traveling together. Lieutenant, naturally, in first class. When I boarded, the private took off back into coach. Seemed fair to me." After a brief search he found a smile, but lost it when there was no response.

"Somewhere, between Hickam and Clark, the lieutenant starts talking to me. At first I thought he was talking in his sleep. But he wasn't asleep. He was just talking to me without looking at me. No eye contact. No body language, not like you'd expect in a conversation between strangers. Took me a few seconds to come up to speed." It was apparent to his two listeners that Winter was still enthralled with the event.

"Just out of the blue. He began right in the middle of a story, something that had happened to him. And it was, by all accounts and definitions, a *non sequitur*, in the sense that I said nothing to prompt it. And it was also, if you can bear the added tension," Winter said with humorous irony, "an instance of *déjà vu* of the most vividly recent kind.

"Somewhere in the telling, it came out that his name was Dan Dewey, and he, too, had just come from his home, en route to 'Nam. Told me . . . said he'd been sick, caught a bug or something while traveling with a friend, and while he was laid up, his niece and his housekeeper—don't ask; I don't know why a first lieutenant, unmarried, would need, or for that matter, could afford, a housekeeper, but that's what he said . . . these two women in his life—had taken all his books out of his library, piled them in a courtyard, and set fire to them. Burned them. *Farenheit Four-fifty-one*, be damned. Burned them!

"Lot of history books. Especially big collection of books on the Crusades, and chivalry and such. Lot of books about Spain and the Spanish in the New World. All of 'em. *Burned!*" Winter let the word hang on the dead silence that had prevailed since Glencannn's outburst. It had an almost tangible essence, examined by his two listeners.

The connection was made.

Smiley first, then Glencannon, attempted to speak. To ask the obvious questions. Neither seemed able to enunciate the words. The connection was made, a connection so bizarre as to render both speechless.

Finally, "Kinda weird ain't it, troops?" Winter said waggishly. "Brenner would be in hog's heaven. Latin up the ass. A *non sequitur* and *déjà vu*, all working in one and the same instance. Not to mention this officer who's an anachronism. Another literary device. And he was. A literary device. Antiquated. Out of character. His story worked for me and it scared the downright be-Jesus out of me because of what had happened with my books in Long Beach. I couldn't speak. I sat there, trapped at thirty-five thousand feet, nowhere to go, checking out the outdated officer "pinks" this old man lieutenant was wearing. And he was an old man. A first lieutenant, he had *gray hair*. Where he had hair. He was partially bald. Skinny. Almost frail, but there was about him the feel that . . . he might have been infantry. You know the old-time kind of N.C.O., man who's spent his life in the ranks. Probably drinks way too much. A bachelor, loner. But, drunk or sober, when you order him out, he can take a platoon of hardcore soldiers and leading, can run all friggin' day long. He had that look. The lieutenant had that look up close." Winter would not allow the subject to be sidetracked.

"And I could almost swear, that's him over there. And his sidekick, too. The round one." Winter did not mention that his sparse acquaintance with the pair went back even further. To his first tour in 'Nam. He glanced back toward the corner of the almost empty mess hall, emptier now by at least two men since his last look. The lieutenant and his companion had disappeared.

Glencannon said in a relieved voice, "Well, we'll never know now, will we? Who gives a shit?" he asked into the void, echoing Magic Marvin, Winter thought . . . for all the world like Magic Marvin. Who gives a shit? For sure, GI.

* * *

Winter pondered the conundrum as he left the mess hall, and crossing the parking lot with Smiley, discoursing on the ambiguous nature of security arrangements for the vehicles parked there, he walked past a tall, disheveled staff sergeant and knew in an instant that he knew him, too. It seemed that kind of night. Again, from somewhere . . . sometime, but the man seemed elusively unidentifiable. There was about him an air of confusion, and yet his pace was resolute. The sergeant looked through him, did not speak, and ambled past without saluting. He was obviously and gloriously drunk.

Saunders! The name popped up like a target on the range. Staff Sergeant Wicklow B. Saunders. Member of a relatively small group of enlisted men whom Winter had known who'd held specialist grade above E-five level. But it was not that for which he was unforgettable. On the edge of memory, Winter blanked the details from his mind. He fled from the memory of the unfortunate specialist. And the ephemeral lieutenant.

* * *

Winter and Smiley worked their way through the aviation companies of the 224th. "Into their hearts," Smiley disparaged, mulling on the lack of enthusiasm of most pilots and operators. Pilots and operators in all four companies shared the attitude that the Standardization duo were pissing up a rope, attempting to bring order to their acceptable worlds of chaos.

Returning to Tan Son Nhut-Sai Gon, they wrote findings in clear language which encompassed the full range of their mission interests, and recommended logical, simple fixes. Their thoroughness assured that nothing would ever come of their work.

A massive disconnect, the S-3's efforts to standardize the four companies' operational techniques, was doomed by one irrevocable factor: terrain. I Corps and II Corps pilots and ops would continue to spend their flying hours, straining for competence on fixes by flying as low as profitable, while staying high enough to avoid the ubiquitous peaks of those mountainous regions of Viet Nam. Airmen still clung to the notion, however frivolously expressed, that altitude—the separation of one's ass from Mother Earth—was the antidote to all evil. And in III Corps, a target-rich environment, things were different. So too in IV Corps, with their unenviable navigation and "fix" problems. But in the minds of all involved, the lack of standardization was mired in greater swamps than merely geophysical differentiation.

* * *

Winter continued amazed that the majority of Vietnamese youth still, in late 1968, had not fallen prey to the military draft. It was a thing GIs bitched about during his first tour. There were millions of men and women under arms in Vietnam, but the forces were still largely volunteer. The fighting, largely being done by Americans, was paid for by Americans—including the cost of supporting Korean forces, Filipinos, Thais, and others—and only the Australians represented any meaningful addition to armed assistance, any kind of return on investment.

Autumn was in full swing elsewhere in the world, north of the equator. In Viet Nam, there was only one season—miserable. Everyone basked in unequivocal misery.

* * *

In Gia Dinh, downscale suburb of Sai Gon, a young woman snapped the side closures on her black *aow dai*, cupped her hands and pressed her substantial breasts aggressively upward and out, smiling indifferently at the effect. She removed a large, black American service automatic from a small sandalwood cabinet and slipped it into a Parisian-style evening bag with beads. Snuffing the oil lamp, she pushed a worn Solex motorbike out of the shed that served as her home and garage, onto the street.

* * *

Winter lived a staid life. After four weeks in-country, he still resided in the 509th billets in Cho Lon, made daily trips back and forth to Tan Son Nhut on the Navy bus, or in an Army Jeep or truck. Meals in the mess facility in Cho Lon usually accounted for breakfast and dinner, though occasionally he visited Cheap Charlie's for Chinese, the Mayflower for French, or the Punjab for Indian cuisine. Lunch was the airport restaurant, the 509th mess hall, Circle 34 Mess, or once in a great while just for a change, Open Mess Number One, a laconically named eatery of little significance which also doubled as a senior officers' billet near Tan Son Nhut's Gate 2.

Jack Albrecht caught up with Winter as he was boarding the bus in the Davis Station motor pool at the end of a working day. "Wanta make din-din at Cheap Charlie's tonight? I gotta get off this station." His eyes had taken on a peculiar luminosity that, even in the afternoon light, added an element of intensity to his aura.

"You not going home tonight?" Winter asked, thinking of the small apartment Jack kept on Tu Do Street, above the Royal Thai Airways ticket office.

"Nahh. Thuy and the kids are in Bien Hoa, visiting her grandmother. I been bunkin' out in spare beds around Davis. But the messhall's about to do me in."

"Sure. Let's catch a cyclo," Winter offered. "Everytime I try to get off this Navy bus, anywhere but at the prescribed stops, the goddamned driver has kittens."

They walked out the gate of the motor pool and down the road toward the soccer field. They'd gone less than a hundred yards when a small three-wheeled motorized *dzong* cart drew up before the ARVN Ranger battalion and let off several Vietnamese NCOs and EM. Without waiting for it to stop as it drove past them, the two Americans hopped aboard, and the driver accelerated in a cloud of happy blue smoke, making for the front gate.

"Sai-*Gon*, you bloody Viet Cong. *Di-di* fucking *maow!*" Albrecht urged the driver. The Vietnamese drove with a mad grin.

* * *

Fifteen minutes after he had picked them up outside Gate 2 in the 100-p Alley strip, another cart driver dropped the two soldiers near the Catholic cathedral, downtown Sai Gon. The massive church marked an invisible border defining the extent of his legal fare range, the area in which he was allowed to carry passengers. Only the blue-and-cream taxis and military vehicles, plus vehicles of a certain level of important civilians, were allowed in the downtown heart of the city. Winter had bad, fiery memories of that square.

Cheap Charlie's, a slyly disingenuous name for a restaurant, sat on a street behind the national assembly building known as the Opera House, across from the Brinks BOQ and the Continental Palace Hotel, near the Caravelle, adjacent to the Navy BEQ and PX. Serving this bevy of elegant doss houses, Cheap Charlie's enjoyed a central location that could not miss with GIs; but it was the quality and quantity of food and the ridiculously low prices that drew the crowds of Americans to the restaurant. A dozen clams in butter sauce, small ribeye, fries and a salad: $2.50 equivalent.

Very near Cheap Charlie's, around the corner, was another restaurant of equal quality. But in that other eatery—where there was decor, not just space—the name of which Winter could never remember, prices were more than twice Charlie's rates and the servings were meager. Winter had gone through most of his first tour before he discovered an open secret known to everyone else in Sai Gon: the two restaurants served from the same kitchen and were owned by the same ex-whore and her husband, a police captain in the river district *arrondissement.*

* * *

The slim young *Co* idled her Solex up to the curb where a lone GI stood. He was obviously drunk, a disorderly soldier. In his wrinkled, sweat-stained khakis, he appeared out of sorts and would not be much of a conquest. But, she served a master whose value judgements were not qualified by fashion.

"Hey, GI, you wan' boom-boom? Makee love? Fuckee fuckee. I numbah wan."

He looked owlishly at her, his gaze traveling down her frontage. "Those can't be *your* tits, honey. Sorry. Go 'way." The soldier, who was drinking but not drunk beyond functional competence, turned away and began to walk along the sidewalk. "C'mon, big man," he called softly but clearly to no one visible. "Positive ID." The woman did not hear what he said. She pushed the Solex forward to catch up with him.

* * *

"You ever eat around the corner in the other place," Winter asked Albrecht as they came out of Charlie's and ambled along the walk.

"You mean, the back side of Charlie's?" the NCO laughed. "That's a kicker, ain't it?"

"May be a kicker, but I used to eat at one, then the other, for almost a year last tour, before I knew they were the same kitchen. And they even used the same menu, except for prices. I never noticed." Winter remembered with amusement how it changed the taste of the food for him when he learned the truth.

* * *

The girl in the black *aow dai* drew up before the soldier again, rested the Solex against a traffic sign, and reached into the saddle bag on the back fender. She pulled out a handbag, and slid from it a pistol that looked ridiculously oversized in her hands. Without a further word, she grabbed the butt with both hands, thumbed back the hammer, and jerked the gun up toward the soldier's head.

* * *

Winter and Albrecht strode along the wet sidewalks where shop owners and residents sloshed the concrete with buckets of filthy water to wash away the filth of a day's myriad passings: spittle, dirt, ash, bird droppings, fruit peels, flower petals from the tiny jasmine flower necklaces sold by children as a hedge against unsavory smells of the city. Early evening occasionally offered this still, calming remedy, as if people were not dying by the hundreds within a dozen miles of this spot. As if the war was a thing of the past, instead of a thing of constant horror and presence, and a week from now, an hour from now, a moment from now, this same sidewalk might be scattered with the blood and body parts of human beings intent only on wending their way homeward after a day at work.

* * *

As the girl with the impressive bosom used all her strength of hands to hold down the safeties and depress the heavy trigger, a hurtling black shape of deadly proportions exploded from the alley behind her, striking her broadside, knocking her across the bike and well into the street. But dazed and on the ground, she retained her grip on the gun.

The big man followed her, his impetus from the blind-side block carrying him forward into the street, and he grabbed her gun hand, weapon and all, and jerked her to her feet. She was dazed, but well indoctrinated. He wrenched the gun from her hand, and when she clawed at him with her left hand, the only one not numb from the impact, he back-handed her into semi-consciousness with one swipe of his huge paw.

* * *

The two American soldiers walked down a dark street parallel to Tu Do, intending to cut over to the main street when they reached the area of Albrecht's apartment. They had agreed to stop off there for a drink; Albrecht would remain for the night, Winter would take a taxi to Cho Lon to the BOQ before the curfew witching hour. Passing a store that had been closed down for weeks, its front glass gone to a grenade blast, its stock ruined by the explosion and seasonal heavy rains, the two men were at the mouth of an alley that ran back into the recesses of the city block when they felt the concussion.

Blast echoed out of the alleyway. Winter and Albrecht knew from the concussion it was a grenade. Albrecht was unarmed, but

Winter reached for his .45 and had his hand on the butt when, from around the corner, he leaned forward and stared down the alley.

A madly pounding figure burst from the darkness and, rounding the corner, smashed into Winter. Both men went down. A second dark shape, much bigger and alternately growling and laughing, ran past, almost colliding with Albrecht. The big figure stopped, jerked the first runner back on his feet, and went on his way, all without breaking his fluid movement.

"Winter. Goddamn! Winter. Goddamn! Go man, go!" The first runner, who had fallen, grabbed the warrant officer's hand, pulled him up, and sprinted away, yelling back at Albrecht: "Get it, asshole, or you're white mice meat."

Taking in the unaccountable sequence, from the blast to the disappearing GIs, Winter dashed off in pursuit. Albrecht was already moving just behind, and Winter saw ahead of him, in the light from a store window, the unlikely appearance of a ghost from the past, sprinting madly.

Ratty Mac MacGantree, when Winter caught up to him, was picking 'em up and putting 'em down in the same crazy-legged, spastic shuffle that had made him an unenviable acquisition for the softball team in Asmara. Crazy Bruce, bigger than the proverbial, lumbered along at some speed exceeding fast. Just an old linebacker, getting into the game.

They rounded the corner onto Tu Do, yet a block from Broddard's, and slowed to a walk which they maintained on to the cafe. When the four of them had settled at one of the spindly metal tables, conspicuous in the glassed-in coffee bar on the street corner, breathing heavily, they knew they were safely divorced from events back in that alley. Whatever those were.

Winter knew only that something bad had happened in the alley. He also considered that there were no witnesses but themselves to whatever Mac and Bruce had been a part of. There was no indication anyone had seen the four of them running on the street. They had slowed to a walk on Tu Do and elicited no interest. Now, looking around him, Winter remembered the first time he brought Mac here. A lifetime ago.

The quartet ordered coffee and dessert, Cokes with ice, and Bruce wanted ice cream. After a few minutes of silence, there still was no sign of excitement; and when the QC sirens started, no one viewed the GIs suspiciously. The group indicated no interest in whatever was going on outside.

"And what the hell was that all about?" Winter asked Mac in a low voice.

"Well, hello to you, too, Dave. Is that any greeting for old friends?"

"Mac. Bruce. What the hell?"

Bruce wrinkled his nose. His Indian eyes were flat black and disinterested. Whatever he and Ratty Mac had done was a thing done.

"Bruce doesn't want me to talk about it," Ratty Mac said. He glanced at Albrecht. Winter got the message.

"Algernon MacGantree, Bruce Phillipson, this is Jack Albrecht. Jack, Ratty Mac and Crazy Bruce are two old cronies from Asmara and times past. Guys, Jack's a fellow bagger from my first tour here. Hell, both of you probably know Jack; he was here the same time we all were. But where the hell did you two come from. What are you doing . . . how is it that you're here?"

"I know Jack from my first tour here," Mac said. "Long story. I don't—"

"What happened back there, Mac? Seriously."

"Well . . . uhh, Mister Winter," he said, glancing at the bar. "I guess . . . this was, like, payback." Mac played it out for effect.

"Payback."

"Yeah. You know. Gettin' some of our own."

"Explain."

"We just out-dragoned the Dragon Lady. We just eliminated the bitch from the game." The grin threatened to split his sun-blistered lips. " 's not right when the players start usin' unfair tactics—and suckerin' in GIs with the offer of poon tang, just so's she could blow 'em away, is unfair tactics. So we . . . ejected her from the game."

Mac told them he and Bruce had, for several evenings now, been on the streets, trolling for the Dragon Lady, and then the events tonight that led up to the tackle by Bruce, who'd been in the alley taking a leak. Then he finalized the felony.

"When Mac told her to pull down her pants, even half conscious she thought she was gonna screw her way out of it. Huh!" There was a tiny glimmer of life in Bruce's eyes. "He just pulled the pants up over her *aow dai*, tucked it in like a shirt, and dropped the frag down the baggy front. Then we run."

"Jesus!" Albrecht's mouth was an open chasm.

"You're shitting me, Mac. Bruce?" Winter said, hoping it was true.

"I shit you not, *Mister* Winter. What's the matter? Where's your sense of humor. Did you give that up when you became an orificer?"

"Dave," Mac said, "she's killed four, five, maybe more G.I.s. If we'd held her, turned her over to the white mice, they'd just screw her silly, then shoot her. Hell, we just cut corners." He believed it.

"Sense of humor, Bruce? How can you know it was Dragon Lady? You might have just killed a pissed-off whore. Maybe you said 'No' in a way that offended her. Do you think she was going to shoot?" Winter knew his questions were pointless.

"Another half second," MacGantree said, "old Mac woulda' been history, my friend. No shit. I mean, Dave, come on. I done a lotta things, but I don't kill a hooker for kicks, not after all the business I give 'em."

"Ain't no sense makin' over it, Winter. It's a done thing." Bruce applied all the logic that he would ever expend on the matter.

Winter tried out-staring the Indian, and failed. "And where the hell did the grenade come from?"

Neither said anythings.

"Did you steal that out of the arms room, Mac? Or trade for it? What'd it cost you?"

"Nope. Never stole nothing, Dave" he said defensively. "Snuffed it off a litter-bound Marine on a chopper ride from Duc Hoa. Hell, had to make the aircraft safe for the flight. I been keeping it, just for a special occasion." He snickered nastily.

Two Army MPs came in the door, looked casually about, and took seats at a nearby table, effectively ending further discussion.

When the QC found the dismembered body in the black *aow dai*, found the damaged but well-described Solex nearby in the street, and the .45 on a nail in a door, the questions simply faded. And the killings on the street stopped.

chapter fifteen

The Get Down, Downtown, Low-Down Nikon Boogie

Vietnam: October 1968

The Blue Moon was desolate. Half the bargirls were absent, ostensibly vacationing, but in actuality observing a hiatus in service while being treated for the clap after a US Army doctor had examined them and threatened to put the bar off limits. Mama-San bowed, pleaded, hustled the offending social workers out the back door, vowing a clean house. *Disgraceful creatures, they would never work again in the Capital Military District!*

But in the end, all the madam had done was pull the old razzle-dazzle, the Sai Gon shuffle. She sent the six diseased *filles de joie* to the San Francisco Bar and borrowed six of their girls who, if truth be known, were working off the same sentence in their own establishment. The doctor knew it. The MPs knew it. It didn't matter; just keeping the straphangers happy.

X-ing blocks, checking squares. Dogging it!

When he understood the epidemic proportions of the Blue Moon's malaise, Winter said to Ito, "I think, young sir, we'll just shuffle on down the *Strasse*."

"Seems right to me, G.I.," Ito said, and they did, drifting up Tu Do, down the Street of Flowers, until they settled on the Casino Bar, an oasis of undistinguished attractions just off the main.

In the old days, Winter told Ito referring to his first tour, the bar had been a hangout for the 3rd RRU, mostly ops and pilots and mechs of the Air Section who did their socializing there. In the old days there was no need for grenade screening on windows or guards on doors; in the old days the Cong had not really learned how to hurt the foreign devils.

Winter still wore the 3rd RRU Air's patch from that assignment on his fatigue jacket pocket. The logo, a black cat with a lascivious grin, sitting atop four golden spheres and transfixed by a lightning bolt, was centered on a round red background. The Air section's motto, not found in any heraldry tome but posted conspicuously on the latrine walls of every bar in III Corps, declared 3rd RRU Air to be a "four-balled electronic tomcat who prowled its bloody field of conflict undismayed." By late 1968 the tomcat was reduced to a spayed pussy, the lightning bolt to a weak spark; only the field of blood was valid. They'd counted their losses, though admittedly relatively meager, drowned their sorrows, and marked off the days in their favorite bar.

Now the Casino was open ground, frequented by Rangers and airdales, tattooed fuzzy-cheeked brown water sailors off the Riverine patrols, MAC-V office apes, and select other drudges. The territoriality of individual units was submerged in the crushing onslaught of troops, and there was neither sufficient *Ba-mui-ba* beer nor enough bargirls to go around.

But not all was bad. Winter had made the transition from quarters in Cho Lon to the Newport BOQ just outside Tan Son Nhut, and was grateful for that move. It was nice to be living where he could take advantage of some amenities he was at least familiar with.

Inside, the dingy bar was the same as Winter had first known it. The ceiling fans didn't turn; the ashtrays were thin aluminum disks which served no purpose other than as a target to be avoided when outing a butt; and the flies, if they had talked, could have related generations-old memoirs of French soldiers, Japanese, Tonkinese before this current American infestation. The stench from the latrine out back was ever the dominant feature. The bar mirror, layered over plywood backing, was bolted through several bullet holes, part of the price for profiteering off young, armed warriors who didn't know the limits of the formaldehyde-laced beer. The lighting was poor, but considering the decor that was not all bad.

Like the Blue Moon, there were few customers in the Casino, but all the girls were on station here—that was something. In a back room, separated from the bar proper by dangling strands of beads that served only to tease the flies, a tight little squad of Vietnamese men in civilian clothes sat around a poker table without the pretense of cards. They looked up quickly, black marble stares assessing the two GIs who walked in, then ignored them and resumed whispering. Winter recognized the pattern: black-marketeers! Or pimps. Or drug entrepreneurs. Or any two . . . or all. Opportunities for betterment were boundless in the wartime city.

An American Air Force sergeant, in sweat-stained but beautifully starched khakis, was pitched forward across a table along the wall on the left. Flies meandered in and out of his open mouth at will, undisturbed by his whistling snores. Some nostalgic wag had written on the rough mahogany wall above the table, "Kilroy was here." Scrawled beneath in felt-tip-marker response: ". . . and fucking loved it."

A Special Forces Spec-5 sat at the bar, beret tucked under his left epaulet. A Kabar with a nine-inch blade was strapped to one boot. The butt of a nickel-plated automatic protruded from beneath the edge of his jungle fatigue jacket. He was primed for whatever, but he drank quietly and ignored Winter and Ito when they came into the bar.

Ito nudged Winter and muttered stiffly aside, "Snake eater. Green Beanie." Winter shrugged him off.

Winter had developed a necessary caution. Following assignment to quarters in the Newport BOQ, he belatedly learned the Newport had no mess facilities. His choices were to eat at the 34th Group mess or at BOQ Number One. In his initial run on BOQ #1 he encountered Warrant Officer Fred Ito, whom he'd last seen on the bus from Long Binh to Sai Gon-Cho Lon on arrival in country. Ito, it turned out to Winter's disgust, had been assigned quarters at BOQ #1 his first night in town. He was a Chief Warrant Officer-Two, same as Winter. To add to Winter's chagrin, BOQ #1 was the essential habitat for O-5s and above. There were enough lieutenant and full colonels in #1 to staff your own Pentagon, Ito said. A crap shoot, Winter groused—getting quarters or anything else in the Army, considering his banishment to Cho Lon.

Leaning on their mutual experience of arrival in-country, both assigned to the 509th Group, Winter and Ito found themselves dining together, traveling to and from the base together, and socializing in the broader world together. So Winter had developed caution.

When he bar-hopped with Ito, he frequented only establishments where they were known. The Hawaiian officer was such a study of the Oriental *type* he might easily have been anything, genetically and culturally—even Vietnamese. His diminutive size suggested it, and he spoke the language.

Sai Gon bars, heavily dependent upon American trade, did not encourage the patronage of their own nationals. Winter understood, even empathized with the unwelcome Vietnamese troops more than he did the businessmen of the city; but he knew, too, that the blame for the prevailing attitude could be shared by all. Still, it made of Fred Ito as drinking partner a potential hazard in the nervous Sai Gon of the times.

In the early war years, while the kids from Tampa and Des Plaines and Cottonwood were drafted to go off to fight a war the

American public still wasn't sure about—jerked out of Biology 312 for a failing grade, off the docks, out of the cornfields, and sent off to the strange, hostile land with the miserable climate—the Vietnamese had laughed up their sleeves. "Let the foreigners fight if they wished," mocked their attitude. The Americans, strangely, took offense at this state of self-preservation.

But those of the newly conscripted Vietnamese youth who did go, with training support and decent weapons—when the old caste system of selecting officers by family connection and the practice of appointing commanders for cash or politics, was abolished at the insistence of US command—that blasé attitude had changed to some degree.

Among some Vietnamese.

Never all.

But the memory of inequity was still there, and when there was drinking and the soldiers of both armies faced off, there was trouble in the river city. Guards were hired by bars as much to keep out the blank-faced young ARVN as to fend off attacking VC. Terror was where you found it, Winter was aware: lose some on the battlefield, some at the cashbox.

Ito slid up onto the stool two seats over from the Special Forces soldier. The way he did it suggested stealth and cunning. A devious Oriental invasion. The Spec-5 turned, checking Ito out—the curious ensemble of Hawaiian shirt, army fatigue trousers, Ho Chi Minh sandals—looked back at Winter accompanying the slight figure, then back at Ito. The Spec-5 was tall and heavy through the shoulders. His forearms propped on the bar were sunburned an angry bronze, and his state of mind showed in the cords of muscle that stood up in tight rows from the wrist back.

"You from the islands?" he asked Ito.

"What islands?"

When Ito answered in English, the Green Beret turned away and went back to staring into the broken bar mirror, sipping silently at the San Miguel. Winter watched this identification process with mild annoyance, though aware he might have done the same in similar circumstances. He sat down on the stool next to Ito.

The little Hawaiian turned to Winter and nodded behind himself at the soldier. "Enlisted swine wants to know if I'm from 'the islands.' Subtle, isn't he?"

"Yep!" Winter replied. "Hey, Mama-San, two *Ba-mui-ba*." He held up two fingers to aid her slight English. "If you weren't such a skinny little piece of shit, dressed like a Cho Lon slickie boy, you wouldn't be hassled for a local."

"Up yours, Round Eyes."

"Snappy retort there, Fred."

"You *haole* fuckers just wait. When Charlie comes skulking through the front gate, any night now, I'm slipping into my black jammies and coolie hat and moving out with them through the wire. We'll be halfway to Cambodia before those mothers figure out they picked up an extra hand. By then, I'll be off in the bush on my own."

Winter stared at him, incredulous. He shook his head. "Jesus, Fred. You got Tet jitters or something? You get lost in City Park in Honolulu. What the hell you gonna do in the jungle, G.I? Gonna turn killer, sudden-like? Gonna kick ass? Shee-it, you wouldn't even make a good meal for a leech. If Charlie caught you, he'd throw you back. You ain't even a keeper."

"Aaaahh—"

"Man, when you gonna put some meat on them little yeller bones? Only sustenance you ever get is booze, and that ain't staying with you. Don't you ever eat solid food, inscrutable one?"

"Get off my case, Winter Man. I'm at fighting weight now. Solid muscle and bone—"

"Muscle! Shit, it takes all the muscle you can muster to push the pins of those bars through the collar of your fatigue jacket every morning. By the way, where do you buy those toddler-size jungle suits, anyhow?"

The diminutive officer scowled and the slits that served as eyes became thinner. "Now you've done it. Now you've hurt me."

"Sorry 'bout that!" Winter laughed. They drank in silence.

"Mama-San, *hai Ba-mui-ba! Di di!*" Ito's singsong order caused a flurry behind the bar, swapping fulls for empties, raking in the military scrip.

* * *

The front door of the Casino swung open. It was a heavy-framed door; the wood panels cut out and replaced by glass with an embedded pattern of wire, so that guards and wary drinkers could see out. On the street side a screen of heavy-guage wire was attached; and inside the door a second, finer mesh was stretched. Where idle drinkers had once sat and watched the parade of Asian life outside, the glass was gone from the tall, narrow windows alongside the door, replaced by plywood with corrugated metal nailed to the inside in a curious reversal of transparency. From the street the place had a deserted, forbidding look; but to GIs in the nervous city, the quasi-protective construction of the bar was a drawing card.

* * *

A man entered the bar. He hesitated, then eased the door shut behind himself. Small, Oriental, his pin-stripe silk suit was conspicuous among the sea of wrinkled khaki and olive. His shirt of watered silk, white on white, and the four-in-hand tie were elaborate in a land where open collars were fashion. He squinted in the semi-dark of the bar, but wore large silver-faced sunglasses, though the sun was down beyond the western bank of the river. He resembled some small, prim form of goggle-eyed insect.

He smiled timidly in the gloom as he approached the bar. Slung around his right shoulder was a leather camera case, a sincere looking device, heavy and black. It appeared upwardly functional. Winter read NIKON across the face of the lens protrusion. The contents of the case were completely hidden.

Mama-San scrutinized the stranger with hard eyes.

The Special Forces troop's eyes swung to the door at the man's entrance, staring hard at him as he approached the bar. The small man smiled again, an effort that extended no further than his mouth; his eyes were silver mirrors. He dipped a quick bow in the Americans' direction.

Ito gave the same quick nod in return, a modern excuse for the honorable amenities—countless generations of Japanese formality. Ito turned away from the man, frowning.

Watching him climb onto a stool, Winter wondered if the newcomer was really Japanese or merely meant to convey that impression. He looked too slick, too much like a Japanese businessman to be a Japanese businessman. Winter felt a sense of disquiet.

The alert trooper stared at the man in the mirror back of the bar. He did not ask if the newcomer was from the islands.

In halting English, the Oriental asked for a beer. He carefully unslung the camera case from his shoulder and set it on the bar. He moved the case about with his elbow several times, then reached, took it off the bar, and tried to place it on the ledge beneath. The shelf, for cigarettes and change, was not deep enough to hold the case. The newcomer placed the Nikon package back on the bar cautiously as his beer was served. Throughout his manipulations, the man appeared nervous and Ito, embarrassed for him, turned from staring.

Frederick Ulysses Ito was born to a Japanese family new on the island of Molokai during the anti-Japanese hysteria of early World War II, while the family was being held in detention in a camp within sight of their own home. Ito's father—his reading of the classics was the inspiration for the child's middle name—and mother insisted that little Fred speak only English, though they had to rely upon neighbors to teach him. They had been humiliated, treated as foreigners, and would do nothing to mitigate their distance. They might have returned to their homeland in shame, but the war was on and they were incarcerated in the government camps; and too, once in America, they had seen the vast resources and knew Japan would lose and there would be nothing to go back to. So, disdaining a struggle with the unfamiliar language, they fought to ensure their son's place in the new land.

Fred Ito grew up, attended the University of Hawaii, and joined the Army with only a trace of bitterness inherited from his once-incarcerated family. In service, he was assigned to Army Security Agency and language trained, first in Korean and then some years later, in Vietnamese. What the Army didn't know, though the question never arose, was that Ito didn't speak the Japanese language native to his parents. But he felt guilty about that as he grew older.

Now, in the shabby bar a few steps off Tu Do Street—French expatriates insisted on calling the street Rue Catinat—Ito felt the compromise of his origins. He couldn't speak to the stranger in the bar in what he was sure was the man's native language, and he was ashamed to use English. He would not consider Vietnamese; Korean would be demeaning.

"Ain't that a bitch," Ito whispered, staring blindly at the bottle of "33" beer before him..

"Ugh!" *Ba-mui-ba* beer bore the reputation of being recycled mongoose piss, but it was cold. Winter frowned and took another swallow, letting the ambiguity slide.

"I mean, hell, man. I can't even talk to the little yeller mother. I think he's a Jap. I'm a Jap. And I can't even talk to him. I wonder if he speaks French," Ito said, brightening.

"I didn't know you spoke French."

"I don't. But he might."

The *non-sequitur* jarred Winter's concentration. "Leave him alone, Fred. For Christ's sake, he might be Burmese or Thai or something. Malay. Cambodge. What makes you think he's Japanese?" Winter wanted no part of a brouhaha in the bar because of a language barrier. The Green Beanie Spec-5 was tense; all he needed was an excuse.

"Look at the way he's dressed. A fucking tie! I mean, really!"

"Might be a Zip, scouting for *GQ*."

"Yeah, right. Shit, Winter, he ain't no Zip. Too much class. Look at the suit."

"Try some Cong talk on him and see."

"Bullshit!" The slits of his eyes narrowed again. "I'm not going to embarrass him and me with that kind of jerk-off play." He turned back to the bar.

"Okay," Winter grumbled. "Then shut the hell up and leave him alone. I got enough to worry about, targeting myself here on this stool, being seen in public with you, without worrying about some U.I. Oriental's ancestry."

"Well, fuck you very much, G.I."

Winter had mentioned targeting jokingly, but it was not a subject to be dismissed lightly. They both knew it, and beneath the banter at the bar there was tension in every move. It was why grenade screening was on the doors, why guards were necessary, why unaccompanied packages and objects were suspect.

Bars were particularly hazardous. The Viet Cong were running the ultimate protection racket in the midst of the war. Bar owners paid stiff "taxes" to the revolutionary people's army, or they would find themselves in a prime slot on the VC hit parade. "Hit," in the venacular of the war zone, was not just slang. A bar, blown by a grenade in real time, or a landmine planted after hours with a timer detonator, was not a popular watering hole for GIs who came to Sai Gon from the field to get away from such threats for a few days. So, they'd take their business elsewhere. It was a harsh judgement which pointed out that the GI was subsidizing the VC by his select bar patronage, but there was more than an element of truth in the charge.

The hold-outs, such as the Phillie Bar in Gia Dinh and the My Canh floating restaurant on a barge in the Sai Gon River, had their own cadres of bad asses, troops, and hardcore politicians who ate and drank in defiance of the VC. These few redoubts of integrity employed their own hit teams of thugs and slickie boys to root out

Cong plots and ward off attacks, and they did it with a viciousness, thus efficiency, that even the barbarism of the local military or police could not match.

As he watched the well-dressed stranger step off the stool, Winter realized he didn't know where the Casino Bar placed in that safe-hit spectrum, whether they paid their VC taxes or not, though he had never been given reason to believe he might be bombed in the old hangout. That some form of accommodation was in effect seemed obvious.

The pseudo Japanese glanced around the bar the way a man will search desperately when he's two beers past his bladder's limit. He motioned toward the camera case and patted it for Mama-San, ordaining her with its security, then headed for the curtained doorway at the rear of the room. The case remained, prominent on the bar.

Something—some other sense—told Winter he'd missed a trick. He felt a spasm of alarm. What was it? He raised the bottle . . . what had tweaked his brain? Something one of them had said? Who said?

He sipped the beer. Something he was thinking? . . . it was why the bars had grenade screening . . . why guards, why—

It was why packages of any kind, shape, or size were suspect in the hands of strangers, or delivered by hand, or left lying about in the vicinity of American personnel!

His eyes sought the quasi-Japanese. The man had disappeared into the back hallway leading to the stinking relief troughs. Winter knew there was a door at the far end of that hallway that led outside into an alley, eventually onto the Street of Flowers. They were all familiar with the Casino's ins and outs.

Winter tried not to look at the case on the bar, as if his radar-like, piercing gaze would somehow trigger the device inside. He turned uneasily back toward Ito, allowing the case privacy in which to go away.

Ito studied the camera case, slit-eyed and inscrutable. He alternately watched the rear hallway and stared at the black shape, as if willing the case away, or bringing the owner back.

A silent but unified wish for reappearance of the stranger hung in the air of the bar. Glancing about, Winter saw every pair of eyes in the place playing the same shifty game. But the rear hall remained empty and silent.

Winter's eyes were increasingly drawn back to the case. He scrutinized the strap where it had torn and been carelessly mended with fishing line. It was a sloppy job, unlike anything he would expect from the silk-suited Asian. The case itself looked shiny and new. There were no scratches there from use, no spots where the dye was worn off the leather from contact with a hip or belt buckle. The case was tightly closed, its contents hidden from examination.

A hush hung over the bar, deepening with each passing second. Winter looked beyond the object, forcing his eyes away from it; still, it hulked at the edge of his vision, black and threatening, emanating a hostile presence. He watched the Spec-5, saw the young Special Forces soldier's eyes grow increasingly round, increasingly large with surprise. All those months—years even—the specialist had spent in training, preparing for just this kind of situation, for action, Winter thought, and now it was here and the young soldier was caught out. Was he prepared for it? Were you ever ready for it?

The Special Forces trooper looked as if he had confirmed a long-nagging suspicion. There was a touch of smugness in his posture; there was, too, suddenly fear.

Winter suffered a brilliant pre-vision, a flashing burst of fire and death, in the pupils of the young man's eyes. Was it the Spec-5's fear he saw, or his own? There was no time, he knew, suppressing the vision.

The Vietnamese gangsters at the table in the rear glared in silence at the case. Their onyx eyes widened as if they would bring the magic of Oriental ESP to bear and vanish the thing. They had failed to consider such a development, choosing to meet like this in a place frequented by Americans. A risk out of hand. The odds were formerly always in their favor.

Without warning, Mama-San had begun edging front-doorward. It was as if they all could hear the ticking now, and it grew louder as long seconds crept by.

Suddenly, in a choreographed reaction, the bar leapt into life. Ito shouted, *"Bomb!"*

Winter, torn between sacrifice and self-preservation, without consciousness of the polarization—between grabbing the case or hurling his body the other way toward safety—vacillated for a moment in a spastic exercise, then dove from the stool, rolled once across the floor, and came up on his feet, sprinting toward the curve of the bar leading outside.

Mama-San stopped her waddling progress toward the door and flowed limply to the floor behind the bar. The black market-pimp-drug dealers in the back booth disappeared out the same door the bomber had taken, leaving in their wake a tumble of chairs, a crash of bottles and glasses.

Only the Spec-5 did as trained. Only he responded in an attempt to marginalize chaos. Only a Green Beanie, thought Winter later, was silly enough to do that. Or conditioned enough. Or bold enough. He should have fled the bar while he could, like ordinary people.

No! Answering a higher calling, he should have responded as he would.

And he did.

And it cost him.

The Spec-5, echoing Ito, screamed, *"Bomb!"* and grabbed the camera case in both hands, turning without hesitation toward the front door, walking gingerly but rapidly, holding the sinister leather container before him.

From his place behind the curving front of the bar, Winter saw the Snake Eater coming. He jumped up again without thinking and hit the grenade screen of the front door, running. He slammed the door back, hearing the glass shatter between the layers of wire, feeling shards splinter out like shrapnel. Plastered to the outer wall, he held back the shattered door to give clear passage to the soldier with the bomb.

As he brought his forearm up to cover his face—vainly seeking to make his body as small as possible—he saw the old crone soup-and-noodle vendor chopping vegetables at a cart just beyond the door of the bar. She was always there, he realized in a flash. He'd eaten from her service, but had never really noticed her before. He screamed at her: *"Di di mau!* Get the hell out of here!"

She stared at him blank-faced, an opiate film of distance across her mind, and she did not move. Winter could clearly hear the isolated *chun-nk* of her cleaver as she chopped through the greens, undisturbed, accustomed to the prevailing American violence.

The Spec-5 stepped out through the door, holding the case in both hands at waist level, strap dangling, dragging on the ground.

He's carrying it all wrong!, thought Winter, wanting to shout. But he knew there was no right way to do what the Green Beanie was doing. Any second . . .

If it did explode before he could dispose of it, the Spec-5 would be a permanent decoration on the front wall of the Casino. So would

Winter. He couldn't watch . . . couldn't *not* watch. He wanted to be somewhere else, somebody else. He wanted—

The soldier stopped on the walk, repositioned his right hand tightly about the camera case, then grasped the case even tighter in his left hand. When it was securely fixed there, he released his grip with the right. Winter watched the young soldier reach down and grab the strap—*Take it farther from the door!* he longed to scream, but he feared what the sudden shout might do to the Beret's concentration—and in one fleeting mini-scene vision as he dove for the sidewalk, he saw the soldier suspend the camera case by its strap, then whirl it around his head by the strap, saw a group of Vietnamese sailors on the opposite sidewalk scatter as they intuitively realized what was happening, saw the black hallmark of terror go sailing across the intervening street and erupt against the wall of the concrete-faced office building-porno studio opposite . . .

* * *

Winter awoke to dimly remembered strains from a song: ". . . dawn comes up like thunder out of China 'cross the bay." He gleefully imagined several special hells for pilots, co-pilots, jet mechanics, aeronautical engineers, airframe manufacturers, tower controllers, radar and GCA operators, baggage handlers, runway maintenance crews, strike planners—everyone associated with aircraft proliferation. His head, stuffed with barbed steel wool, reverberated with pain.

The Mandalay he remembered was a Chinese restaurant in Salinas. The thunder came, not out of China, but from twin J79-GE-15 jet engines as sleepless crews launched dawn strikes from Tan Son Nhut. The wind had shifted in the night and the sorties were coming off runway Zero-Seven. Weather fickleness had Winter at the ass-end of the Phantoms, and he suffered the full range of decibel destruction as he listened, hearing the F-4Cs turn into the wind, poise, then take to the sky, lining up their afterburners on the Newport BOQ as they overflew. You could have tac air, or sleep; not both.

Winter pulled himself from the bed and lurched to the window holding his head. He parted the louvered slats, staring into the dark sky to the west. Another rumble built as a second pair of Phantoms rolled into their tandem race down the dark strip between rows of flickering blue. He covered his ears to the deafening crescendo as they pulled max and thundered up over the roof of the billets.

Tracking them by their exhaust, he watched them arc away north and east into the darkness, some time yet until the red-going-gold-pink-mauve dawn of the song. And they *were* the thunder.

Really decent! He could recognize that, despite his head. They were graceful, he grudgingly admitted, as the powerful engines thrust them heavenward: eight thousand, five hundred feet in less than a minute, though loaded and deadly with ordnance. In the air they were . . . odd. Unexpectedly more awesome even than their imposing grandeur poised on the ground. Winter, watching one taxi by him on the strip at Da Nang, had felt as if he had come suddenly upon a rhino in toe shoes that, in launching, had leaped, ungainly, onto point and become beautiful in transition.

Jesus! He was getting flaky. He needed sleep. He looked at the time and groaned: less than two hours since he hit the rack after an evening he wished he could forget. That goddamned Casino!

He leaned over the edge of his bunk, holding his head in his hands. The consecutive booms of another Phantom's afterburners, followed closely by those of his wingman, made Winter's entire body throb. He felt shaky, tentative. Sick.

The heat of the coming day was hours away, too, but it did not matter; the heat of yesterday was still on the land, the humidity still cloying. The sickly stench of *nuoc mam* pervaded the BOQ, a statement of disregard for USARV regulations which proclaimed that housegirls might not cook their meals in the billets areas. The halls and stairways and rooms reeked of their disdain.

Winter reached over and flicked on the bedside lamp. His new UI captain roommate, who had come in during the previous day, dropped his bags and gone out, was still not back. Winter hung his head and watched the pattern in the floor tiles emerge as his eyes focused. No sleep, he'd settle for quiet.

But there was no respite. The short spell was broken as a flight of prop aircraft rose from the Tan Son Nhut runways and broke out of the pattern directly above the BOQ. The Skyraiders were not as loud as the F-4s, but the throbbing insistence of the recip engines was in a way more deadly than the jets.

And no breathable oxygen. Only residual blue smoke from cyclos and taxis, the sodden heat with its own odor; grey smoke from charcoal-burning buses and late cooking fires, rotting fruit on the ground, and the reek of back-alley urine, excrement, vomit, and spilled beer. He held his head and pushed in on his temples, trying to still the incessant devils there. He tried in vain to blank from his vision the previous night.

Behind closed lids he saw, in a staccato series of single-frame movie shots, the high arcing path of the black camera case lobbed into the concrete front wall of the tall building across the street from the Casino. He saw it strike the wall. He heard—he would keep on hearing—the smash of metal and glass and levers, gears, film and mirrors, of screws and plating and lens caps and coupling rings, and the long, drawn-out cascade of those parts as they showered down on the already thoroughly littered street.

The Nikon camera exploded from the case and spread in a shower of junk, and for an instant the burst radius of the finely crafted mechanism was as impressive as any bomb might have been.

When his astonishment was stilled, when he and the Special Forces SP5 looked at one another—uneasy, embarrassed, relieved they were alive—and turned to find the Japanese businessman standing in the door of the bar, twisting the glasses in his hands like a revolving silver propeller, Winter had felt the horror of the moment . . . only horror, not humor. No one had laughed.

Now he drew a blank on what had come after, until he had realized he was walking along Tu Do Street and Ito was calling to him from behind, hurrying to catch up, and he could hear, farther back, around the corner, the high shrill screams of the Nipponese businessman who had come to the old whore city on the river in the wrong season.

Winter'd felt guilty about leaving the Spec-5 at the Casino to catch all the flak. But after all, anybody who volunteered for his kind of grief ought to be able to withstand a little minor aggravation. After several more drinks toward solace at another bar on Tu Do, Winter and Ito had taken a taxi back near the Third Field Hospital and split up. Winter walked the block to the Newport. Ito scuffled his way through the side street muck and trash back to BOQ Number 1, each to seek his own vision of unwarranted grace from a bottle of his choosing.

chapter sixteen

Penthouse Schmoozin'

Vietnam: October 1968

He flicked off the light and lay back on the damp bed. Closing his eyes, he tried again to sleep, but his hands leapt back in front of his face each time he almost dropped off, shielding him from— something. The explosion rang in his ears, the one that never came, echoing through lapses of wakefulness, ringing out in fragmentary dreams. When the real stuff began impacting in the distance, off toward Ben Cat on the horizon, it was mixed up with nightmares and with the screaming never-happens of the camera-bomb.

When his mind had slammed through the shift several times, evolving each time into *Alert!* Winter forced himself finally from the terrifying and fitful sleep. Like pulling a dead weight up out of the mud, tentacles of slime and sinuous roots and vague, living hazards gripping, pulling back against the effort. With a mighty surge, he freed his mind of the morass. He was awake.

Steady, rolling reverberations trembled the bunk and he felt his heart pounding, pounding and pumping madly, and for one harrowing moment he envisioned it ripping from his chest and bounding into the night, away from explosions and fear.

When he was thoroughly awake, when he recognized what he was hearing, what he felt, he could tell the rounds were falling far off and he did not bother to go to the window. He would see only a rosy glow along the skyline, he knew, and starshells and parachute flares would hang, draped in the hot night sky like evil Christmas lights. Still, he would not sleep.

It would be Ben Cat . . . he listened . . . or Phu Lai. It was always Ben Cat or Phu Lai. Poor bastards! The Vietnamese Panther Division might have been deployed on an artillery range impact area for all the incoming they caught. But if they weren't good, it would not have been worth Charlie's time and precious ammo.

Winter marveled at the dedication required to live that life, thankful he didn't do it anymore. Once, in another life, that had been what his war was all about. But this way was better. As he cynically gave in to the preference for creature comforts, he knew that very issue was a major factor in America's inability to better deal with the struggle in this third-rate country. He had disturbing images of huge tails manipulating small dogs.

He pushed the conflicts of conflict from his mind, slid into clammy fatigue trousers, and pulled a Tee-shirt over his head. He found the clogs in the dark and flip-flopped out the door into weak, flickering hall light. He shivered as he realized, despite his own casual evaluation, he *was* living that other kind of life.

He stopped at the elevator, thinking of the three flights of stairs from this second floor to the roof. One shot in ten the lift would be working, he knew, but when he released the button the 2 lit up, and he heard the cage rise from the ground floor. The car shuddered to a stop at his floor and the doors sprang open.

A wildly staring naked woman was propped back in the right corner of the car. Chief Warrant Officer-3 Jackson Spain, in mufti for whatever devious purpose he worked on the nude, red-headed nurse, snarled out at him. Winter stepped back. The doors zipped shut. The car continued north. He admired Spain's taste.

He shivered, and walked up the stairs. Passing the fourth floor, he saw down the hall the pilot, Spanish Jack, propping the nurse's white, recumbent body against the wall, holding her clothes bunched in that same hand while he opened the door with the other. Winter looked away and kept climbing.

When he stepped out of the stairwell on the roof, the air struck him with the welcome force of the first beer on a hot day. The Sai Gon air was not cool, it didn't smell good; but it was fresher than the dank, close atmosphere that ranged about the lower floors. Leaning on the parapet looking out onto the war was better than lying between clammy sheets fighting 'mares.

Winter's eyes roved the skyline to the north, his mind musing on the economy of the word. 'mares! *Night*-mares. Out of some vague classroom of the past he dredged up fragments, the origin of the word, something arising from mythology or literature—succubi and incubi, horses of the night, some such innocuous drivel. Probably Brenner could explain it. But Brenner was drinking Maxlrainerbräu in Mietraching or Gross-Karolinefeld.

Now he was sure. The target was Phu Lai, nearer than Ben Cat, still a comfortable distance away. Strange relativity, that.

Artillery shells walked along the horizon, taking each step in a blinding flash of beauty. He watched in awe, knowing that each blossoming flower of fire grew over the dead and the maimed and dying. There was no way to equate the sensations and he steeled himself against the need. As he watched the distant show, Winter grudgingly admired the precision with which some tiny alien revolutionary worked his magic, calling in compliant devils from afar, bringing down a storm of destruction. He knew, too, it was likely done with primitive tools: bamboo poles for aiming stakes; a French hiker's compass, likely as not, for fire control. How could he not be impressed.

"Infantry may be the Queen of Battle," he recalled a gunner's sage comment, "but it's arty'll blow your nuts off." He no longer sought immutable verities in such philosophies, but neither could he deny the essential truth. The lean, ignorant sergeant who had passed on those immortal words was an artilleryman. A tender of the guns. No one mentioned him in that light; in the world beyond his craft, no one considered him in those terms. A man in his career, as aptly titled as Chekhov described his dandified Czarist soldiers, labored without the knowledge of why he was or was not so labeled.

To be an artilleryman in the war age of mechanization and computerization was somehow anachronistic, though he still served the guns that delivered the ordnance that rent and violated and conquered by fear and intimidation and the purest form of destruction. He did know, and would have reaffirmed the statistic, that eighty percent of all casualties in the Big One, World War II, were the result of artillery fire—in its many variations. It was a calling, and the artilleryman had pride in the crossed tubes on his collar brass.

Winter watched the fireworks with a craftsman's pride. He too had served the guns and knew quality work when he saw it.

"Who goes?" The voice from the dark, sharp and anxious in the reflected flashes, startled him.

"Chief Winter. Who's that? Hermann?"

"Private First Class Printer, sir. You're not supposed to be on the roof, sir. Especially when there's activity." The guard came into view, framed against the light from the upper floors of Third Field Hospital beyond; the helipad across the road was a contrast in black. The guard walked toward Winter with an M-16 thrust before him, angled to the side. Sandbags were stacked kitty-cornered at the junction of the north streetside parapet and the east wall. The black silhouettes of an M-60 machine gun and a spotting scope were framed, like the guard, against the glow. Beyond the structure to the east and south flared the uneasy nimbus of Sai Gon.

"Does that mean I'm never supposed to be up here, period? Or am I just not to be here when there's activity? You new here, Printer? Hell, there's always activity."

"Sir, excuse me, sir. My orders are that no one but guards and the staff of the BOQ are to be on this roof. I'm new on this assignment..." his hesitance begging understanding.

"Winter. Chief Warrant Officer Winter. Yeah, I know, Printer. But nobody pays any attention to that shit." He walked toward the east wall. The young PFC insinuated himself between Winter and the wall, and raised the M-16 halfway in front of his chest.

"Relax, Printer. I know what they told you at guard mount. They tell every guard that. But I live here in this B.O.Q.—"

"Sorry, sir. They specifically warned us about you flyers."

"Now just a goddamned minute, Printer," Winter bristled. "You watch your mouth. Sweet Jesus! Do I look that weird? I'm in the 224th; I am *not* a pilot. Give me a break, man. I'm just a real American lad, red, white, and blue, through and through." He nodded over the parapet toward the large villa below, on the opposite side of the small secondary street. "I even respect the old bastard."

Ignoring the rifle almost touching him, Winter leaned on the stone-topped ledge and looked down into the compound of General Vetter's quarters. The general, commander of all US and allied forces in Vietnam, lived better than your average warrant officer. "Besides, can't you tell . . . I'm unarmed. I'm unlegged. Un-assed . . . man, I am un*done*." He propped his chin on his crossed hands, but took small comfort in the guard's uneasy indecision.

"Hey, Dave!"

The guard whipped about, rifle at the ready. The voice was a whisper, but it carried across the open roof, borne on a night breeze that smelled of cordite and dead fish and the line of whorehouses in Hundred-P Alley up the street: the cold stars above; the hot, sour world below. Even Hundred-P Alley was a lie; the cheapest ass began at 200 piastres.

"Who's that?" Winter said to the dark.

"Prue."

"Hey, Fat Man. Where are you?" speaking to the void. A goddamned staff meeting.

"Behind the tank. C'mon over."

"Sir," the guard began anxiously, "I didn't know there was anyone else up here. You gentlemen—"

"Go back to your post, Printer. Watch the honcho's palace. We won't tell; you don't tell. We won't bother The Man, I promise you; you don't bother us. We're just gonna sit behind the water tank and watch the fireworks. Like we always do. And pray for peace . . . like we always do. You just pray they don't move this way and start dropping them in here like they did in Tet. This flat roof is no place to be, with incoming." Winter was conscious of the lie implicit in his warning; the facts were correct, but he wasn't even in country for the Tet offensive. "And, Printer . . . watch who the fuck you're applying that term to—gentlemen."

But the hint worked. The guard moved rapidly back into his semi-private bunker, put his semi-automatic weapon on safety, and became semi-catatonic. Winter sat down by the hulk that was CW3 Carl O. Prue and reached for the bottle he knew had to be there.

"Whatcha want?" Prue asked indignantly.

"Gimme a drink, Prue. I really need it."

The fat man, a pilot who might have used both pilot and co-pilot seats for himself, hedged a bit, then reached behind rolls of belt-line fat and passed over the fifth of JD. "Didn't think you liked bourbon, Dave," he murmured.

"I don't. Drink anything tonight, though."

He told Prue the story of the Great Casino Bombing, and when he was finished the pilot was rolling on the graveled roof, his breath ragged gasps, catching in hysterics, tears streaming down his fat cheeks. He didn't even reach for the bottle back, and Winter had a couple more before Prue sat up wiping his eyes. "Great fucking day! That Nip is probably still ricocheting off the walls downtown in some Q.C. station. Called out the White Mice, no doubt. He'll probably put out a contract on that Snake Eater." He went into another spasm of laughter. "You, too," he grated out between deep sobs of breath.

"Yeah, probably," Winter agreed. "But that's all right—that Beanie had the balls to do what I didn't do. Or maybe I had more sense or something. But he did it. Know what I mean? He did it while I waffled. So did Ito. And the pimps and Mama-San boogied. And—" He sat up suddenly. "Oh, shit!"

"What?"

"There was another G.I. in the bar . . . I just remembered." He described the face in the beer. "Nobody warned him, nobody moved him. It that had been a bomb—if it had gone off in Gallant Man's face—that drunk'd never have known what hit him."

"There're worse ways to go," Prue observed. "No anxiety, no fear, nothing. One minute you're blissfully blown away, the next, you're just . . . blown away." Looking at him in partial darkness with the glare of artillery bursts reflecting off low-hanging clouds, pulsing off his round, sweaty face, even the most dedicated romantic would have failed to recognize in Prue a warrior. Bedrock of real heroism. Not some mock variety contrived for show, displayed when the photographers or generals were swarming; a spontaneous, unconscious kind of caring. But it was true: he didn't look the part.

Carl Prue was on his third consecutive tour in Vietnam, three years without a break from the war, except occasional R&R to some other Asian port. He had an astronomical count of combat flying hours, and he was the recipient of two Silver Stars, two Distinguished Flying Crosses, the Bronze Star with "V" device and three Oak Leaf Clusters, eighty-seven Air Medals, and several Army Commendation Medals. He called the latter his "didn't get caught" markers, considering them officers' Good Conduct Medals.

He didn't count yet the Distinguished Service Cross, which he'd been recommended for but had not received through channels; and he dismissed the five Purple Hearts, arguing that any dumb sonuvabitch could get a chunk blown out of his ass—didn't take anything special for that, and he didn't relish the award. The DSC had been written up personally by a brigade commander after observing, in person from his command chopper, Prue's actions, landing his bush plane on a grass strip in the Michelin Plantation near Tay Ninh during a fire fight. Prue had leapt from the plane and flogged his bulk over sixty yards of open ground under fire, manned a machinegun while grunts dragged their LT out of the fire. He then carried the wounded officer on his shoulder back to the plane—by then a target for every weapon in III Corps—and with the help of his ARDF operator loaded the WIA, boarded the Beaver, and took off downwind through a hail of fire that left Prue wounded, his operator wounded, and the wounded officer wounded all over again. All three survived.

Prue had the awards, but the only time he ever wore his medals was when he was called up on one charge or another before some transient, one-tour commander, or by some unknowing Provost Marshal for an indiscretion. Then he would don full dress, complete with medals, Senior Aviator Badge, Master Parachute Badge, Combat Infantry Badge, and display himself before the astonished court. When they saw him in flight gear, they saw a fat clown; when he decked out, they saw a warrior. A *large* warrior. He had never been disappointed at their reaction, and suitable disposition to his case inevitably followed.

The Army would have discharged Pruitt for gross obesity had he not played his cards exactly right. His main reason for staying in Vietnam was that he was known there by his record in the combat zone, by his flying ability. He always managed to be manifested on a flight when physical exams were scheduled, and by stalling, lying, various forms of chicanery, he extended the reviews into the twilight zone and he was never pinned down for the physical. A similar arrangement allowed him to miss any kind of personnel inspection. Generals pinning medals on him never had the nerve, staring at that massive chest of rainbow colors, to comment on his weight problem. If he had returned to the US, or shipped to Okinawa, Europe, Japan, or Korea, the ubiquitous curse of medical regulations would have banished him from the life he loved.

As he grew increasingly larger, Prue found buckling two web belts together to reach around his girth a demeaning act, so he refused to wear a belt. He could not wear his shoulder holster in the prescribed manner; his bulk would not permit it. But that didn't bother him. He stuck the bare .357 down in a cargo pocket and dumped half a box of truncated-cone ammo into his side flight suit pockets before each flight. He'd had the fire-retardant suit specially crafted for him by an Indian tailor in Sai Gon out of the remnants of three other suits. It cost him five cartons of Salems.

Prue's three tours had seen him decline from the premier role for his skills—flying helicopter gunships—to what he considered a less-demanding, thus less attractive role: flying *slicks*, choppers without organic firepower. Later, he transitioned into the large support CH-47 Chinooks, and eventually into fixed wing where he now found himself. And here, his bulk had grown such that he could not make it past the equipment racks in the U-21s, so he could not fly the new mission birds. He had difficulty even climbing onto the wings of the U-8s unaided, so he was generally reduced to flying Beavers and Otters which sported exterior ladders. Though he liked those old high-wing, single-engine bush planes designed for use in Arctic terrain, he pretended disappointment. He'd begun to believe someone *at the top* was out to get him, but so long as they—the Army—felt he was miserable, maybe they would leave him alone. And so they had, thus far. Just another pilot, burnout, been in southeast Asia too long. 'round the bend!

"What else's going on?" Prue asked Winter. "I heard some sirens come up from Gia Dinh and head down Plantation Road. Something I oughta know?" His moon face was middle. Not happy, not sad; neither angry nor calm. Just middle. It was how he said he always felt, as long as he could fly. He wasn't flying the cream of the fleet anymore, but he was flying.

"Who knows! Can't see shit from the second floor, and I was trying to sleep." Winter watched the pyrotechnics along the horizon, noting with mild interest the sudden appearance of a red beam, like a ruby searchlight that illuminated the perimeter of the flickering fires where the shells fell. It might have been a skysweeping Boy Scout with red cellophane over the lens of a powerful flashlight. But he knew it was Puff, the Magic Dragon.

Puff was friendly. The beam was not a flashlight or laser, and it did not emanate from the ground; it was a stream of cannon fire, the rounds fired so rapidly that the tracer trajectories appeared like a solid stream of red flame directed from the converted C-47 platform. Puff was doing a number on enemy pincered around Phu Lai—in the daily briefings at The Pentagon East, nearby MACV headquarters, the enemy was always described as "pincered around friendly elements at Phu Lai" or the enemy was "attempting to establish a pincer envelopment of Ben Cat." The NVA, now attacking, not knowing a pincer from a pissant, had waited until their own mortar fire lifted before leaving spider holes and bunkers and ditches and buffalo wallows in the dry rice paddies, charging *en masse* into the remains of the bombarded hamlet defenses.

And Puff, with omniscient knowledge and the stoic patience of mythical dragons, had waited in turn.

Winter grunted and nodded toward the conflict. Prue followed his lead, took a drink and smiled. His face for a moment was not middle.

"Saw Spanish Jack bringing Doris up in the elevator," Winter murmured.

"She have any clothes on?"

"Nope. Drunk. That time of night." The fires were dying on the skyline. There were fewer flares and the colors of the starshells were changing. At first white, then green; now there was a red one, a green, then another red. Puff's dragon breath became sporadic.

"How the hell you reckon he manages that? Every time he takes her out," Winter said.

Prue took another swig and passed the bottle back to Winter. "Jack said she gets horny on gin, and he has to get her out of wherever they are, because when she's had more'n a couple, she's drunk and wants to screw. Most women have subtle signals they give their mate—taking off earrings, a certain smile, something. Doris's signal is ripping off her clothes. Not a subtle bone in her fine body. Mad! Mad!"

"How bad is that?"

"Know what you mean, but Jack's afraid to take her out anywhere where there're people. So he just hangs around with nurses and pilots and other whores."

"Harsh, Prue. Harsh."

The fat man smiled grimly. "Not my judgement—Jack's. He says he tries to keep her off gin—she can drink anything else without bothering her that way—but wherever they go, she finds the Bombay and goes for it. He's had to flee some mighty fine parties. Hell, she even started whippin' them off at the O Club on Tan Son Nhut one night and General Vetter was there with a party of Gook bigwigs. Vetter thought she was a paid stripper and started fooling around, offered her to the Zip three-star who was obviously taken with her. Jack had a hell of a time getting her out of that fiasco without them both winding up in L.B.J.," he laughed, then changed tack. "Christ, why don't he drop her, Dave? He can always get a nurse. Or that doughnut dolly from the Zoomie side."

"Says she's too good. I believe him, too. He thinks he loves her." Winter nodded in admiration. "Gotta be worse ways to go through a tour here."

"Hmmm." Instant and unwarranted shift. "Heard from Nickie?"

There was a long pause. Prue wasn't looking at Winter. "A week ago," Winter finally said. "One of my boys, Jeremy, is having some ear problems. The other one's fine. Good news."

"How about your . . . *situation?*"

"Apparently still a situation."

"Ain't that a bitch!" Prue said softly.

"Second time tonight I've enjoyed that little epithet."

"Say what?"

There was silence for a while after that. The red beam went away and the rumbling along the horizon tapered off.

Winter, cast into the amphitheater of personal pain, indulged a fond reminiscence of a time when he and Nicole were not a situation, but were a mated pair, joined at the heart, and jointly enamored of their tandem-ness. Then he thought better of it and sought distance.

Winter pulled occasionally at the fifth of JD, glancing finally at his watch. "Aarrghh! Oh-four-thirty, plus. And to you skulkers out there in the night, the big hand's on six and the little one's . . ."

Prue snored reproachfully at him. Winter stood, picked up the poncho he'd been sitting on and spread it over the mountainous figure, slipping the almost-empty bottle beneath. He walked toward the stairs, avoiding proximity to the nervous guard.

Back in his room, Winter reached into his *faux* wall locker and pulled a letter from the pocket of a jungle fatigue jacket. A crackling sound arose from the locker, a flimsy box-like structure made from uncured mahogany that threatened to wrench itself apart as it dried. He turned on the 25-watt bulb at bedside, and in a move that he had already sworn not to commit to again, sat down to read for the twenty-third time the latest missive from the home front.

David: *Oct. 3rd*

Just a note to keep you up on the boys, and things in general. Jeremy has been to the Dr. twice with ear infections. We may have a drain put in. The Dr. says he is a bit old for this procedure, it is usually done mostly on infants. But if it will help—He is doing well in school, especially reading. I know you would want to know that. He's a good boy, helps his mother a lot, especially with Adam. Adam is just Adam; never gets sick, and without the rigors of school, seems happy but dare I say it? somewhat disoriented for lack of his dad.

I am well and we are doing as well as we can in this too-familiar scenario. In a sense, I am sorry that we did not get to talk more about the <u>real problem</u> before you left. I know I was being a bitch, and I do apologize about your beloved books, but I wish you had not moved up your departure as you did. We do need to resolve this <u>stand-off</u>. For the boys, if not for ourselves. That sounds a bit smarmy, but I was sincere when I said what I did, about whatever happens to me is not so important, but that we have them to consider. Thinking back on my behavior, you probably think this is just another form of self-

serving, being a martyr, or such. You may not be wrong, but I don't think you're right.

Be careful. Whatever our state of relations, I would not want to have something happen to you. Again. Something final! I cannot even bring myself to write it, you know what I mean. That would be taking too much from the boys' lives.

Nicole

Winter stifled a slight shudder. The letter was missing a lot of phrases, a lot of words.

A lone Jeep, headlights doused against the curfew, sped down the road below. Winter heard a clink as a beer can hit the asphalt, a loud giggle, and the Jeep disappeared toward Gate 2. A scream echoed back on the tormented night: *"I hate this fucking place!"*

chapter seventeen

The $100 Caribou

Vietnam: October 1968

Winter looked up, thinking to get up, but it was impossibly early. Across the room a preview of emerging sun brought out a bit of exotica hanging between a wall locker and a foldout from a men's magazine. The piece taped to the wall, a faded calendar print he had only vaguely noticed before, seemed a compulsive exhibition. The wall locker—that was familiar: it had no door, its hinges ripped off in some midnight requisition. The marvelously endowed pinup with San Miguel bottle tops taped over her nipples had caught his eye, too; more gynecologically astounding than beautiful, she was well suited for the purpose she served. Both items—the wall locker and the pinup—were the remains of previous BOQ tenants who had served their time here and gone back to the world, or gone up country, or down. Or died. Or changed back into a prince.

Neither wall locker nor, strangely. the pinup, was of interest.

But between them the calendar photo, badly framed in bamboo, held Winter's gaze. The courtyard of a Buddhist temple with shiny, intricate roofs slightly out of focus, fierce but hazy plaster dragons guarding wide doors. In focus, in the foreground nearer the camera, a simple vase holding a handful of long-stemmed joss sticks intruded into the scene, the tips of the sticks glowing with subdued fire. These votive offerings, rather than the temple background, caught the viewer's eye. Staring at the joss sticks in the jar, an elegantly plain Zen artwork in the dim light, Winter thought he could smell the smoke that wisped in a thin plume upward from the portrayed silent courtyard where there was no wind. He caught the scent of jasmine where unfocused blossoms on vines hung from a bough above the fiercest dragon. He sensed the serenity of the courtyard; he knew the bamboo and willow leaves on the tiled courtyard under his feet, dry and crackling in the quiet.

An accomplishment, that picture.

* * *

He was up now, the events of the night only a bad dream behind him, and with more corporeal Phantoms shattering the dawn, launching from the nearby Tan Son Nhut runways, sleep was no longer an option. Finally back in the rack after the rooftop follies at 0430, now it was just turning over six.

He yanked a towel off the mosquito bar, damp and heavy from yesterday's shower, cold with minimal evaporation. In the shower the water was tepid: he could get it neither hot nor cold. He scrubbed off the surface layer, sponged himself with the moist towel, and crawled back into the same jungle fatigues for the second day. The rank odor of last night's mud, threats, and fears enveloped him tighter than the jacket.

He was standing at the foot of the bunk buttoning his jacket when full sun broke the uneven horizon of surrounding buildings and shone through the slatted window. A shaft of light fell directly on the picture of the temple court he had so admired upon waking. Winter, drawn to the wall, inspected the picture, this time in the light of day without the overweening influence of the hob-goblins of the night.

It really was an ugly picture, he decided. Cheap, maudlin, bourgeois . . . just plain ugly.

* * *

Winter worked the cipher lock and entered Headquarters, 224th Aviation Battalion. The guard was at his post, the duty sergeant in the S-1 shop asleep at his desk, and down the hall another light shone from the Three shop. Beyond that, the building seemed deserted. Outside, it was full light at 0630 hours and moderate, the heat just beginning to build against the promise of another tropical cooker. Inside, the hall was chilly from the air conditioner that ran twenty-four hours a day. In the chill, artificial air he felt the fatigues where they stuck to his body. He tracked a drop of perspiration as it trickled from his collar, down the length of his spine, until soaking into his damp beltline.

Winter walked into the S-3 Operations shop and watched silently as Boyd Smiley performed his ritual calisthenics. The Warrant Officer pilot, unaware of his audience, continued the sit-ups, counting aloud each repetition, working in a little patter between counts: "Sixty-seven . . . ugh! Sixty-seven dirty witches . . . whuh! Sixty-eight . . . ugh! Sixty-eight slimey bitches . . . whuh! Sixty-nine . . . ugh! My kinda number . . . whuh! Seventy . . . ugh! Seventy limber switches . . . whuh! Seventy-one . . . ugh! Seventy-one switched tushes . . . whuh! Seventy-two . . . ugh! Seventy-two tushie pushies . . . whuh! Seventy—"

From the corner of his eye he spotted Winter but his rhythm did not falter.

"—three . . . ugh! Seventy-three winter pussies . . . whuh! Seventy-four . . . ugh! Seventy-four pussy munchies . . . whuh!"

"*Mister* Smiley, if you please."

"Ugh!"

"This cannot be. You? Abroad at this hour?"

"Seventy-five, finitos! *Whewf!*" The officer arose from the desktop, flat-bellied, muscles rippling along his slim extremities: poster model for lean and mean. Closer to merely skinny and aggravating, Winter knew his acidulous friend Brenner might have argued. Smiley drew the one-piece NOMEX flight suit from where it belled about his waist, slipped his arms into the sleeves but didn't zip it up; he pulled an olive drab handkerchief from his flight suit pocket, mopped the sweat from his face and neck and seemed to deliberate.

"Secret mission, Dave. Can't tell you." He grinned, waiting for Winter's come-back.

"Secret mission's ass. It'd take more than cloak and dagger to drag your reluctant bod out of the rack." Winter turned away, feigning indifference. "Coffee ready?"

"Yeah, back there." His grin faded quickly, as if suddenly remembering the joke was in poor taste. "Honest, this is deep stuff." Or the joke was on him. Or it was no joke. "Get your coffee. I'm glad you're in. I gotta tell somebody. I'm so pissed I can't see straight, and if something goes wrong, I don't want to leave my history in the hands of the colonel. I want his ass hung out to dry."

When Winter returned to the office with undisguised curiosity, Smiley was packing his .38 and maps into a desk drawer. He looked up and Winter saw challenge overridden by evasion in his eyes. "Dave, you heard from Nickie?"

"Not since last time," he said, shutting *that* door. What was this Ann Landers shit? Did all his friends think they needed to—"Thought you were flying," he countered, nodding toward the open drawer.

"Yeah, I am. But man, this ain't like no flight you might want to book on." He looked around to ensure the office had not been invaded by the colonel's latent spirit. He went to the door, glanced up and down the hallway, shut the door, and sat on the edge of a desk near Winter. Still breathing hard from the calisthenics, he spoke softly. "Listen, man, don't utter a word of this to anybody. *Any*-body, I mean it. That wacky colonel would have my balls on a prop blade. This is truly weird stuff, son."

"Well, hell! Get on with it!"

"Hold your horses. Gotta get my shit straight." His breathing leveled out. When he spoke, there was a timbre in his voice of tales told around childhood scout camps, when counselors would build huge roaring fires and bewilder-terrify youngsters with tales of ghosts and murderers and dead Indians and such, the counselor voices filled with awe and wonder. "Mister Winter, you ever heard about Two-seven-four? Caribou, tail number Two-seven-four?"

"No. Air Force bird? Army don't have anymore Caribous, do we?"

There was a hush. "We got one," Smiley said softly. His eyes would not hold still. He continued to empty his pockets into the desk. He set aside a single chart with navigational markings and one grease pencil. The rest of the maps and charts went into the drawer. Winter waited, saying nothing, staring at Smiley's flight helmet on the desk, stenciled with his name. The pilot picked off a rack a second helmet, a battered and scarred relic bearing the name of a pilot who had contracted malaria, shipped out to the states, and died en route. His gear never caught up with his body. The helmet had become a spare in the 224th/146th, but the dead airplane driver's name, Ames, still marked it. No one wanted to wear it; even new enlisted ops shunned it when they knew its history. Smiley held up the headgear in silent comment and slipped it into his helmet bag.

Winter continued waiting, knowing he would hear about Caribou 274 when Smiley was ready, and bracing himself for a story. Pilots were a superstitious lot, their lives re-runs of terror and tales of that terror, and worse. Winter, because he flew with them, was accepted on their terms, up to a point. That included sharing the myths. He was entitled to Smiley's revelations.

* * *

Smiley's tale was a subtle mix of his own angst and verifiable history.

In November 1966, American military presence had grown to more than a half million troops in Vietnam. Since October of the previous year, when American forces had defeated main-force North Vietnamese Army regulars in a major engagement in the Ia Drang Valley—such conventional warfare alien to their guerrilla philosophy—the communist forces avoided large set-piece battles, falling back for the time on the precepts of Ho-Giap-Mao guerilla strategy. This did not mean avoiding combat, merely avoiding combat when the good guys were liable to pose an even-or-better threat.

But over the ensuing months, Americans and South Vietnamese forces lost sight of their strategic goals. Command became enmeshed in a numbers game, and the emboldened communist forces began to press their advantage, choosing time and place for confrontations.

Winter, familiar with this history, thought it pedantic in Smiley's bitter telling, but he listened with aroused interest to the pilot's denunciation of the ARVN forces, a fault he attributed to a failure of their officer corps. Tragedies on the battlefield were commonplace and the most tragic aspect was that the wrong people paid the price.

Major Dan Barlow was adviser to an ARVN infantry battalion in III Corps. In OPERATION JUNCTION CITY, that battalion and its sister battalions in the ARVN 29th Regiment suffered major casualties: 11 percent dead; 36 percent wounded, captured, and/or missing.

When the battle was over—when the North Vietnamese broke contact and evaporated into the jungle along the Cambodian border—Major Barlow, severely wounded in the right hip, the right shoulder, and the left periphery of his neck and head but adamant about sustaining his advisory role, called on his own countrymen for ultimate support. He held his Vietnamese infantry—enlisted men, NCOs, and some junior and company grade officers—in warm regard. The allied ARVN regimental commander and his staff, however, and the commanders and staffs of two of the three battalions, including his own 2nd Battalion, had managed to be absent from the battlefield during festivities. Recognizing for themselves an obligation to spare the Vietnamese Army and government the embarrassment that loss of such august personages might provide, they had fled.

Barlow was not shocked; he was on his second tour in an advisory role. But his anger and a sense of shame shared with the Vietnamese soldiers kept him in a hyperactive state, even after wounding, helping him avoid medical shock which, on the aid-deficient battlefield, might have proven terminal. He stayed alert, denying himself the comfort of morphine for the pain, until all the wounded were evacuated, and as a final gesture, ordered an airlift for the remains of the dead.

But due to priorities, American Graves Registration personnel and South Vietnamese medics brought in on a Chinook CH-47, along with bundles of body bags, began their work in earnest a full twelve hours after the battle. The Chinook could not wait, but wafted off toward Plei Ku with a wave of the pilot's hand and the implicit promise of returning.

The JUNCTION CITY hoo-hah was still on-going in adjacent AOs, and every chopper in III Corps and beyond would be busy in shuttle fashion for days to come. Thirty-Fourth Support Group offered to lift out cargo nets of bodies and transport them to Sai Gon or Plei Ku—customer's choice—but someone else must gather the dead into the nets, hook the slings aboard when the Chinooks hovered, and someone must be at the terminal point with recovery personnel.

There were, mixed in the horrifying muddle of battle residue, South Vietnamese soldiers and Marines, some civilians by default, and Viet Cong and North Vietnamese Army troops. Two American advisors were MIA and could also be a part of the mix.

Most enemy dead were bulldozed into shallow trenches, limed over, and covered with dirt. Barlow refused evacuation for himself until he was assured there would be no common bagging of his ARVN troops with the enemy; and in any case, the American dead had to be exempted, if they could be found. So the body bags came into their own.

But no transport was available when the bags were filled.

ARVN Graves Registration could not cope in the field with such numbers, such carnage. They were filling bags as quickly as they could with any degree of propriety, but in some cases, individuality was a declining privilege. Some bags got a more-or-less single, whole body, depending upon the wound. Some got the best of a mix-and-match effort: two legs, two arms, head, and trunk. Some even made up legitimate matches.

As the sun bore down, the bodies of the Asian soldiers began to swell. Their regular diet included vast amounts of garlic, peppers, and the pungent, ever-necessary decayed-fish sauce, *nuoc mam*, and such natural demonstrations of the converse of Boyle's Law of the physics of gases pertained. Gases formed and expanded, distending the bellies that were whole until they ruptured. Graves Registration, in horrified response, became less demanding, less persistent in their seeking for one-ness. Then, too, mix-and-match accounting for each body was based on a premise that two legs, two arms, a head, and a trunk were present for each bag candidate.

The violence of sustained mortar and RPG fire, mines, booby traps, and satchel charges on both sides; the uniqueness of napalm, 250-, 500- 750-, 1,000- and 2,000-pound high explosive bombs; air-to-ground rockets; as well as artillery of every conceivable caliber; Claymore mines, and other high tech wonders used by both sides, had completely changed that equation. The unaccountable violence thus unleashed made accounting for the enemy and enemy parts in the mix a representation of the norm.

The bags, swelling in the heat, began to assume unlikely, ambiguous shapes as the recovery teams filled them in haphazard economy: trunk, one leg, three arm parts, no head; two arms, three leg parts, no trunk, partial head; two trunks, two legs, two arms; two heads—the combinations became more creative as the building blocks became less evenly available. Parts were more anonymous then requisite.

As he is listening to Smiley's hushed tale, envisioning the hell of that LZ, Winter flashed on the hog-killing days in the first frosty days of Autumn back home. There was no similarity..

But he understood that in Smiley's revelations, during the trying period of Major Barlow, the battle raged on not far away. Aircraft were committed, their crews exhausted by a continuing flight schedule that sapped life energies and wore out components at an exponential rate. By the time the bodies were bagged and ready to be moved, there was only one possibility for transportation in any kind of realistic time frame. A Caribou utility transport aircraft, lo-lexing ammunition, plasma, and water into a hot LZ near the fighting, offered to drop in where the bodies were gathered, on their way back from off-loading, pick up the bags, one load each flight, and return them to Plei Ku. From there, they could be transshipped to the Sai Gon or Da Nang morgue on strategic, rather than tactical transports.

The CV-1, called Caribou, was another of the utterly reliable and functional aircraft built by DeHavilland of Canada for bush-country work. It had the critical facility for landing and taking off on incredibly short strips, not necessarily of a hardened surface: cleared fields, roadways, dry rice paddies—almost anywhere it could develop forward motion up to 40 knots without hitting something larger than a water buffalo was enough to ensure launch.

The recovery teams, Vietnamese medics, and security elements looked up and watched this high-winged craft descend almost vertically onto the dirt road along the edge of the jungle. A huge vertical stabilizer protruded into the air bearing the numbers Two-seven-four. When it had landed and taxied close to the grim cargo piles, the rear ramp dropped and every person on the LZ, with the exception of four men providing security, began hauling bags, stacking them in the fuselage like cordwood.

There were approximately one hundred forty-one body composites altogether, and they would in no way fit on one aircraft, but when the Caribou was as loaded as could be managed, the Army Captain piloting the craft yelled out the hatch to Major Barlow's replacement, an infantry captain, that he would alert other supply aircraft to make stops on the way back from a drop, as he had done, until the black, rubberized mountain was reduced to zero. He turned the aircraft into the wind, ran up the engines, released the brakes, and seemingly within a short walk was airborne with his grisly cargo.

As the Caribou gained altitude, decompression caused the bodies to swell even more. Most of the bags were zippered tight, forming closed containers like the bodies they bore, and having lain in the sun the material had softened. The bags, too, began to swell. At twenty-six hundred feet, the first tiny explosion occurred inside one of the bags in the middle of the stack near the rear ramp. At three thousand, five hundred feet the bodies were exploding like small land mines, and the mound of bags expanded as individual bags became distended with expanding gases.. At thirty-six hundred ninety feet, some of the bags began bursting. The smell, despite clean air at that altitude, was indescribable.

The loadmaster, seated on an ammo crate in the cargo bay, was caught by the hellish assault and driven forward into the flight deck. The flight engineer, drafted away from a lucrative but insulated career in cosmetics distribution, went instantly mad when he realized what was happening. He tried to jump from the plane and it took the loadmaster and co-pilot to hold him down. The bags continued to burst, until the pilot, realizing his complicity in the horror, dropped the nose, and brought the aircraft back down to a hazardous twelve hundred feet and held it there all the way to Plei Ku.

Everyone in the aircraft was on oxygen. The pilot wanted to drop the cargo ramp and pull the nose up into a steep climb, dump everything out the rear. But there were possibly Americans among all the others and there would be sincere upset over such an action. The pilot informed the tower at Plei Ku of their load; control there directed them to by-pass that field and proceed to Tan Son Nhut, far off their intended route, where they were directed to the remote end of a parking ramp off the end of the active runways. The pilot, on the ground, reported by phone to his First Aviation commander, who ordered him to fly back to Plei Ku, continue his lo-lex flights and continue to haul the bags until that job was finished—not to alert any other aircraft to join him in evacuation of the KIAs.

While the morgue ghouls had filled nine ambulances and two six-bys with bodies and departed, the pilot took on fresh oxygen and taxied back to the quickly organized cargo loading point. The squad humping ammo and rats walked into the cargo bay, dropped their supplies, and fled from the plane. The deck was slippery; dark, viscous, coagulated dross coated half the cargo space. Substances still liquid ran in rivulets in the bracket channels in the deck.

The pilot taxied the ship to a separate, major cargo ramp and the aircraft crew loaded most of the cargo before a master sergeant, threatening the loading gang on the ground with severe bodily harm, got them some help, and they were loaded and gone in minutes. In the air, they flew with the ramp half open, all hatches open from the cockpit back, and the crew remained on oxygen. The die was set.

* * *

"I don't want to think what it must have been like in that field morgue, but that ship was ruined. I flew it on my last tour, sometime after the body haul. Always on oxygen. The ship was a pariah. After that first time, it was used for hauling bodies almost exclusively. Most of the time, it was logged 'down for maintenance.'"

Smiley shuddered, the saga of 274 vivid in his memory. "They tried to use it to haul cargo regularly—no troops would board the bitch for transport; no commander would be silly enough to order them to—and even the cargo handlers wouldn't go near it. Only thing it was good for was policing battle fields. The smell had seeped into everything, even in that brief, original flight. The canvas, everything made of rubber or fiber . . . seat cushions, parachutes—couldn't get the parachute loft to take the 'chutes back; far as I know, they've never been re-packed, so nobody will ever use them." Smiley spoke with detachment, as if recalling a vaguely remembered joke, but had forgotten the punch line.

Winter wondered at the veracity of this remarkable tale.

"You remember the story of the hundred dollar Cadillac?" Smiley said. "Heard it all my life, thought it was a joke. The kid who runs across a Cadillac for sale on a small-town lot in Texas? Dealer wants a hundred bucks for it, three-year-old Caddie. Tells the kid the reason is that the car held bad memories for the previous owner who lost his wife, so he had to sell it. When the kid, who figures there's a scam, buys the car anyhow, it smells a bit odd, even though it's perfumed to high heaven, and it's nighttime and cool on the lot. Guy tells him it might be a field mouse got caught up in the fan or something, maybe a bird, and he can have it steam-cleaned for fifteen bucks and it'll be fine. But after he bought it, and it sat in the sun a bit . . .

"Eventually the kid learns the previous owner's in Huntsville on death row for killing his wife. Hid the Caddie with her body on the back seat in a cane break along a swamp near Longview for seven hot months."

Winter had only the vaguest notion of relevance.

"Two-seven-four's like that Caddie. Couldn't quite ever get that smell out, and it's worse in the sun. They've scrubbed the metalwork and decking, replaced everything that would come loose, tried vinegar from the messhall, cleaning polish, bleach, sprays, fumigation, deodorants—everything. No dice! The bitch is marked. After April last year, when the fucking Air Force got Congress to give over all our Caribous to them, it's been sitting on the far end of the ramp. Air Wogs wouldn't accept Two-seven-four for the same reason no one but recovery crews would touch it in the Thirty-Fourth or First Aviation. The Army can't keep it, Air Force won't take it, so some block-checking, paper-shuffling asshole at Mac-Vee is making motions to force a happening. Wants to ree-solve this issue, I 'spect."

He pulled the scarred helmet from the bag, turned it in his hand, inspecting it, pushed it back into the bag and zippered it shut. "Ames," he said, shaking his head, thinking briefly of the dead pilot..

"So, nifty story. Is it true? Never heard it before. But what about it? " Winter said to Smiley.

"I'm the one gonna drown the bitch."

Winter goggled at him.

"No shit, man. First Aviation borrowed me for the job. Me and Johnny Gregg are going to fly her out to sea and ditch her. We're both jump qualified, both rated in the Caribou. So we'll fly her out to sea, set her on a course for Australia, trim her nose down, and hit the silk. Navy's agreed to run a boat a couple of miles out, 'just in case we have some aircraft trouble while test flying this old bird.' Navy don't know what's going on, but they'll be around." He smiled grimly.

"We come back, file a report, claim engine failure, ground fire, something. Colonel hasn't decided yet just what he wants it to be, and man, it's not like he has a lot of time to make up his mind. He doesn't want another combat loss on our record, but he doesn't want an accident board either."

"That's insane!"

"Never said it wasn't. Ain't arguing that. Nobody in the command will challenge our report, whatever it is, 'cause it's one great big, gigantic fucking conspiracy and everybody's in on it, from the goddamned oxygen technician in the maintenance hangar to General Debbins in First Aviation. Airdales, too, they'll go along. They won't take the whore and we got to get rid of her. Two-seven-four, the plane without a country." His face was without expression. "And the silliness just goes on and on."

Winter found he could not speak to the whirling madness in his mind.

"One thing nobody's touched on, though. What the hell happens the next time they want some stiffs hauled? Do we break in a new hearse? Use a U-21, or some choppers? 'cause you know, ain't no buncha airdales gonna haul dead grunts." Smiley was nothing if not serious.

"That's bullshit! Boyd, you don't have to take that kind of order," Winter said. "That's not a legal order. You guys could lose your ass. In the jump, in the pickup. It's insane."

"Yeah, but it's Army, old buddy. Pure Army!" Smiley hoisted the zippered bag, and headed up the hall toward the entrance. "Don't mean nuthin'," echoed back. The steel-plated door slammed shut behind him, the metallic epithet echoing in the cold hallway.

* * *

Winter walked down the flightline to the mess on Davis Station, but found he could not eat. He waited for any word on the ill-fated, final flight of Two-seven-four. He didn't know if his friend was alive, or if he'd become a part of 274's grim legend. But he couldn't just wait. He walked back to the 224th, convinced of the truth of Smiley's tale . . . at least convinced that Smiley was convinced of it.

He started writing a letter to Nickie without thought, writing on the back of a blank tasking sheet. He'd written only three sentences when he was brought up sharply by an overpowering sense of sadness.

He tore the page in strips and trashed it. This was not something to write to Nicole about; it was the essence of her distance.

It was still early; only a few personnel were in the building. He fought the usual battle to get a phone call through to Air Search and Rescue, hoping to get brought up to speed on Smiley and the other pilot. No one answered the phone. Winter wondered what their hours were.

chapter eighteen

Joss Sticks and Temple Dragons

Vietnam: October 1968

Colonel Sizemore burst through the front door. The colonel always exploded through doorways, much as he thrust himself at every subordinate—like a challenger rather than commander. He saw the group of officers in the hallway by the door of the S-3 and demanded, "Anybody seen Smiley this morning?" The colonel's shiny, blank black face was hard to read. Inscrutable, Winter thought. Like Fred Ito's.

"He's flying, Colonel. He took a Caribou out for the Thirty-Fourth, or some such. About an hour ago," Winter answered him evenly.

"Oh, okay. Fine. Yeah, good." He swivelled his head from side to side, muttering to himself, and dashed into his office. Winter heard the smack of boot heels as the colonel's clerk leapt to his feet and saluted.

The colonel's face emerged around the doorframe. "Mister Winter," he shouted.

"Sir!"

"Need to see you. Now!"

"Yessir." Winter looked at the other pilots, shrugging his shoulders. They dispersed with blank faces.

* * *

On the chopper en route to LANDING ZONE MADRID, Winter tried to recall at precisely what point in the discussion the colonel had decided that the situation required an officer on the spot. *Our man in Madrid.* Before Winter could offer a single reason why the idea was preposterous, he was boarding the chopper.

Was it something he'd said? Did I step on my own crank, he wondered. By God, I did not!

He thought briefly of Smiley. Winter considered the magnitude of the conspiracy that the colonel had hatched to rid himself of Warrant Officers in the 224th, while at the same time recognizing the magnitude of his own paranoia. The wild swing of logic did not exceed his burgeoning sense of incredulity.

The Huey fluttered on across the airspace of III Corps.

"Get out to L.Z. Madrid," the colonel had ordered. "There are a lot of Tropic Lightning troops on that piece of ground . . . should be cold. They're going to build a firebase there soon's we get the heavy equipment and the Seabees on it. Or Army engineers. Meantime, we've got a Five-oh-nine Group team operating out there, working with Twenty-fifth's close-air-support people. The target coordinates they're sending back are worthless, and we can't make radio contact to do anything about it. They're not keeping net skeds. We sent a message through the battalion they're with, and they farted that off. So you get your butt on a chopper and get out there and find out what the hell kinda rinky-dink operation they're running. I already informed the S-3. Fire somebody. Replace somebody. Do something, but fix the problem. Do it now!"

"Uh, right, sir. Who's in command on the L.Z.? Our team, I mean."

"Hell, Mister, I don't keep that trivial crap in my head. He's one of *your people*. Some sergeant. Check in S-3." The colonel picked up a message from his desk and held it between himself and Winter, scanning the yellow tearsheet, ignoring the Warrant Officer. Winter realized the interview was terminated.

"Your people" did not resonate with Winter. He didn't have any people, being a staff weenie, so it couldn't be him personally the colonel meant. Must have meant some ground ops, because neither two two four's S-3 or the 146th had enough airborne ops to go sit in the woods with grunts. Did he mean someone from S-3 Operations? Or merely one of the 509th RRG noncommissioned officers. Probably the latter.

On the whole the colonel was mistrustful of intelligence personnel. He was a pilot, pure and simple, an airplane driver who knew nothing—did not want to know—about the finer points of reading other people's mail.

Colonel Sizelove, being suspicious of security operations, held them in awe and fear, terrified of security violations. What he didn't understand, he struck out at. He was an intolerant commander at best to the RRG troops assigned under him, another enemy for them to fight along with the Cong, the NVA, the mosquitoes, the weather, loneliness and deprivations. The commander was not the least of their afflictions.

* * *

Winter looked down on the blur of green and brown land. A series of muddy streams passed beneath, normally trickles, swollen now by the rains to angry brown torrents, swirling floods that robbed the land upstream and overflowed their banks, spreading across the flat country like greedy fingers. They flew at 3,500 feet; he never knew if they drew groundfire or not and was grateful for the ignorance.

The chopper swung in a giant circle and the door gunner nearest him jacked a fresh round into his M-60 slung on a bungee cord. Winter could hear nothing but the pulsing throb of the blades and the high-pitched whine of the turbine. A strong smell of kerosene, hydraulic fluid, and burnt oil filled the ship. He looked forward past the pilot and co-pilot out the bubble and saw a raw, red gash along the ground, surrounded by a cleared field of fire, surrounded in turn by the darker, jungled growth at the perimeter.

The LZ was talking them in. He could see the jaws of the pilot working and he looked about the cargo space for a headset. *Hav-va no!* As the pilot confirmed their approach, green smoke popped in the clearing. Cold!

No sign of Charlie. Swell.

The UH-1D slid into the wind and broke over the edge of the bunkers. Looking out the port side past that gunner's legs as the young corporal braced himself into the gun and fought the Gs of spiraling descent, Winter saw a quick ripple of white across the bunker area: heads turned, faces skyward, watching their approach. He saw in the clearing below two more Hueys, one with blades whipping lazily in idle. Both helicopters hunkered in deep, waving grass, their skids hidden in the lush growth. The field, burned over just days before when the LZ was cleared; already was knee deep in green. Interminable rain manifests lawn success.

The pilot, cowboying it, shot a hot approach though there was no hostile fire, flaring at the last moment, settling the slick into the grass with a soft thump. Winter was the only passenger. The crewchief/ gunner yelled in his ear: they would leave him to his mission while they delivered mail, ammo, beer and water at a smaller LZ nearby, and return for him in an hour. He had vague misgivings about being stuck on strange LZs; precedent gave substance to his disquiet.

Winter dropped through the open door onto the skid, on into the grass. Crouching beneath the blades, he sprinted toward the bunkers. It was quiet on the LZ. Troops lay about on sandbags and in the grass without shirts, some even *sans* trousers, jungle skivvies for the most part uniform of the day. Behind him Winter heard the pitch of the turbine whine increase, the flutter of the big blades chopping increasingly faster for lift-off, and he knew the instant the ship broke ground without looking up.

He did not see the first RPG round when it penetrated the engine housing and exploded.

He heard the blast a split second after he felt it, lifted from his feet and cast forward. He sat up, stunned, looking toward the field. Part of the ship's bubble canopy spun off through the air like a giant frisbee. Pieces of fuselage sprayed out like loose asbestos siding in a high wind. Winter numbly felt over his body for parts missing, and began to understand that he was untouched. Just concussion.

He stared, uncomprehending, as the blades stuttered, the helicopter tilted back down and fell into the slowly revolving blades of the idling chopper on the ground, whose blades cut through the falling ship, slicing through the cockpit and the light metal frame like a cleaver, bisecting the pilot on a forty-five degree angle from one shoulder to the opposite thigh. A large, ill-defined section of the stricken chopper fluttered away from its impact point. The idling Huey on the ground, its blades caught up in the chopper lifting off, spun around on its skids and crashed into the third ship nestled in the grass nearby. To Winter, still behind the curve with the first explosion, all this occurred in a spectral silence.

Rocket propelled grenades struck quickly now among the thrashing helicopters. Giant windmill blades whiplashed the sky, the earth, men, and steel frames. An engine caterwauled mechanical death screams. Mortar rounds began their walk across the clearing, impacting on the bunkers. The TOC was the prime target: most of the Tactical Operations Center was buried beneath the surface with thick log-and-sandbag overhead . . . but still the rounds fell.

The attack in daylight caught the infantry by surprise; the soldiers scrambled for holes, for ditches, bunkers, a fold in the ground. Chaos and devastation grew upon the LZ as the treeline nearest, more than a hundred yards away, erupted in fire. A sergeant in skivvie shorts and flak jacket yelled steadily, a stream of profane commands, but his voice and the message it carried were unintelligible. A burst of machine gun fire went over Winter's head, driving him into the grass. Was that directed at him? He was still fifty yards from the bunkers; did they take him for the enemy?

No shit! He was from Headquarters—to them, he *was* the enemy.

In the opening hysteria of the attack, he knew that no one would associate him with the chopper. There was no time to assess what he had been dropped into, no need to question. He crawled toward the bunkers seeking not understanding but cover,.

The second Huey exploded, hurling a gunner and the co-pilot clear of the craft; they lay where they fell. A gunner and both pilots—including the halved one—of the ship he'd arrived in were trapped in the ship where the fire spread to them. JP-4 fuel raged, and flames, spreading to the third helicopter, ravaged across the LZ. From his low crawl, Winter could hear screams of someone in the choppers: the trapped gunner or pilot, he knew with a shudder.

The mortars had the range down to a gnat's-ass precision. Several rounds exploded on bunkers, on the TOC. Direct hits. Still the RPGs rained in. No more cover on this MADRID than there was shelter from the blazing sun on that distant Iberian plain.

The Huey that was hit in the air cartwheeled across the field—what was left of the ship after the first rocket and the machine gun fire, burning—spinning away toward the trees. Winter lay in the grass and watched, hypnotized by the graceful, slow-motion breakup of the ship. Everything seemed to be happening very slowly. But he knew that effect, knew its deceptive hazards.

A squad from weapons platoon raced across the open ground from a bunker that was burning to another with a commanding sweep of the trees, carrying a 106mm recoilless rifle and a pair of machine guns. Winter crawled in their direction.

There was a multitude screaming now, a formless, meaningless, unanswerable protest. Winter listened to the chorus as he crawled. He could hear each individual voice like an isolated stereo track before they blended into cacophony. The first Huey seemed to go on and on, flopping crazily about the LZ and along the bunker line, like a wrung-neck chicken in its death throes. To the warrant officer the terminal dance seemed to take forever.

Or had it already stopped and he was in frenzied recall?

Winded, he lay flat in the grass, seeking to crawl beneath it, and watched helplessly. The growing chorus of screams, of orders and weapons fire and explosions and curses, mounted in his consciousness until his head pulsed with reverberations.

He knew later it was a matter of short seconds, but in that peak of conflict everything stretched out like slow motion, and the movement of soldiers was like that of mechanical toys. Even the stupefying din of explosions and gunfire, the screams of those hit and those missed close, the whirlwinds of shock and fear—the sounds, though obvious now to him, seemed to be distant, unconnected to the scene before him.

Winter started again toward the bunkers. *Gotta move!* his instincts urged. Indefensible in the open, a target for anyone, friend or enemy. "Give 'em a movin' target, nothin' but a movin' target," he recalled the lesson pounded into his head at Parris Island and in the trenches and bunkers of another Asian land. "Make 'em go for the movin' target. Burns up their ammo, scares hell out of 'em, so that only occasionally do they blow your ass off."

He tried to get beneath the grass but was denied. He hugged the helmet to his head; it fell off repeatedly as he crawled, before he thought to hook the strap. Why hadn't he simply hooked the chin strap? he thought. His canteen had somehow gotten twisted around until it was beneath his stomach. He couldn't breathe with the hard lump pressed into his belly, but he could not raise his body even one millimeter to free the canteen. His muscles would not respond to his urge to elevate his body; his muscles knew better than he what was *up there.*

Sudden recall—following an infantry dictum, he unsnapped the strap, lest the helmet take his head off under concussion.

The barrel of his M-16 was full of mud and grass. Staring at the unmilitary condition of his weapon, he couldn't think why that might be important. And he couldn't recall how he had come about carrying an M-16. Sweat rolled down his face and into his eyes, carrying with it a plague of tiny black gnats. He kept wiping his face with the muddy sleeve of the fatigue jacket, but it didn't help.

Every exploding round seemed to lift him from the ground. His ears funneled sharp pain into his head. He feared his eardrums might be ruptured and put his hand up to feel for blood. The rounds that impacted around him sent waves of concussion rolling over his body, sweeping upward from the ground.

In a move that validated his prescience, concussion jerked the helmet away from his head; he felt a complacent smugness, earned in earlier apprenticeship, as he reached out, chasing the steel pot.

He felt each tremor and tickle of movement, sensations he had never noticed on his body before: the movement of blood in his veins, throbbing in his temples; the itch of a mole on his hip since birth; a pain behind his right kneecap from a baseball injury when he was fourteen. Immersed in a barrage of stultifying horror and fear he froze. Immobilized in his time and place, at the same time electrified by the sensations he experienced, each isolated and pure, he could not move. He couldn't tell if it was he screaming, or if it was someone in the grass near him. He thought likely it was he.

The bunkers continued taking hits while RPG rounds whooshed across open ground like the dawn's earliest light. Explosions of mortar rounds appeared like a single elusive entity, leaping about like a huge, vengeful child playing deadly hop-scotch, leaving behind havoc. There was no predicting where the next round would land. They fell in barrages, in sheaves, in waves. And they fell and fell and fell. . . .

* * *

Three kilometers away, a battalion of the 25th "Tropic Lightning" Infantry Division troops were blown out of their training camp blasé that some had called a "don't-give-a-shit attitude," when the 396th NVA Battalion opened fire in the cover of the dripping rubber trees. It had been raining over the plantation moments before, an isolated downpour, and mist and ground fog swirled through the trees cutting vision, transforming bushes into enemy, enemy into innocuous undergrowth. Shattering, long, barrel-melting bursts of return machine gun fire carried a message of panic; fire discipline was a myth. Beyond the line, mortar and blooper rounds arced out with loud *Plop!*s and the crump of grenades echoed down the orderly ranks of rubber trees.

Long sinuous creeper vines webbed down into the little bit of maneuver room the troops had, choking out the paths between the trees along the deadly rows. Heavy fire enfiladed down the shaggy-columned avenues, and it was worth a life to try to bring fire to bear, or to aid the wounded, or just to watch . . . or to run away and simply leave it all behind:

In for a penny . . . in for a penny.

Artillery was useless; the rounds detonated high in the trees, and the splintered mangroves and palms along the fringe of the groves were as hazardous to friend as to foe. There was no air support.

"Rainforest? Goddamn, shrapnel city!" Crazy Bruce yelled at no one. The jungle canopy around the edge, between the main house of the *Tresiême Administratif* and the mass of the Michelin groves, was so thick it did not rain beneath, not even during the heavy tropical squalls of October. But always, beneath, always it dripped, as in the caves in Kentucky where Bruce's uncle with tuberculosis had taken him once as a kid. When he was in junior high. The sergeant wondered briefly if that old man with the gentle voice was still spitting blood and defying all the doctors back in Indiana. He thought of the beauty of the caverns, the colors of the rock formations, how they sparkled. Bruce felt fortunate to have the presence of mind, at this hazardous juncture, to recognize the Rosetta Stone connection to this moment. The crystal glitter around him in the trees now was a deceptive reminder; it was not mineral reflection, but the insistent winking of small arms fire.

Hot weather, cold, rain or shine, windy or calm, it never seemed to matter in the rainforests. Beyond the fringe of mangroves that stood tall about the edge of the plantation, beyond the creeper vines and the elephant grass and the hedge rows and kraits, out into the deadly relative open order of the rubber trees, the new recruits, old hands, draftees, and lifers of the 25th Division were buying rubber trees at a cost of one hundred seventy-five dollars and two point three men per tree. Civilian damage compensation was a bitch, but in the rainforest they didn't think about the spiraling inflation of the groves; neighborly concerns were a luxury they could not afford.

Crazy Bruce burrowed into the roots of a mangrove, sharing the space with lizards and leeches that lurked in the puddles of stagnant water there. In the midst of the firefight he experienced a flash of memory: something he was supposed to do today, something Colonel Sizemore had said in a message. Someone coming out to investigate something.

Just what he needed now. He hoped the investigator brought ammo, water, and an airstrike. His sponsoring grunt company would no doubt appreciate that.

Screw it! If the investigator came now, the problem, whatever it was, was solved.

Dull reverberations, tunnel rats clearing sappers from tunnels and spider holes, washed over him; he felt the intensity of fire moving away from him. He had an urge to get up and walk, go somewhere. Maybe shopping in Cu Chi with a friend.

Maybe he would stay where he was a while longer. . . .

* * *

The boot lay alongside the trail, just where it had fallen on the scarred, red earth. The nearest troops—the new machine gunner and Specialist Martin, caught in the frenzy his fourth day in country, en route to join his assigned team—effected a casual attitude. No one in the squad would make a move toward the footgear. Not a soldier would speak of it, but every eye was fixed on it, its crafted functionality, the blatantly false innocence. The laces were still interwoven like tiny Z-shaped snakes that twined in and out of the dull brass grommets. The gloss from some recent inspection shine back at a lately departed basecamp—dazzling in the leaf-dappled light, holding every gaze—still shone on the toe.

Sergeant Glasgow had been leading a patrol along the Suoi Bei Da riverbank and heard the incoming RPG and mortar fire on LZ MADRID only seconds before the ambush was sprung on his own squad. It happened fast. Coordination between more than one enemy element meant a major attack, but the patrol could only deal with their own little corner of crisis. No one in the squad had seen the face of the enemy yet, though Valdez and Linskyy were dead; Butts, Filiano, and the new medic wounded at least—the medic probably dead too; they couldn't get to him—and Glasgow had seen his radioman go down in an explosion. Fire still poured in on them, heavy, deadly.

Glasgow knew the only way to deal with an ambush was to attack, as best and however they could, but here, strung along the path with the dikes intervening, they could not bring to bear any significant fire. The squad froze. For a long time after Rocco dragged Melton's unconscious body back up the trail toward the LZ, while sporadic fire crackled through the elephant grass above them, every man lay . . . and stared . . . and knew what had to be done. Nobody wanted to be the one to do it.

Sergeant Glasgow stared at the boot at arm's length, mesmerized by the pattern of cleated rubber sole, seeing no evil there in its well-designed comfort and utility. He marvelled at how clean the boot was. Melton had not been with the squad long enough for the ochre-tinted soil to fix its patina of stain inexorably into the footgear as it had stained all their bodies and their souls. Embraced its creases, deep into the nylon flex fibers, coloring the leather. The red soil was like a talisman, marked on them by the gods for transgressions they weren't aware of. It was everywhere. It came from the brush they walked through, the muddy ditches they crawled through, and the rice paddies they waded through; it was in the air they breathed. Pervasive. Corrosive. Equalizing.

Glasgow listened and judged the target of the mortars. Crazy Bruce had the RR team over on LZ MADRID, working out of there, just about where he judged the rounds to be impacting. Winter was somewhere in country. Martin, here with him. Ratty Mac . . . A quick roster of past companions ran through his mind. He prayed.

* * *

Winter reached the treeline behind the bunkers on his knees. He had the momentary sensation of entering a cathedral when he looked up at the canopy of branches above him, the architecture of the rubber trees giving way upward to the mangroves, like outbuildings propped against a towering main structure. Dependent upon them. He fell to the ground, breathing in shuddering gasps.

Incoming was still heavy, but he was out of the pattern for the moment. The rounds fell in the open field and along the bunker line. The three helicopters blazed like giant smudge pots along the edge of the trees, their heat unnoticeable, superfluous in the climate.

He saw no one in the trees, no one moving anywhere about him. He lay for a moment, feeling the pounding in his chest against the ground. Under the mangroves, occasional paths traversed the underbrush tangle, but under the rubber trees the ground was mostly clear.

Concussion had done its work. Wild orchids and frangipanni, jasmine, and flowering creepers grew wildly through the mangroves and underbrush. After the recent rains the blossoms swelled, the vegetation pregnant with new life, so loud with color and scent they begged for symbiosis with bees and parasitic creatures. But concussion took precedence.

Winter slithered forward and crouched on the edge of a small clearing among the trees. Before him in the gloom of the rainforest stood the remains of a courtyard. The wooden gate hung askew, the crude iron ideographic symbols on the arch rusting. The temple had taken a direct hit in some earlier conflict and there was only rubble where the walls had stood. He saw in the dim light, and in the conformation of the crumbled walls, the temple of the calendar print on his BOQ wall. He knew it could not be the same—this temple had never known an artist—but somehow it was.

There were no guard dragons. No one had prayed here for a long, long time. The urn for the smoldering joss sticks had been taken by one military unit or another—ARVN or American, French or Cong—for a water jug, a wash basin, a souvenir or bed pan. And the artillery thunder had rained down all the blossoms onto the hidden trails. The trees were only green now, and the jungle floor a palette for mad impressionists.

Through the mystical panorama, hazy with shifting light, obscured by wisping smoke and mist, two figures advanced in languid fits and starts. They moved slowly and used the cover of the trees only incidentally. The tall, emaciated soldier's body armor was shattered, his clothing torn and powder-blackened. He had lost his helmet. He carried no weapon and walked forward with his face angled upward as if scanning the tops of the trees, his tousled hair white in the patchy light. He clearly was somewhere other than on this battlefield.

The man with him was also without helmet. He wore an old-fashioned fatigue cap, the issue item that was called a KP hat in WWII, with a soft brim all around, shapeless. He was short. And round. He carried a rifle slung muzzle down, and if Winter could have seen clearly in the dense growth, he would have recognized a vintage M-1 Garand. The short, round soldier also carried a Thompson submachine gun. And all the ammo for both weapons. In addition, hanging from his belt were two canteens, a medical field pack, and pouches for the submachine gun's heavy drum magazines. On his back was a knapsack that bulged with hidden treasure, and two blanket poncho rolls. He followed the tall soldier in apparent contentment.

But for the businesslike weapons the private carried, albeit of another era, and their familiarity with terrain—and if not that, a disdain for direction, going wherever fate seemed to take them in a search for encounter—the two could have been delivered intact from the pages of some Rabelaisian tale. Velazquez would have painted the tall one as an ascetic, his upturned face seeking God in the flowerless trees of the jungle. The short, round one he would have cast as a fool. Or the painter may have reversed the roles. Velazquez was a student of human nature.

The two men drifted from Winter's field of vision, and with their passing he felt a twinge of familiarity, as if he'd seen an acquaintance out of some past life, or he had experienced the dream-like sequence of *dèjá vu*. In the immediate aftermath of the destruction in the field and on the bunkers, his mind sought distractions. He thought he could hear the two mystical soldiers' deliberate conversation as they made their way through the jungle, though he could no longer see them. Their's a mission he would not have believed or understood had he heard clearly.

"Sam, my good man. Can you look on the face of the compass and tell me if we are proceeding by favored impulse." The tall one spoke kindly, but left no doubt he expected instant compliance. He wore a single silver bar on his collar. He disdained the black cloth fatigue symbol of rank that was both camouflage and mark of leadership; such a device was fit only for those who would hide their true worth from the world, and for those too poor to dress their part. The officer's name was Dan Dewey.

"Sir, we're on the right course. I think we should take respite up ahead and eat while we may." It was apparent from Sam Fellows's appearance that he missed few meals. Only since he had joined up with Lieutenant Dewey had he suffered.

The officer was a madman. He never thought about food. Or sleep. Only his duty. But he had managed to get them through some tight scrapes, and Sam thought if he was going to get anywhere in this military world, he would do well to follow the man. The officer had some old-fashioned ideas, but he was sincere and serious about them, not inconsistent. And if Sam Fellows had to pretend to be able to read a compass, and to effect a comradely attitude in the face of ridiculous adversities, so be it.

And then of course, there was the promise of the island.

* * *

A tiny strand of vapor curled up occasionally from the eruption in the footpath by the paddy, a trace of phosphorous, dying reluctantly. The boot itself no longer gave off smoke as it had following the explosion, though nine pairs of eyes watched it for any such sign, retaining some hope it would suddenly burst into flame, turn to stinking ash, crumble to dust, and blow away, cleansing the ground at the bend of the trail where the tiny band of soldiers was pinned down.

Glasgow listened to the AK-47 rounds snapping over his head, and he marked anew how the peculiar sharp whine of the bullet made the Kalashnikov assault rifle stand out in a firefight. One could estimate range, fire blind almost, on enemy positions by that sound alone . . . providing some dumb-ass GI was not playing John Wayne and using a captured weapon. His mind leaped back to the boot again; at the same time, he was fascinated by how easily he allowed himself to be distracted from the real problem.

He stared at the troops he had once commanded, and led again now that Sergeant . . . he couldn't remember the interim platoon sergeant's name, the dead one, the one in numerous pieces back at the river. The troops were hunched over like statues, frozen in fear, and he knew he could not continue to focus on inanities; it was something he should not have to do. He'd trained them differently. They would not have frozen if—

He had to get off his ass, take the innocuous boot that lay like a startling harbinger of destruction, and do something with it.

But what? The Dustoff was already gone with Melton, and the discarded item would never catch up with him, though it might track him to the 3rd Field Hospital in Saigon, to the Phillipines, and eventually into San Francisco and Letterman General. Or to Arlington's green slopes: destination still in doubt when Melton was choppered away, though likely Arlington.

It wasn't as if Melton's foot was *in* the boot or anything; the casualty had both feet. The blast had merely blown the boot off his foot without disturbing the laces. It was his abdomen that took the brunt of the explosion and the shrapnel; the abdomen . . . and his stomach, and chest, his hands—hardly any part of him that wasn't shredded when he fell on the grenade. They all owed him something—the grenade fell in the middle of them—though Melton had had no intention of performing such an outrageous act as it subsequently appeared. Indeed, not even aware of the grenade, he had tripped and fallen on it, unawares. But somehow it had to start with the boot.

Glasgow began inching forward.

* * *

Winter lay in the shadow of the mangroves, looking out into the light in the field, his face stupid in shock. Beyond him in the clearing and where the bunkers had been, the carnage was complete. The world before him was tinged blue-green, shifting, transmuted in the swirls of dust and smoke that eddied about the fresh-pocked earth. He tried to stand, to walk, but some elusive constraint admonished him with mild severity to lie still. His eyes roved the scene in awe, in silence.

The edge of an illusion intruded into what he saw before him. Children screaming in mock terror. Chasing across a similar field where balls were hit and races run. The children fled. He heard their feet pounding the dirt, stirring the hot summer dust, and he sought to reach through a screen of bamboo to warn them. The limber, clattering growth sprang aside and closed behind the passage of his arm, distended and detached from the eyes that followed it.

He could identify the sound of gunships as they arrived to work the treeline, pushing the diminishing enemy farther and farther from him. He knew vaguely there was something he had to do, but the ringing in his ears and the echoes of screams and the sounds that did not belong to the jungle—were not of the rubber trees—held him. A sensation of limpid green translucence, pulsing and receding, washed over him as he tried to stand. The M-16 was still in his hand; he leaned on it; he pushed erect and hefted the weapon. The rifle weighed nothing, but the grass and mud in the flash suppressor and in the barrel was a burden.

He observed with care how the same green growth that was around him as he had lain in the field now sprouted from the muzzle. It was ridiculous that it did so. He was hallucinating and knew it. He giggled. He threw the rifle aside, useless. Can't fire a green gun! he giggled again.

Nearby lay the upper half of a Vietnamese Ranger sergeant's body, hands still gripping an M-2 carbine. Vaguely he realized he hadn't known there were ARVN troops on this LZ. The remainder of the soldier was nowhere in evidence, as if he had been issued only the trunk, arms and head of a body. Without thinking, provoked by instinct, Winter wrenched the smaller, older weapon from the dead man's grip and checked it automatically, cleared it, and flicked the safety off. The sharp, crisp click sounded loud in the cathedral silence.

He pulled two banana clips of .30 caliber ammo from a muddy pouch on a web belt slung around the soldier's neck, wiping the blood and gouts of tissue from them abstractly. He carried the weapon and ammo loosely in his hands.

Winter walked up onto the cairn of stones where the small temple had once stood. It was just at the edge of the trees and he could see the entire field in the blazing sun. Under the trees, the dappled light seemed cool.

But out there . . . out there . . .

* * *

When he was nine years old, Davey Winter had traveled with his mother to visit her cousin in Abner, Arkansas, in the late summer of the year. That town of 2,300 in the tornado belt of the Mississippi Valley boasted only two industries: the mines and a doll factory. The mines were dug for the limited Arkansas diamond trade, but they were played out. The doll factory was a high, ugly wooden structure of ancient vintage that had once been a shirt factory, before that a furniture factory, and originally a cotton gin. Only the gin had provided enough work to employ the few in town who did not depend upon the mines; but following the decline in mine fortunes, when the cotton market failed, everything else in the town failed too. So the owner tried furniture, sold out to a shirt maker, and when he went under, the wife of the town's only service station operator opened the doll factory to capitalize on a family cottage industry.

In the doll factory the tall gin shaft served as storage space for the completed dolls. They waited on four levels in regimented poise for shipment to the various doll houses and battlefields of genteel southern darlings.

On the day in August of 1944 when Davey and his mother arrived, a tornado warning had been issued. As they stepped off the train they could feel the warm, quick rush of winds presaging storm. Aware of the impending tornado, most of the townspeople rushed to the mines for shelter. Those too far away, or disdainful of the threat to the degree they would not demean themselves in the filth of the mines, moved to a hope of safety in the school gymnasium. It was a county school, large for the community, and the gym was able to accommodate the entire six hundred-plus people who poured into it in a slightly festive mood. They crowded into corners, huddled with loved ones, played cards, joked, laughed, and for the most part stoically awaited the passing of the storm.

As the winds grew louder and the building began to shake, those who were believers began to pray. Those who were not, prayed for the conversion that might put them in a category to be saved. Neither prayer could stop the winds.

When the twister had finally passed, miraculously lifting away the walls and half-domed roof of the gymnasium and revealing to God's own view and judgement the six hundred sudden Christians inside, either He was satisfied with their state, or so disgusted He chose to ignore them. He took their gymnasium as token, and with a touch of contempt, left all six hundred-plus untouched as a huddle of fakirs.

The doll factory two hundred yards down the road was taken in sacrifice, a sudden inspiration on the part of the frivolous God out for an afternoon's tornado, with the implicit understanding that expiation was the common goal of the community. Boxed and cellophaned whole dolls, pieces of little bodies, tiny dresses and coveralls and uniforms were flung into thirty acres of sweet potato vines some five miles from the town, scattered like fallen leaves; the first few coloring sumac leaves of the season fell with them, among them. Broken, dismembered, shattered beyond repair; little dresses and boots and blouses, tiny Sam Browne belts and swords, unrecognizable in the vines of the mis-labeled yams, the dolls in their destruction created a fallout like tiny human confetti.

His mother and cousin had taken him along when they went out to see the strange and wonderful sight, gawking like other townspeople, believers and renewed skeptics. Little Davey Winter, like most boys—though he would have denied it then, and for years afterward—had played his share of girls' games and created his own fantasies. God-like, with bits of stuffed cloth and clothespin arms and legs, he'd created living worlds responsive to life on another level.

When he saw the littered sweet potato field, standing by the gravel road that ran along the ditch with the air oppressive and close in the aftermath of the tornado, Davey grew frightened. The same fiction in his mind that allowed him the fantasy of the dolls on that long-ago afternoon had played him false here in this other green field.

The transposition had confused him then, and his mother was forced to take him back to the house before she could deal with his fear. A dish of ice cream had stopped the quavering chin, but the picture remained, deep in his psyche, and all the glossing-over of later years was futile now on this different field that was somehow the same.

Real as that scene had been to him that late summer day, that day he had his first view of apocalypse, so *un*-real was the scene before him now. He must remember, his mother had chided him gently but repeatedly; they were only play. They were not real people.

As far as he could see in the gloom of the forest and the rubber tree plantation, there was no movement at all. Turning slowly about, scanning the ruins of the bunkers and the littered field beyond, Winter could hear no sound.

chapter nineteen

Lonely Ringer

Vietnam: November 1968

Smiley, with Winter in the co-pilot seat of the RU-8D, landed on runway zero-seven, a long taxi from the Tan Son Nhut Army ramp. Rumbling across a patch of perforated steel plating, their tiny craft became the victim of road rage. A large, gray-and-white, twin-recip-engine aircraft with two slung jet boosters bore down on them, forcing them to stop on the PSP until the larger craft lumbered by. The big fella, too, made for the Army ramp and jerked to a halt, rocking on the axis of its landing gear for several moments before the semi-violent oscillations dampened out. The propellers still turned.

"That a P.-two?" Winter asked, nodding at the airplane, the likes of which he'd not seen before. From the perspective of the U-8, it looked monstrous.

"Oh, yeah. That's gotta be Jernigan." CWO Boyd Smiley checked for traffic and eased forward onto the taxiway.

"Who's he?"

"Major Frank-lin Double-U Jernigan. C. O. of the First Rah Rah. In his mighty, mythical flying steed, Pegasus." Smiley's eyebrows became one solid arched line.

"Seems a bit . . . *careless?* Aggressive."

Winter was still finding his way about the hierarchical relationships among the officers, pilots and otherwise, of the 224th Aviation Battalion. His learning curve was apt to be short, for he understood the sometimes strange, quasi-military, often slip-shod world of pilots and other air-oriented performers. He could do this, he knew, again grateful to be in the air world. His recent manhandling on the new LZ, two weeks before when he flew out on a chopper for a liaison meet with Crazy Bruce, convinced him his chances with aircraft exceeded his chances on the ground. He hadn't a good record with LZs.

Smiley interrupted his musing. "Jernigan is Jernigan. Force unto himself. Probably came down here to ping on Colonel Sizelove."

There was a story not being told. "Problems?" Winter, ignoring the intercom, shouted over engine noise.

"Hmmm. Not racial. I doubt Jernigan's ever noticed Sizelove's black. Jernigan just . . . he runs the First like his personal fiefdom. Because they fly these humpin' big relics, he looks down on the rest of us puke-and-pedal drivers."

Winter was familiar with the self-derisive references to pilots in the 224th who flew the small U-6, U-8, U-1, and U-21 aircraft. The faux self-denigration was generally related to the flying of those very aircraft, and *not* flying Hueys, Loaches, and Cobras—the killer elite. These pilots and planes made up four of the five aviation companies in the battalion, and all flew a similar mission. The 1st Radio Research Company, a rogue outfit that flew an outdated, cast-off Navy aircraft on different and dicey missions, had taken unto themselves the role of something unique, mutterings about which were common.

"Count my blessings," Winter mumbled.

"What say?" Smiley shouted, as he shut down contact with Ground Control.

Winter, shucking the harness, said, "I was on orders to go to the First. I got co-opted for this standardization thing. Maybe it's not a bad exchange."

"Man, bite your tongue. Don't even think it. If you get a chance for Cam Ranh with the First Rusty Rifles, jump on that sucker like stink on shit. Jernigan's do-able with his people. Treats his pilots and his mechs and ops great. It's the head shed, especially the boss—" nodding toward the battalion headquarters building beyond the flight line, "—that keeps his kettle boiling."

The U-8 rocked to a halt some fifty feet from the P-2, and Smiley shut it down. The two props spasmed to a stop, asynchronously. It was quiet on the ramp. Winter saw both huge reciprocal engines on the Neptune still rotating in idle, but the big bird was downwind and he could hear nothing. As he watched, the two four-blade props cycled to a synchronized stop. A little blue smoke eddied back from the port engine. No sooner had the props stopped than a pair of boots appeared through a hatch at the front tricycle wheel of the aircraft. Another hatch, like a bomb bay, opened farther back along the belly of the fuselage and three men in gray flight suits dropped to the tarmac. The feet at the front hatch grew a body, became a chunky man with wet, spikey hair who wore senior pilot's wings. As his feet hit the ground, he slapped a fatigue cap on his head bearing a major's gold leaf. He headed immediately for the headquarters building.

"Yep, Jernigan!" Smiley said. "That's him," reservation in his voice.

The two warrant officers, returning from a 3-day TDY to Phu Bai and Danang, carried their gear—flight bag, ops bag and secure pouch, two AWOL bags, two parachutes, two flight helmets, and a bag of trash from a box lunch they'd eaten as breakfast en route—from the aircraft, past the maintenance hangar, and across the busy street to the 146th company Flight Ops building. Winter dropped his gear there and went back across the street into the 224th battalion headquarters carrying the classified courier pouch. The startling effect of air conditioning, after traversing the white concrete ramp where temperatures fluttered between 115°-120°, shocked, discomfited Winter. It felt wonderful . . . but something in the back of his mind . . . somehow, in a moderately elusive manner, a sense he couldn't put into words, the comfort caused him *dis*-comfort over his war effort.

Bullshit! He tried to muster up an argument: don't have to suffer like grunts, just to contribute. His subconscious remained unconvinced. He recalled his initial confrontation of that mind set early in his first tour. It was not conducive to a happy camper's profession of faith.

In the hallway Winter encountered CW2 Ito coming out of the S-3 office. When he saw his friend, Ito's eyes expanded from their exaggerated oriental slit toward a *haole's* ocular configuration. He glanced behind him and stepped farther up the hall, pulling Winter along by the sleeve. Winter could hear raised voices behind in the S-3's inner office; the loudest voice not that of Colonel Sizelove as would be expected, nor indeed of the man whose office it was, the S-3, LTC Northcutt. It was a sound like an overheated chainsaw; a voice Winter did not recognize.

"Dave, boy, stay out of there," Ito urged him, towing him down the hall.

"I wasn't going in there. What's up?"

"You. Well, maybe you."

"Whaddaya mean, me." What, now?

"You know who's in there?" Ito whispered.

"I give a shit! Who?"

"Jernigan. And Sizemore. *And* Northcutt. All of 'em, wrangling over your sad, round-eyed bod."

"Bullshit!"

"I shit you not, G.I. I didn't hear it all, but Jernigan came in with a full head of steam, coming on to Colonel Northcutt about him 'stealing' you from the First's allocation. Sizelove heard the commotion, came in, got in it. Sorta surprised me: Sizelove usually shies away from Jernigan if he can. Anyhow, it's a three-way fight for your butt. I think," he smirked, "it's only that none of them want you and are trying to foist you off on one of the others."

"Huh. Well, I came over here on orders for the Two-twenty-fourth, with a directive from The Hall for further assignment to the First. But because of a security hold, Group wouldn't assign me to Cam Ranh, and I wound up doing this standardization shit for the S-3." Winter looked back at the open door. "Maybe I'll stick around and listen to this."

"Not your best notion, G.I. But . . . man's gotta do what a man's gotta do." Ito shuffled away with tiny, controlled, sliding steps, his hands stuck inside the opposing arms of his jungle fatigues, a small mandarin of unquestionable probity, shutting out the cares of the world.

* * *

Smiley broke onto final at Cam Ranh Bay, stabilized the aircraft and checked his rate of descent. It was a clear morning and Winter, from the co-pilot's seat, could see all the way north along the scalloped white beaches flanking the South China Sea, well past Nha Trang, and back south past the point at Ca Na. Smiley slipped the Seminole onto the strip between launches of two successive pairs of F-4s, exiting the active runway short at the first high-speed taxiway. It was that, or get run down. The second pair of Phantoms passed close behind them and thundered aloft as the RU-8 scurried off the main strip.

The instant Smiley cut the engines and lifted the hatch, sunny Viet Nam poured into the cockpit, inundating the two warrant officers. They were drenched with sweat before they could grab their gear and exit the plane. As they climbed down onto the ramp, a Jeep screeched to a halt behind them and the driver, wearing torn-off levis and an olive drab, sleeveless T-shirt with a silver, first lieutenant's bar pinned at the level of his sternum, shouted, "You boys want a lift to the Sandman?"

"Indeed," Smiley answered.

"And the Sandman is . . .? Winter queried the chauffeur as they threw their gear aboard.

"The finest li'l ole waterin' hole in the southeast of Asia, good buddy. Hey, I'm Bimbo Billingsgate," the driver announced without reference to rank. "Bar fly, raconteur, musician, purveyor of games of chance and, probably of more interest to you, billeting officer. You would be—" he looked closely at Smiley's wings, confirmed they were aviator's, and opined, "Boyd Smiley." He held out his hand, shaking the pilot's as he stamped on the gas. He yelled back over his shoulder, ". . . and welcome to you, Dave Winter. Glad to have you aboard. Hot damn!"

They raced across several acres of PSP, past a number of P-2V Neptunes bearing a shield-shaped logo: a yellow-eyed, dark gray pussycat a-straddle a flying white, winged stallion, the cat holding a long lightning-like spear, all superimposed on a large black numeral 1. Across the curved top of the shield was the block-lettered nominator, "CRAZY CAT." There were aircraft ID numbers in medium-size letters on the vertical stabilizers, but otherwise, the aircraft—white underneath; dove gray above—bore few markings: a small block of letters recognized Army affiliation, no other usual aircraft company advertising.

"Uhh, Lieutenant—" Smiley began.

"Bimbo!"

"Yeah. Bimbo. Maybe we'd better go check in at the orderly room, or with the C.Q., First Sergeant, somebody. Try to see the boss, if he's not flying."

"Jernigan'll be in the Sandman, if he's on base."

In the lounge? Winter checked his watch. At oh-nine-forty in the ay-em?

The Jeep left the edge of the flight line and sped past a couple of two-story buildings that more nearly resembled stateside billets than anything Winter had seen in Vietnam. Billingsgate switched off the Jeep and let it coast to a jerky stop between two buildings. There were large signs identifying the Naval Air Facility, and other logo-ed signs denoting various Navy VP squadrons. Across from the VP areas, Winter spotted a unit designator for a Sea-Bee company, and saw from its identification that it was part of the Construction Battalion from Gulfport, Mississippi, down the road a few miles from the new home where he'd left his wife and kids. He felt a disquieting tremor across his shoulders.

They followed a sidewalk around the building; above them a balcony followed the same path on the second level. Doors to the rooms opened out directly onto the walkway, and there were latrines and stairs at the center of each building. Where individual billets elsewhere in-country were screened to allow any breeze, each room here was completely enclosed. Individual air conditioning units hung over the walk and balcony, condensate a steady drip.

The three officers walked through the center of the nearest building, through the latrine, and close by, around the corner on the far side, came to an open door. It faced onto a small concrete patio with a tall lattice-work board fence shielding it. A barbecue grill, made from half a 55-gallon fuel drum, rested on pipe legs on the lanai. Canvas patio chairs were scattered about. Billingsgate stopped before the open door and pushed the two warrants inside before him.

Winter's first reaction was astonishment, followed immediately by hilarity. Two men in boxer shorts and T-shirts stood at a homemade bar, San Miguel Export bottles beading moisture before them. "Chiefs," said the stouter of the two, a man in his mid-forties with a shock of gray-flecked black hair standing straight up in spikes. He reached his hand out: "Frank Jernigan." He nodded to his left: "Nickel Nuts there."

Past the CO the entire inside walls of the room, a space which Winter estimated to be some twelve-to-fourteen feet square, were covered with full display centerfolds from *Playboy* and other skin mags. Professionally lettered signs expressing everything from the poetry of e e cummings to trite aphorisms of a military nature filled the spaces between: *INFANTRY: The Queen of Battle,* and someone had written in small red letters beneath, *Old fag that she is.* Next to it, a professional-looking, medium-size sign in Day-glo orange proclaimed: *Signal Corps: An organization of technically inept malcontents which lends chaos and bureaucracy to an otherwise orderly means of communications.* Another combat arms branch came into it where *Armor: A noisy compendium of moveable foxholes, all designed to attract the eye!* was stated succinctly. And a pus-blue plaque with ornate script rounded off the general service-bashing: *The Air Force assures accuracy. All their bombs will reach the ground.*

Winter looked up. A paddle fan, suspended from the center of the ceiling on a shaft that passed through the crown aperture of a camouflaged cargo parachute, turned slowly, jerking spasmodically. The chute was pulled to the ceiling and stapled there, around the periphery, and down three feet on each wall, except at the front where the open door encroached. Winter was inundated with memories of his old 3rd RRU billet on Davis Station, Tan Son Nhut, on his first Viet Nam tour. Wonder if that ceiling chute was still collecting dust and scorpions.

Superimposed on this chute were some forty-or-so hats, each one stapled to the ceiling through the back of the hat and through the chute. Army fatigue caps with varying rank, from PFC to bird colonel; several Army dress garrison caps—one bearing the two stars of a major general—and one barracks hat; a dozen or so Air Force covers—fatigue, beret, baseball cap, dress hat, and one flight helmet that bore an Air Force squadron insignia of the 614th Tactical Fighter Squadron from Phan Rang, and sported what appeared to be a bullet hole through the side—Marine and Navy covers; and a baseball-style civilian cap with a logo and "Rutgers University" on it. It was an intriguing display.

No sooner had the warrant glanced up than the man who answered to Nickel Nuts jerked the fatigue cap from Winter's head. "That's where they come from, Chief. Can't you read?" He pointed to a tiny sign, one inch by one inch, secreted on the inside wall, just above the light switch. Winter leaned close to read the 2-pica lettering: "Hats: Wear them in here, lose them."

Winter started to open his mouth, saw Smiley jerk his own cap from his head, and kept quiet. He didn't know who Nickel Nuts was, but Jernigan was the CO and he said nothing to deter the loss of Winter's cover. He was in an alien land.

Then Jernigan spoke up: "Let's call that a practice grab, Nichols. These guys are our guests; they didn't know the rules." Nichols! The 1st RR's Executive Officer. *Major* Nichols. Winter waited, curious, as the man designated Nickle Nuts said, "They can read, can't they?" nodding at the tiny sign.

But Major Nichols, his T-shirt a tie-dyed swirl of blues, greens, and purples handed the hat back to Winter. He reached around the end of the short bar, scrambled a bit, and handed Winter a beer. "Keep that in mind, Chief." And he smiled. "The boss must have taken a liking to you. I don't think he's ever gone back on a cover grab." He pointed up at the glitter of bars, two-color oak leaves, eagles, and stars that covered the ceiling, and said, "We bag 'em all.".

* * *

Major Jernigan let the door slam shut behind him as he followed Winter into a chilled office space in the corner of a Quonset hut on the edge of the parking ramp. Still in shorts with a damp T-shirt, the Commanding Officer seemed unaffected by the cold air which, to Winter's unaccustomed body, felt sub-Arctic. "Grab a chair. Anywhere, Chief."

The warrant officer, acclimated enough by now to senior grade officers, still held Jernigan in awe, whether a result of the rumors about him, approaching the status of legendary lunacy, or the very real threat of his presence as potential commander and signer of his Officer Efficiency Report—his Army report card. Winter said nothing, leaving it to the major to set the ground rules.

"Chief—what is it, Dave or David? Whatever. Chief, you're coming to work for me."

Winter waited. It wasn't what he would have called a warm welcome.

"Uhh, sir. I thought I was sent up here to take a look at operator procedures in the First, look for common ground to operations in the rest of the battalion. I assumed—"

"We got no fulltime oh-five-eights in the First; we don't do ARDF. That was so you get a look at our operation, the site, and for you'n me to have a session. You got a problem with that?" His bland countenance, evidencing no antagonism, invited confidence.

"No problem, sir. But I don't und—"

"You'll pardon me if I dispense with the military proprieties: That fucking light colonel running the Two-two-four is out of his tree. You came to 'Nam on orders containing a specific directive for assignment to the First. My Controller, the operations leader for the mission crews, is short. Something like forty days. You're his replacement. I've got to get you up here in time to fly overlap missions for familiarity, and that, young chief, does not allow me much time. Screw this hot body piracy shit." He reached for a fatigue jacket and shrugged into it.

"Sir, I don't have a problem with that. I wanted assignment to the First, but the major issue—beyond Colonel Sizelove shanghaiing me—is that I'm barred from combat missions for security purposes, due to a project I worked in Europe." Winter couldn't even explain the project; the major was not cleared for it.

"You're flying now. How's that work with security prohibition?"

"It's supposed . . . I'm technically not flying real missions, but training flights and so-called planning flights. Somehow . . ."

"You're flying missions, right?" That spiked hair was straight up again.

"Yes, sir. I make regular, scheduled flights and do my observing and training while on mission." He hadn't expected to be called on this, and he dare not do anything to open himself up to security violations.

"This is what you were ordered to do, right? I mean, Northcutt gave you this directly?"

"Sir. But I think it came from Colonel Sizelove. His grand plan . . . which he likely pirated from Colonel Northcutt." In for a penny, in for a shekel.

"Thought so. Well, I *did* know about your prohibition, matter of fact. My Mission Ops officer, Lieutenant Kerwyn, is checking with The Hall to find out just how long that security block's supposed to remain on you. You've been out of the European theater now, what? Three, four months? Probably no longer even applies. But you can't do anything about that." He kicked a foot up on his desk. "I want you to take a mission flight, today-tonight, if possible; look around, check things out; look over the station—" he waved his hand about, designating everything for 360 degrees "—then let me know how you feel about a transfer, and you can hop on back to Sai Gon tomorrow afternoon. 'kay?"

"Uh, yes, sir. I mean, going out on the bird is, in effect, violating the prohibition against my enemy overflight . . ." It was a specious argument: he was already violating the letter of the law, as well as the spirit. Why was this any different? And he was curious about the mission, about the First. ". . . but when do we launch?"

* * *

Back at the Sandman, Smiley was on his third beer. Winter related his dilemma: Jernigan had said the mission launch was at 1245; it was now 1120. He hadn't time for much, certainly not the time, nor the inclination, to open *that* can of worms—calling S-3 for clarification and/or permission—so he asked for a soda and stood drinking it in the doorway of the bar.

There were more unfamiliar faces present now, and several more bodies lying about on chairs on the patio. Officer personnel, Winter had to assume, without rank or nametags introduced themselves as they came and went. Smiley, ever the social doyen, introduced Winter to CW4 Ransom, CPT DeGrandcourt, and a black Navy pilot, Lieutenant Ivory. Before him where he leaned on the bar and sipped the soda, occupying center place on the back wall of the club, was a large, front page clipping from a browning, eight-month-old

Stars and Stripes military newspaper, proclaiming in 60-point type, the Marines' taking of the Citadel in Hue, the final ringing down of the curtain on the misfired Tet offensive. He had a flash of memory, another wall in some dayroom in the not too distant past. Almost a year after the events Tet was still the main topic of conversation.

Winter looked about at the wealth of literary aphorisms, the pulchritude of countless centerfolds, the infinite wisdom of a long line of disdainful pilots and officers who had passed through the Sandman Lounge on the way to one battle or another—*sans chapeaux* or not—and realized he would have to spend a full tour up here to work his way through all the postings.

* * *

Winter flew the impromptu mission, got his first look beyond the DMZ, overlooked Laos, and returned at 0125 the following morning, thirteen flying hours later, feeling, as he said, "Like a hundred eighty-five pounds of hammered shit." It was a boring mission, however; for the most part they drew no ground fire they were aware of. The linguists who handled the mission spent half their time trash-talking ballplayers and bar girls while they twiddled knobs and fought sleep. The one event of interest occurred during the Late Show hours: a crackle of static brought a mystery message across the ether, perking up the flight crew for a period.

Winter, during a period of quiescence in radio traffic, and lingering on Guard Channel, heard clearly a broadcast made in a calm but forceful voice. "GUNFIGHTER Eight six, this is CRICKET. I copy your MAYDAY. Request A.O. again. Are you *in* STEEL TIGER EAST, or just en route?" Winter noticed other ops around him, suddenly sitting up straighter, reaching for tuning knobs, heads turning. Op chatter. He could not hear the other end of the communication, though there was some breaking squelch right on the edge of his range. Because he had heard CRICKET's query, he could make out some reference to STEEL TIGER but nothing to clarify its meaning.

Winter was sitting at the Communicator's console; he leaned across the aisle and shouted above the engine noise at the Controller, Mister Voskov. "Who's CRICKET? And what's STEEL TIGER?" It was the first words he'd had with the warrant officer who had slept the first five hours of the flight, then took over the Controller's position from an SFC, who rotated to a voice op's console, freeing a specialist there to sit aft station watch in the rear of the plane. Voskov let hooded eyes drift slowly to Winter; he didn't answer for a long minute.

"CRICKET's emergency control. Call sign of A.B.-triple-C. STEEL TIGER's a classified area of operations in our neighbor." His sleepy gaze drifted back to his console.

"Our neighbor? . . ."

"Laos." Stingy with words. Or hung-over. Winter wondered about ABCCC, but didn't ask.

"Somebody's in the shit beyond our reach. Not that we could do anything anyhow, except maybe relay traffic if they couldn't hear one another. GUNFIGHTER's the callsign for Air Force F-4s out of Da Nang. Got one loose in Laos with horizontal controls shot up. Don't know if he can make it back to—"

"GUNFIGHTER Eighty-six, CRICKET," broke across the 243.5 megahertz band. "I copy you 'feet wet' about Pork Chop Lake. Take a heading of one-five-zero degrees and remain on Guard Channel. If you punch out, give me final coordinates."

"Roger," the Phantom's reply came back clearer, "I have two wingmen, Huns, courtesy of MISTY. They will provide coordinates. Thank you, CRICKET. Now ejecting . . ." It was the last Winter heard of the drama.

Voskov grimaced, a facial signal that apparently served him as a smile. "If you want to chase the rest of the rescue, switch to two-niner-niner point five. They're off Guard now."

Other than macabre voyeurism, Winter couldn't think of a legitimate reason to do so; he couldn't contribute anything, and he was just beginning to get the hang of Communicator.

After the courier drop at Da Nang at midnight, a quick refuel, then a rapid sprint down the coast to Cam Ranh Bay, Winter hit the rack in the empty room of a pilot who was on R&R in Singapore, and had the first completely relaxed night's sleep he'd had since arriving in-country. What deadly or minor activities might have taken place in surrounding Indian Country was filtered out by the soothing murmur of the air conditioner, and he was cool for the first time, delighting in the covers pulled over his head. He was amazed to find, in the morning, that his sheets were not even damp

* * *

Back in Sai Gon, no one even questioned him or Smiley; just another check mission, doing the standardization thing for the First as they had for the other four companies it was assumed. Winter knew now, though, that given the opportunity, he'd kill to get to Cam Ranh Bay. He'd spoken only briefly with CW3 Voskov, the current Controller whom he would replace and was assured of the criticality of the job, requiring a warrant officer with operations background, and especially useful was one with flight and ARDF experience. But all he could do was wait.

Rocket barrages and occasional mortar attacks broke the night calm around Tan Son Nhut, and from the roof of the Newport BOQ, impacting fire and secondary explosions and fires lit the horizon. Over the next week there was a sudden, vehement series of sapper attacks on select bars in the Sai Gon-Gia Dinh area, and Winter limited his downtown restaurant explorations. Not a deprivation, though; he was either flying or gone on TDY much of the time.

* * *

While on a TDY to Da Nang Winter encountered a Sergeant he'd known at the Defense Language Institute in Monterey, who told him that another mutual friend was in Nha Trang. On a trip to the 144th RRC (Avn.) in Nha Trang, at the end of the first mission day, Winter went to hunt up Duke Raidler, now a sergeant first class, non-flying, Ops NCO. When he asked a sergeant in the Orderly Room about Raidler, along with the information that Duke was "always in his hooch," he got a strange look, as if he'd asked about the best road to Transylvania.

Crossing the compound, Winter scuffled along in the white, gritty dust of the roadway, late in the afternoon when the sun setting behind the mountains left a dark sheen on the ocean and cast a discolored pall over everything. Chow was over and troops had taken refuge in their hooch or in the shower, the club, or some palace of delights in downtown Nha Trang. There were few bodies on the street. Winter reached a junction where the company street crossed another, narrower walk at right angles; Raidler's hootch was down this way, he'd been told.

"Winter! Dave Winter, I do swear. Man, is that you?" A body materialized out of the gloom, grabbing him by the jacket as he rounded the corner. He stared at the unfamiliar Duke Raidler, slimmed down now from when he'd known him six years before in Asmara. The man was naked but for a dripping OD towel about his waist and shower clogs, carrying a shaving kit of green leather.

"'scuse me. *Sir!*" The sergeant had just seen Winter's collar brass in the light, and he mockingly saluted with the dop kit. His voice sounded sad, sepulchral; deep with a quality Winter didn't remember and didn't recognize. They reminisced as Raidler continued to his hooch. Inside, he stashed his kit, dropped the towel, and slipped into OD skivvies while Winter recalled several common acquaintances and where he'd last encountered them, or heard of them.

But after the initial spate of glad-handing and "remember old—" and "where's old so-and-so, now," conversation dropped off, severed from any interest. Winter felt awkward, as if he found himself in a room full of hostile strangers. He suddenly couldn't remember anyone else to talk about, had nothing else to say. He became as quiet as Raidler.

The NCO sat on the side of his bunk, pushing the mosquito bar back, thrusting his bare feet onto a foot locker. His head slumped forward. He said nothing.

After a few moments, ill at ease, aware of an air of discontent about Raidler, Winter said, "Duke. What's up, man? Some kind of bad news or something?" He had not been a close friend of The Duke in Eritrea, but he knew him, had shared shift work with him, even went down the mountain to Cheren once on a hunting trip together, an event of which he now could remember no details.

After a long delay, when Winter thought the man would not respond, Raidler said, "I guess you could say that."

"What?" Jesus, it was like pulling teeth.

"Just that . . . I'm going to die." Profound. Explicit. No smile, no invitation to further discussion. No hint that he invited concern.

Winter felt out of synch. Trying to put a light spin on it he said, "Well, hell! Aren't we all." He watched the man's face. No indication he'd heard.

"Soon."

"Soon?"

"Maybe tonight."

"Duke, you sick? Something wrong with you?" Winter sought explanation, but suspicioned, almost immediately, that he would get none. The sergeant had that thousand-yard stare that takes over men sometimes who have seen too much combat, men who can no longer distinguish between what they see that is real and what they see that is dredged up from some deep well of anguish and pain and fear, fatigue, hunger . . . a life in decline, a soul in stasis.

But how could that be? Few Radio Research troops had been exposed to that kind of direct combat. A few maybe, working with a team assigned directly to support of one of the combat divisions. Certainly not Raidler. As far as he knew, Raidler had spent his entire tour—and this his first and only tour in Vietnam—at Nha Trang in a relatively secure environment. What had brought him to this pass? Where did his personal chimera derive from?

"Not sick," the sick man said. "Just gonna die. Soon." He sat on the bunk, kneading his hands as if washing them. Just out of the shower, he gave off a sour odor.

Winter tried to talk to him; he wouldn't respond. After more than an hour of fruitless and frustrating entreaty, Winter left the billet and sought out the company commander. Major Dorcas shook his head, commiserated, told Winter they'd had his friend to the shrinks, to the flight surgeon even though Raidler didn't fly, and up to the Navy hospital in Da Nang. Nothing physical; nothing they could find amiss. But they could not talk him out of his state of mind. They were going to ship him out soon in a rubber suit, back to the world.

Winter returned to the transient quarters, told Boyd Smiley about Raidler, and lay for a long time in his bunk before falling into an uneasy sleep. In the morning, after an early mission-standardization flight, while their own plane was being fueled and readied for return to Tan Son Nhut, Winter sought out Raidler again. He went through every likely space in the company. The NCO was not to be found. Winter and Smiley were airborne at 1335 and he never saw Raidler again.

* * *

The fat man's act exploded before he got the tale out, and he sprayed cheap scotch over half a dozen bystanders, then trumpeted, "The First Sergeant shouted, 'Listen up, troops. Announcements: Baker, your leave's approved. See the clerk. Hermasillo, go by the dispensary for blood work; they have the forms. Wozlinski, your mother's dead. Hopper—'

"'Jesus Christ, First Sergeant. C'm'ere,' the CO said, pulling the First Shirt to the side of the formation. 'You can't drop something like that on a soldier, man. You gotta ease into it, go 'round-about. Show some sensitivity, some tact, for God's sake.'

"So the Top steps back before the formation, looks at his roster, and says, 'O. K. Moving right along. All you guys with fathers living, take one step forward. Hey, hey, not so fast there, Hopper.'" The jokester began laughing, a deep cigarette-phlegmy, hacking laugh, his round, red cheeks aflame and sweating.

"Ahhh, man, that is so ancient," the wire correspondent responded. "That's historic. I heard that one in Navy boot camp in nineteen and forty-seven." The correspondent, his safari jacket unreasonably clean and pressed, made an imposing picture, the projected epitome of a media mump, Winter thought. He could tell the daily press briefings were as close as the newsie got to the front; but man, did he have an *image*—the way he dressed, carried himself—but more damning, the way he wrote what he wrote. Winter had read the journalist's tripe in several papers. "The man's syndicated," he said to Captain Darren in a tone of astonishment..

"The man's an asshole," Darren replied. He was from the S-4 Shop in the battalion; he knew an asshole when he encountered one.

"Well, he's a syndicated asshole, then."

The daily press briefing, the "Five O'clock Follies," was already started. A poster-boy major danced his way through statistics, trite phrasing, and clichés, while behind him at the briefing wall chart a sergeant posted stick-on symbols and wrote with grease pencil, changing the face of the war as they watched. Winter had accompanied Lieutenant Colonel Northcutt to provide operator perspective if needed as background for the S-3's briefing to General Vetter; Winter was not asked for input, and he and his boss, dismissed, lingered to hear how the briefing would be translated into "squeak speak," the official word. Some kind of selling language for the media at the Follies..

"I wonder we even bother," Winter grumbled, disdain for the pack mentality of the crowd of newsmen and -women projected.

The colonel, now a pilot, had, like Winter, earlier carried a rifle, in the colonel's case in the big one, WWII. "No wonder there. Ever since Bill Mauldin put on civvies and went back to drawing cartoons with corporate targets, I've not had much respect for the Fourth Estate."

They had wandered out among the clogged pathways filled with media and staff hangers-on, but Northcutt did not lower his voice. Captain Darren, whose job sometimes required he interface with the media, peeled off and disappeared. Outside, Winter pushed through a cluster of Vietnamese enlisted soldiers wearing red scarves and freshly-white-painted web gear and belts, part of an honor guard for the Vietnamese General who sat in on part of General Vetter's briefing—the Unclassified portion, Winter was relieved to note.

At the Jeep, Private Mladcjik V. Woijczek popped a salute and aided the colonel in mounting to the front passenger seat. The colonel turned and stared at him in amazement. Winter climbed over the gas can on the back and stepped down onto the back seat, then onto a pile of grease-stained canvas on the floor behind the driver. There were other comments Winter felt he should make regarding the news people he despised, but the colonel was silent on the subject, and Winter didn't want to come across as hysterical. They all held their own views of the media.

There was silence between the two officers, both fixed on Woijczek's low-voiced recital of fuse characteristics for 155mm artillery shells as he drove. The source of his inspiration . . .?

Winter interrupted, speaking to the colonel, "I just read, a week or so ago, a correspondent who used the phrase, '. . . and the war was far away then.' Sounds so Hemingway-esque. Sounds so bullshit! The war is never far away." Except, he thought, perhaps for these Caravelle Commandos but kept it to himself when the colonel did not respond.

* * *

"What's this *Lonely Ringer* crap, Ito? The Battalion motto. Where's that come from?" Winter asked Ito later as the two walked up the littered sidewalk past 100-P Alley toward the Newport BOQ.

"Where you eating?" the diminutive warrant officer asked.

"Does it matter? Circle Thirty-Four, I guess. OK with you? *Lonely Ringer?. . .*"

"Fine. Not up to BOQ Number One. The motto? Some *haole* schmaltz. Like a lone ringer in horseshoes, it stands alone. I'm not sure what the message is ... I guess it has to do with our uniqueness of mission, but as with most of this hype and cockamaimee crap, it's supposed to send a flurry of fear through the little yeller muthas . . . not to mention the enemy."

* * *

Dear Nickie: *16 November*

Here we are in November and the big news is still the Tet Offensive. Sorry/glad I missed it, but it must have been something. Very little is back to normal, whatever that is, as if anything's normal in this country. I sense the great fear is that this holiday season will bring a repeat of last.

One thing which is daily coming home more forcefully to me is the lack of wisdom in our policy of one-year tours. I've seen so many examples of why that's just downright dumb. Sure, it's good to know when you'll have your tour finished, and to have a date to look forward to. It's good for the individual. Not, I think, a good thing for prosecution of the war.

For one thing, it takes a year to get a soldier really competent at his job, to have learned enough to do the job right, and protect himself. Then he's gone! He's no good, for the most part, for some time even before he's gone. Knowing they're short, too many troops start getting overly cautious, overly concerned, and they don't do their job. Some weasel out of patrols and flights; some just flat refuse to go. It's become practice to let it slide. That means new guys coming in as replacements don't get the training and overlap they need. They take the brunt of hostile engagements.

And young officers. Six months in the field, then they rotate into a headquarters rear-echelon job where they're technically safe. They're just learning their job and becoming valuable to the war effort. I know all the arguments: It's not fair for the same guys to just keep on fighting the same war, while others never see combat. But the fact is, it's become just a game to survive the 12 months, often without regard to completing the mission.

Actually, I don't have the answers. All I know is that I want to complete my 365 and get back to you and the boys. Despite all the things you said—we said—you know we love each other and belong together. We have to be there, together, for the boys. And for each other.

I'm not, as you said, a zealot who wants to just keep on going to wars. I do think the U.S. had a reason to come over here, and though little has improved with all the input of troops and arms, I don't think that reason is gone away. It's something we can disagree on, surely, without tearing our marriage apart. It's not like we're either one of us involved with someone else, or have lost sight of our primary commitments.

Please write. I've gotten no mail since I got here.

Looks like I will be moving north to Cam Ranh Bay soon. The C.O. there has made it his own personal Grail, if for no other reason than to confound the battalion C.O. I'll get you an address if/when I transfer.

Love, Dave

As he folded the letter, looking about for the envelope he'd already addressed, he wondered if he had made a mistake, bringing up the very subject that had torn them apart. And having had no response, indeed no letter at all, from her, was he just pissing up a rope?

* * *

Mean Mutha Ashfinian stopped Winter in the map shop at headquarters. "Dave, my man, enlighten me."

"As to what?"

"I was in the PX this ay-em and saw the strangest pair of dudes I've ever come across. I mean, I see Zips of all kinds in there, Vietnamese, probably some of them VC and NVA, and there's Filipinos, Koreans, Thais, Aussies . . . so it's not like I'm unaccustomed to foreigners, you understand. But there was a pair of guys who looked . . . well, one was dark but not a black, maybe like a Latino or something. The other was a tall, thin, white guy, dressed in old fatigues—both were—and I could swear speaking Spanish. Seemed really out of place."

The warrant's description nudged an elusive memory for Winter that seemed somehow bothersome; but his mind was on briefing for the afternoon flight and he said to Ashfinian, "Could be Puerto Ricans. Lots of Puerto Ricans in today's Army." He had a brief flash, a hazy and indistinct aura of the bizarre he thought was associated with his first tour in 'Nam. But there were too many bad memories and unwelcome associations; he waved and turned away to grab his mission bag.

* * *

That evening, long after Winter had secured from the afternoon flight and had eaten, then stuck around for two hours in a nowhere movie at the Circle-34, and was in his mosquito-barred rack trying to read, a ripple of 82mm mortar rounds fell on Cho Lon, one of them impacting on the 509th transient billets. One round wounded a first lieutenant, who was in his room, and his enlisted aide asleep in the hall outside. An aide for whom no one could find an explanation; nor why an enlisted man was there in an officer's billet. An aide? the curious queried. What first lieutenant has an aide? For what reason? Sounded like something out of the Middle Ages.

And though the orders file and registration log were examined repeatedly, no one could find the names of either. In the settling dust of the attack, after both had been wheeled away to the Third Field Hospital, enquiry there revealed no such patients, and no trace of either man could be found in the III CTZ.

chapter twenty

Chucklin' Chicken

Vietnam: November-December 1968

Beware, thee, a multitude of ground fire,
for it shall surely lay thee low.

"Jesus! Aviator humor hasn't improved much in three years," Winter, unsolicited, informed anyone within hearing, including the CW2 pilot. "That aphorism was popular, right here in this building, in 1965. The sign looks at least that old. Has it just remained?"

"Stupido come l'aqua calda!" the pilot said scornfully, turning away in dismissal.

Winter gazed about; nothing forthcoming. "What did Travaglia say about stupid? Was that a slam at me?"

"Who gives a shit?" asked a sergeant sitting by the black box.

"You said . . .?" Winter invited, turning toward the speaker who was unknown to him.

"Oh. No . . . sir. That wasn't directed at you. Your statement . . . question. I meant, who gives a shit about such infantile humor?" He failed to look contrite.

"Infantile? Hmmm. Yet to be seen . . . but my clerk, back at B.A., that was his favorite expression. The answer to anything. Everything. 'Who gives a shit?' indeed," Winter reflected.

The sergeant looked up from a classified document upon which he had cast his eyes at the realization of his *faux pas*. "Wouldn't have been Magic Marvin, would it, sir?"

"You know Marv? Were you at B.A.?"

"Yessir, right after you left . . . Got there just in time to be levied over here."

"From one route-step organization to another, am I right?" Winter looked at a blank space on the sergeant's jungle fatigue jacket where a nametag should have been. "What's your name?"

The sergeant rose from his chair and stood at a relaxed position of semi-attention. "Stamps, sir. Staff Sergeant Montgomery O. Stamps." He looked as if he would offer his hand.

Winter did. "Marve have that effect on you? Coloring your perceptions, as it were?" *And* your discourse, he thought. They shook hands perfunctorily.

Stamps offered a wry smile, "Doesn't he have the same effect on everyone, Chief?"

"I guess he does. What do you do, Stamps . . . your MOS?" Winter asked, realizing the man's initials were M-O-S, but surely didn't stand for his Military Occupational Specialty.

"Oh-five-eight. Nine-eight-two trailer." Stamps said. He had had that ironic equation, his initials, pointed out to him too many times to accept it with equanimity. But the warrant officer did not comment.

"So-o-o . . ." Winter looked around in query: "Where're you going to work?" Except for the flying ops in the 146th Radio Research Company (Aviation.), there were no 058s assigned anywhere near. Stamps, FNG that he appeared, didn't have enough time-in-country to qualify for Air. And there were no 982s closer than Bien Hoa.

"Going up to Plei Ku, the Three-Oh-Third, for a few days' mission orientation. I'm assigned to LAFFIN EAGLE when it gets in-country next month." He smiled, satisfied with his lot.

But Winter knew it was not a given: "*If* they get here. Those U-twenty-ones have been *on the way* now for more months than I can tell you." He looked over at Travaglia who was back and motioning to him from the door. "But good luck. If I see you around anywhere, we'll grab a cup of coffee and talk about Magic Marvin. Behind his mousey little back."

"Uhh-h, right, sir. Yessir." Winter realized Stamps mightn't understand the rodent allusion.

When he caught up with him in the hall, Winter demanded of the Italian flyer,

"*Wha-a-t?*"

"Ween-ter. You hav-va mean streak to yourself."

"Hey, shit-for-brains, is that anything to say about a friend?"

"*Dagli amici mi guardi Iddio . . .*"

"Now what the hell's *that* mean?" Winter stopped, hands on his hips in exaggerated chagrin.

"Hey-y-y, don't eat with me, Ween-ter. *You* speak *Italiano.*"

"I know ten words of Eye-tie, J.C. And it's not 'eat with me.' You mean, 'Don't *mess* with me.'"

Travaglia looked puzzled. "But thee messing hall is thee eating hall. I say eat. I like thee soun' better."

"But it's not the same sense. 'Don't mess with me' means . . . oh hell, drop it. I've forgotten what we were talking about. Where are we going?"

A voice spoke up from behind Winter: "He said, 'God protect me from my friends . . .'"

Winter turned, confronting the rare sight of the Piltdown Pilot. The first lieutenant who flew with the 146th RR Co. (Avn.) was almost never to be found in the 224th headquarters. "What?" Winter said. He must have missed a line of dialogue.

The lieutenant patiently reconstructed: "You asked him, 'Is that anything to say about a friend?' and he said, *'Dagli amici mi guardi Iddio . . .'* Which means, 'God protect me from my friends . . .' The rest of the saying is, *'ché dai nemici mi guardo io'*—'for I can take care of my enemies.' Colloquially, 'With friends like these—meaning you—who needs enemies?'"

Winter glared at the lieutenant. "P-Square, how the hell come you're suddenly a linguist? I never heard you speak Italian before."

"Well, gee whillakers, Chief, you probably never saw me wipe my ass either . . . but I do it. *Almost* regularly. And with that kind of response, I probably don't want to enlighten you all the way back to what you two were originally talking about. But as to where J.C. was taking you, I asked him to get you and me together. I wanted to see you about something." The lieutenant suddenly began patting the pockets on his Nomex flight suit . . . and there were many pockets. He had been the first aviator in the battalion to don the Nomex. When the fire-retardant suits—in color "shit-brindle brown," according to Mister Smiley—first became available to Army pilots, many, out of some sense of macho disregard, or simply a reluctance to change habits, chose to continue wearing the established gray, one-piece Air Force flight suits. But Piltdown Pilot was no fool; he chose safety over image, and shortly after his appearance on the flight line at Tan Son Nhut, the Army green safety garments became the order of the day. And then USARV published an edict taking away any options, choosing not to allow individual pilots to unnecessarily put themselves at risk from fire and explosions.

"Stick around, will you," the lieutenant whose name in quasi-civilized circles was William Mabry said, glancing back down the hall while he slapped at his pockets inquiringly.

"What'd you lose?" Winter asked. Travaglia waited as if the answer was important.

"My car keys."

"*Car* keys?"

"Jeep, then. I've got Two-six-three, the one with the padlock. Gotta have the keys to make the sucker go. Be right back." He faded down the hallway..

Winter rolled his eyes and leaned against the wall, turning to Travaglia. "J.C. How long you been in country now? All along? Since you came? . . . which was late July, early August of 'sixty-four? I remember. It was about the time I made Staff Sergeant and moved over to the Air Section."

A short, bald major whom Winter had never seen came from the S-1's office, stared at the two of them without stopping or speaking, and marched out the front entrance, an Army barracks hat worn at a jaunty angle, like the 50-mission-crush Army Air Corps pilots' hats from World War Twice. But with the stiff inner rim present it did not present a "crush" and therefore looked silly, Winter thought..

"Four year, three month. Long time, no?"

"Long time, yes, you silly shit. How come you keep extending?"

"Why not? What I'm goin' ta do? Cannot go back to *Italia*; the Carabiniere still seek me. Can't get into h'America with no green card. Get shot here, get shot in Civitavecchia. What's the oddment?"

"Difference."

"Yes, what's the deeference?"

"Why do the national police of Italy want you?" You never know, do you, Winter thought. Giancarlo "J.C." Travaglia seemed the least likely individual he knew to be in trouble, the least offensive of any number of Italian-Americans he knew. And of pilots he knew.

"Tha's a leetle joke. But not too much. Commandante Bivolo, the Carabiniere boss in my town, still looks for me, I am sure. He is the uncle of a very sweet, ver-ry fragile *signorina*, who, by now, has take the veil. Cut off her life. He—the commandante—is not forgiving of young *amore*. He is not, at least, forgiving my part in this tragedy." He raised his head and sniffed speculatively. "*Il bruto!*"

Winter chuckled. Now he knew. Four years, three months ago, no one had a clue about J.C., how he came into the clutches of the Army, the Warrant Aviation Program, or The International Brigade. He started to ask odd-man-out if he knew where his two other compatriots, the rest of The International Brigade, were now after all this time, but the Piltdown Pilot interrupted, speaking as he walked past him.

"The answer to your question, regarding my use of Italian, is that I spent more than two years flying out of Vicenza. I spent a *lot* of time cultivating social niceties there," he said knowingly. "C'mon. We'll take my Jeep." Travaglia was apparently a part of the package; he followed along and climbed into the back of -263.

Lieutenant William Mabry, the Piltdown Pilot, drove as he flew: the only aircraft in the sky, the only vehicle on the road.

* * *

When they crossed the main strips of Tan Son Nhut—Zero Seven/Two Five, the twin 9,000-feet strips oriented to bearings 070 and its reciprocal, 250, degrees magnetic north—Mabry slowed and stopped at an Air Force check point. Beyond, in an area called the "Air Force side," a venue into which Winter had not ventured since some business in 1964, he saw a forest of aircraft vertical stabilizers scattered amongst a parallelogram-shaped puzzle of revetments and armored bunkers. C-130 Hercules and C-7 Caribous were parked haphazardly along the fringes of an area denoted priority; the cargo planes did not rank with the quality of the air fleet—the fast movers.

He recognized the entrancing slant of F-4 Phantom tails, as well as vertical evidence of F-100 "Huns," F-5s with Vietnamese Air Force markings, and a lone F-104 Starfighter. "The One-oh-four must be lost," Piltdown Pilot commented. "Hardly see them outside NATO." The air policeman handed Mabry his I.D. back, saluted, and waved the Jeep through the gap.

They crept down passageways that led ever deeper into the maze of parked tactical aircraft. He stopped finally and pointed to a small executive-looking aircraft, all alone, diminutive in the large revetment. It had Army markings and was painted pale gray and white, with blue trim. Winter and Travaglia stared in question, until Winter noted the dipole blade antennas on the wingtip, supplemented by a veritable forest of vertical antennas protruding from every horizontal surface. "It's a flying antenna farm," Winter offered.

"LAFFIN EAGLE, gentlemen." Mabry exhibited a kind of pride, as of ownership. "The first of many."

"No kidding. So that's Chucklin' Chicken. Have you flown it?" Winter wanted to know. He stood so he could see clearly over the windshield. Windshields in the Capital Military District usually lay flat, folded down to avoid flying glass from projectile damage, but

Lieutenant Mabry, Pildown Pilot or no, would not drive his Jeep in that configuration. The wind mussed his hair.

"Not this one. Flown U-twenty-ones, though. Got a couple hundred hours in Utes." He pointed.

"That the nickname for the U-twenty one? Ute?" Winter asked, trying to place the allusion to an Indian tribe in the euphemistic sequences of aircraft. Bad as GIs with their war names, there were those effecting Indian tribal titles, birds, animals, weather configurations.

Piltdown Pilot did not answer, but nodded, a movement which directed their eyes to a sentry. An Army SP4, armed and watching them with curiosity, was on guard by the sand bag wall that surrounded the new plane. They got out of the dirty little vehicle and walked toward the aircraft. The guard, slipping the M-16 from his shoulder, held it at port arms and watched their approach.

In the shadow beneath his cap brim, the guard's eyes were indistinct but unwavering. Winter recognized the man, an airborne operator from the 146th who was recently grounded. He couldn't remember why the man was off flying status, but it was something medical.

"Hiser," Winter nodded to the guard.

"Sir. Mister Winter, Lieutenant, . . . uhh, Mister Tra-*vag*-leeyah," he acknowledged, carelessly shifting his rifle to a moderately recognizable effort at a rifle salute, then let the rifle drop back into a non-aggressive position.

"So you get first close-up on this baby, huh, Hiser? Gonna fly on her?" Winter asked.

"Don't know, sir. Grounded. May not fly again."

"It'll be some time before EAGLE's activated. Maybe by then you'll be back on status," the lieutenant reasoned aloud.

"Doubt it, sir."

"What's your problem, Hiser. Why'd they ground you?" Winter asked.

"Got some kind of irritated bowel or something; they're not sure. But everytime I fly, I get the shits." They looked at him with horrified sympathy. "Yessir, get the screamin', runnin' shits. From the time we leave the ground. Doctors said it may have to do with decrease in pressure as we gain altitude. Whatever, pilots won't fly with me. And the mechs have threatened to frag my quarters if I mess up another bird. So, I'm probably grounded for good." He smiled. He did not seem anxious to reverse that medical judgement.

"Gee, yeah. That's terrible, Hiser. Well, good luck . . . I mean . . . however it works out," Winter murmured and moved away with the other two. Hiser went back to staring across the baking airstrip, adjusting his aviator sunglasses, and moving determinedly about the shiny new U-21.

No one said anything as they walked around the bird. Winter didn't know what Hiser's instructions were, *vis-à-vis* curiosity seekers, but he didn't particularly care to approach the aircraft to get a look inside, anyhow. Like Hiser, he would never fly on it. Through the side port he could see equipment racks and banks of receivers, analyzers, generators—the whole fucking tutti-frutti, as Ratty Mac would have put it. Winter caught Mabry looking at him, pensively. He smiled, shook his head. They moved away from the isolated bird, mounted the Jeep, and left.

Back on the perimeter road, Mabry said, "That's what I'm up to, if you cared. That's why I asked you to come see the bird, Dave."

"I'm not following you. You're not talking about Hiser, are you?"

The pilot shook his head. "When LAFFIN EAGLE goes operational, initial tasking will be Two Corps. Practically all the ops in the one forty-sixth, working primarily in Three Corps, have no mission orientation for Two Corps. The one forty-fourth in Nha Trang is short-handed; they can't break anyone loose for the preliminary training sessions. I have to go to Plei Ku, make a presentation that we hope will entice some ground ops with Two Corps experience to go Airborne. You probably know some of those ops, and you're experienced in DF. Colonel wants this done A-SAP. Said I could take whoever I need."

"And . . .?"

"So, are you going with me? Your boss says he can 'spare you,'" he said dryly, "for a couple of days. Okay?" He pulled up and parked the Jeep as close as the security limit would allow before battalion headquarters

"Same rules apply? Ops still gotta have six months in-country, in-mission, and then extend for six?" Winter wanted confirmed. He unlimbered himself from the joyless vehicle with the cast iron suspension.

Piltdown Pilot shook his head. "Gonna waive the six months in-country, if they're otherwise experienced and capable." Mabry knew it would not be a popular point with the warrant officer who'd had a major hand in putting ARDF practices in place three years earlier.

"Don'cha know, I love that so much I could just shit," Winter grated.

"Means we'll have a bigger field to draw from," Mabry said soothingly. Winter responded as if the officer did not understand the disparity.

"It also means we get newks who don't know the mission. Makes for a lot of wasted airframe time."

The lieutenant sniffed, looked across the barbed wire, and murmured as he walked away, "There *is* no waste when *I'm* flying. Flying's where it's at."

* * *

First Lieutenant William Mabry had come the long way 'round. He'd been ready for military service in 1961 when he graduated from High School in Vermont. He was from just outside Island Pond, a small town in The Northeast Kingdom, which was, he realized, like being from Nineveh. He always gave his origins as Sussex County. So they were, but such ambiguity also discouraged hassles with insistently ignorant Army clerks trying to distinguish "near" Island Pond from "just outside" the village, as a militarily definable location.

Mabry had no provenance he could claim. He had been found, a two-year-old waif, by all other measures just brought into the world, warmly dressed in good quality winter clothing, sitting on a slab of Vermont granite in an abandoned quarry a couple of miles from Island Pond in 26-degree weather. The village was too small to count a social services staff among its payroll. The police sergeant who responded to the startled moose hunter's CB radio call, went to the quarry and picked up the child, took him into his home for, as he offered, "a few days," hoping for discovery of the parents in short order. When that resolution failed to materialize, the child had been taken by the state and eventually adopted out, returned to the same area in the care of a dairy farmer and his barren wife.

The youth's adoptive father, having the best interests of the child in mind following his graduation from High School, urged him into college, primarily to avoid growing concern over a tiny southeast Asian hot-spot. Mabry reluctantly went to school, declaring no major at Johnson State College, attending enough classes to maintain his student status. But he couldn't maintain the fraud for long; he knew he was wasting time and his father's money. When he failed two subjects in the same, second semester in his junior year, he was urged by his counselor to "consider some other line of work." What the unkind counselor meant was, find another scheme to avoid the Draft. And so he had.

In the early summer of 1964, Mabry enlisted in the Army. After Basic, when he learned of the warrant officer flight program, he applied, was accepted, graduated flight school, got his Warrant Officer-1 bar, and shuffled off to Buffalo. In those years, every helicopter pilot surviving the training was on a slick slide to Vietnam. Mabry spent his first tour with the First Aviation Brigade.

Army aviation units were overstaffed with warrant officers who could not hold positions of command; the Army needed commissioned officers as company commanders and high-level staff officers. Warrants were traditionally seated, for their period of servitude, metaphorically "below the salt," whatever their pedigree. But noting the young W-2 had almost three years college, the Army tendered him a direct commission to second lieutenant.

Along with the promotion, and upon departure from the First Aviation Brigade, came the assignment to Vicenza. It was while he was in that command that some clerk, reviewing his records for promotion to first lieutenant, overdue after more than a year in grade, could find no records of his flight school graduation and certification as a flyer. This, after a year spent flying slicks and Dustoffs in Eye Corps. His promotion followed quickly, but the lack of pilot pedigree was allowed to fester, leaving him without definition—worse, without a calling—while distant personnel clerks in the Hoffman Building sought validation for him.

It was while in this star-crossed mode that the adjutant, a captain whose own antecedents would not bear inspection, reflected on a serendipitous bevy of facts that *were* known about the young lieutenant. He was from Sussex; he had an unknowable history but was found in a quarry in that county; and in the sense of advancing from enlisted to warrant officer to commissioned officer, all within a two-year period, was a new kind of animal. The adjutant, a physical anthropology major in civilianary for want of an ambition in life, quickly likened Mabry to a scientific scandal still new enough to occupy the minds of interested souls: Piltdown Man.

Enthused with his own esoteric grasp of facts of the anthropological hoax, the adjutant labeled Mabry "Piltdown Pilot." The title, without the piquant supporting story, followed the young lieutenant to Viet Nam and into the quirky lexicon of war names, with one of which almost every man equipped themselves, or was so labeled by insensitive associates..

* * *

CW4 Claude Riché, the senior warrant officer in the 224th Aviation Battalion, piloted the damaged Beaver with studied disdain for the threat. Between him and Winter, they could count seven holes in the RU-6A, but had no idea what the final count was since they could not see beneath the craft. Two rounds, at least, had come through the floor, subsequently through the overhead, where they passed on through the bird without striking either the pilot or the operator, a role being played by Winter in what had been designated a training/familiarization flight for the pilot. Mister Riché, the "Mad Cajun," recently transferred from the 138th RR Co. (Avn.) in Hue-Phu Bai to battalion headquarters for cross-training in preparation for the new RU-21Ds expected "any day now," had not been exposed to the battalion's standardization scheme. Though he despised flying the single-engine Beaver, there were no RU-8Ds available and airworthy on this day, and he reluctantly agreed to use the U-6 for his initial exposure. Boyd Smiley, scheduled to fly with them as "instructor" for the Mad Cajun, had weaseled out. Winter had heard Smiley express the opinion that he ". . . would just be goddamned if I will fly with the Cajun, who has Methusalah's own years behind the stick, and *instruct him* in anything." It was a matter of respect.

"Mister Richie—" Winter began.

"Rish-é," he corrected Winter, accenting the second syllable. "It's Cajun. French. Acadian. Besides, I'm Claude to you."

"Sorry . . . Claude. Don't we want to try to get this bird down somewhere before it falls out from under us?" He was glancing nervously around the hazy landscape, waiting for a friendly wave, an invitation from some emergency strip.

"Nah-h-h. Don't smell no smoke. Don't see no fire. And the fuel guage's not goin' sout' on us. Maybe, even with that slimey little bastard's unfo'tunate skill, or luck, with the machine gun, we might-a dodged a bullet. In a manner of speaking." Riché's diction was a haphazard mix of improper grammar and shortcuts and a decent vocabulary, with Cajun overtones. He fiddled with the trim control and the aircraft waddled on through the heavy, humid air, seeming to take itself seriously in this new role of combat warrior.

Winter, who did not share the same sense of *laissez-faire* regarding their state of being, unconsciously tightened his harness.

The Mad Cajun saw the move as what it was, and said, "Don't worry 'bout it. I got dis piece-a shit covered. Nothin's what it seems." At Winter's skeptical look, the pilot snorted and waggled the yoke mischievously.

After a bit, the pilot glanced over his shoulder, saw Winter in slack mode, and said, "In the absence of work, let me tell you a story, ' bout t'ings not bein' what dey seem."

"I can live with that."

"Back when I was in school—we didn't live out on the bayou den; we was 'city folk,' living in Baton Rouge—there was a whole passel of young 'uns in my class, Coon Asses. The teacher was not. Not of the Cajun persuasion. She was one of de old line whites, just a cut above us and niggers and yankees . . . anyone who didn't fit her notions of birth and heri-*tage*. But we didn't recognize dat den, being kids and snotty and jus' didn't give a fuck about school or most t'ings grown-up.

"We thought Miz Letty—*Miss* Leticia Thorndyke, never married, a teacher forever—we t'ought she was pretty special. About once a week she brought in platesful-a homemade cookies for her classes. Unless you'd screwed up pretty bad, you got to take two cookies . . . and man, dey were good cookies. Even if you had screwed up, if you made up like you was sorry enough, she let you have de cookies anyhow. Dis was something she been doing for years, almos' long as she been teaching. Long time, 'cause my Aunt Gertrella had her thirty-some years before."

Winter had begun to inch away from the threat of consummate destruction, caught up in what was not necessarily a captivating tale, but one holding enough allure to preclude fixation on fiery death. But he had trouble seeing the Mad Cajun as a student. He must certainly be in his fifties, he thought, old enough he did not fit the model. But consistent with the tone of the tale of the baker-teacher.

"Ol' Miz Letty turned 'round from de blackboard one day when we was doin' fractions, pointed her finger at Johnny Beauclaire, who was acting up, opened her mouth . . . and fell over dead. *Dead!* As last week's news. Shook us up pretty good, I can tell you—"

A loud burst of white noise washed over the two warrant officers as something close and powerful transmitted a burst, then squelched away to ambient hiss. Riché squinted his eyes against the aural assault and switched the radio out of Stand-By mode.

"—shook us up. Lotsa students went by her house, mostly curious. She was dead, and she lived wit' no one.

"Miz Thorndyke had kept birds. Had a parrot, I know; I saw him. I heard she had some others, t'ree or four cages of different breeds. Well, a few days later, when some relative of hers came to town to take care of t'ings, she asked around if anyone wanted these birds. Had a couple of takers, all right, but during the various negotiations and pawning off dese birds, de relative told the wife of the next door neighbor—they were talking and the neighbor commented on how Miz Thorndyke must-a really loved kids to spend so many years putting up with them and all their shenanigans. The teacher's relative said that was all fiction, that Miz Thorndyke hated kids; but because she never married and had no other income and didn't know nothin' else but teaching, she had to stick to it to live. But she had been getting her own back for years." Turned sideways, caught up in the tale, Winter noted the middle-aged pilot's look of curious smugness.

"Ev'ry week, makin' a fresh batch of cookies for her students, she take the newspapers out from the floor of de birds' cages and shake off into the cookie dough de bird shit and whatever had fell there. The goddamned ol' bitch had been feeding us on bird shit for years. Everybody in that town, practically, had eaten dose damned cookies at some time over the years."

The tale finished, *denouement* accomplished, the Mad Cajun went quiet.

The single engine droned on despairingly, the thrumming high-pitched roar cycling up and down while plowing ever onward. Neither man spoke. Winter swallowed convulsively. The picture occupying his vision gagged him. The Cajun pilot seemed to have come to an accommodation with what was, for Winter, a disgusting and unforgettable image.

Ahead, Winter could make out the emerging shapes of Sai Gon; just beyond, farther north, was the welcome white concrete strips of Tan Son Nhut. To think of that as home was a stretch for Winter, but at this time, anything was a welcome get-away from the tale of the cookies and fear of the possible bleeding fuel lines on the Beaver. Now if the Mad Cajun could just keep this sucker in the air for ten more minutes. . . .

chapter twenty-one

Piltdown Pilot Proselytizes Plei-ku

Vietnam; December 1968

The Mad Cajun taxied the Beaver into its slot along the Army ramp. With the throat-cutting slash from the ground crewman, he shut down, immediately flinging his door open. The incessant engine roar died, followed in moments by damping oscillations of the propeller. Winter, breathing deeply for their salvation in the sudden windfall of noise abatement, clearly heard a plaintive query from someone not visible: "Have we won the war?"

The voice cut through the background of distant airborne engines, the clatter of dropped tools, a double-time cadence in Vietnamese, and the enveloping witch's medley of airbase sounds. Winter searched nearby, but could see no one who appeared to have been the winsome speaker. CW4 Riché appeared unaware of anything untoward.

Walking toward the 146th ready hut, they were forced to circumvent an Air Force F-4 Phantom, just off a mission, in an unusual location far from jet fighter tie-down. It was poised, shut down at the junction of the parking ramp with the taxiway. Not parked; it appeared too ready to take to the skies. Winter's first impression was of the smell, a heady, noxious compendium of burnt-kerosene JP-4 jet fuel and hot taxiway tar, bubbling in the sun.

The pilot and back-seater sat in their tandem cockpit seats in a five-way conversation with a mechanic and two people with cameras who stood on the wing fairings. Despite the ambient heat concentrated on the white concrete, Winter felt a coldness about the aircraft. As if it brought the lofty heights to earth with it; as if it were not really a part of things earth-bound.

Passing in front of the fighter-bomber, staring into the twin J-79 intakes as into the bottomless shafts of a void, Winter discerned through the background noises a vast orchestration of airplane sounds in a diminutive range. The surreal moment came on him suddenly, as if he had been transposed slightly to a new earthly plane, this one anticipatory, fraught with symbolism. The serenade, its insistence overriding logic, mesmerized him with a steady, arrhythmic flurry of clinks and crinkles, like beer cans crushed, wrenched backwards and forwards in the hands of bored bar drones. A mad percussion of cricket sounds, dry and allied with no other rhythm, accompanied the same atonal cacophony. Soft, sibilant hissings of pressure bleeding off hydraulic vascular systems, interrupted by occasional crisp, crunching eruptions, like someone stamping on ping-pong balls. Electronic blower motors, tiny whirlwinds siphoning heat from power-deprived modules, laid a patina of normalcy over the resting airframe.

Smells, even beyond Winter's first visceral contact, seemed a physical attachment to the Phantom. The raw, fresh headiness of oxygen, burnt oil and scorched metal, the dominant kerosene vapors of jet fuel blended with the stench of smoldering rubber—not quite burning, but heated beyond specs—and the cold, ozone absence of aroma that was space. The odors emanated from the metal wings and fuselage and vertical stabilizer, the dive brakes, and bomb racks, nacelle fairings and Plexiglas of the twin-seat cockpit.

The Phantom was more than a physical presence: it exuded its own metaphysical tenderings to the skies. It was an awesome vehicle, deliverer of death, maker of myths and mystique, purveyor of power and fear and gerrymandered politics. Winter felt almost a giddy envelopment of awe. Of . . . *sense.* He also had the awareness to realize that was silly.

Riché had stopped on the roadway, looking back at Winter. "Kinda takes your breat', don' it?" he said.

"Yeah, so it does. Mean mutha. I've watched them working, up in Eye Corps, but I've never made the acquaintance close-up before. Impressive. Truly impressive." Winter took in the odd, unbalanced look of the plane; but he saw, beyond the airframe, the pilot and GIB—the guy in back, the electronics warfare officer, EWO—saw in his mind's eye the awesome impact of thousand-pound bombs, the scythe-like harvesting of enemy troops with scattered anti-personnel bomblets, gnat's-ass accuracy of rockets and missiles, and the seared battlefield following the delivery of napalm and a vast conspiracy of weapons.

As he caught up with the senior pilot, Winter heard Riché effecting a lyrical recital in a soft, sing-song voice, a litany of warrior-shared compassion: ". . . and a plague came upon de tribes of Mekong, and He rain down on dem ROLLIN' T'UNDER an' ARC LIGHT. And dey were sore afraid." The pilot concluded, "No shit!"

Winter felt an unaccustomed diminishment, a demeaning recognition that he was not making war at the height of its demands. As a fighter pilot, he might have. . . .

But, hell. He'd never have made a fighter pilot, he admitted. He didn't possess enough of the killer instinct, maybe, or his reflexes and eyes were not good enough. Biggest reason, he told himself, sharing Brenner's rationale—the disdain at having to wear blue uniforms and being part of the Air Farce.

Maybe.

The bird was one mean mother goose, nevertheless.

* * *

A runner came to the BOQ and woke Winter. He was in Can Tho with Boyd Smiley on a protracted training/evaluation mission and they had four days to go. When he answered the phone in the 156th company office, the signal from Tiger Exchange, part of the awkward and unreliable in-country military telephone system, was missing.

The military phone net resembled a web woven by a nine-legged spider on speed. Each unfortunate intersection of wires and intents had a unique name, but it was common fallacy that one could dial up and reach the object of one's communications.

Nevah-hoppen, GI.

When he had come within microns of ripping the phone from the patchboard on the studs of the headquarters hut, Tiger Exchange miraculously reappeared, asking, "You working, Can Tho six?"

"Yes. Yes, Tiger. I'm working," Winter irritably assured the Vietnamese female voice. Probably a *Viet Cong Co*, Baby-san. The real meaning of *Gooks in the wire!* Nothing could have been a bigger detriment to US aims than to have the communications system discretionary on the whims of charlie.

Suddenly, Ito's voice was in his ear. "Yo, Haole. Get your butt back to the head shed."

"What? Now? In the middle of—"

"Man said, 'First flight.' Not my doing."

"What man?"

"Now shit, Winter—"

"Are you working, Can Tho?" The interruption must be that of a VC.

"Yes, goddammit, Tiger. I'm working," Winter growled, insisting there was a live person on this end of the link.

Sounds on the line settled down again. "Ito, you still there?"

"Where you left me in your snit. Now would I call you in the middle of the night for anyone but The Man?" He sounded as if Winter had made a bad joke or questioned the virgin birth. Nothing more to say, Ito hung up.

* * *

Winter was at the Air Force transient counter early the following morning. Smiley chose to remain in Can Tho and carry out some of his more extensive duties with the unit Maintenance Officer. Winter had to find another ride up-country. He approached the counter, surveying the board on the back wall where scheduled flights were chalked in without any apparent scheme.

"Wha'cha got going to Tan Son Nhut, sergeant?" he asked the Air Force two-striper, giving him the benefit of a promotion.

"Nothing, sir. Not this morning." He waved at the posting board.

In a visual disclaimer, a C-130, including tail number, was posted for a 0745 takeoff, destination, TSN.

"What's that, sport?" Winter asked, nodding toward the blatant note.

The airman gave a perfunctory glance and said, "That's been cancelled."

"Why's it still posted?"

"Been too busy to change it," he said, sliding his paperback novel beneath the counter.

"What about the later one. The Pilatus Porter tagged for fourteen hundred?"

"That's Air America. You can't fly with them," he smirked.

"Your ass. Where's the bird parked?" It was still not yet 0700.

"Out there, somewhere. Sir."

"Why do you have them posted if nobody can fly on the friggin' CIA birds?" Winter was getting an early start on a case of red ass.

"I don't know that they're CIA, whatever, Chief. *They* post their own skeds. Shit, they don't even file a flight plan—"

"And the C-one-twenty-three with open sked time?" Winter asked desperately.

"That's cancelled, sir. Like—"

"Yeah. Like the C-one-thirty.

"Yes, sir."

A tall, deeply bronzed older man in gray flightsuit, wearing Navy/Marine pilot's wings, who was leaning on the counter, growled over at Winter: "How bad you need to get to Sai Gon, Chief?"

Winter noted the small, black metalized insignia of a Marine master gunnery sergeant tacked discreetly under the loose flap of what passed for a collar on the baggie "PJs." Jeezus, he thought; he'd assumed—an unwarranted assumption, it seemed—that all the flying sergeants in the Marines were dead by now. Although, as he later reflected, they flew in the heady gull-wing days of WW-Twice in the Pacific, as little as 23 years before. This airplane driver, with a voice like a DI, looked as if he could go on forever.

"Bad. Got a 'come home' call from my commander, and my ride is no longer available."

"Check with Sergeant Smith. He'll get you on the Marine round-robin."

"Sergeant Smith's gone up-country on that flight, Sarge," the Air Force clerk offered.

"When?"

"Oh dark thirty. Flew the run early this morning. The bird was laid over here last night. Maintenance problems. Had to wait for a Marine mech to fly down—"

"Well, shit." The Gunny sniffed, shifted a chaw to the other side of his mouth, and said, "Sorry 'bout that." After spitting ruinously on the semi-buffed tile floor, he returned to whatever engaging endeavor brought him to the Operations desk.

Winter walked back down the flight line, found Boyd Smiley in the mess hall, and told him of the dilemma. Smiley drained his coffee cup, said, "Let's go, Winter Man. I can get you back to Sai Gon, be back here before my scheduled ten-hundred." It was now 0713.

Walking out to the flightline, Winter described the gang-bang at the Air Force terminal; Smiley didn't even grant him commiseration. "Hey. You know the game. Air Farce gets their share of the budget, first thing they do's build air-conditioned billets for the Zoomies, with hot and cold running. Service club, library, motion picture theater, B.X., pool. If they have money left over, they go to the airplane auction, bid on a coupla birds. Scrounge a little fuel from the Army. Borrow some bullets from the hard-up Marines. Look around, see if there are any personnel not committed to one of the earlier-listed pastimes and, if they find one, politely ask him if he would mind flying a mission. But only if he's not too busy. Don't want his goddamned union getting their skivvies in a twist."

Winter didn't say anything. There was no evidence that Smiley did not know of which he spoke, even if he spoke through tight jaws.

* * *

Landing at Tan Son Nhut, Smiley dropped Winter and his gear off on the far side of the strip from the Army ramp, in an area accessible by ground vehicle only in a long, round-about drive around the perimeter of the field. When he'd called ahead to inform the S-3 of his in-bound state, Captain Willoughby had informed Smiley that Two Five-Right was closed to traffic, due to Crash Crew operations. A VNAF A1E prop job had run up the tail of his wingman on takeoff, and both planes and pilots were undergoing a session of rehabilitative scraping and sorting. The Three would send a driver for Winter.

Without confirming Winter had a ride, Smiley wheeled his aircraft about on the taxiway without tower concurrence, asked for clearance, and began his take-off roll before he got a reply.

A driver from the 146th, SP4 Mladcjik Woijczek, was waiting near where Winter de-planed at Tan Son Nhut. Winter remembered Woijczek as a private, just before he left Bad Aibling four months ago. Last week in Plei Ku, he was wearing PFC rank. Today he was here at Tan Son Nhut, a Spec-Four. Join the Army . . . Find a home . . . Move ahead!

Winter stepped briskly to prevent the very proper Woijczek from hoisting him bodily into the Jeep with all the finesse of a family-treasured gentleman's gentleman. He shoved his two bags at the driver and let him deal with them while he climbed in the passenger seat.

As the Jeep began a circle to head back to the perimeter road, a medium-size creature that resembled something in the cat family, making a screaming noise, ran across the path of the vehicle. The critter was lucky and disappeared in the grass. Woijczek had made no effort to avoid it, but he did feel constrained to comment in his own insidious fashion.

"The most dangerous animals in the world are responsible for an inordinate number of deaths each year. Defined by number of humans killed, the most dangerous are snakes which account for more than one hundred thousand deaths each year, most in India and Africa. Next in line are bees, who kill more than ten thousand a year. Then, crocodiles, a scary third with two thousand kills per year.

Scorpions are next, though the numbers are hidden in undiagnosed deaths, mostly in third world countries. Elephants kill more than one hundred a year; big cats—lions, tigers, leopards, mountain lion, *et cetera*—close to a hundred. Jellyfish take more than fifty lives; and sharks still account for some. Hyenas get some, though there are few records kept, and, despite what you might think about them being North American in habitat, bears kill a fair number of people, mostly in Soviet satellites, which again goes unaccounted for."

Silence in the Jeep.

"Don't you find that interesting, Mister Winter?"

"Uh, yeah. Really fascinating." Actually, he did find it interesting. But more, thought Winter, that's the first time I ever heard Woijczek engage his audience directly,. Not that he did much engaging.

The rest of the short trip was made in silence.

* * *

Winter reported into the S-3 shop. The boss was gone, but Spec-5 Mangrum was able to enlighten him as to why he'd been recalled to Saigon. Someone, reviewing Winter's records for transfer to the 1st RR, had noted that his qualifications for flight status were not up to date in the medical arena: he needed a hearing test. Shit. I've not been run over by taxiing aircraft on the field; I can still copy skeds; I must be able to hear, he reasoned.

Mangrum pointed out that the hearing test facility was just around the corner from the big Army hangar, located in a trailer, back in amongst other trailers and storage buildings. Winter remembered searching out the same facility three and a half years before when he first was placed on flight status. He had an idea where it was.

But when he found the general area described by Mangrum, it no longer appeared as he remembered it. Pallets of supplies, expendables, airplane parts, and unidentifiable items, were hidden under tarps, concealed within packaging, or merely not identifiable, stacked within the semi-confined limits of the space between two hangars. He saw no trailer that appeared to offer aural testing services.

At the back end of a corridor between stacked crates, up against a concrete block wall that closed off the long, narrow space at the end of an unsurfaced track stood a large tent, what had been known in his Marine days as Tent, G.P., Medium. General purpose and larger than a breadbox. The track ended at the closed flap of the tent.

In a rare moment of airfield silence, Winter heard slight sounds of movement inside the tent. Maybe they would know where the medical trailer was. He would ask.

As he approached the tent, the quality of the hot, humid, close air about him, worsening in the confines of the corridor, took on a different aspect. The usual fetid stench of Vietnam was exacerbated, and with each step toward the door-flap, the fetor increased exponentially. Winter did not make the association until the instant he pulled back the flap, bent forward, and stepped in.

"Aw-w-w-w, Jee-e-z . . ."

A concentrated stench of feces and urine, with the added attraction of roasted meat and the overwhelming, defining smell of decaying human flesh, overlay the field morgue with a miasma of wretchedness, a vaporous exhalation right out of hell. Before him in the weak light of a half-dozen 40-watt bulbs, Winter stared at mounds of bodies, rounded heaps of body parts, pyramids of unidentifiable matter, and beyond that lingered things he could not even get his mind to examine. A fleeting memory stabbed through his mind, a tag line from a Magic Marvin utterance regarding things he thought existed *two steps from reality*: "Like a bad painting of a wooden duck." Winter could never have expressed it so, but it was, somehow, how he felt.

There was no one in the tent. The sounds . . . the sounds he had heard from outside, must have been some movement caused by . . . Aw-w-w, Jeez-us! He had subliminal flashes of chemistry lab in high school, an ugly, smelly place: properties of gaseous matter, exponents of chemical versus physical displacement, the breakdown of matter . . . Aw-w-w, Jeez-z . . .

Wondering why this all seemed so familiar, he tried to retreat before his eyes and brain registered permanent images. He had a brief encouraging thought that if he could regain the outside world faster-than-a-speeding-bullet, he could somehow eradicate the horrific compendium of sights and smells and sounds of the tent. Reverse his memory accountability.

Even as he staggered back into the open air, in his mind lingered snapshots: unmatched pairs of limbs, sometimes arms, sometimes legs, tumbled and unattached to a body. A head—part of a head, at any rate—squeezed under a rather organized stack of body trunks, some with appendages, some without. A sheen of blood, some dried, some gelatinous, overspread the uneven piles, hi-lighting viscera and occasional oatmeal-like brain matter. A hand was visible, seemingly reaching up out of the pile of . . . *things* . . . and Winter equated its prominent poise as significant, as if some dead-and-on-his-way-to-subterranean-bondage Vietnamese private was giving him the finger for his unwillingness to follow.

It was a visceral realization of Smiley's hundred-dollar Caribou . . .

Sights ever more devastating and on the very edge of recognition, lapping over into his imagination, hustled him out the flap and away from the tent. He stumbled backward, tripping on a heavy rope net that lay unattended in the dirt. He noted dark stains on the ropes, some remnants of fleshy bits caught up in the fibers of sisal that reminded him of—

Jesus, was he mad? Had he lost it? Why did he suddenly remember the night streets of Tijuana, jokes about the omnipresent taco stands and why you never saw cats on the streets in that border town. Now he knew the provenance of this charnel house—charnel tent, he reminded himself—of horrors. He took it in with unavoidable klieg eyes.

Some poor bastard chopper pilot, probably flying a Chinook, maybe a Huey if he had no other cargo, had sling-loaded the remnants off a battlefield within the past few days. Maybe soon after the fight; maybe later. Time enough for the advancement of nature's play. It was like with the Koreans, who also ate lots of garlic and peppers. The breakdown of comestibles in the body, living or dead, proceeded apace in the hot weather. It gave a spice to battlefields in the Orient that had no match elsewhere.

He flashed again on Smiley's Caribou Two-seven-four.

Aw-w-w, Jeez-us!

* * *

When Winter was driven to the Hearing Test Center the following day, it did in fact emerge as a trailer of ancient vintage, located within fifty yards of the hellish tent. His mind was so inundated with the images of the day before, he could later recall nothing of the test itself. It didn't matter what they asked of him as part of the procedure; if the test determined anything, it was that the trailer was not the best venue for testing hearing. The location, within a hundred meters of an active runway constantly launching tandem jets on strikes, was not conducive to one hearing anything. Winter could not have heard a 105mm artillery piece being fired just yards from his head. But then, neither could anyone else tasked with having their hearing tested. It was a block-checking exercise. If it was a measure of actual aural discretion, the U.S. Army—and the Air Force who used the same facility—employed thousands of deaf pilots and aircrewmen.

* * *

Winter and Lieutenant Mabry flew to Plei Ku. The Maintenance Officer at the 224th at Tan Son Nhut, CW4 Lester Vintle, euphemistically called "Brother Dave" for his amazing likeness of voice to the Southern comedian of that title, rolled his woeful eyes at Mabry's request for an aircraft ". . . for an admin mission."

"I already heard about Piltdown Pilot's recruiting mission to the three-oh-third, and I gotta tell you, I got nothing air-worthy but an Otter. You won't make a sterling impression if you fly in there in one of those old relics." The DeHavilland U-1, one in a line of venerable bush planes, was designed by practical Canadian aviation types to fly the challenges encountered in that northern wilderness. It was a remarkably able craft in its environment, and resilient, sustaining inordinate damage before succumbing to the status of "grounded." But it would not impress the average run-of-the-mill non-aviator seeking elegant transportation or suffering visions of deadly combat assault aircraft. It was just ugly!

So when Mabry landed the Otter with Winter at Plei Ku, they were geared up to suffer the gibes and taunts of ground wonks . . . but another set of circumstances ensured their transport was not even noticed.

Rain or shine, peace or war, the Dow-Jones up or down—didn't matter. One thing the Army did not avoid or pass over or delay or ignore was doctrinal commitment to the annual IG inspection. Every unit in the US Army, stateside or overseas, brown-boot Army or dilettantes, at least once a year underwent a thorough inspection by the Inspector General of that organization's parent headquarters. In order to acquit themselves by satisfactorily passing that annual look-see—which ostensibly was to ensure all personnel and units were maintained and operated, trained and indoctrinated, in the Army manner—all units endured run-up inspections as preliminaries. The preparatory inspections, and pre-prep inspections, and pre-pre-preps could back up a unit into the fallout from the previous year's final, formal IG. Such, it seemed, must have been at work in Plei Ku in the baliwick of the 303rd Radio Research Company.

The first hint the two officers had of something not quite in focus was the Jeep driven by the SP5 who met their plane and drove them to Operations. In most respects, it was a standard Army Jeep: four wheels; two bucket seats up front, one bench seat in the back; windshield folded forward onto the hood; gas and water five-gallon cans strapped to the rack on the rear; unit markings and serial numbers on the bumpers, front and rear—painted a glossy purple. Not mauve, not maroon, not periwinkle, nor any of the shades of the color spectrum which could, with strain, perhaps be arrogated to a mistake for, or a close approximation of, legitimate Army-issue paint.

No! This was a glaring, shiny, *royal* shade of purple.

Piltdown Pilot didn't seem to notice; he was mumbling over the manipulative presentation he had written out for himself to aid in his soul-saving ministry-to-come, head-hunting someone else's troops. Winter was afraid to ask, and the enlisted driver offered nothing in the way of explanation for the violet-gentian paint job.

This aberration took on more epic dimensions when they pulled up before Operations and the two officers stared at the orderly, stacked walls of purple-painted sand bags and roofing tin. The wooden posts at the corners of the building, visible through gaps in the sandbags at corners and junctions, shone with royal distinction. Stones set into the red, gritty soil as a footpath echoed the same color scheme. There was no variation, no shades ranging from a lighter to darker; none capturing other colors due to reflecting lights of different colors. Just the same purple everywhere.

While Lieutenant Mabry moved about the compound and throughout the Operations building, seducing, threatening, entreating potential turncoats, Winter went about the area seeking anyone who could explain the purple statement. But it happened, even in the cross roads of Viet Nam, that Winter could find no one he knew. No one to whisper a few sibilant words of explanation to him. He asked a couple of questions into the open maw of strangerhood, but nothing satisfactory resulted. It was as if all hands had committed to an obscure religion, the doctrine of which was inexplicable, and though they couldn't explain it, adherents were content to continue paying homage to it.

He did manage to put together a possible scenario, partly on-site in Plei Ku, and partly later, back at 509th headquarters. The major who commanded the 303rd, and who accompanied Mabry about the site, making no comments on the potential manpower drain, what might have been seen as a personal affront, had apparently been recently rendered an annual Officer Efficiency Report that fell somewhat below the norm, a death knell for career ambitions. Anything short of maximum was a killer. And Major Wexfort's report card reflected badly as a result of the previous year's IG, when some officious NCO with a personal hard-on for Wexfort, had written up the unit as ". . . in physical appearance, drab and uninspiring; infrastructure obviously not painted in several years; requires a thorough going-over with attention to personnel morale and cleanliness." He avoided the "Cleanliness is next to godliness" tag only by oversight.

Major Wexfort, apparently, had no intention of suffering the same critique at the upcoming IG. As to what Major Wexfort *would* suffer, some sort of divine retribution no doubt, Winter chose not to dwell upon. He focused on a Zen-like exchange he'd overheard in the Morse bay, one senior op leaning over a man engaged in copying code and saying, "I cried because I had no shoes . . . until I met a man who had no feet."

The unabashed answer came without the op breaking his rhythm on the mill, "I cried because I had no feet . . . until I met a man who had no Guccis." A hollow burst of appreciative laughter followed Winter down the hall.

* * *

Piltdown Pilot took the seven names he'd acquired, making deals no one wanted to know about, ignored the *pallette de violet*, and was not disappointed when they broke ground and flew away from the II Corps mountains, avoiding overflight of the colorful kingdom below.

chapter twenty-two

Silent Night, Wary Night

Tan Son Nhut, Viet Nam; December 1968

Back from Plei Ku and feeling the end of the year, Winter walked to BOQ Number 1, found Ito at odds, and they spent the evening together, shuffling down the crowded streets of Sai Gon, in and out of crowded bars, peeking into crowded restaurants, until Winter led Ito to Cheap Charlie's Chinese eatery, also crowded, yet unchanged in the face of economic growth. Hanging over the evening's festivities was the incipient threat of the imminent curfew.

They sat at a table jammed close to other tables. Ito, his first time in the five-star slophouse, scanned the terrain to take it all in. He locked his Oriental gaze on a soldier in fatigues seated by himself at the next table. The private wore a shoulder patch of the 25th Infantry Division. Ito's interest was elsewhere as he stared at the soldier's chest.

"Hey, Tropic Lightning G.I. That's essentially a no-no," he said.

The private glared mutely at him.

"Wearing ribbons on fatigues. Just not done. Violation of the uniform code."

"Yeah, well, what the fuck. Just shoot me."

"Hey, Ace," Ito reacted with irritation, "how about a little play-the-military-game here. In case you failed to notice, these are warrant officer bars . . . or rather, this one is. This other is—"

"Gotcha. Go away."

"Young troop," Winter interrupted. "You'd do well to get your head out of your ass, *and perhaps*, get on your feet and respond properly to this officer."

"Yeah? Whatcha gonna do? Send me to 'Nam?"

Winter sized him up. "Strange as it may seem, there are worse places, Private." His eyes roved over the shabby soldier, noting the rotted, torn fatigue jacket and only a hint of a history of a haircut. "Though from your looks, you might already have spent a tour there."

"Make you feel better, jammin' me up?"

"Makes a shit to me. Just another Visigoth burnout, right?"

The private stared, morose and silent.

"Just out of curiosity, why have you chosen to sport a Bronze Star with combat 'V' and an oak leaf cluster, *and* . . . seven—let's see, silver oak leaf cluster and one bronze—yep, seven Purple Hearts? No D.S.C?"

"'cause they're mine. 'bout the only things the bastards can't take away from me."

"You mean you earned them?" Winter asked skeptically.

"Bethchur ass, Dude."

"You're a grunt. Right? What's your MOS? Your job?"

"Tunnel rat. Eleven Bravo."

There was a long, expectant silence. "Dragon bait." Ito murmured.

The soldier dipped his head back toward his empty glass.

Winter turned to Ito. "Anything to add?"

"Not for me."

"Mama-san," Winter shouted, holding aloft three fingers. He spoke to the Tropic Lightning soldier: "Have a *Ba-mui-ba* on me, *Dude.*"

* * *

Waking up to the fact that he needed one more mission, minimum, to earn his flight pay for the month, Winter moved to get himself scheduled on a mission;. No need waiting to the end of the month. But, though he had no date for it, if in fact it happened, what if he was transferred meanwhile? .

There was no problem finding an op in the 146th to stand down. Checking the sked, Winter chose an early morning flight with CW3 Jackson Spain, flying the Hook. The Fish Hook, a J-shaped incursion of South Vietnam into Cambodia, was extremely hostile Indian Country, notorious for heavy engagements in the ground war. Consequently there were ample targets to keep the ARDF flyers busy over the weekend. Winter could still handle the Op's job, he thought, better than anyone in the 146th . . . except perhaps Laughin' Louie Wilmot. Then he quickly admitted the existence of several more veteran ops who fit the bill.

Waiting for Spanish Jack in the "ready room," a tongue-in-cheek euphemism for the corner of the 146th office, Winter mused on the sign that filled an otherwise empty space on the wall above the coffee pot, reading aloud, "Avail thyself of everything here, in this, our G.O.D." He wasn't struck by a sense of outrage or disapproval for what appeared a slight blasphemy—as he remembered it, he and

Matusczak had gone down that road: was any blasphemy slight?—for he was aware the trick, the lack of religious disparagement, was in the periods. Abbreviations. G.O.D. Garden of Delights. Not a word but an acronym, a euphemism for the entire Sai Gon-Cho Lon-Gia Dinh-Tan Son Nhut chihuahua.

Spanish Jack trailed in the door, carrying a flight helmet that might have been used by Orville at Kill Devil Hills. It had been worn and subjected to maltreatment to the point that no paint remained. The 146th logo was scratched and unrecognizable, and the visor semi-opaque. "Get your shit, Hot Shit. Let's go. I got your skeds for you, oh *Military Intelligence* weenie."

Damn, Winter thought. Sure, he was the best op in the battalion except Wilmot, but he hadn't remembered to pick up his sked sheet at intel briefing. Would have been embarrassing, cranking that U-8 all the way out to The Fish Hook, and having to tell the pilot he didn't know where to direct him, and he had no notion of his targets.

Once they cleared Tan Son Nhut airspace, Spain clicked the intercom and said, "Why am I enjoying the high-priced spread today?"

"Need one more to keep my hostile fire pay; can't afford to lose sixty-five bucks, and I couldn't ask someone to booger-up a manifest for me. Why?" Winter asked. "Afraid I can't hack it?" He had flown with Spanish Jack when he and Smiley initiated standardization.

"Worried you'll chuck your cookies in my bird. I did note, however, that you're dressed for the ball."

"Come again."

"Got your forty-five Excaliber there, I see. Why do you drag that big hog around? Can't hit shit with a forty-five, and it's just extra weight. Everybody in the One Forty Six carries a thirty—."

Spain suddenly rolled the U-8 into a steep bank to port and watched a Mohawk clatter past them closer than was comfortable, inbound for Tan Son Nhut, leaking fluids and trailing smoke and fire. He grimaced. "Hard Luck Harry," he said.

Winter, in the right front seat for the outbound flight, said, "You know him? The pilot?"

"Nahh. Anyone who has to drive those goddamned death traps."

They flew in silence for half a province. Winter said, in a reach, "Speaking of sidearms . . . when I was in school, Central High School, back in Jackson . . . Mississippi . . . I had a math, a geometry teacher. Old "Scottie" Prescott. Mister Prescott, a Scot, flew in W.W. One for the fledgling R.A.F.

"He was a good old shit. Had mostly boys in my class, and Scottie was fond of tall tales. Not that I didn't believe them . . . Matter of fact, some years later when he died, my mother sent me a newspaper clipping with his obit, and damned if he didn't do all those things he told us about. At least, he was in the time and place and circumstances to do them. But he could spin a yarn. As he told it, in the early days of that first air war, before aircraft got all spiffy with machine guns and rockets and such frivolities, the birds were all unarmed. But Prescott carried a big old Webley point four fifty-five pistol. Mostly, he said, what they did was surveillance and try to force observation balloons of the Germans to be cranked back down to earth—they were teatherd aloft on cables—but after a while, when the Krauts figured out that the airplanes couldn't hurt them unless they crashed into them, the balloons pretty much ignored the planes.

"He was out on a late afternoon patrol, he said, flying with two other guys. They came head-on right into two Fokker aircraft. They danced about a bit, and he saw one of the Germans dive toward one of his buddies, and a Kraut in the front seat leaned out and threw a wrench at his buddy's prop—all wooden props, then—and damned if he didn't hit the thing. Of course the prop shattered, and his buddy was left with a glider. Scottie got so pissed, he pulled his Webley and flew at the Germans and started firing. He didn't hit anything, but the Krauts got the message. They spun away and split for home."

Spanish Jack had been silent. Winter could tell by the cant of his head that he was closely listening.

"His buddy, it turned out, just floated on down, dead-stick, and landed in some French farmer's cow pasture. He rode back to the A.E.F. lines in a wagon full of hay, then took a train back to his airfield. That might have been the beginning of aerial combat. *My words*; Scottie didn't claim that. But he did say that not long after, they began arming the second man in two-seaters and the pilot in single-seaters with a rifle for more accurate results. And then, someone discovered that if you fire at one of those honking big dirigibles, filled with hydrogen, they go up like a roman candle. Turns 'em into little pieces of pollution."

"That's a helluva story, Dave. Any truth to it?"

"Like I said, I read the obituary, and from his history I think it might have been. The old man was too straight to lie about something like that."

"A Scot flying for the Brits?" Spain said it with faux astonishment.

Winter bit, responding, "Scotland's part of the British Empire. The Brit forces are full of Scots, Irish, Welsh—"

"Irish? I thought the Irish hated the Brits." The pilot seemed determined to play it to the end.

"From Northern Ireland. Protestants." Winter thought his chain was being pulled, but he was into it now. "They're part of the empire. Sikhs from India, Kiwis—New Zealanders—and Australians. Lots more. Just one great big happy cookout. They all fight for the glory of the empire."

"Shit, men don't fight for empires. They fight for something concrete." Spain trimmed the tabs and Winter felt a shiver pass through the aircraft. "For money, for a buddy, for a piece of ass. To save your own ass. Flags, testimonials, such shit don't get much play when the balloon goes up. So to speak."

"Yeah, well you're dead wrong about that. Here I am, over here now, a mercenary, fighting for the lucrative pay and bonuses and stock incentives we Army pukes get." Winter managed to say it without sounding bitter.

Spanish Jack had been around the block, too. "Gotcha."

They engaged in the mission long before reaching the Hook's environs. Winter intercepted and recognized a priority target, and began working it. They were subsequently late on station; but he knew the tradeoff was worth it. They were busy and hadn't spoken for a while when, in a fallow period, awaiting one final sked, Spanish Jack used the intercom.

"Dave, Christmas is Thursday this week. You doing anything Wednesday eve?"

"Christmas eve?"

"I thought I said that."

Winter pictured the calendar, shook his head, keyed his mike: "Nothing. Why?"

"I notice on the roster you've got O.D. New Year's Eve. I wondered if you'd trade off and take the Christmas eve duty, then I'll take yours for New Years'. I gotta date for a dance at the Zip 'O' Club." Spanish Jack was squinting into the sun, the harsh rays fractured and amplified by the grease-streaked cockpit windshield.

"Battalion give a shit? I've not traded before." In most outfits, common practice was that persons assigned rotating duties might trade with other persons having duty on other days if both parties agreed. The only caveat to such practice was that if no one showed up to pull the assigned duty, the one whose name was on the roster was the one who got the ass-kicking, regardless of private deals.

"They don't care. I could probably get one of the Zip corporals from the Motor Pool to pull the duty and they wouldn't notice," he added facetiously.

"Then go for it! Who's the date?" he asked, though he knew better. It had to be "Gin Sling" Doris, the nurse. He wouldn't stand in the way of true love. Spain confirmed it.

They wound down the mission reporting a crash: a VNAF A1E, making a strafing run on some ground activity just outside Moc Bai, followed its tracers straight into the rubber trees. Spanish Jack never saw any enemy fire—Winter was in the back seat doing operator things and saw nothing—and the crash site showed no fire, no smoke; nothing to mark it. Spain gave the site coordinates to the ASR people, reporting that he saw no survivor, no sight of a parachute.

* * *

Jackson Spain, pseudo civilian by virtue of dress, came from the elevator and paused in front of the duty officer's table-desk, a new acquisition recently stolen from the Navy Logistics Compound in Sai Gon. Winter had been at the desk for only minutes. At 1815 hours he'd had his evening meal, a discouraging porridge of unidentifiable meats, unrecognizable plant life, whether vegetables or fruit, and a delicate sauce of viscous muck. Now, resisting comment on his gustatory experience, he looked up at Spain, and remarked on the change that had been wrought by his dress in mufti.

"Gotta look my best; tonight's the night," he said mysteriously. Winter didn't want to know.

"Well, gotcha covered, Jack. I'll just sit here and hope Santa and his helpers don't come bearing arms." He smiled. "But then, he's just apt to," he said, thinking back on last year's Tet holiday, though that wasn't Christmas. He wasn't concerned he'd made a bad trade; he had nowhere to go, and his duty on New Year's was just as likely to be problematic. That would now be Spanish Jack's problem.

Spain hung about, awaiting another pilot's arrival. Double-dating, Winter thought with a chuckle. He and Spain made small talk: home, Christmas pasts, family . . . Winter realized he didn't know anything about Spain's background.

"You married, Jack?"

"Isn't everyone?"

"Kids?"

"Doesn't everyone?" Spain seemed to be deliberately closing that road. "But I got some family, still living. Back in Utah." He pulled his wallet out, removed a hand of photos, and pushed the five, one at a time, across the desk at Winter. "My mom. That's dad. And my brother, Bernard." He stared at each one longingly before passing it to Winter.

Winter received them gratefully. *Anyone's* family was welcome in this season.

"Nice looking family. Bernard looks enough like you to be a twin."

"Easily explained. He is . . . but he's an old geezer. Older'n me by almost seven minutes."

"What's he do?"

"Do?" he looked strangely at Winter. "Nothing. He works for the government."

Winter avoided the opening. Spain pushed another snapshot over. "Here's my uncles, my dad's two brothers, Ernesto and Henrique."

Winter stared at the sepia-toned picture that showed two men standing on opposite sides of a large, arched gateway in a brick wall. Through the opening, in the background could be seen a couple of horses standing before a shack with a sign reading "Gristmill" on it. One of the men was tall and thin, almost emaciated, with skin that looked like leather. The other brother was short, fat, and dressed like he was trying for a part in "The Treasure of the Sierra Madre." They looked familiar to Winter. He stared at the two for a long, silent period, ignoring Spain's out-thrust hand with one more photo.

Feeling uneasy, Winter laid the uncles' picture on the desk and reached for the last one. This photo, also in sepia, showed the two brothers and a woman, all three dressed for a celebration of some sort, the kind country people put on celebrating the seasons or the crops or something equally bucolic. He handed this photo back to Spain quickly.

"Yeah, I know. When my family gets together, dresses up for a shindig, they're uglier than a sounder of warthogs." He didn't smile.

Winter thought Spain had captured them perfectly, and made no response. Though Spain offered, his willingness to share his Christmas cards and letters was turned down. He didn't seem offended.

After Spanish Jack had gone with his pilot friend to make merry with the Zips, as Jack put it, there was no traffic in or out of the Newport BOQ for a while. At 2200, Piltdown Pilot came down from his room and stopped to chat with Winter. Said he couldn't stand being in that room as Christmas descended upon the world. Conversation led around to Mabry's origins, and he spoke fondly of New England memories of Christmastide.

His hometown of Island Pond, Vermont, sounded a perfect nostalgic note for Winter. He'd never been to Vermont, but Mabry had the ability to convey strong visual images. When he talked of accompanying his father on moose hunts as a child, he said the only memory he had of any particular hunt, was when he'd gotten some new boots one year, a pre-Christmas gift so he'd have them for the hunting season, and he'd worn them and almost lost his toes to frostbite. His father had felt really bad about that and had taken the boots back to Crawford's in nearby Derby, and forever after, his father would buy nothing from the man who'd sold him crappy boots.

One of the Vietnamese mechanics who worked for the 146th came by, bearing a box wrapped in garish paper, and asked for Mister Eason, the Maintenance Officer. Winter walked over, shouted up the stairwell to the third floor, and returned to his seat and conversation.

Piltdown Pilot, dexterously using his hands like an Italian speaking Chinese, painted a winter scene so vivid that Winter almost felt a shiver. He described winter sleigh rides in old horse-drawn conveyances around the perimeter of The Pond. Winter knew from his time at Fort Devens with nearby Walden Pond, that in New England a pond was not a small muddy pool for watering stock, seining for crawdads or fishing for perch, but could be quite a large lake by Southern standards. Spain painted a Currier & Ives motif for the desk-bound officer.

He could envision the cabins about the pond, buried in snow, the few businesses in the small community that were open in the off-season showing the yellow glow of kerosene lanterns because the winter snows and freezing rain often brought power outages. An almost total absence of automobiles on the road. A few Jeeps—Police cars were 4-wheel-drive Jeeps—and the rest farm trucks with tractor-like tires. Most travel was done on cross-country skis and snowmobile. Island Pond was 15 miles from the Canadian line.

"I cannot even imagine the kind of cold you have up there," Winter said, effecting a shiver of body parts. "But when I was a kid in Mississippi, we had cold weather. Sometimes, it'd get down to freezing."

Lieutenant Mabry snorted.

"Yeah, not very impressive is it? But in our climate, where it's over a hundred for days at a time in the summer, even freezing is bad news. One fond memory of Christmas and winter was the one time I remember we had snow, and in Raymond, my older cousin taught us how to make snow ice-cream. And I remember how we got our feet warm before going to bed, and kept them warm until we'd gone to sleep. I guess these memories come from the big old house we lived in, just outside Raymond where I was born.

"In that old house, our heat was from fireplaces. Just before bedtime my mother, or my cousin who we lived with, used to put a clean brick on the hearth, right in front of the fireplace, and let it sit there, turning it, until it was pretty-well warmed through. They'd wrap the brick in a towel, and after I'd gotten into my jammies or long johns and gotten my feet and butt warm before the fire, I'd crawl in bed between those old rough, icy sheets, and the adult would place that wrapped, warm brick next to my feet. That was delicious."

"Hard to beat country living, isn't it?" Piltdown Pilot commented.

"Yeah," Winter agreed, his eyes focused beyond the world before him. "That's where we lived when my brother burned to death in the open fireplace."

There was stunned silence. "Eight months old," Winter murmured. "Just learning to walk in an old, homemade walker. Wheel tipped into a void where a brick was missing in the hearth." He returned to the conversation. "I could never warm my feet with a brick after that. Never."

* * *

· *1800 hours, 24 Dec 68: Assumed the duty for scheduled CW3 Jackson Spain., OD, Newport BOQ. Ho! Ho! Ho!*
  —SP5 Bullock duty driver, courier, messenger, dogsbody

—Signed for 27 asst'd keys on a ring (?), Duty weapon, .45 cal. auto. pistol (dirty) w/2 mags. ball ammo (dirty); one vehicle, believed to be a Jeep beneath mud coating, Ser. Nr. 66965... (remainder missing)

· *1922: Star in the east. Quaint cliché. Really bright star!*

· *1957: Jingle . . . of sleigh bells? Red arc at 3K ft. (est.) across northern sky . . . Rudolph?*

· *2015: Three kings are late. Distinct absence of wise men. Fantasies!*

—Eastern star vanished, dropped to ground, small parachute crumpling into prized heap dangling burnt flare in some bamboo thicket

—Small brown children will seek it out at first light

—Sleigh bells: tinkle of spent brass swept from a gunship on 3rd Field's pad—crewchief doing scut work

—Northern red arc, just Spooky on a killing spree. Merry Xmas, charlie! (Flying the Fishhook yesterday. III Corps rife w/pine trees; dropped down to view some seasonal evergreen. Substantial groundfire. Grinch bastards.)

· *2138: Duty Sergeant/509 walk-in. Wants help changing a tire, up by 100-p alley. Right!*

—No, seriously.

· *2225: 3rd Field Hospital chopper pad quiet. Business down; things looking up*

· *2250: Checked building. Nobody on roof. (How odd!) I worry about Cong paratroopers.*

—Alien personnel on 4th level. Smells female. Can't be—this is a male BOQ

—Quiet

· *2310: Shots fired next door/ARVN vehicle park, JGS. Who knows? Who cares!*

· *2356: Getting close now. I can smell reindeer shit.*

· *0001: Now Xmas morn. Best present I can hope for—make it through the night. Alive.*

—One at a time. No sweat.

· *0040: CW3 Jackson Spain disembarked a cab at the front entrance; stiffed the cabbie and ripped the door off the Renault. Seems a bit testy (I took Spanish Jack's OD tonight in exhange for New Year eve duty; he wanted to take his woman to a Xmas dance at nurses' BOQ or the Zip O Club, one or the other. Short night for him; must be that time of month.)*

—Still waiting for Santa; hope he's not wearing a cone-shaped, bamboo boater.

· *0156: Sky lit up, northeast. Gotta be Ben Cat. Hel-lo, Cease Fire*
   − *Season's best, you poor beggers*

· *0210: Duty driver back. Dog robbers at Circle 34 Mess wouldn't part with so much as a bacon sandwich. "They ran out." Uh huh! Mess cooks' families and bar girls, at least, are eating, no doubt*

· *0245: Cleaned the .45, put it back together. Voilá! No leftover parts. What next, elves?*

· *0320: Brought down old family photos on my last walk-thru. Jeremy and Adam will be so much more . . . Nickie . . .*

· *0321: Quiet*

· *0339: Column raggedy-assed APCs from 25ᵗʰ Div just came up Plantation Rd past here−Going where? Can't go downtown. Nobody needs them in Gia Dinh. Lost!*

· *Four o'clock: That's 0400 for you night skulkers*
   − *Still, if it were colder . . . No! Never mistake this for a holy land. No way*

· *0444: Firing beyond Gen. Vetter's quarters. Checked roof: guard there and both front/side gate guards at his quarters seem OK with it; nobody disturbed. Revelers!*
   − *Sleep well & merry, General*

· *0522: Sky lightening*
   − *Can't help remembering other Xmas morns: kids clattering down stairs, bright expectant eyes, hair like brushfire, baggy-toed jammies*
   − *Heart breaking memories . . . and I look up, there's Kingston. Hung over. Scuffling out to the flightline. Looks like Death's vomit. Seen better conditioned bodies dragged behind tracked vehicles. Enough weaponry for WWIII. Now there's an Advent calendar.*

· *0605: Adjutant called: I'm relieved of duty. Duty weapon and log to head shed with Bullock .*
   − *Officially on Xmas holiday . . . for one hour, 25 min.*
   − *Manifested for first mission flight of the day at 0730 w/Sky Queen. (Should have sent this journal "accidentally" to the Adjutant, kept the official log. Merrick would have a shit fit.)*

[Private journal of Chief Warrant Officer David D. Winter, W3431247, Tan Son Nhut/Saigon, Republic of Vietnam; Christmas 1968]
   − *Looky, looky, you be pleasing!*

* * *

Once relieved of duty that Christmas morning, Winter walked upstairs to his room. He had a 0730 flight. The overwhelming stench of *nuoc mam*, the pungent fish sauce prized by the Vietnamese and eaten with every dish, hung in the halls like a plague. *Merry Christmas!* GI-san.

On every floor were signs posted in Vietnamese and English forbidding the cooking of food within the BOQ. The housegirl violators of those rules might argue that they couldn't read; but that was a lie; the rate of literacy in Vietnam was higher than in the United States. And despite housegirls being fired for those offenses, the illicit practice continued. Winter worried that he might get airsick on the flight as a result..

"They must not realize that posted statement is signed by a bull colonel," Ito had observed trenchantly one day when visiting.

"And would they give a rat's ass if they knew that?" Winter had asked.

"Well, of course. Vietnamese are very law-abiding—" He couldn't abide Winter's loud guffaws and shuffled off down the corridor, sniffing the air suspiciously as if pleased.

Since it was Christmas, and Charlie was paying token homage to the Christmas ceasefire, and Winter had learned his designated mission aircraft was broken, he had the rest of the day off. He thought he'd drop by the Circle-34 mess for the holiday doin's and stay to catch the early movie. *Dr. Zhivago.* He'd seen this magnificent adaptation of Pasternak's epic twice already in the past week, and until he left for Cam Ranh Bay—he still didn't know when that would be, precisely—he would probably continue to sit through it again and again. Not like that was hard to do.

When near the end of his Russian language training three years before, the movie had shown in the Steinbeck Theater in Monterey with Russian Cyrillic sub-titles. He chuckled recalling how, after seeing the film the first time, overly impressed with his own capabilities in his new language, he set out to read the book in the original Russian.

It was assigning Hamlet to a third grader.

* * *

Winter walked back from the movie with new Lieutenant Prisbauyou, just in from Fort Sill. Lieutenant Gorby, the Lost Soul from Con Son Island, staggered through the lobby of the Newport as the two officers returned, stared blankly at them, and asked, "Were you there?"

Fully cognizant of Gorby's plight, though not enough convinced of his true madness to feel sympathy, Winter refused to be drawn out. Prisbauyou stared in ignorance.

The warrant did not elaborate for the new lieutenant, who headed for his room.

* * *

Walking up the stairs to the second floor, Winter thought about his up-coming transfer. If, in fact, it transpired. He really hoped—

His mind, momentarily unfocused, swept back to his constant companion: sadness. Not even a Christmas card from Nickie or the kids. One from a third cousin in the Air Force, stationed at some grim outpost in the Dakotas. Nothing from anyone who counted. He pushed away from self-absorption.

His transfer. Possible transfer. *Likely* transfer; he had to believe Major Jernigan. The man didn't joke worth a shit.

His . . . which transfer? What was the ordinal number, if this one eventuated. He began to run down transfers, reassignments, moves, permanent changes of station versus temporary duty over his fifteen-plus years' service. For Beelzebub's sake, pass on the TDYs.

When he'd made the mental circuit, starting with leaving Jackson, Mississippi, in 1953 for Camp Pentleton, and had come full circle to the move to Cam Ranh Bay, he was astounded. He stopped on the stairs.

Can that be right? Twenty-seventh permanent change of station coming up? He knew it must be so. He remembered each and every PCS, dislocations of lesser or greater impact—thirteen during the seven years in the Corps, fourteen in the Army's nine years.

His grandfather had always hedged when questioned, dealing with the issue of his and his forebears' life in the *Ould Sod*. Maybe there *was* a Tinker in the family tree.

Be that as it may—or may not—he still couldn't be assured of the move to Cam Ranh Bay.

Merry Christmas, GI.

Epilogue

Sai Gon, Viet Nam: December 1968

Varykino lay dormant under a snow field that swept away smooth, unbroken and unhindered as far as vision allowed. At the limit of the sun-flared white plain, the tumbled crests of the Caucasus punctuated the brilliant sky, their evergreen mantle sheathed in white.

The vast house, regal as a ship on smooth seas, surmounted the otherwise unmarked scape. Inside the decaying mansion was little different from out: walls, furniture, chandeliers, paintings, statuary, and floors were etched with frost and ice crystals; snow, settled through broken glass overhead paneling, made tiny mountains on the carpet.

Antonina Alexandrovna was radiant. The fur hood framing her curious beauty was rimed with her crystalline breath. Yurii knew what she did not: that her effusive well-being sprang from the new life growing inside her. He would not tell her yet; let her discover this primal truth in an epiphany of her own divining. He adored her; he would do what would please her most.

Yurii Andreievich kissed her passionately, turned and waded through a drift at the front of the steps to the sleigh. He nodded to the driver, Old Mishka, as the servant wrapped a heavy cloak around him. The road to Yuriatin was entirely obscured, not even utility poles to mark the route; the new commodity of electric service had not made its way to this remote region. As the runners broke free from the ice with a crack, and he left Tonia behind, Yurii's mind quickly gave over to anticipation of the coming tryst with his love, Larissa Feodorovna, in the town scarce ten leagues away.

Even as Winter gazed, mesmerized by Lean's exploitation of the doctor's bold deceit, transcribing Pasternak's flowing prose into visual splendor, he unconsciously but empathetically steeled himself against the mantle of cold the impatient lover must feel, the deceptive and dangerous climate of the steppes. Winter, fully mired in the scene—his favorite of the film—was transported, blissfully shivering in the blast of Russian winter, until his entrancement was broken by a loud voice behind him: "Is there a Chief Winter here? Winter. Two-two-four."

The warrant officer reluctantly drew himself back from the revolutionary tale of love, war, and infidelity, back into the hated reality of a hot and humid Christmas, after-lunch movie in the Circle 34. By the time he reached the bar and overcame the obstructions of the Viet military telephone communications, he had totally forsaken the tale of the enigmatic Russian poet-doctor. Now the day after Christmas, he'd already sat through the film four times. Actually, three-and-a-half. He patiently awaited telephonic connection. With that miraculous accomplishment, he was not surprised when Sergeant Albrecht informed him that his mission flight, cancelled yesterday, cancelled again this a.m., re-scheduled later in the day, then cancelled again, was back on. Again.

* * *

The post-Christmas week crawled by. Winter re-visited Zhivago as the movie was held over at the Circle 34 and, as he considered it, in his "spare time" worked to schedule training for the 146th. He flew two training missions, relegating the remainder to Jack Albrecht. On the last day of the year, a suitable finale to a bitching four months, he flew an early afternoon mission flight. Boring to a fault. Only one target appeared—as if all the elves were on strike.

Shucking his flight gear and leaving his pilot to close out the books, he caught a ride along the flight line to Davis Station where he would check his mail—anticipating nothing—but hoping to score a lift to the Newport BOQ. No mail, and nothing forthcoming for a ride, he joined two sergeants from the 146th and ate a burger and greasy fries at the NCO club.

Above the cacophony in the club of irate voices, off-key musical ditties, and the tinny crinkle of Black Label cans, he heard again, like an off-color postscript to the year, an unwelcome announcement crackling over the PA: "Mister Winter. Phone." As the warrant picked up the antique handset, the bartender—a truck mechanic in disguise—would not look at him, content to wreck the officer's evening without amendment.

* * *

Winter prowled the lobby of the Newport, his second shift as duty officer in eight days. The SDO brassard hung contemptuously from a buttoned strap at the waist of his jungle fatigue jacket. He fumed.

If I get my hands on Spanish Jack, he vowed fervently, that Mickey Mouse, sometime pilot is apt to find himself medically grounded.

He recalled the astonishing conversation over the phone at the club. When he'd picked up the receiver, an unfamiliar voice had rasped out, "Mister Winter?"

"Yes. Who's this?"

"This is the voice ending your career."

A joker. "So, which voice of doom—"

"This is Captain McChord, smart ass. The Group Adjutant."

Oh, shit! "Yessir. How can I help you?"

"Help me? Help *me!* You'd better concern yourself with helping yourself."

"Sir?" Why didn't the captain say something with content?

"Don't play dumb shit with me, mister. Why aren't you at your goddamned post? Why are you not, at this red-hot moment, performing duty as O.D. at the Newport? You're A-WOL!"

"Uhh, sir, C.W.O. Spain and I swapped duties. I took his on Christmas eve; he's doing mine tonight."

"He's doing jack-all. If he was standing your watch, why the hell would I be breaking your balls?" A reasonable question, Winter thought in panic.

"Get a grip, Winter," the adjutant went on. "Spain's loose on the wind. Your trading don't mean shit to me. All I know's your name is prominently listed in my O.D. roster. And you're not at your post."

"Well . . . fuck!"

"That's about it. You're coming into focus. Get your ass over to the Newport."

"Aye, aye, sir."

* * *

At 2035 hours, as Winter paced and fumed, indiscriminately surly with anyone who approached him, he watched as an unfamiliar captain entered the BOQ lobby. The officer walked directly to where Winter leaned on a shelf staring out into the garishly lit street beyond.

"Chief Winter?" the officer said.

"Yes, sir. O.D."

"So you are. I'm McChord, Group Adjutant."

"Oh. Well—"

"I thought, since I had perturbed your day a bit, I might as well stop by and totally destroy the rest of it."

"Sir . . .?"

"You're going to have a busy night, Chief. Not only are you relegated to this boring and irritating nowhere duty, but you're going to have to pack. That is, unless you're still not unpacked, living out of your duffel bag."

"Uhh, no sir. Pack? For what? Where'm I going?" Winter could barely keep up with the shifting focus of the bizarre dialogue.

"You're going—P.C.S., I might add—to the First R.R. Cam Ranh Bay. Early flight tomorrow morning. Now does that ruin the rest of your day?" The hint of a smile edged into the captain's demeanor.

"Cam Ranh." Jeez-us, Cam Ranh. Tomorrow. "But I don't—"

"Of course you don't know shit about this. That's the way things are done in this route-step outfit."

"Sir?"

"David, I came to bring your orders." The adjutant's voice approached a reasonable tone as he proffered a sheaf of wrinkled papers. "They were only cut about half an hour ago. Gives you only a smidgeon of time to prepare. You and Chief Ito are being chauffeured to Cam Ranh at zero seven-forty-five by none other than your own S-three. Colonel Northcutt offered to fly you up, since we couldn't find another convenient way to guarantee you'll get there tomorrow. And that's gotta happen."

"Ito, too?"

"Did I speak too fast for you, Chief?"

"But, what about O.D.? I can't pack while I'm on duty. And I won't be off until seven."

"I saw Ito at Number One, dropped off his orders, and told him to come over and spell you long enough for you to pack. I'll relieve you by phone at oh-six-hundred, and have a Jeep here to ferry you two over to the head shed and Davis Station for check-out." The captain smiled, a faded remnant of sincerity. "Sorry 'bout the harangue over your duty mix-up. Spanish Jack's known for taking advantage in similar circumstances. Sucker skates out of more details than you can imagine. But I hope Cam Ranh Bay might make up for the double duty."

His tone indicated he didn't give a rat's ass if it did or did not; the captain had transmogrified back into an adjutant. But Winter had a bus to catch.

End

CPSIA information can be obtained at www.ICGtesting.com
Printed in the USA
LVOW06s1009310713

345459LV00001B/33/P